Limerick City Library

3 0002 50051912 9

# She was no longer out of reach.

She was right there. So close.

He turned fully toward her, almost helpless. and caught her chin in his fingers.

"I was getting you back." Logan recognized his mistake. He was letting this case get personal, and that was the last thing he should be doing.

Let her go. Hands off. Get her on the plane. Deliver her home.

Walk away. But it had been so long since he'd held her.

Even longer since he'd kissed her. One moment of weakness. Would it really hurt? Would it really—

She rose onto her toes and kissed him.

Yes.

CANCELLED

D1448579

# ALPHA ONE

### BY
### CYNTHIA EDEN

CANCELLED

MILLS & BOON

All the characters in this book have no existence outside the imagination of the author, and have no relation whatsoever to anyone bearing the same name or names. They are not even distantly inspired by any individual known or unknown to the author, and all the incidents are pure invention.

All Rights Reserved including the right of reproduction in whole or in part in any form. This edition is published by arrangement with Harlequin Enterprises II B.V./S.à.r.l. The text of this publication or any part thereof may not be reproduced or transmitted in any form or by any means, electronic or mechanical, including photocopying, recording, storage in an information retrieval system, or otherwise, without the written permission of the publisher.

This book is sold subject to the condition that it shall not, by way of trade or otherwise, be lent, resold, hired out or otherwise circulated without the prior consent of the publisher in any form of binding or cover other than that in which it is published and without a similar condition including this condition being imposed on the subsequent purchaser.

® and ™ are trademarks owned and used by the trademark owner and/or its licensee. Trademarks marked with ® are registered with the United Kingdom Patent Office and/or the Office for Harmonisation in the Internal Market and in other countries.

First published in Great Britain 2013
by Mills & Boon, an imprint of Harlequin (UK) Limited,
Eton House, 18-24 Paradise Road, Richmond, Surrey TW9 1SR

© Cynthia Roussos 2013

ISBN: 978 0 263 90349 2
ebook ISBN: 978 1 472 00701 8

46-0313

Harlequin (UK) policy is to use papers that are natural, renewable and recyclable products and made from wood grown in sustainable forests. The logging and manufacturing processes conform to the legal environmental regulations of the country of origin.

Printed and bound in Spain
by Blackprint CPI, Barcelona

CITY OF LIMERICK
D14633
PUBLIC LIBRARY

*USA TODAY* bestselling author **Cynthia Eden** writes tales of romantic suspense and paranormal romance. Her books have received starred reviews from *Publishers Weekly,* and she has received a RITA® Award nomination for best romantic suspense. Cynthia lives in the deep South, loves horror movies and has an addiction to chocolate. More information about Cynthia may be found on her website, www.cynthiaeden.com, or you can follow her on Twitter (www.twitter.com/cynthiaeden).

# Chapter One

"You don't deserve to die here."

Juliana James looked up at the sound of the quiet voice. She couldn't move her body much because she was still tied hand and foot to the chair in the dimly lit room. Tied with rough ropes that bit into her skin. Though she'd struggled for hours, she hadn't been able to break free. She'd done nothing but slice open her flesh on the ropes.

"If you tell them…what they want to know…" He sighed. "They might let you go."

Juliana swallowed and felt as if she were choking back shards of glass. How long had it been since they'd given her anything to drink? After swallowing a few more times, she managed, "I don't know anything." She was just trapped in a nightmare. One day, she'd been soaking up the sun on a Mexican beach, and the next—

*Hello, hell.*

It was a nightmare all right, and she desperately wanted to wake up from it. *Ready to wake up—now.*

John Gonzales, the man who'd been held captive with her for—what was it now? Three? Four days?—was slumped in his chair. She'd never met John until they were thrown together in this hell. They'd both been kidnapped from separate areas in Mexico. The men who'd abducted them kept coming and getting John, taking him.

Hurting him.

And she knew her time was coming.

"I'm not…perfect," John's ragged voice whispered to her. "But you…you didn't do anything wrong… It was all your father."

Her father. The not-so-honorable Senator Aaron James. She might not know who had taken her, but once her abductors had started asking their questions, Juliana had figured out fast that the abduction was payback for something the senator had done.

Daddy hadn't raised a fool. Just, apparently, someone to die in his place.

Would he even care when he learned about what had happened to her? Or would he just hold a press conference and *look* appropriately saddened and grievous in front of all the cameras? She didn't know, and that fact made her stomach knot even more.

Juliana exhaled slowly. "Perfect or not…" She didn't know the things that John had done. Right then, they didn't matter. He'd talked to her when she'd been trapped in the dark. He'd kept her sane during all of those long, terrible hours. "We're both going to make it out of here."

His rough laughter called her words a lie.

She'd only seen his face a few times, when the light was bright enough in the early mornings. Appearing a bit younger than her own thirty years, John had the dark good looks that had probably gotten him plenty of female attention since he was a teen.

Not now, though.

"Do you have any…regrets?" John asked her. She saw his head tilt toward her as he waited for her response.

Juliana blinked against the tears that wanted to fill her eyes. *Regrets?* "A few." *One.*

A pause. Then "You ever been in love, Juliana?"

"Once—" and in the dark, with only death waiting for her, she could admit this painful truth "—but Logan didn't love me back." Pity, because she'd never been able to—

The hinges on the door groaned as it opened. Juliana tensed, her whole body going tight with fear. John was already swearing, jerking against his binds, but...

But the men weren't coming for him this time.

They were coming for her.

Juliana screamed.

LOGAN QUINN FELT A TRICKLE of sweat slide down his back. He didn't move, not so much as a muscle twitch. He'd been in position for the past forty-three minutes, waiting for the go-ahead to move.

To storm that building and get Julie out of there.

*Hold on, baby.*

Not that she was his baby. Not anymore. But the minute Senator James had contacted him, asking for his help and the help of his team, Logan had known that trouble, serious trouble, had come to hunt him down.

*Julie's missing. You have to get her back.*

That was all it had taken. Two sentences, and Logan had set his team up for a recovery mission in Mexico. His unit, part of the Elite Operations Division, didn't take on just any case.

But for her, he'd do anything.

"There's movement." The words whispered into his ear via the comm link that all members of his recovery team used.

Logan barely breathed.

"I have a visual on the target."

His heart raced faster. This was what they'd been waiting for. Movement and, hopefully...visual confirmation. They wouldn't storm the place, not until—

"I see her. The girl's being led down a hallway. There's a knife at her throat."

*Visual confirmation.*

Logan held his position even as fury pulsed within him. Juliana would be scared. Terrified. This was so far from the debutante balls in Mississippi that she knew. So far from the safe life she'd always wanted to lead.

He'd get her back to that life, then he'd walk away. Just as he had before.

"South side," that same voice whispered in his ear. Male. Gunner Ortez, the SEAL sniper Uncle Sam had recruited for their black-ops division. A division most said didn't exist.

They were wrong.

"Second door," Gunner said, voice flat and hard as he marked the target location.

Finally, Logan moved. A shadow in the night, he didn't make a single sound as he slipped into the building. To his right, Jasper Adams moved in perfect sync with him. The Ranger knew how to keep quiet just like Logan did. After all their training, stealth was second nature to them now.

Logan came up on the first guard, caught the scent of cigarettes and alcohol. One quick jab, and the guard's body slumped back against him. He pulled the guy into the shadows, dropped him in the corner and signaled for Jasper to keep moving.

Then he heard her scream.

The blood in Logan's body iced over. For a second, his vision seemed to go dark. Pain, fear—he could hear them both in Juliana's scream. He rushed forward, edging fast on Jasper's heels. Jasper knocked out the next guard, barely pausing.

Logan didn't pause at all. He drew out his gun and—

*"Please, I don't know!"* It was Juliana's desperate

voice. The voice he still heard in his dreams. Not soft with the South now, but high with terror.

They passed the first door. The second was just steps away. *Hold on, hold on...*

"Company!" Gunner's terse warning blasted in his comm link. They barely had time to duck for cover before the *rat-a-tat* of gunfire smashed into the wall above them.

*Made.* Logan fired back, once, twice, aiming with near-instant precision. He heard a choked cry, then the thud of bodies as two men hit the ground. Jasper covered him, moving quickly, as Logan kicked open lucky door number two. With that gunfire, the men inside would either flee...

*Or try to kill their prey.*

Option number two damn well wasn't going down on his watch.

But as Logan burst into the room, three men turned toward him. He fired at the guy on the left as the man drew his gun. The guy's body hit the floor. Then Logan drove his fist into the face of the attacker on the right. But the one in the middle...the one with his knife pressed against Juliana's throat...

Logan didn't touch him. Not yet.

*"Deje a la mujer ir,"* Logan barked in perfect Spanish. *Let the woman go.*

Instead, the soon-to-be-dead fool cut her skin. Logan's eyes narrowed. Wrong move.

*"Vuelva o ella es muerta,"* the guy snarled back at him. *Step back or she's dead.*

Logan didn't step back. He'd never been the type to retreat. His gaze darted to Juliana. She stared at him, eyes wide, body frozen. A black ski mask covered his head, so he knew she had no idea who he was. But Logan knew she'd always had a real fine grasp of the Spanish language. She understood exactly what the man had said to him.

*"Step back."* Her lips moved almost soundlessly. "Please." Then she repeated her plea in Spanish.

Still, he didn't move. Beneath the ski mask, his jaw locked. He kept his gun up and aimed right at her attacker's head. *One shot...*

*"Vuelva o ella es muerta!"* Now the guy yelled his warning and that knife dug deeper into Juliana's pale throat.

Instead of backing up, Logan stepped forward. Juliana screamed—and then she started fighting. Her nails clawed at her captor's hand, and she drew blood of her own. The guy swore and yanked back on her hair, but that move lifted the knife off her throat. Lifted it off just enough for Logan to attack.

He caught the man's wrist, wrenched it back. Even as Logan yanked Juliana forward, he drove the guy's wrist— and the knife—right back at the bastard's own throat.

When the body hit the floor, Logan didn't glance down. He pulled Juliana closer to him and tried to keep her attention off the dead men on the floor. "It's all right," he told her, attempting to sound soothing in the middle of hell. More gunfire echoed outside the small room. The sound was like the explosion of fireworks. The voice in his ear told him that two more men had just been taken out by Jasper. Good. The guy was clearing the way for their escape. Logan's hands tightened on Juliana, and he said, "I'm gonna—"

She kneed him in the groin.

Logan was so caught off guard by the move that he let her go. She lunged away from him, yelling for all that she was worth.

"Damn it," he growled and hissed out a breath, "I'm not here to hurt you!"

She'd yanked the knife out of the dead man's throat.

She came up with it clutched tightly in her white-knuckled grip. "You stay away from me!"

"Easy." They didn't have time for this. Logan knew that if he yanked up his mask and revealed his identity, she'd drop the weapon. But he had mission protocol ruling him right then. Their team was to stay covered during this rescue, until the target had been taken to the designated safe zone. No team member could afford to have his identity compromised at this site. Not until everything was secure.

"Back up and get out of my way," Juliana snapped right back at him, showing the fire that had first drawn him to her years ago.

He hadn't obeyed the dead guy. Did she really think he'd obey her?

But then Jasper leaped into the room at the same instant that Gunner barked on the comm link, *"Extraction. Now."*

Logan caught the whiff of smoke in the air. Smoke... and the crackle of flames. Fire wasn't part of the extraction plan.

"Two hostiles got away," Jasper grunted, shifting his shoulders, and Logan wondered if he'd been hit. He'd seen the Ranger take three bullets before and keep fighting. One hit wouldn't slow him down—Jasper wouldn't let it slow him down. "And I think those fleeing hombres want to make sure we don't get out alive with her."

No, they wouldn't want her escaping. Too bad for them. Logan spun for the window. Using his weapon and his fist, he broke the glass and shattered the old wooden frame. He glanced down at the street below. Second story. He could handle that drop in his sleep, but he'd have to take care with Juliana.

"Clear," Gunner said in his ear, and Logan knew the guy was still tracking the team's movement. "Go now... 'cause that fire is coming hard for you."

Juliana's captors had probably rigged the place for a fast burn. The better to leave no evidence—or witnesses—behind.

Logan grabbed Juliana's hand. She yelped. He hated that sound, hated that he'd had to hurt her, but now wasn't the time for explanations.

The knife clattered to the floor.

Now was the time to get the hell out of there. He wrapped his arm around her waist and pulled her close against his body. "You'll need to hold tight," he told her, voice low and growling.

But Juliana shook her head at him. "I'm not going out that window. I have to—"

"You have to live," Jasper said from his post at the door. "That fire's coming, ma'am, and you need to get through that window *now*."

She blinked. In the faint light, Logan saw the same dark chocolate eyes he remembered. Her face still as pretty. "Fire?" Then she sucked in a deep breath, and Logan knew she'd finally caught the scent of smoke and flames. *"No!"* She tried to rip out of his arms and lunge for the door.

Logan just hauled her right back against him. Now that he had her safe in his arms, he wasn't about to let her get away.

"Area's clear," Gunner said in Logan's earpiece. *"Extract now."*

Logan tried to position Juliana for their drop. The woman twisted against him, moving like a slithering snake as she fought to wrench back and break free. "I'm not leaving!" she snapped at him. "Not without John!"

Who?

*"Extract."* Gunner's order.

"Stop fighting," Logan told her when she twisted again. "We're the good guys, and we came to take you to safety."

She stilled for a moment. Heaving a deep breath, she said, "Me…and John."

Seriously, who the hell was John?

"He's back there." Her hand lifted and one trembling finger pointed to the doorway. The doorway that was currently filling with smoke. "We have to get him out."

No other civilians were in the building. Only Diego Guerrero's killers. Logan's team members were pulling back and—

"I'm not leaving without him!"

An explosion rocked the building. Juliana fell against Logan's chest.

Jasper staggered. "Go time," Logan heard him say.

And yeah, it was. Keeping a hold on Juliana, Logan tapped his receiver. "Is there another civilian here?" He had to be sure. He wouldn't leave an innocent to burn.

He motioned for Jasper to take the leap out. He had Juliana; there was no need for the other agent to stay any longer. Jasper yanked out a cable from his pack and quickly set up an escape line. In seconds, he began to lower his body to the ground.

"Negative," Gunner responded instantly. "Now move before your butt gets fried."

Gunner wouldn't make a mistake. He and Sydney Sloan had the best intel there was. No way would they send the team in without knowledge of another innocent in the perimeter.

Juliana blinked up at him. "Y-your voice…"

Aw, damn. He'd lost most of his Southern accent over the years, but every now and then, those Mississippi purrs would slip into his voice. Now wasn't a good time for that slip.

"You're goin' out the window…" Another explosion shook the building. Her captors were packing some serious firepower. *Definitely don't want her getting away alive.* "Your choice—you goin' through awake or asleep?"

"There's a man trapped back there! He's tied up—*he'll burn to death.*"

She wasn't listening to him. Fine. He grabbed her, tossed her over his shoulder, held tight and dropped down on the line that Jasper had secured for him.

By the time she'd gotten any breath to scream, they were on the ground.

"Take her," Logan ordered, shoving Juliana into Jasper's arms. "Get her out of here." She was the mission. Her safety was their number one priority.

But…

*He'll burn to death.*

Logan wasn't leaving a man behind.

He grabbed the cable and started hauling his butt back up into the fire.

"WHAT THE HELL is he thinking?"

Juliana stared around her with wide eyes. She was surrounded by two men, both big, strong, towering well over her five foot eight inches. They had guns held in their hands, and they both wore black ski masks. Just like the other guy. The guy that, for a moment, had sounded exactly like—

"Alpha One," the hulking shadow to her right said into his wrist. "Get back here before I have to drag you out of that inferno." Wait, no, he wasn't muttering into his wrist. He was talking into some kind of microphone.

Alpha One? That had to be the guy who'd jumped out of the window—with her in his arms. Her heart had stopped when he'd leaped out and she'd felt the rush of air on her body. Then she'd realized...he'd been holding on to some kind of rope. They hadn't crashed into the cement. He'd lowered her, gotten her to safety, then gone back into the fire.

"There's someone else inside... John..." Juliana whispered. The fire was raging now. Blowing out the bottom windows of that big, thick building. Her hell.

They were at least two hundred feet away from the fire now. Encased in shadows. Hidden so well. But...

But she couldn't stop shaking. These men had saved her, and she'd just sent one of them right back to face the flames.

She couldn't even see the men's eyes as they glanced at her. The sky was so dark, starless. The only illumination came from the flames.

Then she heard a growl. A faint purr...and the man to her right yanked her back as a vehicle slid from the shadows. Juliana hadn't even seen the van approaching. No headlights had cut through the night.

The van's back doors flew open. "Let's go!" a woman's sharp voice ordered.

The men pretty much threw Juliana into the van.

"Where's Alpha One?" the woman demanded. Juliana's gaze flew to her. The woman had short hair, a delicate build, but Juliana couldn't really discern anything else about her.

The man climbing in behind Juliana pointed to the blaze.

"Damn it." The woman's fist slammed into the dashboard.

But as Juliana glanced back at the fire, she saw a figure running toward them. His head was down, his body moving fluidly as he leaped across that field.

The van started to accelerate. Juliana grabbed on to

the side of the vehicle. Were they just going to leave him? "Wait!"

"We can't," the woman gritted out as she glanced back from the driver's seat. "That fire will attract every eye in the area. We need to be out of here yesterday."

But—

But the guy was nearly at the van. One of the guys with her reached out a hand, and her "hero" caught it as he leaped toward them. When he landed on the floor of the van, the whole vehicle shuddered.

Juliana's heart nearly pounded right out of her chest. Her hero was alone. "John?"

He shook his head.

"Logan, what the hell?" the woman up front snapped. "You were supposed to be point on extraction, not going back to—"

Logan?

A dull roar began to fill Juliana's ears. There were thousands of Logans in the world. Probably dozens in the military.

Just because her Logan had left her ten years ago that didn't mean...

"There was no sign of another hostage," the guy— Logan—said, and his voice was deep and rumbling.

A shiver worked over her.

Juliana sat on the floor of the van, arms wrapped around her knees. She wanted to see his eyes, needed to, but it was far too dark inside the vehicle.

One of the other men leaned out and yanked the van doors closed. The sound of those metal doors shutting sounded like a scream.

"'Course there wasn't another hostage!" This came from the woman. "She was the only civilian there. I *told* you that. Don't go doubting my intel."

He grunted as he levered himself up. Then he reached for Juliana.

She jerked away from him. "Take off that mask." She could see now. Barely.

He pulled it up and tossed it aside. Not much better. She had a fast impression of close-cropped hair and a strong jaw. Without more light, there was nothing else to see.

She needed to see *more*.

"You're safe now," he told her, and his words were little more than a growl. "They can't hurt you anymore."

His hand lifted, and his fingertips traced over her cheek. Her eyes closed at his touch and Juliana's breath caught because... *His touch is familiar*.

His fingers slid down her cheek. Gentle. Light. It was a caress she'd felt before.

There were some things a woman never forgot—one was the touch of a man who'd left her with a broken heart.

This was her Logan. No, *not* hers. He never had been. "Thank you," she whispered because he'd gotten her out of that nightmare, but she pulled away from his touch. Touching Logan Quinn had always been its own hell for her.

The van rushed along in the night. She didn't know where they were heading. A heavy numbness seemed to have settled over her. John hadn't made it out.

*I'm not...perfect.*

"We're the good guys," one of the other men said, his voice drawling slightly with the flow of Texas in his words. "Your father sent us after you. Before you know it, you'll be home safe and sound. You'll be—"

*Rat-a-tat.*

Juliana opened her mouth to scream as gunfire ripped into the vehicle, but in the next instant, she found herself thrown totally onto the floor of the van. Logan's heavy body covered hers, and he trapped her beneath him.

"Get us out of here, Syd!" Texas yelled.

Juliana could barely breathe. Logan's chest shoved down against hers, and the light stubble on his cheek brushed against her face.

"Hold on," he told her, breathing the words into her ear. "Just a few more minutes…"

Air rushed into the van. Someone had opened the back door! Were they crazy? Why not just invite the shooters to aim at them and—

Three fast blasts of thunder—gunfire. Only, those shots came *from* the van. The men weren't just waiting to be targets. They were taking out the shooters after them.

Three bullets. Then…silence.

"Got 'em," Texas said just seconds before she heard the crash. A screech of metal and the shattering of glass.

The van lurched to the left, seeming to race away even faster.

Juliana looked up. Her eyes had adjusted more to the darkness now. She could almost see Logan's features above her. *Almost.*

"Uh, Logan, you can probably get off her now," that same drawling voice mocked.

But Logan didn't move.

And Juliana was still barely breathing.

"Missed you."

The words were so faint, she wasn't even sure that she'd heard them. Actually, no, she *couldn't* have heard them. Imagined them, yes. That had to be it. Because there was no way Logan had actually spoken. Logan Quinn was the big, strong badass who'd left her without a backward glance. He wouldn't say something as sappy as that line.

*Backbone, girl. Backbone.* She'd survived her hell; no way would she break for a man now. "Are we safe?"

She felt, more than saw, his nod. "For now."

Right. Well, she'd thought they were safe before, until the gunfire had blasted into the back of the van. But Texas had taken out the bad guys who'd managed to follow them. So that had to buy them at least a few minutes. And the way the woman was driving…

*Eat our dust, jerks.*

"Then, if we're safe…" Juliana brought her hands up and shoved against his chest. Like rock. Some things never changed. "Get off me, Logan, *now.*"

He rose slowly, pulling her with him and then positioning her near the front of the van. Juliana was trembling—her body shaking with fear, fury and an adrenaline burst that she knew would fade soon. When it faded, she'd crash.

"Once we get out of Mexico, they'll stop hunting you," Logan said.

Juliana swallowed. Her throat still felt too parched, as if she'd swallowed broken glass, but now didn't seem the time to ask for water. Maybe once they stopped fleeing through the night. Yes, that would be the better moment. "And…when…exactly…do we get out of Mexico?"

No one spoke. Not a good sign.

"In a little over twenty-four hours," Logan answered.

What? No way. They could drive out of Mexico faster than that. Twenty-four hours didn't even make—

"Guerrero controls the Federales near the border," Logan told her, his voice flat. "No way do we get to just waltz out of this country with you."

"Then…how?"

"We're gonna fly, baby."

*Baby.* She stiffened. She was *not* his baby, and if the

guy hadn't just saved her, she'd be tearing into him. But a woman had to be grateful…for now.

Without Logan and his team—and who, exactly, were they?—she'd be sampling the torture techniques of those men in that hellhole.

"We'll be going out on a plane that sneaks right past any guards who are waiting. Guerrero's paid cops won't even know when we vanish."

Sounded good, except for the whole waiting-for-twenty-four-hours part. "And until then? What do we do?"

She felt a movement in the dark, as if Logan were going to reach out and touch her, but he stopped. After a tense moment, a moment in which every muscle in her body tightened, he said, "We keep you alive."

# Chapter Two

Her scream woke him. Logan jerked awake at the sound, his heart racing. He'd fallen asleep moments before. Gunner and Jasper were on patrol duty around their temporary safe house. He jumped to his feet and raced toward the small "bedroom" area they'd designated for Juliana.

He threw open the door. "Julie!"

She was twisting on the floor, tangled in the one blanket they'd given to her. At his call, her eyes flew open. For a few seconds, she just stared blindly at him. Logan hurried to her. She wasn't seeing him. Trapped in a nightmare, probably remembering the men who'd held her—

He reached out to her.

Juliana shuddered and her eyes squeezed shut. "Sorry."

His hands clenched. The better not to grab her and hold her as tight as he could. But this was a mission. Things weren't supposed to get personal between them.

Even though his body burned just looking at her.

Faint rays of sunlight trickled through the boarded-up window. Sydney had done reconnaissance for them and picked this safe house when they'd been planning the rescue. Secluded, the abandoned property was the perfect temporary base for them. They could hear company approaching from miles away. Since the property was situated on high land, they had the tactical advantage. They also had the firepower ready to knock out any attackers who might come their way.

And with that faint light, finally, he could *see* Juliana. She'd changed a lot over the past ten years. Her long mane was gone. Now the blond hair framed her heart-shaped face. Still as beautiful, to him, with her wide, dark eyes and full lips. She was still curved in all the right places. He'd always loved her lush hips and breasts. The woman could—

"Stop staring at me," she whispered as she sat up.

Hell. He *had* been staring. Like a hungry wolf who wanted a bite so badly he could taste it. Taste her.

She pulled up her knees and wrapped her arms around them. "Is John dead?"

Logan didn't let any expression cross his face. Here, he had to be careful. The team wasn't ready to reveal all the intel they were still gathering. *Another reason we aren't slipping out of Mexico yet.* They could have gotten her out faster, but his team didn't like to leave loose ends behind. So a twenty-four-hour delay was standard protocol for them.

"I searched down that hallway," he told her, and he'd found the room they'd been holding her in. Seen the ropes on the floor near not one, but two chairs. *John had been there.* Only, no one had been in the room by the time Logan got there. "I didn't find another hostage."

"They got him out?"

He didn't want to lie to her. "Maybe." He'd been trained at deception for so long, sometimes he wondered what the truth was.

He took a slow step toward her. She didn't flinch away. That was something. "Did they…hurt you?"

She touched her cheek. He could see the faint bruise on

her flesh. "Not as much as they hurt John. They'd come in and take him away, and later, I'd hear his screams."

Another slow step, almost close enough to touch. "So they took you, but they never questioned you?"

"At first, they did." She licked her lips. Now wasn't the time to notice that her lips were as sexy as ever. It wasn't the time, but he still noticed. He'd always noticed too much with her.

*Not for me.* Why did he have a problem getting that fact through his head?

They were thrown together at the moment, but once they got back to the United States, they'd be going their separate ways. Nothing had changed for him. The senator's daughter wasn't going to wind up with the son of a killer.

And now he was a killer, too.

Logan glanced down at his hands. No blood to see, but he knew it stained his hands. After all these years, there was no way to ever get his hands clean. Too much death marked him.

He was good at killing. His old man had been right about that. They'd both been good....

*Too* good.

Logan sucked in a deep breath. *Focus.* The past was buried, just like his father. "So when they were...questioning you..." The team needed this info and he had to ask. "Just what did they want to know?"

Her chin lifted. "They wanted to know about my father." She paused. "What did he do this time?" Pain whispered beneath her words. Logan knew that Juliana had long ago dropped the rose-colored glasses when it came to her father.

As for what the guy had done this time...

*Sold out his country, traded with an arms dealer, took*

*blood money and thought that he'd get away scot-free.* A normal day's work for the senator. "I don't know," Logan said. The lies really were too easy. With her, it should have been harder.

She blinked. "You do." She stood slowly and came close to him. Juliana tilted her head back as she looked up at him. At six foot three, he towered over her smaller frame. "But you're not telling me."

Being the guy's daughter didn't give her clearance. Logan was on Uncle Sam's leash. The job was to get her home safely, not blow an operation that had been running in place for almost two years.

"What did you tell them about the senator?" Just how much did she know about his dark deeds?

"Nothing." Her eyes were on his, dark and gorgeous, just like he remembered. "I didn't tell them a thing about my father. I knew that if I talked they would just kill me once they had the information they needed."

Yeah, they would have. He hated that bruise on her cheek. "So you didn't talk, and they just left you alone?" Her story just didn't make sense. Unless Guerrero had been planning to use her as a bargaining tool and the guy had needed to keep her alive.

For a little longer, anyway.

Juliana shook her head and her hair slid against her chin. "When you found me…they'd taken me into the torture room." She laughed, the sound brittle and so at odds with the soft laughter from his memory. "They were going to *make* me talk then. The same way they made John talk."

But they'd waited four days. Not the standard M.O. for Guerrero's group. All the signs were pointing where he *didn't* want them to point. "This John…what did he look like?"

"Tall, dark…late twenties. He kept me sane, kept me talking all through those long hours."

Yes, Logan just bet he had. But "tall and dark" could be anyone. He needed more info than that.

"You get a good look at his face?" Logan asked.

She nodded.

He offered her what he hoped was an easy smile. "Good enough that you could probably talk to a sketch artist back in the States? Get us a clear picture?"

A furrow appeared between her eyes.

"We'll need to search the missing-person's database," he told her. *Liar, liar.* "A close image will help us find out exactly who John was."

She nodded and her lips twisted. "I can do better than meet with your sketch artist." Her shoulders moved in a little roll. "Give me a pencil and a piece of paper, and I'll draw John's image for you."

He tried not to let his satisfaction show. Juliana was an artist; he knew that. Sure, she usually worked with oils, but he remembered a time when she'd always carried a sketchbook with her.

She'd always been able to draw anything or anyone… in an instant.

"We'll want sketches of every man or woman you saw while you were being held."

Now her shoulders straightened. "Done."

Hell, yes. This could be just the break they needed.

"I want these men caught. I want them *stopped*."

So did he, and Logan wasn't planning on backing off this mission, not until Guerrero was locked up.

The mission wasn't over. In fact, it might just be getting started.

He turned away from her. "Try to get some more sleep." They could take care of the sketches soon enough. For the moment, he needed to go talk with his team to tell them about his suspicions.

But she touched him. Her hand wrapped around his arm and every muscle in Logan's body tightened. "Why did you come for me? Why *you,* Logan?"

He glanced down at her hand. Touching him was dangerous. She should have remembered that. He'd always enjoyed the feel of her flesh against his far too much.

With Juliana, only with her, he'd never been able to hold back.

Maybe that was one of the reasons he'd run so far. He knew just how dangerous he could be to her.

"The senator came to our unit." Yes, that was his voice already hardening with desire—just from her touch. "He wanted you brought to safety."

"Your unit?" Her fingers tightened on him.

He gave a brief nod. "We're not exactly on the books." As far as the rest of the world was concerned, the EOD, or Elite Operations Division, didn't exist. The group, a hybrid formed of recruited navy SEALs, Rangers and intelligence officers from the FBI and CIA, was sent in for the most covert missions. Hostage retrieval. Extreme and unconventional warfare. They were the ones to take lethal, direct attacks…because some targets had to be taken out, no matter the cost.

"Does your unit—your team—have a name?"

Not an official one. "We're called the Shadow Agents." Their code name because their goal was to move as softly as a shadow. To stalk their prey and complete the mission with a minimum amount of exposure.

They always got the job done.

"My father really came to you? How did he even know you were—" Her hand fell away, and he missed her touch. Close enough to kiss, but never close enough to take.

It was the story of his life.

"He didn't come to *me* for help." The senator had nearly doubled over when he'd seen Logan sitting across the desk from him. "He came to my division, the EOD—the Elite Ops Division." Because the FBI had sent him there. The senator still had power and pull in D.C., enough connections to get an appointment with the EOD.

Juliana shook her head. "I didn't think he'd try to get me back." A whisper of the lost girl she'd been, so many years ago, trembled in her words. Lost…but not clueless.

She knew her father too well. The mission to Mexico hadn't just been about her. And if Juliana knew the full truth about the trade-off that had been made in that quiet D.C. office, she'd realize that she'd been betrayed by them both, again.

As if the first betrayal hadn't been hard enough for him to stomach. For years, he'd woken to find himself reaching for her and realizing that she'd forever be out of his hands.

*But she's not out of reach right now.*

He turned fully toward her, almost helpless, and caught her chin in his fingers. "I was getting you back." Logan recognized his mistake. He was letting this case get personal, and that was the last thing he should be doing.

*Hands off. Get her on the plane. Deliver her home.*

*Walk away.*

But it had been so long since he'd held her. Even longer since he'd kissed her. One moment of weakness…would it really hurt? Would it really—

She rose onto her toes and kissed him.

*Yes.*

Logan let his control go. For that moment with her, he just let go. Logan's arms closed around her as he pulled her against him. Her breasts pushed against his chest, and he could feel the tight points of her nipples. She had perfect breasts. He remembered them so well. Pretty and pink and just right for his mouth.

And *her* mouth…nothing was better than her mouth. At twenty, she'd tasted of innocence. Now she tasted of need.

Seduction, at that moment, from her, wasn't what he'd expected. But it sure was what he wanted. His hands tightened around her, and he held her as close as he could. His tongue thrust against hers. The moan, low in her throat, was a sound he'd never forgotten. Arousal hardened his body as her hands slid under his shirt and her nails raked across his flesh.

She was hot. Wild.

But this was *wrong*.

So why wasn't he stopping? Why was he putting his hands on her curving hips and urging her up against the flesh that ached for her? Why was he pushing her back against the wall so that he could trap her there with his body?

*Because I need her.*

The addiction was just as strong as ever, just as dangerous to them both.

He jerked his head up and stared down at her. Juliana's breath panted out. Her lips were red, swollen from his mouth. He wanted to kiss her again. One hot minute wasn't close to making up for the past ten years.

A taste, when he was starving for the full course.

*Get her naked. Take her.*

She'd been through hell. She didn't need this. Him.

He sucked in a sharp breath and tasted her. "This can't happen," Logan said, voice growling.

At his words, the hunger, the passion that had been on her face and in her eyes cooled almost instantly.

"Julie—"

But she shoved against him. "Sorry."

He wasn't. Not for the kiss, anyway. For being a jerk and turning away? Yes.

But making love then, with his teammates in the next room? He wouldn't do that to her.

"I don't even know what I'm doing." She walked away from him and didn't look back. "I don't want this. I don't want—"

She broke off, but Logan stiffened because he could too easily finish her sentence.

*You.*

Adrenaline. The afterburn. He understood it, had been through enough battles and enough desperate hours after them to know what it was like when the spike of adrenaline filled your blood and then burned away.

He headed for the door and kept his shoulders straight, like the good soldier he was supposed to be. "You should try to get some more sleep."

They weren't out of the woods yet. Until they were back in the United States, until death wasn't hanging over her head, he would be her shadow.

That was his job.

Since they'd been forced together, he figured she deserved the warning he'd give her, and he'd tell her only once. "If I get you in my arms again like that…" His hand closed around the old doorknob, tightened, almost broke it off. Logan forced himself to exhale. *If I get you in my arms again…* He glanced back and found her wide, dark eyes on his. "I won't stop. I played the gentleman this time."

Right. Gentleman. Because he knew so much about that bit.

Her eyes said the same.

His jaw clenched. "I'll be damned if I do it again. You offer," he warned, "and I'll take."

Not the smooth words a woman needed to hear after her ordeal in captivity, but there wasn't much more he could say. So he left. While he still could.

And of course, Jasper was waiting for him in the other room. The guy lifted a blond brow. His face, one of those pretty-boy faces that always fooled the enemy, hinted at his amusement. "Now I get it," he drawled.

Angry, aroused, close to desperate, Logan barely bit back the crude retort that rose to his lips. But Jasper was a friend, a teammate.

"You're always looking for the blondes with dark eyes," Jasper teased as he tapped his chin. "Wherever we go, you usually seem to hook up with one."

He was right.

Jasper smirked. "Now I know why." The briefest pause as he studied Logan. "How do they all compare with the original model?"

Logan glared at his friend. *There is no comparison.* Instead of responding to Jasper, Logan stalked off to trade out for his guard shift.

SENATOR AARON JAMES stared down at the gun in his hands. Things weren't supposed to end this way. Not for him. He'd had such big plans.

Easy money. The perfect life. So much power.

And everything was falling apart, slipping away.

The phone on his desk rang. His private line. Jaw clenching, he reached for the receiver. "J-James." He hated the tremble in his voice. He wasn't supposed to be afraid. Everyone else was supposed to fear him.

Once, they had.

Until he'd met Diego Guerrero. Then he'd learned a whole new meaning of fear.

"She's dead." The voice was low, taunting. No accent. Just cold. Deadly.

Diego.

Aaron's hand clenched around the receiver. "Juliana wasn't part of this."

"You made her part of it."

His gaze dropped to the gun. "She's not dead." He'd gotten the intel, knew that Juliana had been rescued. The price for that rescue had been so high.

His life.

"You think this will stop me?" Laughter. "I'll hunt her down. I'll get what I want."

Diego and his men never stopped. Never. They'd once burned a whole village to the ground in order to send a message to rivals. *And I thought I could control him?* Perspiration slicked Aaron's palms. "I made the deals for you. The weapons were transferred. We're clear."

More laughter. "No, we're not. But we will be, once I get back the evidence you've been stashing."

Aaron's heart stopped.

"Did you think I didn't know about that? How else would you have gotten the agents to come for her? You made a trade, didn't you, James?"

"She's my daughter." He hadn't been able to let her just die. Once, she'd run to him, smiling, with her arms open. *I love you, Daddy.* So long ago. He'd wrecked their life together. Thrown it all away but...

*I wasn't letting her die.*

"I want the evidence."

He'd tried to be so careful. He'd written down the names, the dates of all the deals. He'd gotten recordings and created a safety net for himself.

But now he was realizing that he'd never be safe. Not from Guerrero.

CITY OF LIMERICK

14633

PUBLIC LIBRARY

"I'll get the evidence." A deadly promise from his caller. "I'll get you, and I'll *kill* her."

The phone line went dead.

Aaron swallowed once, twice, trying to relieve the dryness in his throat. Things had been going fine with Guerrero until...*I got greedy.*

So he'd taken a little extra money, just twenty million dollars. It had seemed so easy. Sneak a little money away from each deal. Aaron had considered the cash to be a... finder's fee, of sorts.

He'd found the ones who wanted the weapons. He'd set up the deals.

Didn't he deserve a bit of a bonus payment for his work? He'd thought so. But then Guerrero had found out. Guerrero had wanted the money back. When Guerrero started making his demands, Aaron had threatened to use the evidence he had against the arms dealer...

*My mistake.* Aaron now realized what a fool he'd been. You couldn't bluff against the man called El Diablo. The devil would never back down.

Instead of backing down, Guerrero had taken Juliana.

His eyes squeezed shut. Juliana was safe now, but how long would that safety last?

*I'll get you,* Guerrero had said. This nightmare wasn't going to end quietly. The press would find out about what he'd done. Everything he'd built—*gone.*

*I'll kill her.*

Juliana was his regret. He'd pulled her into this war, and she didn't even realize it.

Now she'd die, too.

No one ever really escaped Diego. No matter what promises Logan Quinn had made. You didn't get to cheat the devil and walk away.

The receiver began to hum. Fumbling, Aaron shoved the phone aside. Stared down the dark barrel of the gun.

He wouldn't lose everything, wouldn't be made a mockery on every late-night television show. And even when the public turned on him, Aaron knew he'd still be hunted by Guerrero.

There wasn't a choice. No way out. When Guerrero caught him, El Diablo would torture him. He'd make Aaron suffer for hours, days.

No, no, that wasn't the way that Aaron wanted to go out.

*"I'm sorry, Juliana..."*

JULIANA HELD HER BREATH as the small plane touched down, bounced and touched down again on a landing strip that she couldn't even see. Her hands were clenched tight in her lap, and she didn't make a sound. Fear churned in her, but she held on to her control with all her strength. The men and the woman with her weren't scared, or if they were, she sure couldn't tell.

The woman was flying them. Sydney—that was her name. Juliana had heard Logan call her Sydney once. The group hadn't exactly been chatty, but that was probably due to the whole life-and-death situation they had going on.

The plane bumped once more and then, thankfully, settled down. She felt the plane's speed begin to slow as it taxied down what she sincerely doubted was a real runway. They'd taken off from some dirt road in Mexico, so she figured they were probably landing in the middle of nowhere.

"And we're back in America," Logan murmured from beside her with a flash that could have been a brief grin.

She pushed her fingers against her jean-clad thighs.

The better to wipe the sweat off her hands. "Does this mean I'm safe again?" she asked. He'd been her shadow nearly every moment. Close but not touching. And that was fine, right? She didn't want him touching her.

"This means…" He leaned forward and unhooked the seat belt that had kept her steady during the bumps and dives of the flight. "It means that it's time for you to get your life back." His face came close to hers. The face that she'd never forgotten. His black hair had once curled lightly but now was cut brutally short.

The old adage was annoyingly true—a girl really did never forget her first lover.

Over the years, Logan had grown harder. A thin scar under his chin looked as if it could have been a knife wound. And his eyes now creased with fine lines. No one else had eyes that shade of bright blue.

Only Logan.

Right then, his lips were only inches away. Had she really kissed him hours before? At the time, it had seemed like a good plan. Some hot, fast action to chase away the chill that had sunk into her bones.

*John is dead.* She'd left him behind, and he'd died.

She'd almost died, too, and she'd been so scared. Had it been so wrong to want to feel alive? For just a few moments?

Then Logan had pulled away from her.

Again.

Apparently, it had been wrong. Same story, same verse. Logan Quinn wasn't interested.

And she wanted to forget. She wanted passion, not just him.

*Not. Just. Him.*

They climbed out of the plane. The guy called Gunner went first, sweeping out with his weapon up. Logan stayed by her side. A giant bodyguard who took every step with her.

Two black SUVs waited for them. Logan steered her to the front one. Climbed in and slammed the door behind him.

As soon as he and Gunner were inside, the SUV started moving. The driver tossed back a cell phone to Logan. "Another mission down, Alpha One."

She glanced over and found Logan's eyes on her. Should a man's gaze really feel like a burn? His did.

He had the cell to his ear. Who was he calling already?

"Alpha One checking in," he said into the phone. "Package delivered safely."

Being referred to as a package grated. She wasn't a package. She was a person.

Juliana glanced away from him. Empty landscape flew by them. Miles of dry dirt, dotted occasionally by small bursts of struggling green brush.

"Sir?" Logan's voice was tight as he talked to whoever was on the other end of the line. "Yes, sir. I understand."

The called ended. Short. Sweet.

"Juliana…" He caught her right hand. Oh, now he was back to touching? "I'm sorry," he told her, and he actually sounded as if he was.

Curious now, she glanced over at him. "For what?"

Logan's handsome face was strained and his bright blue eyes told her the news was going to be very bad even before he said, "Senator James is dead."

# Chapter Three

The hits just kept on coming for her. Logan watched Juliana, clad in a black dress that skimmed her curves, as she bent and placed a red rose on her father's closed casket.

No one had been able to glimpse the body—folks didn't need to witness the sight left after a gunshot blast to the head.

His team had been with Juliana for the past four days. They'd stood guard, making sure that she returned to Jackson, Mississippi, without any further incident. Once in town, his team had taken over a group of rooms at a local hotel. He'd insisted that Juliana stay at the hotel, too, so that his team could keep a better eye on her. At first, she'd balked, but he hadn't backed down. His instincts had been screaming at him, and Logan hadn't wanted to let Juliana out of his sight.

He'd expected her to cry at the news of her father's death. After all that she'd been through, she was entitled to her tears.

She hadn't cried once.

Her back was too straight as she walked away from the casket. Mourners began to file past her. One after the other. All offering their condolences and stopping to give her a hug or a pat on the shoulder.

Logan watched from his position underneath the

sweeping branches of a magnolia tree. The fresh scent of the magnolias was in the air. That scent had reminded him of her. The first time they'd kissed, they'd been under a magnolia tree. It had been raining.

She'd trembled against him.

"You know what we have to do," Gunner said from beside him.

Logan spared him a glance. Gunner's gaze was on Juliana, his face tense. Gunner was the quiet type, quiet but deadly. A Spanish father and a Native American mother had given him dark gold skin and the instincts of a hunter. He'd been trained early on a reservation, learned to hunt and stalk prey at his grandfather's knee. A lethal SOB, Gunner was one of the few people on earth who Logan actually called friend. He was also the best SEAL sniper that Logan had ever met.

"Knowing it and liking it…" Logan said with a sigh and tried to force his tense body to relax. "Those are two very different things." But the orders had come down from high above. There wasn't a choice on this one.

With the senator out of the picture, Juliana was now their key to cracking Guerrero.

She'd created the sketches for them. Of Guerrero's goons and of the man she'd called John. Perfect sketches that had even included slight moles on some of the men. Her artist's eyes had noted their every feature. Juliana truly was a perfect witness.

One that Guerrero would never let escape.

It was the picture of John Gonzales that intrigued Logan and his men the most. An innocent man, or so Juliana claimed. Another hostage who'd been taken and tortured by Guerrero.

Except John Gonzales wasn't listed as missing in any database. He wasn't turning up in any intel from the CIA or the FBI. As far as they were concerned, John Gonzales didn't exist.

"You think Guerrero's gonna make a hit on her?" Gunner asked as his gaze swept the crowd.

They weren't there to pay respects to the senator. Neither of them had respected Aaron James worth a damn. They were there for guard duty.

The mission wasn't over. Not by a long shot.

"The boss does." Because Logan wasn't the man in control at the EOD. But this time, he agreed. Every instinct Logan had screamed that Juliana wasn't clear, not yet.

She had to be here today, though. Senator James was being laid to rest. Unfortunately, he wasn't taking his demons with him.

The crowd began to clear away. It was a high-profile funeral, with government officials spilling out for their photo ops. Lots of plainclothes security were scattered around, even some folks Logan recognized from the Secret Service.

In particular, he'd noticed that two men and one woman in black suits stayed close to Juliana. On-loan protection. Those three were so obvious, but maybe that was the point. The Secret Service liked to be in-your-face some days.

"You really up for what you'll have to do?"

Logan paused. He knew what Gunner was asking. Could he look right into Juliana's eyes and lie to her? Over and over again? That was what needed to be done, and because of their past, he was the prime candidate for the job.

The man who was supposed to slip close to Juliana, to stay by her side. He'd be her protection, and she just thought he'd be—

Her lover.

"Yes." His voice dropped to a growl. "I'll do what needs to be done." Another betrayal. But he didn't trust any other agent to get this close to her. Not even Gunner.

Especially not Gunner.

The operative on this mission had to stay with Juliana. Day and night.

*Only me.*

He headed for her. He knew his glasses covered his eyes, so no one would be able to tell he wasn't exactly in the mourning mood. Good. No need to put on a mask just yet.

A long black limo waited for Juliana. The door was open. She'd already turned away from Logan and headed for the vehicle.

As he closed in on his prey, a woman with blond hair—perfectly twisted at the nape of her neck—and wearing a tight black dress wrapped her arms around Juliana. Logan's eyes narrowed as he recognized Susan Walker, one of the late senator's assistants. Logan's team had questioned her for hours, but she'd seemed clueless about the true nature of the senator's activities.

"I can't believe he's really gone," Susan whispered, and a tremble shook her body. "This shouldn't have happened. We had so many plans...."

A tall, dark-haired male walked up behind her and put a comforting hand on her shoulder. Thin black glasses were perched on his nose. Logan knew him, of course. Ben McLintock. Another assistant to the senator. One who hadn't broken during the interview process, but still... he'd been nervous.

McLintock glanced over his shoulder and spotted Logan. The guy swallowed quickly and bobbed his head. *Too nervous.* The EOD was already ripping into his life.

As soon as they turned over some info they could use, something that would tie him in with the senator's illegal deals…

*Then we'll have another talk, McLintock.* Logan wouldn't play so nicely during their next little chat.

"Juliana needs to get home," Ben said as he pulled Susan back. "You can both talk more there."

"Yes, yes, you're right." Susan's thin shoulders straightened. She looked toward the casket again. She shook her head and turned away from the limo. "It just seems like a dream."

Ben took her hand but his eyes were on Juliana. "You have my deepest sympathies."

Juliana's eyes were dry. Her face too pale.

"I never…*never*…thought things would end this way."

The senator had surprised them all. Logan wasn't even sure why the guy had done it. Had the senator thought that if he were out of the picture, Guerrero would back off? That Juliana would be safe?

"I'm truly sorry," Ben told her and bent to press a kiss to Juliana's right cheek.

Logan's back teeth locked. Mr. Touchy-Feely could move the hell on anytime. He could spend some quality moments comforting Susan Walker…

And he could stay away from Juliana.

"I need some time…some air…" Susan said, then staggered back as tears trickled down her cheeks. "I can't leave him…."

The woman's body trembled, and Logan wondered if her knees were about to give way. He tensed, preparing to lunge forward.

But it was good old Ben to the rescue. He kept a firm hold on Susan and steered her away from the vehicle. "I'll take care of her." He offered Juliana a firm nod. "We'll meet you back at the house." Then he glanced at Logan.

Logan gave him a shark's smile. "Don't worry, I'll make sure that she arrives home safe and sound."

Other cars began to pull away. Logan spared a glance for the crowd. Juliana still hadn't met his stare, and that fact was pissing him off. He wanted to take her into his arms, hold her, comfort her. But the woman might as well have been wearing a giant keep-away sign.

The trouble was…he'd always had a problem keeping away from her.

Ben and Susan slowly walked away. They stopped under a big oak, and Susan's shoulders shook as she cried.

"I can't do that." Juliana's voice was just a whisper. "Everyone is staring at me, waiting for me to cry, but I can't." Finally, she glanced at him with those dark, steal-a-man's-soul eyes. "What's wrong with me?"

"Not a damn thing." And he didn't care what the others wanted. The reporters—they were just eager for a clip of the grieving daughter so that they could flash her picture all over their TVs. As for all the senator's so-called friends…Logan knew when tears were real and when they weren't.

Better to not cry at all and still feel than to weep when you didn't feel any emotion.

Her lower lip quivered and she caught it between her teeth. Helpless, Logan reached out and caught her hand. "Come with me," he told her.

She stared up at him. Light raindrops began to fall on them. Did she remember the last time they'd stood in the rain?

*I need to forget.* But that magnolia scent teased his nose.

Sometimes you could never forget.

Logan shrugged out of his jacket and lifted it over Juliana's head. "I want you to come with me."

Juliana didn't move. "You're not supposed to be here." Shaking her head, she said, "I saw you standing under that tree, watching me...but you're not supposed to be here. You should have gone back to Washington or Virginia... or wherever it is that you belong."

For now, he belonged with her.

The rain came down harder now.

"Miss James?" It was the limo driver. He was an older guy with graying red hair. The rain was already dampening his dark suit, but he didn't seem to mind. He stared at Juliana, and there was concern—what looked like *real* concern—in his gaze. Not that fake mask most folks had been sporting for the funeral.

Not hardly.

"She won't be taking the limo," Logan said as he moved in closer to Juliana. "We need to talk," he whispered to her.

She nodded. Drops of rain were on her eyelashes. Or were those tears?

She glanced back at the driver. "Thank you, Charles, but I'll be getting a ride back to the house with Mr. Quinn."

The driver hesitated. "Are you sure?" The look he shot toward Logan was full of suspicion.

After a moment's hesitation, Juliana nodded. "Yes." She cleared her throat. "Thanks for all you've done today... I just... You've always been so good to me."

Charles offered her a sad smile. "And you've been good to me." He gave her a little salute and shoved the back door closed. "Take care of her," he said to Logan.

*I intend to do just that.*

Logan caught Juliana's hand and steered her away from

the grave. "I'm not leaving town yet," he told her. "In fact, I'm going to be staying in Jackson for a while."

Her eyes widened. "Why?"

They were moving faster now. His truck waited just a few steps away. There was no sign of Gunner. "Because I want to be with you."

Her lips parted in surprise. "But— *What?*"

An engine cranked. The limo. It would be pulling away soon, then they could—

The explosion threw Logan right off his feet. The heat of the fire lanced his skin and lifted him up into the air. He clutched Juliana, holding her as best he could. They flew through the air and slammed against the same magnolia tree he'd stood under moments before.

Son of a bitch.

*"Juliana!"* Fear nearly froze his heart.

But she was fine. She pushed against him, and he raised up to see a gash bleeding on her forehead. Her eyes were wide and horrified with understanding. "Oh, my God," she whispered and her head turned toward the burning remains of the limo. "The driver..."

There wasn't anything they could do for the poor guy now. Logan didn't waste time speaking. He grabbed Juliana, lifted her into his arms and raced for his pickup.

Gunner was out there. He'd seen what happened—he'd be radioing for backup and making sure EMT personnel were called. There were injured people on the ground, folks who'd been burned and blasted. Law enforcement who'd been at the funeral were swarming as they tried to figure out what was happening.

Chaos. That was happening.

Logan kept running. Right then, Juliana was his only priority. The others would have to attend to the injured. He had to get her out of there.

"Logan, put me down! We've got to help them! Stop it, just *stop!*" Fury thundered in her words as she fought wildly against his hold.

That fury didn't slow him a bit. With one arm, he yanked open the truck's passenger-side door, and with the other, he pushed her inside.

She immediately tried to jump out.

"Don't." A lethal warning. Fury rode him, too. She'd come too close to death. He could have stood there and watched her die. "Who do you think that bomb was meant for? The driver...or you?"

Juliana paled even more and shook her head. "But... the people... They're hurt..."

She'd always had that soft spot. A weakness that just might get her killed one day.

But not today. "Stay in the truck." He slammed the door and raced around to the driver's side. Two seconds later, he was in the truck, and they were roaring away from the scene.

The limo was supposed to have been swept for bombs. Every vehicle linked to her should have been swept. Someone had screwed up, and Juliana had almost paid for that mistake with her life.

The driver had.

"That was...an accident, right?"

The woman was trying to lie to herself. "I don't think so."

Sirens wailed behind them. Logan glanced in his rearview mirror and saw the dark clouds of smoke billowing up into the air. His gaze turned toward the road as he shoved the gas pedal down to the floorboard. The truck's motor roared.

His hands tightened on the wheel. *A deadly mistake.*

"But…it's safe now." She just sounded lost. "It's *supposed* to be safe."

From the corner of his eye, he saw her hands clench in her lap. Her voice came, soft, confused. "You said…you said once I got back to the U.S., I'd be safe."

"I was wrong."

LOGAN TOOK HER to a cheap hotel on the outskirts of Jackson. She didn't talk any more during the drive. She couldn't. Every time she opened her mouth to speak, Juliana could taste ash on her tongue.

*I'm sorry, Charles.* He'd been with her father for over twenty years. To die like that…

She swallowed. *More ash.*

The truck braked. She followed Logan, feeling like a robot. Only, her steps were slow, wooden. He tossed a wad of cash at the desk clerk and ordered the kid to forget that he ever saw them. Then they pushed inside the last room, the one located at the edge of the parking lot.

A ceiling fan fluttered overhead when Logan flipped the light switch. Juliana's gaze swept around the small room. A sagging bed. *One* bed. A scarred desk. A lumpy chair. The place had *pay-by-the-hour* written all over it.

"You're bleeding."

Juliana glanced over at the sound of Logan's voice. She saw that his stare was focused on her forehead. Lifting her hand, she touched the drying blood. She'd forgotten about that. "It's just a scratch."

Her dress was torn, slitting up a bit at the knee. And said knee felt as if it had slammed into a tree—because it had.

"You're too calm."

What? Was she supposed to be screaming? Breaking

down? She wasn't exactly the breaking-down type. Right then, all she could think was...

*What's next?*

And how would she handle it?

"Shock." He took her hand and led her to the matchbox bathroom. "Let's get you cleaned up."

She wrenched away from him as anger began to finally boil past the numbness holding her in check. "I'm not a child, Logan."

He blinked his sky-blue eyes at her. The brightest blue she'd ever seen. Those eyes could burn hot or flash ice-cold. Right then, they held no emotion at all. "I never said you were."

"I can clean myself up." She took slow, measured steps to the bathroom. Took slow, deep breaths—so she wouldn't scream at him. "Stop acting like I'm about to fall apart."

"Someone just tried to *kill* you. A little falling apart is expected."

Near the chipped bathroom door, Juliana paused and looked back at him. "Why do the expected?"

He stared at her as if he'd never seen her before. Maybe he hadn't. "Your father's gone." Now there was anger punching through his words. "Your car just exploded into a million pieces all over a graveyard. Want to tell me why you're so cool?"

Because if she let the wall inside of herself down, even for a second, Juliana was very afraid that she might start crying and not stop. "Wanna tell me why you're with me now?"

"Because you need someone to keep you alive!" Then he was charging across the room and catching her shoulders in a strong grip. "Or do you not even care about the little matter of living anymore?"

She stared up at him. Just stared. She was finding that being so close to Logan hurt. Over him? Not hardly. Once upon a time, she'd been ready to run away with the jerk.

She'd waited for him in a bus station—waited five hours.

He'd never shown. Too late, she'd learned that he'd left her behind.

Could she really count on him to keep sticking around now? He'd saved her butt in Mexico. Hell, yes, she was grateful, but Logan wasn't the kind to stay forever. Juliana wasn't going to depend on him again. "Call the cops," she told him, weary beyond belief all of a sudden. Her body just wanted to sag, and she wanted to sleep. An adrenaline burst fading? Or just the crash she'd been fighting for days? Either way, the result was the same. "They can keep me safe."

Juliana opened the door and entered the closet that passed for a bathroom.

"Juliana—"

Then she closed the door in his face. She looked in the mirror. Saw the too-pale face, wide eyes and the blood that covered her forehead.

She took another breath. *Ash.* How long would it be until she forgot that taste?

Her eyes squeezed shut. She could still feel the lance of fire on her skin. If Logan hadn't been there, she would've been in that car.

And it would've been pieces of *her* that littered that cemetery.

LOGAN TURNED AWAY when he heard the sound of the shower. He yanked out his phone and punched the number for his boss. "What the hell happened?" he demanded when the line was answered. "The site should have been safe, it should have—"

"You aren't secure." Flat. Bruce Mercer was never the type to waste words or emotion. "We need you to get the woman and get out of that hotel. Backup is en route."

Not secure? For the moment, they were. "No one followed me. No one—"

"There's a leak in the senator's office," Mercer said in his perfectly polished voice. A voice that, right then, gave no hint of his New Jersey roots. Those roots only came out when Mercer was stressed—and very little ever stressed him. "Money talks, and we all know that Guerrero has a ton of money."

More than enough money to make certain one woman died.

"You need to bring her in," the boss ordered. "We're setting up a meet location. Tell her she'll be safe with you. Get her to trust you."

Yes, that had been the plan…until the cemetery caught fire. "We're still going through with this?" He almost crushed the phone. The shower was still running. Juliana couldn't hear him, but just in case, Logan took a few cautious steps across the room.

"The plan remains the same. You know how vital this case is to the department."

"I don't want to put her in the line of fire." She'd come close enough to death.

"That's why you're there, Alpha One. To come between her and any fire…just like you did today."

Yes, he had the burn marks on his skin to prove it.

"Your relationship to her is key. You know that. Get her trust, and we can close this case and finally put Guerrero away."

But could they keep her alive long enough to do it?

A pause hummed on the line. "Does she realize what's happening?" Mercer wanted to know.

"She realizes that she's targeted for death." Any fool would realize that. Juliana wasn't a fool.

Once, she'd been too trusting. Was she still? The idea of using her trust burned almost as much as those flames had.

"Have you told her about John?"

The shower shut off. His jaw clenched. "Not yet."

"Do it. The sooner she realizes that you're her only hope of staying alive, the sooner we get her cooperation."

It wasn't just about keeping her alive. The EOD wanted to use her. They were willing to set her up if it meant getting the job done.

Logan exhaled. "When are we moving her?"

"Ten minutes."

The line died.

Ten minutes. Too little time to convince Juliana that he was the only one she could trust to keep her alive.

JULIANA WAS CLIMBING OUT of the shower when her cell phone rang. She'd washed away the blood and ash, but the icy water had done nothing to soothe the aches and pains in her body. She'd cried beneath that pounding water. Juliana hadn't been able to hold back the tears any longer. Her whole body had trembled as she let her grief and pain pour out of her. Part of Juliana had just wanted to let the grief take control, but she'd fought that instinct. Gathering all of her strength, she'd managed to stop the tears. Managed to get her wall of self-control back in place.

As the phone rang again, she grabbed for the dress

she'd tossed aside moments before and pulled her phone from the near-invisible pocket. Her fingertip slid across the smooth surface. Ben McLintock. Her father's aide. The guy had to be frantic. She answered the call, lifting the phone to her ear as she said, "Ben, listen, I'm all right. I—"

The bathroom door crashed open. Juliana gasped and jumped back. Logan stood in the doorway, eyes fierce. "End the call."

"Juliana!" Ben's voice screeched. "Where are you? I searched for you after the explosion, but you'd vanished! Oh, God, at first—at first I thought you were in the car!"

She almost had been.

"Then a cop remembered seeing you jump into a truck." His breath heaved over the line. "They're saying it looks like a car bomb, it looks like—"

"I'm in a motel, Ben. I—"

Logan took the phone from her. Ended the call with a fast shove of his fingers. A muscle flexed in his jaw. "GPS tracking. Your phone just told him exactly where we are."

His gaze swept over her. Crap, she was just wearing a towel, one that barely skimmed the tops of her thighs even while her breasts pushed against the loose fold she'd made to secure the terry cloth. He'd seen her in less plenty of times, but that had been a long time ago.

Juliana grabbed her dress and held it in front of her body. It was a much better shield than the thin towel. "No one is tracking me, okay, Rambo? That was just Ben. He was worried and wanted to make sure—"

"Guerrero has a man in your father's office. Someone willing to trade you for a thick wad of cash." His eyes blazed hotter, and they were focused right on—

*"Eyes up,"* she told him, aware of the hot burn in her cheeks.

Those eyes, when they met hers, flashed with a need she didn't want to acknowledge right then.

"I know how this works," he told her. "And I sure as hell know that we have to move now."

GPS tracking. Yes, she knew that was possible, but... "Why? Why can't they just let me go?" Her father was dead. Shouldn't that be the end with Guerrero?

Logan didn't speak.

*"Turn around,"* she snapped.

His brows rose but he slowly turned, giving her a view of his broad back. Juliana dropped the dress and towel and yanked on her underwear—a black bra and matching panties—as fast as she could. Her gaze darted to his back and—

Wait, had he been watching her in the mirror? She couldn't tell for certain, but for a moment there, she'd sworn she saw his gaze cut to the mirror.

To her reflection.

"Done yet?" he asked, almost sounding bored. Almost.

Eyes narrowing, Juliana yanked on her dress. With trembling hands, she fumbled and pulled up the zipper. All while Logan stood right there. "Done," she gritted out. *Not even trying to play the gentleman now.* "My father is dead. Why do they want to bury me, too?"

He turned to face her. His gaze swept over her. Made her chilled skin suddenly feel too hot. "Because you're a witness they can't afford." He caught her elbow and led her back through the small hotel room. He paused at the door, glanced outside.

"A witness?" Yes, she'd seen the faces of a few men in Mexico, but...

"Did you know that no witness has ever been able to

positively identify Diego Guerrero? The man's a ghost. The U.S. and Mexican governments both know the hell he brings, but no one has been able to so much as touch him."

She pulled on her pumps. Useless for running but she felt strangely vulnerable in bare feet. "Well, I didn't see the guy, either. The big boss man never came in when I was being held." He'd left the torture for his flunkies.

Logan shot her a fast, hard stare. "Yes, he did come in."

She blinked.

"From what we can tell, he spent more time with you than he ever has with anyone else. You saw his face. You talked to him."

Wrong. "No, I didn't. I—"

"John Gonzales is one of the aliases that Guerrero uses."

*My name's...John. John Gonzales.* She remembered the voice from the darkness. *Who are you?*

"He didn't need to torture information out of you, Juliana. All he had to do was ask for it in the dark."

And they'd talked for so many hours. Her heart slammed into her chest.

"You weren't talking to another hostage in that hell-hole." Logan exhaled on a low sigh. "My team believes you were talking to the number-one weapons dealer in Mexico—the man his enemies call El Diablo because he never, ever leaves anyone alive who can ID him."

Goose bumps rose on her arms.

"That man with you? The one you were so desperate to save? *That* was Diego Guerrero."

Oh, hell. "Logan..."

A fist pounded on the door.

Logan didn't move but she jumped. "I need you to trust me," he told her. "Whatever happens, you have to stay with me, do you understand? Guerrero's tracked you. He'll use anything and anyone he can in order to get to you."

The door shook again. There was only one entrance and exit to that room. Unless they were going to crawl out that tiny window in the bathroom…

"I can keep you alive," Logan promised, eyes intense. "It's what I do."

Her father had told her that he was an assassin. That for years Logan's job had been to kill.

But he'd saved her life twice already.

"This is the police!" a voice shouted. "Miss James, you need to come out! We're here to help you."

Logan's smile was grim. "It's not the police. When we open that door, it might look like them—"

*Nightmare. This is a—*

"—but it won't be them. They'll either kill you outright or deliver you to Guerrero." His voice was low, hard with intensity. "I'm your best bet. You might hate me—"

No, she didn't. Never had. Just one of their problems…

"—but you know no matter what you have to face on the other side of that door—"

Cops? Maybe more killers?

"—I'll keep you safe."

"We're comin' in!" the voice shouted. "We're comin'—"

Gunfire exploded. Juliana didn't scream, not this time. She clamped her mouth closed, choked back the scream that rose in her throat and dived for cover.

Logan jumped for the window. He knocked out the glass, took aim and—

Smiled.

From her position on the floor, Juliana watched that cold grin slip over his face. She expected him to start firing, but…

But she heard the sound of a car racing away. Tires squealed.

And Logan stalked to the door. He yanked it open.

The man he'd called Gunner stood on the other side.

Juliana scrambled to her feet. "The cops?"

"Those trigger-happy idiots weren't cops." Gunner shrugged. "A few shots sent them running fast enough, but I'm betting those same shots will have the real cops coming our way soon enough." His eyes, so dark they were almost black, swept over her. "There's a hit on you. A very, very high price on that pretty head. So unless you want the next funeral to be your own…"

"I don't."

Logan offered his hand to her. "Then you'll come with me."

In order to keep living, she'd do anything that she had to do.

Juliana took his hand, and they ran past the now bullet-scarred side of the hotel and toward the waiting SUV.

Trust…it looked as if she had to give it to him.

Because there was no other choice for her.

DIEGO GUERRERO STARED at the television. The pretty, little reporter talked in an excited rush as the camera panned behind her to take in the destruction at the cemetery.

Smoke still drifted lazily in the air.

"Police aren't talking with the media yet," she said, "but a source has revealed that the limousine destroyed in that explosion was the car used by Juliana James, daughter of Senator Aaron James. Juliana was laying her father to rest after his suicide—"

Juliana's old man had been a coward until the end.

"—when the explosion rocked the service."

No, it hadn't rocked the service. The blast had erupted *after* the service. His sources were better than hers.

"One man was killed in the explosion—"

The driver had been collateral damage. There was always collateral damage.

"—while four others were injured. Juliana James left the scene and is now in an undisclosed location."

His eyes narrowed. The reporter rambled on, saying nothing particularly useful. After a moment, he shut off the television, then turned slowly to face his first in command.

Luis Sanchez swallowed, the movement stretching the crisscross of scars on his throat. The man was already sweating.

"Was I not clear?" Diego asked softly.

*"Si,"* Luis rasped. His damaged voice was often limited to rough rasps and growls.

"Then, if I told you—clearly—that I wanted Juliana James brought back to me alive—" he shrugged, a seemingly careless move, but it still caused Luis to flinch "—why did she nearly die today?"

Luis shifted from his right foot to his left. "I heard… word on the street is that…s-someone else has a hit on her. They're offering top dollar…for her dead body."

Now, that gave him pause. "Who?"

"D-don't know, but I will find out. I will—"

"You will," Diego agreed, "or you'll be the one dying." He never made idle threats. Luis understood that. Luis had been with him for five years—and he'd witnessed Guerrero carry out all of his…*promises* to both friends and enemies.

"Put the word out that Juliana James isn't to be touched." Except by him. They had unfinished business. She couldn't die, not yet. He needed her to keep living a bit longer. "And when you find the one who put out this hit—" he leaned forward and softly ordered "—you make his death hurt."

Because *no one* interfered with Diego's plans. *No one*.

## Chapter Four

The place wasn't exactly what she'd expected. Juliana glanced around the small elevator from the corner of her eye. When Logan had said that he was taking her in for a briefing with his team, she'd figured they'd go somewhere that was…official.

Not so much a hole-in-the-wall.

From the outside, the building hadn't even looked inhabited. Just a big, rough wooden building. Maybe three stories.

But Logan had led the way inside, walking with sure steps. Now they were riding up the creaking elevator, and Juliana was forcing herself to take slow, deep breaths.

She'd cried in the shower. She hadn't been able to help herself. But she wouldn't, couldn't cry now. Now wasn't the time for weakness.

The elevator came to a hard stop, jarring Juliana and sending her stumbling into Logan. The guy didn't so much as move an inch, of course, because he was like some kind of military superhuman, but his arms closed around her.

"I've got you."

That was her problem. Being with him—it was just making everything more painful.

She pulled away and saw a muscle flex in his jaw. "I'm fine." The doors were sliding open. Very, very slowly. "Is this the best that the EOD could do?" The EOD. He'd told her a little more about the EOD on the drive over, but the information that he'd given her regarding the Shadow Agents just hadn't been enough to satisfy her curiosity.

When she'd tried to press him, she'd gotten a just-the-facts-ma'am type of routine. That hadn't been good enough. Juliana had kept pressing. The need-to-know routine was getting on her nerves.

Logan had told her that the EOD was composed of individuals from different military and government backgrounds. Their missions were usually highly classified.

And very, very dangerous.

A situation tailor-made for Logan and his team.

"On short notice, this building was the best we could find in terms of providing us with a low-profile base," a woman's voice told her, and Juliana glanced up to see Sydney walking toward them. Sydney stared at Logan with one raised eyebrow. "We were starting to wonder if you'd gotten lost."

He growled. Was that a response? Juliana guessed so, because in the next instant, they were all heading down a narrow hallway. A fast turn, then they entered an office. One that didn't look nearly as run-down as the rest of the place. Two laptops and a stash of weapons were on the right. Some empty chairs waited to the left.

Juliana gladly slumped into the nearest chair.

*I can still feel the fire on my skin.* Even the cold water from the shower hadn't been able to wash away that memory. Juliana rubbed her hands over her arms and caught Logan's narrow-eyed glance.

The guy watched her too much. Like a hawk.

She cleared her throat, glanced away from him and saw the others file into the room. No masks this time. Just tough, fierce fighters.

The woman was already sitting down near the side of the table. Sydney. Juliana had no idea what the woman's last name was. She was booting up her laptop while a big, blond male leaned over her shoulder.

Gunner closed the door, sealing them inside, and he flashed her a broad grin. Was that grin supposed to be reassuring? It looked like a smile that a tiger would give the prey he was about to eat.

The silence in the room hit her then, and Juliana realized that everyone was just…staring at her. Hell, had she missed something?

"You understand why you must have protection, right?" Sydney pressed. Juliana realized the woman must have asked the question before.

Her breath eased out slowly as her gaze swept over them. "Tell me your names." A simple thing, maybe, but she was tired of being in the dark. From this point on, she expected to be in the loop about everything.

"I'm Sydney," the woman said with a slow blink, "and I…um, believe that you know Logan pretty well."

Too well. She would *not* blush right then. She was way past the blushing point. An exploding car made a woman forget embarrassment.

"I'm Gunner," the big guy to the right said. His dark hair fell longer than Logan's, and his eyes—no eyes should be so dark and so cold.

Juliana glanced at the last man. The blond wasn't leaning over Sydney any longer. He'd taken a seat next to her. His arm brushed against hers.

"Jasper," he said. Just that. More rumble than anything else.

Gunner frowned at the guy, and his dark, cold gaze lingered on the arm that Jasper had pressed against Sydney.

Ah…okay. "First names only, huh?" Juliana murmured. That was nice and anonymous.

"For now, it's safer that way," Logan said.

Right. Though Juliana wasn't even sure any of them had given their real names. She put her fingers into her lap, twisting them together. "How are you going to stop the man who is after me?"

Sydney and Logan shared a brief look. Juliana's shoulders tensed. She wasn't going to like this part; she knew it even before Logan said, "Your father…made a deal with the EOD." Logan's quiet voice shouldn't have grated, but it did.

Juliana forced herself to meet his stare. "What sort of deal?" She needed to know all of her father's dark secrets, whether she wanted to hear them or not. It wasn't the time to wear blinders.

"Your safety, your life, in return for evidence that he had against Diego Guerrero."

Guerrero. Her heart slammed into her ribs. The man that Logan had told her was the same guy she knew as John Gonzales.

"What did my father—" Her voice sounded too weak. *Don't be weak.* Juliana tried again. "Just what was my father doing with this Guerrero?"

"Selling out his country." From the one called Jasper. When he spoke and she heard the drawl of Texas sliding beneath his words, Juliana remembered him.

Maybe he expected her to flinch at the blunt charge, but she didn't. She just sat there. She'd known her father wasn't exactly good for a long time.

"The senator facilitated deals between Guerrero and foreign officials," Jasper said with his eyes narrowed on her. "Your father would find the people who needed the weapons, those desperate for power, those ready to over-throw weak governments…"

Her father had made so many connections over the years. He'd been on dozens of committees, and he'd told her once that he'd been working hard to make the world a better place.

Better? Not from the sound of things. Just more bloody, more dangerous.

"We're talking about billions of dollars' worth of weapons," Jasper continued. "From what we can tell, your father took a nice little finder's fee for every deal he made."

She swallowed and forced her hands to unclench. "You're saying my father took a commission from Guerrero? That every time weapons were sold—" *every time people died when those weapons were used* "—he got a slice of the pie."

Jasper nodded grimly.

"He was a good man," she had to say it. Someone did. He wasn't even cold in the ground. "Once." She could remember it, couldn't she? If she tried hard enough, the memories were there. "Before my mother died. He went to Congress to make the world better."

Only, he'd wound up working to destroy it.

Was that why he'd put the gun to his own head? Because he couldn't live with what he'd done?

*You left me behind to deal with everything, all on my own.*

Sometimes it seemed as if he'd left her that hot summer night when her mother died in the car accident on a lonely stretch of Mississippi road.

"He wanted to save you," Logan said, the words deep and rumbling. His hand took hers. Almost helplessly, her gaze found his. "He agreed to trade every bit of evidence he had on Guerrero in order to get you home alive."

"So that's why you—your team came for me." In that hell. "Because my father paid you with his evidence."

"He didn't exactly make the payment...." Gunner muttered as he ran an agitated hand through his hair. "He put a bullet in his head instead."

Juliana flinched.

Logan surged to his feet. His chair fell to the floor behind him with a clatter. Logan lunged for the other man. "Gunner..."

Gunner just shrugged, but he hurriedly backed up a few feet. "Payment was due at delivery, right? As soon as you were brought back safe and sound, Senator James was going to give us the intel we needed. Only, instead of delivering, he chose to...renegotiate."

Juliana could only shake her head. This...*this* was the last thing she'd expected when Logan had brought her in to meet with the other agents. "I *buried* him today."

"And because of Guerrero's deals, hundreds of people are buried every single day," Sydney said, her voice soft and lacking the leashed fury that seemed to vibrate beneath Gunner's words. "We have to stop him. You have to help us."

"How? I saw Guerrero, but..." But she'd already told them that. She'd sketched out half a dozen pictures. Done everything that she could. "Now he wants me dead."

Logan shoved Gunner into the nearest wall. "You aren't dying." He tossed that back without glancing her way. His focused fury was on the other man.

Sydney cleared her throat. "Your father...indicated that you had the evidence we need."

Her words had Juliana blinking in surprise. "I don't. I didn't even know about Guerrero until—I just thought I was being held with a man named John Gonzales, until Logan told me the truth! John said that he'd been kidnapped just like me. When those men put me in the room, John was already there. I didn't know he was Guerrero, and I don't know anything about his weapons." She wished that she could help them. She wanted to make this nightmare end, but she just didn't have any evidence.

"Your father left a suicide note."

She didn't want to hear any more. Juliana pushed to her feet, found Logan by her side. For someone so big, he could sure move fast. She stared up at him. "I wasn't told about a note." He hadn't told her.

He glanced back at Sydney. Glared. "We didn't…want that part leaking to the media."

Rage boiled within her. He was so close. In that instant, she wanted to strike out at him. To hurt him, as she was being torn apart. "I'm not the media! I'm his daughter!"

"Exactly." From Jasper, drawling Jasper. Cold Jasper. "In his note, he said you had all the evidence. We kept that bit from the media, but Guerrero would have put a spy in your father's life, someone who could keep close tabs on him. That someone…we believe he told Guerrero about the evidence."

Her head was about to erupt. The throbbing in her temples just wouldn't stop. "I have no evidence." Could she say it any plainer? "I can't give you anything!"

"Guerrero thinks you can. And he's just going to keep coming for you…" Jasper didn't have to finish. She knew what the guy had been about to say….

*Until you're dead.*

"So you see now why you must have protection," Sydney said with a firm nod. "Until we can recover the information we need, you've got a target on your back."

A giant one. Yes, she got that. "And what happens to my life?"

"With Guerrero out there, you don't have a life." Blunt.

Cold. Sydney could have an edge just as hard as Gunner's—or Jasper's.

"We're going to get him," Logan promised her.

She wanted to believe him. But then, she'd gone for his lies before. Juliana wet her lips. Lifted her chin. "This protection…what does it mean?"

Sydney cast a quick look at Logan before her attention returned to Juliana, then she explained, "It means an EOD agent is assigned to stay with you 24/7. You'll be watched, monitored and kept alive," Sydney told her. "What more could you want?"

Now Juliana's eyes were on Logan. He seemed even bigger to her in that moment. More dangerous. So far removed from the boy she'd known. Maybe she'd never really known him at all. "Which agent?"

The faint lines around Logan's eyes deepened.

"Which agent?" Juliana demanded again.

A beat of silence, then Sydney said, "Given your… history with Logan…"

Did everyone know that she'd given the man her virginity? Had the team been briefed about that? Her breath heaved in her chest, but Juliana managed to speak from between her clenched teeth. "There's a thing about history. It's in the past."

Logan's expression didn't change.

"If I'm giving up my life…" For how long? Until they caught Guerrero? Until the magical evidence turned up? "Then I want a say on my guard choice."

But Logan was already shaking his head. "No, it's—"

Not wanting anyone else to overhear, she closed in on him. "We're done, Logan." A whisper that she knew he'd heard, but hopefully the others hadn't. Juliana turned away from him. Pointed to the man that Logan had shoved up against the wall moments before. Gunner. Then, raising her voice once more, she said, "I'll take him."

"Hell." Gunner's shoulders dropped. "I knew this wouldn't be easy."

Juliana stepped toward him. "Actually, all things considered, I think I'm being pretty agreeable." Another step. "If this is going to work, then—"

Logan's hand wrapped around her shoulder, stilling her. "We're not done."

She saw Gunner's gaze dart from Logan's hand back to her face. Juliana wondered just what he saw, because Gunner gave a little whistle.

"No, I don't think you are," Gunner said.

But then Logan was spinning her back around. He leaned in close, and she could feel the force of his fury surrounding her. "Time to get some things clear."

Oh, what, *now* was the time for that?

"I'm lead on this team." Each word was bitten off.

"That's why he's Alpha One," Gunner said from behind her. The guy was so not very helpful.

"You don't give the orders," Logan snapped at her. "I do. When it comes to keeping you alive, I'm the one in charge. I'm the one who is going to stand between you and whatever hell might come." His gaze searched hers. "You might not like me. Hell, you might hate me, but too bad. This isn't about emotion. It's about getting a job done."

Her chest hurt. Juliana forced herself to breathe. "And nobody else here can—"

"I'm your guard. Day and night. Get used to it."

Her jaw clenched. She didn't want to get used to any of this, and Logan was stripping away all of her choices.

"Unless you don't think you can…trust yourself around me…" This line Logan spoke with a slow, sexy grin.

It took a stunned instant for his words to register with

Juliana. "What?" She almost had to pick her jaw off the floor. There was no way he'd just said that.

"Maybe the old feelings are still there." Now he was barely whispering, talking for her alone. Closing in on her just as she'd done with him moments ago. "Is that what scares you? That when we're alone, you might want… more?"

*Yes.* "No," Juliana denied immediately.

His gaze called her a liar, but he just said, "Then we're set. I'm point. I'll be with you, making sure you're safe. We'll keep you alive."

Promises, promises…

JULIANA STOOD IN THE HALLWAY while Logan and Gunner huddled over a computer screen. They'd called their boss, some guy named Mercer, then they'd gotten busy with their plans.

Plans about her life.

"You're going to be all right."

She jumped a little bit at Sydney's voice. She hadn't even heard the other woman approach, but Sydney was there, watching her with a light green stare.

"Logan's good at his job," Sydney continued, giving a nod toward the men. "The best I've ever seen in the field."

She didn't doubt that.

"He's always cool under fire," Sydney said as she crept closer. "The only time I've ever saw his control crack… it was when we were in Mexico, waiting to get you out." A faint smile curved her lips. "The man wanted to race in, guns blazing, when he knew that wasn't protocol."

Juliana's back was pressed to the wall. Her gaze swept over the other woman. She wasn't sure what to make of Sydney. On the outside, Sydney looked petite, almost breakable, but…but then Juliana looked into her eyes, and she could see the power there.

Sydney was a woman who'd seen dark things, done dark things. It was all there, the memories, the pain, in her eyes.

"I thought he did come in with guns blazing," Juliana said, forcing herself to speak. She remembered him rushing into that room, nearly ripping the door away. Clad in the black ski mask with the big gun in his hands, he'd looked so deadly.

She hadn't known who she should fear more. The man with the knife at her throat or the masked man who promised hell.

"Does he scare you?"

Juliana's lashes flickered. She'd have to remember just how observant Sydney could be. Nothing seemed to slip past the woman. "No." And it was the truth, mostly. No matter how deadly Logan was, she never thought he would physically hurt her.

But she did fear the way he could make her feel. He stirred too much lust in her. Made her want things she couldn't have.

*Sometimes he scares me.*

But the full truth was…*sometimes I scare myself.*

"Good." Sydney's gaze darted back to the men. "And Gunner?"

*Yes.* He made her nervous. So did Jasper.

Her silence must have been answer enough because Sydney gave a little shrug that seemed to say she understood. "Gunner has a special grudge against Guerrero. We were…we were in South America about two years ago. Came on a village that was supposed to be a safe haven for us and for the hostage we'd rescued."

"You do that a lot?" Juliana asked. "Rescue people?"

"We do what needs to be done." Sydney rubbed her palm over her heart in an almost unconscious motion. "The village… I was the one doing intel. I thought it was safe. I didn't realize Guerrero had made a deal with a rebel leader in the area. The gunfire started. It was a bloodbath."

Juliana glanced at Sydney's hand. "You were shot."

Sydney's hand dropped. "Gunner was the one who took four bullets, but he still kept fighting. He and I—we were the extraction team. He got me out, too."

"And the hostage?"

Sydney gave a small shake of her head. "Gunner's brother didn't make it out."

Oh, hell.

"So you can see why he might seem…determined… to get Guerrero."

The men were finished talking. They were heading back toward them. Juliana glanced at Gunner's eyes. Still dark. Still cold. But…she could have sworn she now saw the echo of pain in his gaze.

"It wasn't a sanctioned mission." Now Sydney was whispering. "We went in, just the two of us, because we had to get him out."

There was something there in Sydney's voice. Something… "Who was the hostage to you?" Juliana asked. Gunner's brother, but maybe more.

Sydney just gave her a sad smile. "We all want Guerrero stopped."

Juliana nodded.

"Don't give up," Sydney told her. "Whatever happens, keep fighting, keep working with us. Help us take him out."

Staring into Sydney's gaze and seeing the struggle on her face, Juliana realized that walking away from the EOD wasn't an option. "I will." She'd do her part. Guerrero was a monster, one who was destroying lives left and right.

He had to be stopped.

Logan's arm brushed hers.

*We'll stop him.*

JULIANA WASN'T GOING to like this walk down memory lane. Logan knew it even before the woman's body tensed up, boardlike, in the seat beside his.

"Why the hell are we here?"

The *here* in question would be in the middle of nowhere—or rather, in the middle of the woods in Mississippi. Pulling in front of an old cabin that had seen so many better days, long ago.

A familiar cabin.

He pulled the SUV around back. Made sure that it was hidden. There was only one dirt road that led to this cabin. So when the men hunting Juliana came calling, his team would know.

Logan climbed from the vehicle, swept his gaze past the trees. Jasper and Gunner would be setting up watch points out there, securing the perimeter.

The location was the perfect trap. And Juliana…

"Logan, *why here?*"

She was the perfect bait.

He forced a careless grin to his face. "Because the cabin's secluded. It's secure. And no one in Guerrero's team would think to look for you here."

True enough. They wouldn't think to look for her there, not until they were hand-fed the info.

*Sorry, Juliana.* And he was. He didn't like lying to her, setting her up. But no matter what else happened, he would keep her safe.

That part hadn't been a lie.

She was already out of the SUV, heading up the old wooden steps that led to the front of the cabin. The steps creaked beneath her feet.

Logan followed her. When she paused on the slightly sagging porch, he opened the door for her with a sweep of his hand, and he remembered the past.

*No one's here, Julie. Come inside.*

*Logan, are you sure?*

*The cabin's mine. No one will find us here. It's just you...and me.*

For an instant, he could feel her mouth beneath his. The memory was so strong. Her lips had been soft, silken. Her body had been a perfect temptation under his.

*Here.* It had all happened here.

Locking his jaw, Logan slammed the door shut behind him and secured the lock. Because the team had been planning this move in advance—for days, actually, even before the hit in the cemetery—the cabin was already wired. Cameras had been set up to scan the cabin's exterior. Alarms and sensors were strategically placed outside.

The feed would all go back to Sydney, since she was their tech queen. But Logan had a few monitors set up inside the cabin, too. He liked to keep his eyes open. Being blind in the field had never suited him.

He turned and found Juliana's dark eyes on him. There were smudges beneath her eyes. Exhaustion. She looked so fragile, so very breakable, that his body tensed.

*Go to her,* every instinct he had screamed at him, but he knew Juliana didn't want his comfort. The stiff lines of her body said she didn't want him at all.

The kiss in Mexico had been a fluke. She hadn't come looking for seconds, and she'd been very clear when she told him they were done.

*Not yet.*

So he'd just hold on to his fantasies. They'd gotten him through plenty of long nights, and he could keep his hands off her. He'd try to keep them off, anyway.

"You can take the room at the top of the stairs," he said. It was the only bedroom there and—

Her gaze darted to the staircase. "I'd, um, rather not."

The memories were hitting her, too. He'd pushed her back at the EOD meeting. The idea of her being so close to one of the other agents—*hell, no.* He didn't want her spending any nights alone with Gunner or Jasper. So he'd pushed to see what she'd do.

And maybe because he hoped that deep down she still wanted him. He was on fire for her.

Only, Juliana was turning away. "I'll take the couch."

"Take the bed." He'd gotten a new bed for her. New sheets. New covers. She could rest, take it easy and—

"I'm not getting into your bed," she snapped. Her temper was back. Probably the wrong time to mention he'd always found her sexy when temper spiked her blood and heated her voice. "I might have to stay with you, but I don't have to—"

"You kissed me in Mexico." His words stopped her, but he regretted them the minute they left his mouth. He didn't want to make her mad. He just wanted…

Juliana heaved out a long sigh. "I was half-awake. I didn't know what I was doing." No emotion in her words. "Don't worry, I won't make that mistake again."

If only. "Maybe I want you to do it again." Because they were alone, for the moment. And he was tired of pretending that he didn't ache just looking at her. That her scent didn't make him hard. That her voice—husky, soft—didn't turn him on.

Everything about her got to him. Always had.

Logan was afraid that it always would.

Juliana glanced back over her shoulder at him. A guy could only take so much. She stood there looking so beautiful, reminding him of all the dreams he'd had—dreams that had started right there—and what, was he really not supposed to touch?

He wasn't that strong.

He stalked toward her.

The bag he'd brought in—a bag of clothes that Gunner had prepared for them both—fell at his feet.

"Logan…" She held up her hands. "I said another agent should come. I told you—"

He wasn't touching her, not yet. But he sure wanted to. "You're a liar, Julie." He knew—he'd been lying for so long that it was now easy to spot the lies that others told.

And he'd been watching her eyes when she lied to him. He said, "You don't trust yourself around me. After all this time, you still want me."

She backed up a step. "You're guarding me. Nothing else. Got it? *Nothing…*"

"I remember what you taste like. For years after I left, I remembered…" She'd given him another taste just days ago. For a man who was starving, that taste had been bounty.

But Juliana had stiffened before him. There was a stark flash of pain in her eyes. "But you were the one who left, Logan. I was at the bus stop. Standing there for hours because I was so sure that you wouldn't just abandon me. That you wouldn't walk away and leave me there alone…"

He'd seen her at the bus stop. He'd had to go. She'd held a small black bag in her hands. Her gaze had swept the station. Left to right. A smile had trembled on her lips every time the station's main doors swung open.

Eventually, the smile had faded. When the last train left, tears had been on her cheeks. She'd walked away then.

*And I felt like my heart had been cut out.*

She didn't understand. There were some secrets that he couldn't share.

Because the truth would hurt her too much.

"You always looked at me like I was some kind of hero." A dangerous look, that. It had made him want to be more. Do more.

But the truth, the sad, sick truth, was that he'd never been a hero. He'd been a killer, even back then. And not good enough for her.

*I walked away once. I can do this again.*

So he didn't kiss her, didn't stroke her skin. He sucked in a breath, pulled her sweet scent into his lungs and moved back. "The bed is yours. I'll take the couch." He turned away.

A man could only resist for so long, and if he didn't put some space between himself and the biggest temptation that he'd ever faced, Logan knew his control would shatter.

He could already feel the cracks.

"JULIANA JAMES has disappeared."

Diego turned away from the window and its perfect view of the small city below. A city that still slept, for the moment. "That's not what I wanted to hear." He wasn't paying his men for failure. He paid no one for failure.

Diego walked slowly toward Luis, deliberately keeping a faint grin on his face. Luis knew he didn't accept failure.

Those who failed him paid with their lives.

And often the lives of their family members.

"One of those agents…he took her from the *cementerio,* stopped her from entering the car."

*Sí,* he already knew this. He'd seen the video clips. The

cameras had been rolling when the limo exploded, and Juliana James had been tossed back into the air.

The press had all wanted to be there when Senator James was laid to rest. Then when the car had exploded, the reporters had closed in even tighter.

Those reporters had done him a favor, though. They'd shown him the face of Juliana's rescuer.

Diego strolled to his desk and picked up the photo that he'd had enlarged. The photo that his team had used to track down Juliana's anonymous protector.

Only, the man wasn't so anonymous any longer.

Logan Quinn. A SEAL. A SEAL who hadn't been listed as officially in action for the past three years.

*But I bet you are in action, hombre, under the radar, fighting dirty.*

Diego could almost respect that. Almost. He didn't actually respect anyone. What was the point?

"He's the one we need to track." Diego tapped the photo. This wasn't some random agent. Just a man doing his job by protecting his charge. This was…more.

Diego knew how to get information out of people. Sometimes you used torture. Sometimes lies. With Juliana, he'd enjoyed a game of lies. The torture would have come, of course, but he hadn't been ready to kill her.

He *couldn't* kill her, not until he'd gotten the evidence back. A dead daughter wouldn't have encouraged the senator to give up the secrets he'd stashed away. But a living daughter…one who spilled all her secrets so easily…she'd been a tool that he used.

*Logan.* Perhaps that had been her most important secret to reveal. He just hadn't realized it at the time.

Everyone had a weakness. It was a lesson he'd learned so very long ago. Diego slanted a fast glance at Luis, not surprised to see the man shifting nervously. *I know his weakness all too well.*

The agent, Juliana—they both had weaknesses, too. *Weaknesses that I already understand.*

Juliana had revealed so much to him in those hours spent in the darkness. Sometimes torture wasn't the most effective means of getting what you wanted. Sometimes… sometimes you had to make your target trust you.

Only then could you go in for the kill.

"When we find Logan Quinn, we'll find Juliana." Simple. Diego dropped the photo. *Weaknesses.* They were so easy to exploit.

*"You ever been in love, Juliana?"* It had been a question he had to ask. If she loved, then she was weak. He could use her loved ones against her. So he'd waited, trying not to look eager, then Juliana had said…

*"Once."* Pain had trembled in her voice. A longing for what couldn't be. Juliana had been so sure that death waited for her. And it had. She'd drawn in a ragged breath and said, *"But Logan didn't love me back."*

Diego stared down at the picture. Tough SEALs weren't supposed to show fear. Not any emotion. But… right there, on Logan Quinn's face, Diego saw that the man had been afraid.

Not for himself.

For the woman he held so tightly. The woman he'd shielded with his own body when the car exploded, and Diego knew he was staring at—

Her Logan.

*Ah, Juliana, I'm not so sure he didn't love you back.*

Diego picked up a red marker and circled the face of his target. "You have six hours to find Quinn." The man wouldn't have left the area with Juliana, not yet.

Not…yet.

Diego glanced back up at Luis. "You know what happens if you fail."

Luis gave a grim nod. Then he grabbed for the photo and hurried toward the door.

"Your daughter..." Diego called after him softly. "She's six now, isn't she?"

Luis's shoulders stiffened. *"Sí."* More growl than anything else.

"I'll have to make sure to send her an extra-special gift to celebrate her next birthday."

Luis glanced back. Ah, there it was. The fear. Flashing in the man's dark eyes. "Not necessary." His Spanish accent thickened with the broken rasp of his voice. "You've done enough for her. For me."

Diego's gaze fell to the rough scars on Luis's throat, then after a moment, he looked back up into the other man's eyes. Let the tension stretch. Then he smiled. "She's such a pretty little girl. So delicate. But then, children are always so fragile, aren't they?"

Luis lifted the photo. "Do you want him dead?"

Now the man was showing the proper motivation. Diego considered his question, then nodded. "Once you have Juliana in your custody, kill the agent. Do it in front of her." The better to break her.

Luis's fingers whitened around the photo. *"Sí."*

Diego watched him walk away, satisfaction filling him. His resources were nearly limitless. With Diego's power behind him, there would be no stopping Luis. Money could motivate anyone. The right targets taken out—the right information gained, and Luis could attack.

If someone else was trying to kill Juliana, then they'd just offer more to keep her alive. An insurance policy. Diego liked to have backup plans in place.

And as for the SEAL, they wouldn't need others to kill

him. Luis could send out near-instant checks on Quinn, find any property he had. Find his friends, his family.

Hunt the bastard.

Then kill him.

Luis might be a good father, but he was an even better killer.

Especially when the man was properly motivated…

Logan Quinn was already dead; the fool just didn't know it.

# Chapter Five

"It wasn't Guerrero."

Juliana blinked at the rough words and tried to push away the heavy darkness of sleep that covered her. She blinked a few more times, letting her eyes adjust to the faint light.

*Where am I?*

She glanced around. Saw the old, gleaming wood. Felt the lumpy couch beneath her.

Met Logan's bright stare.

The cabin.

The memories flooded back. Fire. Death. A nightmare that she wouldn't be waking up from anytime soon.

She pulled the blanket closer. "What? What are you talking about?"

He sat on the couch, his legs brushing her thighs. The move made her too aware of him, but then, she always felt too aware when he was close.

*And he expected me to sleep in that bed upstairs?* Oh, no. She wasn't up for that kind of punishment. Too much pleasure. Too much pain waited up there.

She'd bunked on the couch. She wasn't even sure where he'd gone.

"I got a call from Sydney."

Juliana scrambled to a sitting position. Okay, maybe

she was just trying to put some distance between her body and his.

Logan shook his head. "There's a price on your head. Damn high."

"We already knew that...."

The faint lines around his mouth deepened. "The money is being offered if you are taken in alive."

"What?" No, that didn't make any sense. "The car exploded. That's not exactly a way guaranteed to keep me breathing." Or Charles. Poor Charles. Dead in an instant, for no reason.

He ran a hand through his hair. "That hit...Sydney doesn't think it was from Guerrero's crew. The chatter she's hearing all indicates that was from...someone else."

Her heart slammed into her ribs. "You're telling me that *two* people want me dead?" Could this get any worse for her?

Logan touched her. *It could.* The heat of his touch burned through her. His fingers wrapped around her arms. "Guerrero doesn't want you dead. Syd is sure that he wants you brought in alive. And he's willing to pay top dollar to make sure you arrive breathing."

Her breath whispered out. "Because he thinks I have the evidence?"

A slow nod. Did he realize that his fingers were caressing her arms? Moving in small, light strokes against her skin. "I don't have it," she whispered. If she did, then maybe this could all end.

Logan could go back to his life.

She'd go back to hers.

"Syd is working with local law enforcement. They're gonna find out who rigged the car." He exhaled on a rough breath but didn't release her. "The limo was swept before it left the senator's house. It was cleared."

But then it had still exploded.

She'd never forget the fury of the fire sweeping over her.

"I'll be with you. Don't worry. You'll stay safe."

Easy for him to say. He wasn't the one being targeted by two killers. She stared into his eyes.

But...

But Logan had been targeted for death plenty of times before. She knew it. Death was his life. His job.

He was a survivor. A fighter.

If something were to happen, if one of those men hunting her came too close...

*I don't want to be helpless.* "Teach me," she said, pushing away the covers.

Logan blinked in surprise. "Uh, Julie..."

Under the blanket, she wore a loose T-shirt and a pair of jogging shorts. Not exactly sexy, but his gaze still dropped to her legs, lingered.

Her heartbeat kicked up a beat. "Teach me to *fight,* Logan." He'd already taught her to make love years before. *Upstairs.*

When the pleasure had hit her, she'd said that she loved him.

He'd never told her the same.

Maybe there was one thing he couldn't lie about.

Juliana shoved those memories back into the box in her mind. "I want to be able to defend myself if...if—"

"When a bullet or a bomb is coming, there's not much defense."

No. "But when you're trapped in some hellhole and the enemy is coming at you because he wants to *torture* information out of you—information that you don't have—then being able to fight back matters." She'd been helpless in Mexico. If something happened and Guerrero got her again… *I won't be helpless.* "You can teach me some defensive moves. I know you can."

His gaze wasn't on her legs any longer. That too-intense stare raked her face.

"I need this," she told him. She had to have some control, some power.

His nod was grim.

He rose, backing up.

The drumming of Juliana's heartbeat echoed in her ears. She followed him into the opening in the middle of the room. Her toes curled over the old, faded rug.

Light flickered on when Logan bent toward the lamp at his right. Juliana finally started focusing enough to realize that Logan wore no shirt. Just a pair of loose sweatpants. His chest, ripped with muscles, was bare. Only…

Logan was sporting a tattoo now.

She hadn't noticed the tattoo back in Mexico. But then, he'd kept his clothes on there. *Thank goodness.* Now it was tempting…all that bare flesh.

Juliana licked her lips. *Down, girl.*

Her gaze focused on the tattoo. The ink was black, dark, sliding up a few inches over his heart.

Forming a trident.

Why did that symbol look so sexy on him?

Why did she always have to want him?

"I use a mix of martial arts," he told her as he came closer, positioning his body just a few inches from hers on that rug. "I can teach you a few moves to help with CQC."

"Um, CQC?" No clue.

"Close-quarters combat." His words were quiet. His body was too big. She was too aware of his every breath. "You want to be able to kill quickly, efficiently."

She didn't exactly want to kill, just stay alive. But Juliana nodded. She'd never heard him sound so cold before. Her hands pressed against her stomach. "And have you done that?"

He didn't answer. She knew he had. Probably more times than he could count.

*Not the boy you knew.*

She wasn't sure she'd ever known him.

"Can we…can we start easier? I mean…" *I'm not ready to kill.*

He must have read the truth in her eyes. A muscle jerked in his jaw. "When it comes down to it, if it's your life or your attacker's, you'll be ready." Then he moved in a flash, almost too fast for her to see, and in the next breath, Logan's hand was around her throat. "If you hesitate, you can die." His big fingers surrounded her neck, seemed to brand her flesh. She knew with one twist of his hand, he could kill her.

Logan stepped back. "But we'll start easy, if that's what you want."

Had his voice roughened? His eyes had hardened, his body seemed to have tensed.

"Go for your attacker's weak spots. Always make them your targets."

Juliana forced her own body to ease its stiffness.

"When you attack—" Logan was circling her now, making her nervous "—use the strongest part of your body." He stood behind her, came closer. His body brushed against hers. His arm slid around her, and his fingers curled over her hand. "Use your fists." He lifted her hand, punched out with it and turned her arm. "Your elbows." He surrounded her. So big and solid behind her, his arms sweeping out.

He spun her around so that she faced him. His fingers still curled over her fist. He lifted her fist toward his neck.

"Punch at your attacker's throat. Hit hard, with every bit of strength that you have."

His gaze blazed down at her. "You have to be ready to take your attacker out," Logan said.

She tugged her hand. He didn't let go. Her eyes narrowed. "What if I'm just trying to get away?"

Another spin, and her back was to him again. He'd freed her, and she stood there, her body too tense and aware.

"I'll be the attacker," he said.

Her mouth went dry.

"If I come at you from behind…" And he did. In a rush, he had her. His arms wrapped around her body and he hauled her back against him. Juliana struggled, twisting and straining forward, but she couldn't get free of his hold. Her struggles just strained her against him.

*He was getting turned on.*

Juliana froze.

"Hunch your shoulders," he told her, voice gruff. "Don't try to lunge away. Curl in…"

She did, hunching her shoulders.

"Then drop."

She slid out of his grasp. She twisted and turned back up. Her hand fisted, ready to punch.

"When you're free, go for my eyes. My throat." His lips twisted. "My groin."

She *wasn't* going there. Not then. With an effort, she kept her eyes up.

"Use your elbow or fist in a groin attack. Hard as you can hit…"

She managed a slow nod.

"But if I come at you straight on…" And he did. He advanced and those big hands came for her throat once more. His fingers wrapped around her neck. Not hurting her. Again, she felt the ghost of a caress against her skin. "Then shove your fingers into my eyes."

Vicious. Juliana swallowed and nodded. She would do whatever she had to do.

He didn't drop his hand. Just stared at her. The air seemed to thicken with the tension between them.

"I'm not going to let them get you again."

His fingers were behind her ear, caressing. She shivered at the touch and the memories it stirred. In the past, he'd liked to kiss her in just that spot.

"I'll stand between you and any person who comes for you."

She believed that he would. But Logan was flesh and blood. He couldn't stop fire or bullets.

He could die, too.

Then what would happen?

*I'd be without him again.*

Her gaze lifted to his. There was arousal, need, so much lust in his eyes. But he wasn't pushing her, wasn't trying to kiss her, and his hand was falling away from her.

She'd told him no hours before. Told him to keep his distance. *We're done.*

He'd called her on the lie.

She still wanted him just as much as always.

He cleared his throat. "If we just knew where James had stashed the evidence…"

"I'd barely spoken to him in years." Because she'd seen what he'd become. Not the father she knew. He turned into someone cold, twisted. "He wasn't sharing any secrets with me."

Logan's head cocked to the right as he studied her. "Maybe not directly."

"Not *indirectly,* not in any way." She hadn't even seen

him last Christmas. She'd spent the holiday alone. "Wherever he hid the evidence—I don't know."

Logan squared his shoulders. "Okay, let's try this again. I'll come at you and you attack back, as hard as you can."

She pulled her bottom lip between her teeth, hesitated, then said, "Aren't you worried that I'll hurt you?"

He smiled. "I want you to."

Okay, then. If it was pain he wanted… Juliana turned her back to him. She'd give him as much as—

His arms closed around her, tight bands that stole her breath. His last attack hadn't been so hard and she hadn't expected him to come at her full force. Panic hit for an instant. Panic, then—

*I won't be weak.*

She hunched her shoulders, dropped low and slid out of his hold. She came up with her elbow, ready to hit him hard right in the groin, but Logan came at her. His body hit hers, and he pushed her back onto the rug, caging her body beneath his.

She lost her breath at the impact. He caught her hands, trapping them on either side of her head. "Use your feet, your legs," he gritted out. "Fight back with any part of your body that you can. Never give up."

No, she wouldn't. She twisted and her leg slid between his. Her breath panted out. Juliana yanked up her leg, driving her knee right toward his groin.

Logan twisted to the side, and her knee hit his thigh. "Nice," he said. "I knew you had a tough fighter inside."

His breath wasn't coming so easily, either. He still had her hands. Still had his body over hers.

She should tell him to move away. Should say…*enough.* But it suddenly wasn't about fighting. Her heart was still beating too fast, but the ache in her body, that wasn't from fear or adrenaline or anything but desire.

Need.

She'd had another relationship after Logan. It wasn't as if he'd been the only man she'd taken to her bed. Actually, she'd been with two other men over the years.

But the pleasure had never been the same.

And if she was honest with herself, when she'd closed her eyes... *I saw him.*

She hadn't been able to connect with the others, to let go. Not like she'd done with Logan.

"You shouldn't look at me like that." His voice was even deeper now, the sexy growl that she remembered. Lust could always make him growl.

"Like what?" But she knew.

"Like you want me to devour you."

She didn't move. The soft cotton of his sweatpants brushed over her leg. His hands were tight around her wrists but not hurting her. The man was always so conscious of his strength.

So strong, but she knew how to make him weak. Juliana had learned other lessons back in this cabin.

His hands released hers. "I think that's enough for now." He shifted his legs, pulling away from her.

Now it was her turn to grab him. Juliana's hands curled around his shoulders.

Logan froze. "Julie..."

"I did lie." They both knew it.

His pupils seemed to burn away the blue in his gaze.

"I still want you."

The muscles beneath her hands tensed. *Like steel.* "And I'm dying for a taste of you...." He moaned, then his mouth was on hers. Not easy. Not tender. Not like before.

So long ago.

This was different.

His tongue swept into her mouth. Took. Tasted.

He was different.

Her nails sank into his skin.

*She* was different.

The faint stubble on his jaw brushed against her. She liked the rough feel of it on her flesh, liked his taste even more. Her breasts were pushing against his chest, even as her hips arched against him.

The need inside, the need she'd wanted to hold in check, was breaking through, bursting like water out of a dam. She couldn't hold back, and right then, Juliana wasn't even sure why she *should* hold back. Pride?

Fear?

His mouth tore from hers. His lips pressed against her throat. He used the edge of his teeth. Her eyes fell closed, and she couldn't hold back her own moan.

*"Missed...you..."* His words were rough.

Her gaze flew open, but he was already sliding down her body. His fingers had eased under her T-shirt. Rough, calloused fingertips swept over her stomach, sliding over the flesh, shoving up the shirt and baring her to his hungry stare. Then he was touching her breast, stroking the hard tip and making her shudder.

Making her want him even more.

"Stop me," he told her as his left hand fisted her shirt. His right hand kept caressing her.

She didn't stop him. Instead, Juliana whispered, "I want your mouth...on me." In the midst of a nightmare, why couldn't she have her pleasure?

If death was stalking her, then she'd take the life that she could. The pleasure that was right before her.

*Logan.*

Then his mouth was on her breast. Not some tentative

kiss. His lips closed over her. He sucked, licked, and the hand that had been stroking her slid back down now, heading over her stomach, down to the waistband of her shorts.

Goose bumps rose on her flesh. Need electrified her blood. Every breath brought in his scent, filling her with him. She was touching him, learning the hard planes and angles of his muscled body once again. He was bigger now. Stronger.

She wanted to kiss that tattoo.

His fingers brushed against the waistband of her shorts. "Juliana…" he rumbled against her breast.

She arched her hips. There was no stopping. Not now. There was only need. Pleasure was so close, just out of reach.

She caught his hand. Pressed it against her. "I want you."

His gaze blasted her. "And I'd kill to have you."

She believed him. His words terrified a part of her, a part that wasn't wild with need and lust. This man—she knew how dangerous he was. To her and to others. But at that moment…

She didn't care. She wanted his strength. She wanted him.

So when his hand slid under the elastic waistband of her shorts, Juliana arched her hips up, giving him better access. She wasn't going to pretend she didn't want this—him. She needed his touch more than she needed breath right then.

Her whole body was tense. Too eager. Her muscles straining. Then he was pushing his long, broad fingers under the edge of her panties. Touching her in the most intimate of caresses. His name broke from her even as she squeezed her eyes tightly shut.

He didn't touch her with hesitation or uncertainty. He

touched her the way a man did when he knew his lover's body and knew how to give her the most pleasure.

His fingers slid over her flesh, found the center of her need. His touch grew more demanding. Her breath came faster, faster…

His mouth was on hers, kissing, thrusting his tongue past her lips. Her hands dug deeper into his shoulders. The pleasure was so close, driving her, making Juliana desperate for the release that would rip through her and take the pain away.

A shrill alarm cut through the room. The ringing pierced her ears even as she choked out Logan's name. The pleasure hit, fast, brutal, but he stiffened against her.

The alarm's shriek continued and Logan swore.

Juliana's body shook when Logan pulled her to her feet.

"Someone's coming," he snapped.

Her heartbeat was still racing. She swallowed as she tried to ease the dryness in her throat. Her hands fumbled and she attempted to fix her clothes.

"You're safe in here," he told her even as he stepped away and opened a nearby drawer. When his hand rose again, she saw that he was holding a gun.

*Someone's coming.*

Logan caught her hand and pulled her with him into the small room to the right, a room filled with about five monitors. On those monitors, she just saw trees. Empty woods. He must have been using some kind of night-vision cameras so that they could get the view, but she didn't see anyone approaching the cabin.

"Someone triggered the alarm." He yanked on a thick shirt, shoved into shoes.

Juliana shook her head. "They couldn't have found us already." It had just been hours. *Hours.*

Her thighs pressed together. The pleasure had left her

emotions raw, and this—*now?* "They can't be here," she whispered.

But as she stared at those monitors, she saw the men creep from the shadows and close in. Men dressed in black with hoods covering their faces and big guns cradled in their hands.

The images were grainy on the screens. She leaned closer, narrowing her eyes.

And the gunfire erupted. No sound came with the shots, but she saw the men begin to fall. Two staggered back, clutching their chests. The others lifted their weapons. Fired at enemies she couldn't see…even as they raced forward, their images flickering on the monitors.

"Give me a weapon," Juliana said, surprised that her words were so steady.

Logan glanced at her and studied her face with narrowed eyes.

"Give it to me."

Logan's team was out in those woods. She got that. They were firing at the men. But if they didn't take them all out, if someone got to the house…

Logan opened a thick safe on the left, nestled behind the screens. More guns were inside. Knives, too. What looked like a giant stockade of weapons.

He handed her a gun. "Here's the safety. Make sure it's off when you fire."

The weapon didn't feel heavy in her hands. She'd expected more.

It was cold. Hard.

The alarm was still beeping. She could hear the shots now, coming from outside. The battle was nearly at her door.

"Stay behind me," Logan ordered.

She nodded.

His fingers curved under her chin. He tilted her head up and flashed a smile at her.

"Try not to shoot me," he said, then he kissed her. A fast brush of his lips against hers.

His words surprised her enough that a rough laugh slipped from her. Laughing, now? Maybe she was as crazy as he was.

But then the shots came again, and the laughter was gone and only fear remained when she heard the voices shouting outside.

Logan had his own weapon up, ready, and—

Glass shattered. A window. Someone was coming in the window.

"Stand down!" Logan yelled.

Gunshots. They weren't standing down.

Wood cracked. The front door? Being broken down?

Logan pushed her back against the wall on the left. The door to their room was open a few precious inches. He put his gun barrel through that opening. Aimed—

The blast of his gun had her ears aching. Someone groaned, then there was a heavy thud of sound.

Silence, a long beat. Long enough to make her think that the battle was over. Safety was close and—

Gunfire erupted as all hell seemed to break loose in the small cabin.

# Chapter Six

The hunters had arrived too soon. No way should have they already been at the cabin.

The Shadow Agents hadn't even had a chance to leave their trail of bread crumbs for Guerrero yet. They weren't ready for his attack.

They shouldn't have underestimated the man's resources.

A bullet tore right through the door next to Logan. He barely heard the thunder of the weapons, and he wouldn't let himself look back at Juliana. He didn't want to see the fear in her gaze.

He had to focus to get the job done. *To protect her.*

Kill or be killed.

Logan wasn't in the mood to die.

Not wasting any bullets, Logan took aim only when he had a target. When he had a target, his bullet slammed home, taking down another one of the attackers.

Logan panned for another mark.

*Another one hit the floor.*

They should have stood the hell down when he told them to. Logan's breath rasped in his lungs. Adrenaline had tightened his body, pumped through his blood and amped him up for the battle.

He'd always enjoyed the battles, but this time, with

Juliana's life on the line, the tension edging through him cut sharper than a knife.

From his vantage point, he saw when the next man rushed through the cabin's front door, but Logan didn't squeeze the trigger this time.

Gunner was the man in his sights.

Gunner's gaze swept around the room and he gave a low whistle. "Three down…all in the heart."

*Kill or be killed.*

Logan didn't open the door. "Clear?"

"Yeah, yeah, we're clear, Alpha One."

He finally glanced back at Juliana, but instead of the fear he'd expected to see burning in her eyes, the woman just looked mad.

Her fingers tightly clutched her gun, and he wondered…would she have used it, if she'd had to do the job?

As far as he knew, Juliana had never hurt another soul in her life. And shooting at another human, being ready to take a life, that was a line many couldn't cross.

Logan opened the door. *I never saw that damn line.* The kills had come too easily for him.

*Monster.*

He knew what he was, even if Juliana didn't.

A weapon. A killer. An assassin. Senator James had been right about him after all.

Now Juliana had just seen up close and personal how dangerous he could be. Her left hand reached up and curled around his arm. "Are we safe?"

He glanced back to the outer room. Gunner was checking the men. No point in that. They sure weren't moving.

His nod was grim.

Then Logan opened the door, making sure to keep his body in front of Juliana's, just in case. "What the hell," he began, voice lethal, "just happened?"

No way should those guards have gotten this close. Guerrero's men weren't even supposed to know about the location, not until they'd set up a more secure perimeter, but...

"We got slammed," Gunner said, staring at him with narrowed eyes. "Explosives, artillery...they came prepared, but we still managed to take them all out."

So they had. His feet crunched over the broken glass. The cabin was shredded, windows busted. The front door was ripped from its hinges and bullet holes lined the walls.

He'd loved this place once. It had been a sanctuary, courtesy of his stepfather. A place to lick his wounds.

A place to share with Juliana.

Not any longer.

Logan bent next to one of the fallen men. With Juliana so close, he hadn't been able to take any chances. *Kill shots.* If the men had survived, they would have just kept shooting at him.

"Tell me you have someone alive outside," Logan said, not glancing up. If they had one of Guerrero's men in custody, they could try to make him talk. The problem in Mexico was that too many there were too afraid to talk to authorities—really, to those who hadn't already been paid off by Guerrero. The guy wasn't called El Diablo for nothing. People feared him because he could bring hell to their lives.

"The ones still breathing turned tail and ran."

Figured.

Logan's hold tightened on his gun. This was just—

He heard the whisper of cloth almost too late. A rustle of sound that shouldn't have been there. He glanced up at the broken window and saw the barrel of the gun pointing toward him.

Logan started to lunge to the side even as he brought

up his own weapon, but then something—someone—slammed into him, knocking Logan to the floor.

His bullet blasted out, still heading for its target. A man screamed even as Logan grabbed for...

*Juliana?*

She'd been the one to knock into him. He twisted her, shoving her body behind his.

Gunner had already made his way to the window. He flew out with his hands, breaking the gunman's wrist and sending the weapon tumbling through the ground.

Logan's gaze swept over Juliana. *Okay. She's okay.*

He pushed her back and rushed to his feet. In the next instant, Logan was at Gunner's side. Logan grabbed the now-moaning man and dragged his sorry hide through the window.

Gunner kicked the man's discarded weapon a good five feet away.

Juliana had risen to her feet now. She still had her gun out—and aimed right at the moaning man.

Blood streaked down his face. He glanced up at her, and his lips twisted in a sneer. "You're...the one..."

Logan put his own weapon under the man's chin. "Where is he?"

The man's gaze, a dark brown, turned back to Logan. His sneer stretched. "The lover...think you're keeping her safe?" A shake of his head. "You're the one killing her... leading us...right to...*her*." The man's voice was raspy. As Logan stared at him, he could see the jagged scars from an old injury that crossed the man's neck.

"No one's killing her," Logan growled. "You can be sure of that." He shoved the man back. He had to. The temptation to attack was much too strong.

Logan positioned his body near Juliana. He didn't want her to see what was coming, but he couldn't let her leave.

Not with the chaos outside. What if Gunner was wrong? What if there were more men? Gunner hadn't known about this one....

Gunner had shoved the man down to the floor, got him on his knees, and Gunner's weapon rested at the back of the man's head. "Who sent you?" They already knew, yet the question still had to be asked. They needed the man to confess.

But the bleeding man just laughed.

"Tell us," Logan snarled.

The man's laughter slowly faded. He tried to tilt his head to see Juliana, ignoring the gun pressed so close to him as if it truly weren't there. "Ah...little señorita...he'll keep coming for you."

Logan felt Juliana's hand tighten on his arm. "Your voice... *I remember you.*"

Then she lunged forward, trying to get to the man. Logan caught her around the waist and hauled her back.

"You were there!" Juliana yelled at the kneeling man. "That first night in Mexico, you were the one who took me.... You kept saying...little señorita! I didn't see your face, but your voice—I'll never forget it!"

He didn't move. Juliana sure did. She twisted and fought like a wildcat in Logan's arms. He snatched the gun from her hand and held her as tightly as he could.

If Juliana really could tie this man to her kidnapping, and they could link him to Guerrero, make him talk...

"I know your voice...." she snarled.

The voice was distinctive.

"I know *you*," Juliana said. She had stopped fighting, for the moment. Logan wasn't about to make the mistake of letting her go. The woman could just be trying to trick him.

Their captive's head had lowered. His shoulders sagged inward a bit.

"You work for Diego Guerrero," Gunner charged. He'd never once relaxed his stance. "And you're going to tell us everything we want to know about your boss, unless you want to wind up like your friends."

"Who are you?" Logan wanted to know. They'd start with a name and tear the guy's life apart, link him to Guerrero. Find the man and then—

Their captive's head tilted. He actually lifted his chin and shoved the back of his head against Gunner's gun, as if daring the other man to shoot. *"Mi nombre es Luis Sanches."*

Logan nodded. Okay, now they were—

*"Muerte no me asusta."*

Logan's body tensed. *Death doesn't scare me.*

The man's head shoved against Gunner's weapon again. "Do it! Kill me!"

Gunner's eyes narrowed to faint slits.

"El Diablo…he can do so much worse than *muerte* for me." His shoulders shook. "Much worse."

Logan released Juliana. "Don't move." He breathed the words into her ear.

Luis's gaze flickered toward them. "That's why he'll have her… He knows you… Always understands his enemy—"

"We can offer you protection," Logan said. He knew the drill. If you rolled on someone like Guerrero…yeah, you could expect one real short life. "Give you a new name, a new—"

But Luis was shaking his head. "I won't betray him."

Gunner hauled the guy to his feet. "When he finds out that we have you in custody, do you think that's gonna matter? Guerrero will just assume that you sold him out. You'll be finished either way."

Juliana wasn't speaking, just staring at Luis, and Logan realized—Luis was staring back.

"Little señorita, wish…I'd never seen you in Mexico," Luis said. His hands were by his sides. He looked beaten, hopeless.

"I wish you hadn't, either," Juliana said. Her voice was angry, snapping. "I wish none of this had ever happened."

*"Sí…"*

Logan glared at him. "You *will* help us to catch Guerrero." Every instinct that Logan had screamed that this guy wasn't an average flunky. He was older, with shades of gray spiking the edges of his dark hair. His eyes knew too much, had *seen* too much.

"No, I won't help you." Luis's voice held no emotion.

Logan turned away from him, marched over and grabbed his cell. Sydney answered instantly. "What do you see?" he asked her.

A faint hum of sound, then "All enemy bodies are down. Perimeter is secure." Her voice, calm, easy, belied the bloody nightmare that had to be waiting beyond the cabin.

"We need transport," he told her, glancing over at Luis Sanchez. "We've got a live one in here."

But Luis shook his head. "No, you don't."

Then he lunged forward, surging away from Gunner. Luis lifted his hand, and too late, Logan realized that when that man had been kneeling on the floor, when his hands had been at his boots…

*He went for a backup weapon.*

A glinting knife blade was grasped in Luis's hands. Logan brought up his gun in an instant. "Drop it."

Luis wasn't charging with the weapon. Not coming to attack. But—"My daughter...I will miss her...."

Then, even as Gunner lunged for the guy, Luis shoved the knife into his own chest.

"No!" Juliana screamed.

Too late.

Blood bloomed on Luis's shirt. His eyes widened. Not with fear or agony.

*Relief.*

Gunner grabbed Luis from the back. Luis's fingers were still clenched on the hilt of the knife. His legs gave way, and blood sprayed around him.

*"What's happening?"* Sydney screamed in Logan's ear. And he realized that he had the gun in his right hand, and he was still clutching the phone in his left.

He stared down at Luis's body. The man was a killer; he'd known exactly where to deliver the death blow.

"We won't need the prisoner transport any longer."

Luis was still alive, barely, but Logan knew he wouldn't be for much longer. Logan shoved the phone into his pocket as he stalked toward the dying man.

Gunner had lowered him to the floor. He hadn't tried to remove the knife. If he did...well, Logan knew Luis wouldn't even have a few moments left to live then.

They had to get the man to talk, while he still could.

"Where is Guerrero?" Logan demanded.

"My daughter..." Luis said with a smile. "She's... lovely..."

*"Where is Guerrero?"*

"He...won't touch her...now..."

Because Luis had chosen to die instead of rolling over on his boss? Rage burned inside of Logan.

"So beautiful...my sweet..." Luis's eyes flickered. "Marie..."

The man wouldn't be telling him anything more.

Logan glanced at the other bodies. Then his gaze found Juliana's. She was standing just a few feet away, her face too pale.

*They found her already. How the hell did they do that?*

Then he remembered the words that had tumbled from Luis right after he'd dragged the guy through the window.

*The lover...think you're keeping her safe?*

How had Luis known that he'd been Juliana's lover? He watched as Juliana's eyes dipped to the dead men and she swallowed. Her shoulders rolled back as she tried to straighten her spine.

*You're the one killing her...leading us...right to...her.*

He hurried forward and grabbed her arm. "Let's go." Syd would already have a cleanup crew en route, but this location was compromised. No longer the perfect trap, with the bait to lure Geurrero...

*He's the one setting a trap for us.*

And Logan wasn't going to just sit around while that man closed in for the kill.

But Juliana wasn't moving. "Where? Where do we go? He's going to find me. He found me here, after just a few hours and—"

He pulled her close. "Do you trust me?"

Her lips parted.

"Do you?"

Juliana nodded.

The relief he felt had his tense muscles aching. "Then let me get you out of here." He couldn't tell her his plans right then. More lies.

Would they ever stop?

He'd been lying to her since the first day they met, and those lies had torn a hole right through any dreams that he might have ever had.

The day Juliana found out the truth about him, about why he'd first walked into that diner to meet her...

It would be the last day she ever trusted him.

But he led her outside. Jasper already had an SUV idling near the porch steps. They jumped into the back, rushed away. The windows would be bulletproof, the vehicle's body reinforced.

The SUV drove fast, hurtling down that narrow road.

"We've got backup on site," Jasper said, his drawl barely evident. "Syd called in reinforcements. The road will be clear."

It might be clear, but that didn't mean Guerrero didn't have someone out there, watching them, following them.

Guerrero had definitely taken the bait. He wanted Juliana, wanted her alive, because not one single shot had ever been taken at her.

And when a man like Guerrero wanted something... he didn't stop.

*Come for her yourself. Come and face me.*

Because Logan wasn't the type of man to ever stop, either.

SHE DIDN'T KNOW how long they drove. She didn't really care. Juliana sat hunched in the car and saw the image of a man taking his own life flash before her eyes.

That man—Luis—had been so afraid of Guerrero that he'd killed himself instead of betraying his boss.

Logan hadn't so much as flinched.

During the ride, he'd been on the phone beside her, talking to the mysterious Mercer and demanding explanations. He wanted to know who'd leaked their location.

But every now and then, she could feel Logan's eyes on her. And she could have sworn there was suspicion in his gaze.

Why?

The vehicle slowed. Juliana blinked and glanced around even as the engine died away. "Another safe house?" she whispered, and yes, she'd put too much emphasis on *safe*. At this point, she didn't think anyplace was safe. Guerrero was going to keep coming.

The man could track like no one she'd ever seen before.

"Not exactly," Logan said. His voice was guarded, carefully emotionless. In the closed interior of the vehicle, she was too conscious of his body pressing next to hers.

Had she really been moaning in his arms just an hour or two before? That memory seemed surreal. The death, the violence—that had been reality for her.

Then Logan opened his door. She turned away and shoved open the door on her side and rushed out into what looked like a parking garage. A deserted one.

Jasper was by her side, waiting. "You all right, ma'am?" he asked.

He actually seemed worried. More worried than Logan. Juliana nodded.

"It's for your safety," Jasper said. "It might hurt, but…"

Wow. Hold up. She lifted a hand. "What's going to hurt?"

Jasper pointed to the left. Juliana turned and saw a redheaded woman in a white lab coat heading her way. Her gut knotted and she asked, "What's going on?"

"Just a small procedure," Jasper told her. He even put his hand on her shoulder and gave her a little stroke. As if that was supposed to be reassuring. "To make certain that you stay safe."

"So far, I sure haven't felt safe." Her own words snapped out.

Jasper winced. "This isn't the way things were planned.

No one should have found out about your location, not so fast, anyway. We were going to wait until—"

*"Jasper."* Logan's snarl shut up the other EOD agent. Jasper rocked back on his heels.

But it was too late. He'd said too much. Suspicion rolled within Juliana. "Tell me that he's wrong." He wasn't wrong. She knew it, but denial could be a fierce beast.

*We were going to wait.*

Wait and then leak her location to Guerrero? Wait and set a trap for the arms dealer, using her as the unknowing bait?

But Logan didn't speak; the doctor did. "I'm ready for her in the operating room. The implant can be placed immediately."

Implant? Juliana shook her head and backed up fast. Unfortunately, there wasn't anyplace for her to go, and her elbows rammed into the side of the SUV. "I'm not ready for you, lady." The doctor could just back off.

The redhead's lips thinned. "Do we need sedation for the patient?"

"What?" Juliana wasn't sure her voice could get higher than that startled yelp. "I'm not your patient! Stay away from me." Her gaze found Logan's. "You asked if I trusted you." First at that run-down hotel, then back at the cabin, in the middle of all that death. "I said that I did, but Logan, you've got to give me something here. Tell me—tell me that you weren't using me."

He still didn't speak. Maybe because he'd finally stopped lying.

It was Jasper who reached for her. "Come inside with us, Juliana, and I'll explain what's going to happen."

"It's a simple enough procedure," the doctor said.

Juliana felt her face flush. "Lady, I just came from a bloodbath, okay?"

Now it was the doctor who backed up a step.

Good for her.

Juliana ignored Jasper's outstretched hand. Her gaze locked on Logan. "Did you set me up as bait?" Her breath caught in her throat as she waited for his response.

"Yes."

That breath froze in her lungs.

"No," Jasper said in almost the same instant. "He didn't."

Her gaze darted to him, saw his lips tighten as he told her, "*We* did. Our EOD team had its orders. Logan didn't have a choice, still doesn't."

That was a fat line of bull. "There's always a choice." She rubbed her arms, chilled. She was standing there barefoot, wearing shorts and a T-shirt. She smelled like death and Logan's touch seemed to have branded her skin.

How wrong was that?

"Not always," Logan said. She became aware of the others then, men who'd been hanging back in the shadows. Armed. Wasn't everyone in the EOD always carrying a weapon? "My goal is to bring in Guerrero."

Her laugh was bitter. "I thought the goal was to keep me alive." So much for thinking she ranked high on his priorities.

And damn it, she caught a flash of pity in Jasper's eyes. Not what she needed to see right then. Her chin shot up.

"It is," Logan growled. Then he looked around at their audience and swore. In the next instant, he was pulling her toward the double doors on the right. Juliana was marching on his heels, more than ready to clear the air between them.

His palm slammed into the door and then they were inside a small hallway. More guards were assembled. Logan turned to the left and pushed open the door that led into what looked like a small waiting room.

Or an interrogation room. Her gaze darted to the wall on the right. A wall that looked as if it was just a mirror, only, she'd seen walls like that on television shows. Two-way mirrors. "Where are we?"

"Government facility. Off-the-books."

Wasn't just about everything off-the-books these days?

"I'm not… Hell, it's not about using you."

At his outburst, she spun around. "You were going to lure Guerrero to that house! Dangle me in front of him as bait!" She was so angry her words came out rapid-fire.

"I was—*am*—going to keep you under guard. We have to take out Guerrero. You're not going to be safe until he's in custody or until he's dead."

Her breath panted out. "You should have told me the truth." She felt as if Sydney was the only one giving her real insight into what was happening. Yes, they all wanted Guerrero stopped, she understood that. But did they have to lead her around like a lamb to a slaughter?

He shook his head. "There are some truths you don't want to hear."

That did it. Juliana shot across the room and jammed her finger into his chest. *"Don't."*

His brows rose.

"I'm not a child, Logan. I've handled death, disillusionment and betrayal just fine for years." Handled it and kept going. She wasn't going to break, not now and not ever. "So don't make decisions for me. Don't hide the truth from me." Her father had done that for the past ten years. "Just…tell me."

His gaze searched hers, then he gave a slow nod. "You're right. I'm sorry."

Damn straight he should be. And sorry wasn't going

to cut it for her. "Sydney told me about Gunner's brother. About how Guerrero was responsible for the attack that killed him." Her breath heaved out. "I *get* that your team has a personal stake in this, all right? I get it. But we're not just talking about your team. We're talking about my life."

His eyes blazed.

"Talk to me." Now she was the one giving orders. "Tell me what's going on."

His nod was brief. Then "You're in a government medical facility, one that was set up to assist agents in tracking their witnesses."

She realized her finger was still stabbing into his chest. Juliana dropped her hand. "Tracking them how?"

"A small chip is implanted just under the skin. With that chip, we're able to track a person anyplace that he or she goes."

*Anyplace.* "You mean in case Guerrero gets to me—"

"He won't—"

She waved that away. "If he gets to me, this chip is going to help you follow me."

His jaw clenched. "Yes."

Suspicion made her push because the trust she'd had… it was brittle. "Are you going to let his men take me… act like I'm protected but really ease back so they can grab me?"

His eyes chilled.

But she kept going. "Then you can just follow my tracking signal—what, some kind of GPS?—all the way back to Guerrero. You can get him. Get what you want, and hell, maybe all I'll have to do is get tortured or killed so you can bring him down."

His hands wrapped around her arms and Logan pulled her against him. "That's not going to happen."

"Promises, promises?" The taunt snapped out. "Because I don't think I can *trust* you on this, Logan." The pain from the past struck out at her. "I trusted you before, remember? We were going away together. I was there that night. Ready to leave everything I knew behind. I was there for hours." She couldn't hold back any longer. "Where the hell were you?"

## Chapter Seven

His fingers were too tight on her arms. Logan knew it. Taking a deep breath, he forced himself to step back. There was so much anger, no, rage in Juliana's eyes. He hated that.

Even as he knew he could do nothing to change the past. "We were just kids, Julie. Two confused kids."

"I was twenty. You were twenty-two. It's not like we were playing in the sandbox back then."

She wouldn't make him flinch. Terrorists, killers—he'd faced plenty in his time. He'd taken bullets and been sliced by knives. He hadn't flinched then.

*I hate the way she's looking at me.* "We were too young. It wasn't love. Wasn't meant to be forever."

She just kept staring at him, as if she could see through his lies. "No, it wasn't." Her breath rushed out. "I counted the minutes on that stupid clock in the bus station. That stupid, huge clock that hangs over the counter. I counted until midnight, when I had to give up." Her stare was burning him alive. "At midnight, I promised myself I'd never let you betray me again. But…I guess I was wrong about that, too."

The woman was carving his heart out of his chest with every word she uttered.

"Forget it." Then she shoved away from him with more

force than he'd expected. "So I get an implant, huh? That's the next big deal? Someone to slice me open, whether I want it or not."

He wanted the tracker on her, just as a precaution. After the way things had gone down at the cabin, he wanted to make sure he'd have a way of finding her. "Hostages, witnesses—they've been taken before. They're stripped, their bags are tossed. We realized a few years ago that we needed technology that wouldn't be ditched so easily." The tracker was tiny, barely noticeable at all, and easily inserted under the skin. A little piece of tech that Uncle Sam hadn't shared with many others.

"A few hours after the insertion, you'll barely even notice it's there."

She finally glanced away from him. "I'll notice." Her words were clipped. So unlike her usual voice. "But I'll do it anyway because if Guerrero does get to me, the EOD had better haul butt to save my life."

He would.

Juliana had already turned from him and headed for the door. He should let her go but he had to speak. "I really am...sorry." The apology came out sounding rusty and broken.

She pulled open the door. "For what?" Juliana didn't bother looking back at him. "Leaving me before...or setting me up now?"

*Both.* "I wanted you to be happy. You wouldn't—you wouldn't have been happy with me." The line he'd told himself for years. She deserved better. She'd have better. It was only a matter of time until some Prince Charming took her away.

His hands were clenched so tightly that his knuckles ached.

"Don't tell me what I'd be," she said, her spine stiff

and too straight. "I'm the only one who understands how I feel *and* what I want."

Then she walked through the door, calm and poised. So what if she was barefoot and her cute little toenails were flashing bright red? The woman had held court too long in her life not to walk with that easy grace.

"Come on, Doctor," she called out and he knew that Liz Donaldson had to be close by. "Let's get this over with."

Logan exhaled slowly. He looked up and stared straight into the mirror that was less than five feet from him. His reflection stared back. His jaw was lined with stubble, eyes and face worn.

*She wouldn't have been happy.* The words were stubborn, but they weren't his, not really. Her father had been the one to first speak them.

*You can't make her happy. When she finds out what you did, how do you think she'll ever be able to look at you again?*

His teeth ground together, but he managed to say, "Come on out, Jasper. I know you're in there."

After a moment, he heard the slow approach of Jasper's booted feet. Then the Ranger was there, filling the doorway, shaking his head even as he crossed his arms over his chest. "You are one dumb SOB," Jasper said.

"Don't push me now," Logan ordered. Jasper was always pushing. In the field, in the office—everywhere. *Death wish?* Yeah, he had one.

Jasper's mouth lifted in his usual sardonic smile. "Left her there all alone, huh? Didn't even go to see the pretty girl at the bus station. That's cold."

He stared at Jasper but didn't see him. "A blue dress that fell to her knees. A ponytail pulled to the side. A small black bag at her feet." He forced his hands to unclench. "She was sitting five feet from the front desk, turned so that she could see the entrance."

But he'd been there long before she'd arrived, hidden in the shadows, watching what he couldn't have.

A furrow pulled up Jasper's brows. "You were there, but you didn't say anything? Man, what are you—crazy? Why'd you let a woman like that walk?"

"You know what I am." Jasper had seen him at his worst, covered in blood, fighting for his life. More animal than man. He'd seen Logan when his control broke and the beast inside broke free.

*Born to kill.*

He'd been told that for so long.

"No, man, I know what you *think* you are," Jasper said with a sigh. "But I tell you this…if a woman like her ever gave me the look—the kind of look I saw her give you—I'd do anything for her."

He had done anything. He'd given her up. That had been everything. "Don't push me on this," Logan warned. He'd hate to have to kick his friend's butt again.

But Jasper just blinked slowly and kept his smile. "Maybe I should be talking to her, comforting *her*."

"You stay away from her."

"Like that, huh?" Before he could answer, Jasper gave him a long, considering look and said, "At twenty-two, I can still see you being a dumb kid who could manage to give her up. But now, after everything you've been through, after all we've done, I'm betting that sweet slice of paradise is pretty tempting, isn't it?"

She'd tempted him from day one and was still tempting him. When he'd had her beneath him at that cabin. When he'd been touching her skin, feeling her soft flesh beneath his…

"You really think you can let her go again?"

Logan didn't speak.

Jasper nodded. "Thought so." Whistling, he stalked away.

This time, Logan didn't look at his reflection. He didn't want to see the man who stared back at him. The man who just might be desperate enough to try to force Juliana to stay with him.

Even when he knew she deserved more.

JULIANA SAT ON THE small bed in the lab room, her head down, staring at the tiled floor. Logan stood in the doorway for a moment, watching her.

But then her head tilted back, and her gaze found his.

Silence, the kind that said too much.

He hesitated, then said, "I've got clothes for you. Shoes." Logan strode forward and put the bag down beside her. Then, because he couldn't help himself, his hands rose toward her.

She tensed.

"Easy," he whispered. "I just want to check…" He brushed back her hair, knowing exactly where Liz would have placed the implant. His finger slid up her neck, then slipped around beneath the heavy weight of her hair. The bandage was small, barely an inch long, and flat.

"I'm fine," Juliana said. He stood close to her, intimately close. And Logan didn't remove his hands.

He didn't want to. "Are you sure? Any pain, any—"

She shook her head.

*Step back.* He pulled in a breath and dropped his hands. "Once you've changed, we'll head out."

Her hand grabbed his arm. He was the one who tensed then. "Where are we going this time? Another cabin in the woods? Another safe house?"

"No."

Confusion filled the darkness of her gaze.

"No more hiding." The order had come from above. From the man who'd formed the EOD. Syd had picked up rumors online that Guerrero was on American soil. Rumors they suspected were fact. He was close…they just had to make him come in even closer.

And Logan's boss wanted them on the offensive.

*"We need to make Guerrero afraid. We want him to worry that he's been compromised."* Mercer's words. He'd talked to Logan on the phone less than five minutes ago. *"When the woman is hiding, he knows he has the power. Get her out. Put her in public. Make Guerrero think we've got the evidence on him. He needs to be the one running."*

Easy for Mercer to say. He didn't know Juliana. She was just a witness to him. An important one, no doubt, but the idea of putting her in danger wouldn't rip his guts out.

"Where are we going?" Juliana asked again, then her eyes widened. "Unless…maybe there's no 'we' now, maybe the EOD—"

"We're staying with you." As if anyone could pry him away when she was in danger.

She nodded, exhaling.

"But we're not hiding. Guerrero's power is fear. He wants you afraid. Pulling you away from everything you know. He wants to isolate you. That's key for him." The man knew how to intimidate and control his enemies.

And his friends. Luis Sanchez…hell, he still couldn't believe the guy had chosen to shove a knife into his heart instead of talking.

*"Marie…"*

He pushed the memory away, just like he did all the bloodstained memories that wanted to haunt him.

As far as the EOD was concerned, it was time for a new tactic with Juliana. "My boss—Mercer—he wants you seen in public. We want to make Guerrero become the one who's afraid. We want him to think that we've found the evidence. That we're secure. The idea is that he'll get desperate when he thinks we're closing in, and desperate men make mistakes." He'd seen it happen over and over again.

"Do I have a choice in this?"

Her words stopped him cold, and in that instant...

Logan realized that some things were more important than following orders.

"Yes." He kept his voice calm with an effort. "You do. If you want me to take you out of Mississippi, to get you as far from Guerrero and his goons as I can, you say the word."

Her lips parted.

"If you want to stay here, to stand off against him and make him become the hunted, then we'll do that. It's your life. *You* make the choice." He'd back her up, even if he had to go alone, without the other EOD agents riding shotgun.

So Logan waited.

Her hand rose. Touched the small bandage on the back of her neck. "I don't want to spend the rest of my life running."

Logan knew people who had spent years running. That life—it stunk. Always looking over your shoulder, never letting your guard down.

But there was something else she needed to understand before she made her choice. "Mercer's worried we have a leak at the EOD. That if we tried to take you to another secret location..." *It wouldn't be secret.* "Guerrero shouldn't have found us so quickly. Shouldn't have known the things he did."

So Mercer was saying that hiding wasn't an option. No, that hiding *with* the EOD wasn't an option.

Logan was pretty sure he could make Juliana disappear just fine on his own.

He could see the struggle on Juliana's face. Safety... where did it lie?

*With me.* If she'd just trust him again.

"No hiding." Juliana gave a slow nod. "That's not... that's not the way I want to live. I don't want to be afraid, every day, that he's coming after me."

Did she even realize how strong she truly was?

"I want to go after him. I want Guerrero to fear. He took away so much." She swallowed and exhaled slowly. "It's time for me to take away from him."

Damn straight.

"Let him think I have the evidence. Let him think we're tearing his life apart." Her words came stronger now. "And then let's destroy him."

"We will." A vow.

DIEGO STARED AT THE MAN before him. A man who sat, bound, with his arms and legs tied to a chair. A black bag covered his head and the fool was screaming at the top of his lungs.

Did he actually think help would come?

Diego sighed. "Why were you getting ready to leave town, Mr. McLintock?" Because he had been. Diego had sent a man to follow McLintock months ago. Back when he'd first realized that the senator was holding back.

The senator had to trust someone. Someone had been there to help with all the deals.

The someone who'd just stopped screaming.

"I—I was just going to visit my mother. She—she lives in Florida."

It was the wrong response. Ben McLintock should have been asking why he was being held. Demanding to know who'd taken him.

Not rushing to answer with a pat response.

"After all that happened with the senator, I—I needed to get away."

Still wrong.

Diego nodded to his men. The bag wasn't needed any longer.

One man stepped forward and yanked it from McLintock's head. McLintock's gaze flew around the small room, then locked on Diego.

"You know who I am," Diego said as he stared right back at the other man.

McLintock gave a small nod.

"That will make things easier." Diego lifted his hand and gave a little two-fingered wave. His man, Mario, knew what that signal meant.

A knife was immediately shoved into McLintock's shoulder.

The senator's aide screamed.

Diego dropped his hand. "You were working for the senator." The authorities had to know that, too. So he'd had to be so careful when he made his move on this man. But lucky for him, McLintock had been the one to escape from the guards that the government had put on him.

His man had been driving the taxi that picked up McLintock.

"I—I don't know what—"

Sighing, Diego lifted two fingers.

*"No!"* McLintock said. Mario paused and Diego cocked a brow. "I—I was… I just delivered packages for him, okay? I didn't even know what was in them, not until the feds came in and started asking all their questions."

Blood soaked his fancy shirt. "Then Aaron offered me money to keep quiet."

Sure, as if Diego believed that was the way things had gone down. This man had known about the deals. Probably from day one. He'd been taking money, stashing it away just like James had.

But James hadn't escaped. Neither would McLintock.

"Where's the evidence?"

"I don't know. I swear!"

Diego gave his two-fingered wave. The knife sank into McLintock's left shoulder this time. More screams. More blood.

"I'll ask again."

*"I don't know!"*

The knife sank into his left thigh.

"I need that evidence..."

"J-James said he was giving it...to his daughter... s-safekeeping..."

The knife sank into his right thigh.

*"I don't know anything else!"*

He could almost believe him.

*"Please*...let me go..."

Was the many crying now? How pitiful. "I will," Diego promised him. What would be the point in keeping him? A few more moments, and he'd know if McLintock had any more secrets to tell. After that...

He could go free.

"Tell me, what do you know about the bomb in the cemetery?"

McLintock flinched. "Nothing!"

"Lies just make the pain last longer." He knew exactly how to get to this one. Pain. McLintock howled when Mario went to work on him again.

"I didn't set it! I didn't!" McLintock was definitely crying now.

He also sounded honest. Pity. McLintock had been one of the few with open access to the senator's house and to his car. But if it hadn't been McLintock, then that did narrow down his pool of suspects.

Diego nodded to Mario. "You know what to do."

A muscle flexed in Mario's jaw.

"Y-you're gonna let me go, right?" McLintock was soaked in blood and straining against his bonds. "You'll let me go?"

"Of course." Diego turned away. "Once I'm sure you don't have any other secrets to tell…"

Fear tightened McLintock's face.

"So perhaps you'd better keep talking," Diego advised, "or else Mario will keep cutting."

THE MANSION THAT SAT high up on the hill, its stone walls stark and cold, had never seemed like home to Juliana.

The building had felt more like a tomb.

It sure looked like one from a distance.

"We've got a press conference scheduled for eight o'clock," Gunner said from his seat up front. "You're gonna focus on Guerrero during that talk. Time to start rattling the SOB."

Right. She nodded. She'd say or do whatever was necessary. *No more fear.* She wasn't going to stand in the middle of any more bloodbaths. As it was, Juliana had more than enough gore floating around in her mind to give her plenty of nightmares, thank you so much.

The SUV pulled to a stop. A cop car was behind them, another in front. Their escorts. Juliana knew that a large guard force would stay at the mansion. Added cover, sure, but the bodies were also designed to attract extra attention for them.

*Here I am. Come and get me.*

So they could get Guerrero.

Gunner exited the SUV and headed for the main entrance. Juliana knew the heavy iron security gates would have already closed behind them, locking the vehicles inside.

She glanced over at the house. This had been her father's place, not hers.

"Why did you always hate it here?" Logan's quiet question surprised her.

Shrugging a little, she said, "Because it's cold inside. It's just a big fancy tomb." Her palms flattened against her jeans. "My mother died one week after we moved into this house. She was coming home and a drunk driver slammed into her."

Juliana had been twelve. Her mother's death had torn her whole life apart.

And her father—he'd become someone completely different. He'd stopped caring about people. Only focused on *things*. More wealth. More houses.

"It was never home," she said, staring at all the windows. "And it always smelled like a funeral." Because of the flowers. So many had come after her mother's death. For weeks the house had been overflowing.

Then the flowers had started to wither and die.

She glanced back at Logan and was surprised by the pain she saw flash across his face. "Logan?"

"I'm sorry about your mother. I heard…she was a great lady."

This part she could remember so well. "She was." Her mother had been the good that balanced out her father.

She'd always made him be *better*. Without her, he'd fallen apart.

Juliana reached for her door. Her shoes made no sound as she headed up the elaborate walk. Logan was at her side and—

*"You're alive!"*

The woman's high cry had Juliana's head jerking up. Then she saw Susan Walker, her father's assistant, rushing toward her.

Susan caught her in a big, tight hug, a hug that smelled of expensive body lotion and red wine. "I thought you'd died! You disappeared after the explosion and no one would tell me anything...." She pulled back, gazing up at Juliana with wide, worried eyes. "I mean, on the news, they said that you'd survived. But I never *saw* you!" Susan's words tumbled out too fast. "And I was so worried!"

Susan's perfectly smooth face gave no hint to her age. She could have been thirty; she could have been forty-five. The woman had been a fixture in her father's life for the past eleven years.

His closest confidant. The person who organized his life.

And...

Juliana was pretty sure, her father's lover.

"We need to go inside," Gunner said in a quiet voice.

Susan jumped, as if she hadn't even noticed the men surrounding them. Then, after a frantic look around, she said, "Yes, yes, of course..." She ushered them inside the house. She was in a robe. A white silk robe that skirted around her ankles.

When Juliana entered the house, she heard the faint strains of music playing in the background.

They entered the den, and Juliana saw the wineglass on the table.

"I, um...I was just trying to relax a bit." Susan's lips pressed together for a moment. "You knew I moved in last spring, right?" She asked as her fingers nervously toyed with the robe's belt. "I mean, it just... The move gave me better access to your father. There was so much work to do and I—"

"You were sleeping with him." The words just came out. She wasn't in the mood for more lies or sugarcoating. Her mother was gone. She'd known her father had lovers, and Susan—well, the woman had always been kind to her.

Susan paled. "I was his assistant! I was—"

"His lover." Juliana rolled tired shoulders. "It's all right. You don't have to pretend with me."

Logan and Gunner were silent, assessing. She knew they'd run a check on Susan, on all the employees who worked so closely with her father.

All of the employees had turned up clean, no connection to Guerrero. But Logan was still suspicious, and she knew the EOD was still digging deep for dirt.

"Who are these men?" Susan glanced first at Gunner. Then Logan.

"Her protection," Logan said with a smile. "In light of all that's happened, I'm sure you understand why we'll be staying here with Juliana."

"Here?" Susan parroted as her eyes widened.

Right. Well, with her father dead, the house was technically Juliana's. Even if he had been sleeping with Susan. Talk about awkward. She didn't want to make Susan feel uncomfortable, but this was where they needed to be, at least for the next few days. *Just tell her.* "We're going to be moving in for a while." Hopefully, it wouldn't be for long. But in case it was longer, Juliana desperately needed a base to use so that she could get back to her life. She wanted to paint. Painting was her livelihood and she had work to deliver, but more, painting gave her a release. It could help take her mind off all the death.

Logan had told her that supplies would be brought in to her. When he'd said that, she'd almost kissed him. She'd caught herself, though, because she knew just where a kiss would have lead them.

*To us both being naked.* The awareness simmered between them.

"You can't stay here." Susan's rushed denial had Juliana blinking. "This isn't... You've *never* stayed here, Juliana."

It was late. Juliana was exhausted. She wanted to hit the bed and fall into oblivion. "I'm going to be staying here now. So are they." Simple.

Susan just shook her head.

"Which rooms are free?" Juliana asked her. "There should be more than enough for us to use." She was already getting a chill from being inside the house. The place was always so cold. Her father had restored every inch of the old antebellum. Or rather, he'd paid folks to restore the house. Maybe it was cold because the place was so big and drafty.

Maybe.

She knew her father kept a small staff in the house. A driver. A housekeeper. A cook. And—

"Take any room you want," Susan said softly as her shoulders sagged. "Take everything... It's yours, anyway." Then she brushed by Juliana. "I'm in your father's room."

Juliana felt badly about upsetting Susan. She knew the woman was hurting, too. She was pushing into this place—*where I don't belong*—and ripping into Susan's life. Bringing her hell right down on the hapless woman. "Susan..." She wanted her to be safe. Juliana took a breath and though she hated to say it, she forced the words out. "Maybe you should leave for a few days, until…" *Until it's safe. Until I'm not afraid you'll get caught in the cross fire when Guerrero attacks.*

Susan truly had always been kind to her, and when this nightmare was over, Juliana would give her the house. She could take it and be happy.

Juliana sure didn't want the place. She much preferred her small house on the beach. It never seemed cold there.

Susan's pretty face tightened. "You're kicking me out?"

And she'd screwed up. Juliana tried to back up. "No, no, that's not—"

"For your protection," Logan inserted smoothly. "The government will be happy to provide you with temporary lodging for a few days, until the situation becomes more stable."

Susan just shook her head. Her gaze seemed to swim with tears. "I'm not in any danger. No one would want to hurt me!"

"I'm sure that's what Charles thought, too," Juliana said quietly. She'd arranged to send flowers to his family, but she'd do more for them, too. When her father's estate was settled—after the government had their turn to go through everything, she'd see that they were taken care of.

"Wrong place," Gunner added darkly. "Wrong damn time."

Susan flinched. Then her eyes focused on Juliana. "Why? Why is this even happening?"

"Because my father was involved with some very dangerous people." Susan would have been the prime person to realize that truth, only, she seemed clueless. "Now they want me dead."

"We'll be escorting you out tonight, Ms. Walker," Gunner said. "Just show us to your room, and I can help you pack up."

Susan was still staring at Juliana. "I told you. I shared a room with the senator." Then she turned away, moving toward the circular staircase with her head up. But at the stairs, she paused with her hand on the banister. "He was going to marry me."

Juliana barely heard the quiet words.

"We'd planned… He was going to give up his office. Retire. Stay with me." Her head tilted and Juliana saw her scan the house. What did Susan see when she looked around?

Not death and ice, like Juliana saw.

Antiques, wealth, good memories?

"It's all gone," Susan whispered and she climbed up the steps.

Juliana's gaze darted to the closed study door. Her father had died in that room. He'd put one of his prized guns to his head and squeezed the trigger.

Susan had found his body. So that meant she must have found the suicide note, too. She knew that the senator had fallen far from grace.

*It's all gone.*

Yes, it was.

THE LITTLE BITCH was back.

Susan closed the bedroom door behind herself. Flipped the lock—then slapped her palm against the wood.

The pain was fresh, staggering, and it helped her to push back the fury that had her whole body shaking.

Juliana had just marched in…and kicked her out.

After all of these years. After all the work she'd done.

Juliana hadn't stayed around to look after Aaron. She hadn't been there, day in and day out, working to keep the man on a leash. Working to make him look sane when the man hadn't cared about anything.

Or anyone.

Susan glanced at the ornate bed.

*I was here.*

And everything—it was supposed to be hers now. Aaron had promised to take care of her. Only, he hadn't.

He'd been weak until the end. Weak and desperate, and he'd taken the easy way out.

A bullet to the brain. She would have made him suffer more. He'd dangled his promises in front of her for so long.

*It should all be mine.* The money. The houses. The cars. Every. Single. Thing.

She was so tired of pretending. She'd pretended for years. Yanked herself out of the gutter. Pushed her way into Aaron's life.

His weakness had been an advantage for her, at first.

But now...

Her gaze roamed around the room. Right past the paintings that he'd ordered hung on the wall. Juliana's paintings. Her precious work.

Did the girl even realize her father had bought them? That he'd ordered the pieces, paying far too much, and had them delivered back here?

Susan hated them. Storms, dark skies and threatening clouds.

Susan had been so tempted to slice the paintings in the past few days. To just rip them apart.

*Payback.*

But she'd kept up her image, for all the good it had done her. Kept it up even when she'd shattered on the inside.

"Ms. Walker." A rap sounded at her door. "We'll be leaving soon." An order.

She recognized the voice, of course; it belonged to the first man who'd come into her home. The dark man with the darker eyes.

His stare didn't scare her. She'd seen plenty of darkness as a kid.

"Just a minute," she called, trying to keep her voice level. Now wasn't the time to lose her control. Now was the time to keep planning. To keep her focus.

She headed for the nightstand and the small safe that she knew waited inside.

There were files in that safe. A small handgun. Sure, the police and the FBI and who the hell knew who else had been in the house, and they'd searched everywhere, but...

*But they didn't see the papers inside the safe.*

She'd made sure of it. She'd taken those papers, hidden them, then brought them back when the agents backed off.

*I knew I could use them.*

Another rap. "You need to hurry, Ms. Walker. A car's waiting downstairs for you."

Her jaw ached, and she forced her teeth to unclench. She'd recognized the other man downstairs. He'd changed over the years, yes, but she'd still remembered him.

His eyes were the same.

She pulled out the papers from the safe. Flipped open the file.

Logan Quinn's eyes stared back at her.

Once upon a time, Senator Aaron James had wanted Logan Quinn eliminated from his daughter's life.

Susan had taken the necessary steps for that elimination. She'd been the one to do the research. To destroy the budding romance.

She knew all about Logan's secrets. It was time for Juliana to learn about them, too.

*You think you're safe, don't you?* Her gaze darted back

to the paintings. *You think he'll keep you safe. But what happens when you learn about all of his lies?*

Susan left the safe open just a few inches, and she left the manila file pushing out.

Juliana would find it soon enough.

Then she'd be vulnerable.

And Juliana wouldn't survive the next attack on her life.

Susan exhaled slowly and made her way back to the door. She flipped the lock and opened it carefully. "I'm sorry…" A quaver entered her voice. "It's been a…rough few days."

He nodded. "I understand, and the move—it's just for your safety."

She looked at him from beneath her lashes. Not her usual type. Too rough. She'd felt the calluses on the man's fingertips, but…

Sometimes it wasn't about what you liked.

It was about what you could use.

Susan rested her fingers on his chest. "I'll be able to come home again soon, right?"

He glanced at her hand, then back up to her face. The guy's expression hadn't thawed any. "When it's clear."

It would be clear, just as soon as Juliana was rotting in the ground.

JULIANA WAS STANDING at the foot of the stairs when Susan came down. Gunner was just a few steps behind, carrying her suitcase in his hand.

It looked as if Susan had been crying.

*Great*. Juliana shifted her body and blocked the bottom of the stairs. "It's just temporary, Susan."

Susan's eyes were red. She *had* been crying. "It's not going to be my home. You and I both know…in the will, he left everything to you." Anger thinned her lips. "You couldn't be bothered to see him, but it all still goes to you."

"I don't…" *Want it.* "This isn't my home any longer. As soon as Logan and his team stop the man who's hunting me…"

Susan's gaze flickered to Logan. "I remember you."

He was by the door. Arms crossed over his chest. At her words, his head cocked toward Susan.

Susan stared right back at him. "Aaron always told me that you were dangerous."

Juliana eased to the side, blocking her view. This wasn't about Logan. "Susan, when this mess is over, I'll call you. We'll sort everything out. The house, the will— everything."

Susan's lips twisted in a sad smile as her gaze focused on Juliana. "He loved you. Probably more than you'll ever realize. It's too bad you didn't know anything about him." She brushed by Juliana. "Maybe you should take a look at what's on the walls of his room. It might surprise you."

Then she was gone. Gunner followed behind her, shaking his head.

But Juliana saw Logan grab Gunner's arm before he could walk through the doorway. "Find out what she knows."

Gunner gave an almost imperceptible nod.

The door closed behind him with a click.

Juliana rubbed at the bandage on her neck. She'd almost forgotten about her injuries. Her head had finally stopped throbbing. She just—

*"Don't."*

Logan stalked toward her. He caught her fingers, pulled them away from the small bandage. "Don't do anything to draw attention to it."

"No one's here to see." His team had cleared out the

house. They were alone—all of the guards were stalking along the exterior of the place.

Alone with Logan. When he was this close, the awareness between them burned. But she turned away. "I'm… I'm going to shower." She didn't want to see what waited in her father's room. Not then.

She wanted to wash away the memories of blood.

Logan's fingers curled around her wrist. "Are we going to talk about it?"

Her throat went desert dry. "It?"

"You…almost coming…"

There'd been no almost about it. She glanced back, and from the look in his eyes, Juliana knew he realized that truth.

"Or are we just going to pretend that it didn't happen?"

Juliana gave a slow shake of her head. "I'm not that good at pretending."

His gaze searched hers. "You're mad because of the setup. I get that."

Good for him.

"But I swear, I wouldn't risk your life for anything. You're my priority."

She believed that. After all, wasn't keeping her safe his job?

His fingers tightened around her wrist. "You're just going to walk away, aren't you?"

It was what he expected. She knew that. But there was more at stake right then.

Juliana had realized just how vulnerable she still was to Logan. He'd gotten into her heart once, and no matter how hard she tried, she'd never been able to shove him out.

She still cared for him, probably always would.

But she couldn't let herself love him again. It was too dangerous. Too painful.

*Take the pleasure he can give you.* A tempting whisper from inside. *Then you be the one to walk away.*

Only, there was a problem with that plan. If she took him back to her bed, Juliana was afraid she might not want to walk away.

So she pulled her arm free, and before she gave in to that temptation, she headed up the stairs.

*I can walk away now.*

Juliana just wasn't sure that walking away was what she really wanted.

DIEGO SHOOK HIS HEAD as he stared at the man seated in front of him. McLintock couldn't even keep his head up anymore. Blood and sweat coated his body.

"I didn't have anything to do with that explosion at the cemetery. I promise!" Ben McLintock mumbled, voice rasping. He'd already said this over and over, and Diego actually believed him.

Why keep lying at this point? McLintock had no one to protect. No family. No lover. The guy had always just been out for himself.

But if it hadn't been McLintock… Diego's eyes narrowed.

He waved the guard back and strolled toward McLintock. He put his hands on the other man's shoulders and shoved him back. McLintock blinked blearily as Diego leaned in close. "This can all be over," Diego promised him. "I just want to know who's after Juliana James. I want to know who set that bomb in her car." Who'd almost screwed his plans to hell.

*I need that evidence.* Another loose end. There were too many.

"I…don't know! I swear—I don't…"

His hands tightened around McLintock's thin shoul-

PUBLIC LIBRARY

ders. "Did you know that Mario over there—" he tilted his head toward the guard "—has one thing that he's particularly good at? Death. He can kill in a hundred different ways. He *likes* killing."

McLintock was crying. Had been for a while now.

Did he realize that no matter what happened, he wouldn't get out alive? Probably not. People always clung to hope so desperately. Even when they had no reason for that hope.

"Did you see anything…anyone suspicious at the cemetery?" Diego pressed. "You rode over in that limo. Who was there when you got in it?"

"Just…the driver, Charles…"

The man wouldn't have killed himself.

"Cops were…there." McLintock licked his lips. Tried to hold up his sagging head. "Federal…agents. I thought—I thought everything was…safe."

No place was safe.

With the cops swarming around, though, the person who'd planted that bomb would have needed good access—an "in" at the mansion.

"I rode…in the car, just…me, Juliana and…Susan…"

Susan. Diego paused, remembering a woman with sleek blond hair and too-sharp eyes. He'd seen her before, with the senator.

He'd seen Susan, but she'd never seen him.

Aaron's lover. Would a lover kill a daughter?

*Yes.*

"When it was time to leave the cemetery, why weren't you in the limo?" This was the important question. From what he'd learned, Juliana had been about to climb into the limo. What about the other passengers?

"Susan…Susan said she wasn't…feeling well." The words were soft. Weak. The blood loss was definitely taking its toll on the man. "She…asked me…stay with…her. Wanted to get…some air. Said we could get…ride back… with someone else…."

Diego smiled. "Was that so hard?"

Looking confused, McLintock actually tried to smile back even as his eyes flickered closed.

Diego fired a hard glance at Mario. "Find the woman— this Susan. Bring her in to me."

McLintock drunkenly shook his head. "No. Susan… didn't do this… She doesn't know anything about—"

"A man's lover always knows him better than anyone else." That was why Diego made a habit of not leaving his lovers alive. They'd just betray him if they lived.

There was too much betrayal in the world.

His father had taught him that lesson early on. In Mexico, his father had amassed a fortune by dealing in the darkness. The law hadn't applied to him. But…he'd always been so good to Diego. Given him a good life, nice clothes, toys. A home.

Diego had known his father was a dangerous man, but he'd trusted him. A boy trusted his father.

*Until that night*… He'd heard screams. He'd followed the cries. Found his mother dying, and his father— covered in her blood.

*"She was selling me out!"* His father had wiped the bloody blade of his knife on his pants. *"Trying to make a deal with those Americans… She was going to take you away from me!"*

His mother had looked like a beautiful angel. Lying on the ground, her white nightgown stained red.

*"No one will take you from me!"* his father had snarled. *"They think they can use you against me, make me weak!"*

His father had been so good to him before.

But Diego had seen the real man that night.

*No one is good.*

His father had stalked toward him with his knife. The knife he'd used to kill Diego's mother. *"No one can use you against me."*

And he'd known that his father had snapped. He'd cried as he looked at his mother and he'd realized— *He's going to kill me, too.*

Only, Diego hadn't been ready to die.

They'd fought. The knife had cut into Diego's flesh. He still had the long scar on his stomach, a permanent reminder.

*Trust no one.* Especially not those close to you.

But Diego hadn't died. At twelve, Diego had killed his father. Then when he'd walked out of that house, covered in blood, with the bodies of his mother and father behind him...

*El Diablo.*

His father's men had given him a new name—and they'd feared him. Everyone had.

Diego realized that he was staring down at McLintock. The man was barely breathing, and the hope was almost painful to see in his bleary eyes.

Giving a slow nod, Diego stepped back. "You've given me the information that I needed." And he was sure that Susan would be coming to join him very soon.

"You'll let me go? Please?" The man's voice was thready, so weak. No man should talk like that. Diego barely held his disgust in check. No man should beg. His father hadn't begged.

"The knife," Diego said as he opened his hand. Without any hesitation, Mario gave him the blade.

McLintock sighed raggedly. Did he think Diego was going to cut his bonds and let him go?

"You're free," Diego told him and drove the knife right into McLintock's heart.

When he turned away from the body, he saw the fear... the respect...in Mario's eyes.

*El Diablo.*

As long as there was fear, he didn't need trust or loyalty.

# Chapter Eight

The bathroom door opened, sending tendrils of steam drifting into the bedroom. Juliana walked out wrapped in a towel, with her wet hair sliding over her shoulders.

The woman was every fantasy he'd ever had. Just seeing her—arousal flooded through Logan, hardening his flesh for her.

She was looking down when she entered the bedroom, but after just an instant, she seemed to sense him. Juliana glanced up and froze.

Maybe he should be a gentleman and turn away while she dressed. Juliana was probably used to gentlemen. The guys who spoke to her so softly, held her hand and greeted her with flowers.

And didn't constantly think about ripping her clothes away—or her towel—and taking her in a wild rush of lust and greedy need.

The gentleman role wasn't for him.

So Logan kept watching and enjoying that world-class view.

Juliana's eyes narrowed to dark slits, and even that seemed sexy. "Do you mind?"

"Not at all." In fact, this was going on his highlight reel for later.

Her lips tightened. He liked her lips soft. Wet. Open. On his.

"Why are you in here, Logan?"

*Because I want you.* He'd had a taste before, and it had just left him craving more. Their time was limited. He knew that. As soon as the nightmare ended, Juliana would walk away and not look back.

Why couldn't he have her just once more? Before the real world ripped them apart. He needed more memories to get him through the dark and bloody nights that would come.

When he was in hell, her memory got him through the fire.

But he pushed back the flames and said, "I thought you needed to know…Ben McLintock is missing." Syd had called with the news just a few minutes before.

"Missing?"

"Uniforms were on him, stationed at his house." Because anyone who'd worked so closely with the senator was getting extra attention from the government and the cops. "But it looks like he slipped away." Or rather, deliberately ditched the eyes on him and vanished.

She shook her head. "Ben? Ben ran away?"

*Innocent men don't run.* Logan bit the words back and tried to keep his gaze on her face. He shouldn't have to say the words, anyway. Juliana would know the truth.

And sure enough, he saw the painful truth sink in for her. "The car bomb. You said…someone would have needed access to this house. The limo was here."

Ben had been there. The guy had been given 24/7 access to everything the senator had.

Juliana's hands lifted and she clutched the towel closer to her body. "You think…you think he set the car bomb." Not a question.

"It's a possibility." One that Sydney was following up on with the authorities.

"He always seemed so nice." Her words were dazed.

"Nice men can make perfect killers." Because the nice veneer was so convincing. A way to fool others so you could get close.

He realized he was staring at the tops of her breasts. Logan cleared his throat. "We'll find him." The guy had either run on his own…or Guerrero had him. But either way, Logan's team was tracking him now. Ben McLintock wasn't going to just vanish. They wouldn't let him.

He pulled in a breath and caught the scent of vanilla. The scent drifted from the open bathroom door. From Juliana. A sweet but sensual scent.

Logan spun around and headed for the door. "Get some sleep." He sure as hell wouldn't. He'd be thinking about her—what *should* have been.

"Logan." Her voice stopped him at the door. His hand had lifted, and he fisted his fingers before slowly turning back to face her.

Juliana hadn't moved from her spot just outside the bathroom. More steam drifted around her. Her skin gleamed, so smooth, so soft.

"You still look at me—" her chin lifted "—like you want—"

"To eat you alive." Yeah, he knew how he looked. Starving. But Juliana had always made him that way. Desperate for what he wanted, for what he'd taken before.

Her hands were still at the top of the towel. "In Mexico, you told me that if I offered myself to you again…"

He couldn't think about that night right then. Being close to her after all those years—he'd gone more than a little crazy.

"You said you'd take me," she finished.

Logan didn't speak.

"But I've changed my mind."

His whole body had turned to stone.

"I've thought about what I want. What I don't want."

He couldn't hear this.

"I know we don't have forever. I know you'll go back to—to wherever the next battle is, and I'll go back to Biloxi when this is all over."

Biloxi. Her home on the beach. He'd seen it before. After a battle that had taken two of his best friends. When he'd been broken and weak, he'd had to find her.

So he'd gone to her beach. He'd watched her from a distance, gotten stronger just from seeing her.

But he'd stayed in the shadows. After all, that was where he belonged.

"We don't have forever," Juliana said again, the words husky, "but we do have now."

He took a step toward her and shook his head. No way had he just heard her say—

"But I'm not offering."

*Son of a—*

"This time, *I'm* taking." She dropped the towel. His mouth dried up. "I want you, and right now, I don't care about the past or the future. Now—now is all that matters to me."

She was all that mattered to him. Logan was already across the room. His hands were on her, greedy for the feel of her flesh. He pulled her against him, pressed his mouth to hers, thrust his tongue past her lips and tasted the paradise that waited.

The bed was steps away—steps that he didn't remember taking. But they were falling, tumbling back, and he had her beneath him on the mattress.

He'd woken from hot, desperate dreams of her for years, and part of him wondered...*just a dream?*

Then her nails bit into his back. Her legs slid over his hips and she pulled him closer.

*No dream ever felt this good.*

His mouth was still on hers because he had to keep tasting her. His hands were stroking her body because he needed to feel her silken flesh.

But she wasn't just lying passive beneath him. Her body arched against him, and Juliana caught the hem of his shirt—and then she yanked the shirt off him.

Their lips broke apart and the shirt went flying. A wild smile pulled at his lips. Only Juliana. She was always—

*His.*

He caressed the pert curve of her breast. The nipple was tight, flushed pink, and when he put his lips on her, she whispered his name.

And scored her nails down his back.

He should go slowly. Learn her body again, remember every inch.

But her scent was driving him out of his mind. She was pulling him closer. She was all he could feel. All he could breathe.

Everything.

He yanked down the zipper of his jeans. Found protection for them, then he positioned his aroused length at the delicate entrance of her sex.

Logan caught her hands and pushed them back against the mattress. Their fingers threaded together, their gazes locked.

The years fell away.

*The only girl I ever loved.*

"Logan..." She whispered his name. "I've missed you," she confessed.

Then there was nothing else but her.

Logan pushed into her moist, hot core, driving deep and steady, fighting to hold on to his control when he just wanted to take and take and take. But he had to show her pleasure. He had to make sure she went as wild as he did.

Her legs wrapped around him. No hesitation. No fear. She smiled up at him.

His hips pulled back, then he thrust deep. Her breath caught and the smile faded from her lips. The passion built between them, the desire deepening. The thrusts came faster, harder, and the control he'd held so tight began to shred.

The pleasure filled her eyes, making them seem to go blind. He'd never seen anything more beautiful than her. Nothing...no one...

Her climax trembled around him and she cried out in release. Her breaths came in quick gasps as her legs tightened around him.

The release hit Logan, not a wave or a rush but an avalanche that swept over him with a climax so powerful his body shuddered—and he held on to Juliana as tightly as he could.

And when his heartbeat eased its too-frantic pounding, he stared back into her eyes and realized just how dangerous she still was...to him.

THE SCENT OF BOOZE HUNG *heavily in the air. Beer. Whiskey.*

*But even more than that...he could smell the blood.*

*"Dad?" Logan called out for him even as he pushed against the dashboard. It had fallen in on him, and he had to twist and heave his body in order to slide out from under the dash. He yanked at the seat belt, his hands wet with blood, and finally, finally, he was free.*

*His dad wasn't.*

*Logan stared at the wreckage of the pickup. Twisted metal. Broken glass. And his father pinned behind the wheel, head craned at an unnatural angle.*

*His fingers trembled when he put them to his father's throat. No pulse. No life. Nothing.*

*"Help..."*

*The barest of cries. So soft. A whisper. But he stiffened and whirled around.*

*That was when he saw the other car. A fancy ride, with a BMW decal on the front—and the entire driver's side smashed inward.*

*"Help..." The cry came again, from inside that shattered wreck. A woman's voice.*

*And Logan remembered...*

*The scream of tires. The roar of crunching metal.*

*The sound of death.*

*He tried to get to the woman. Cuts covered her pretty face. She was so pale. So small.*

*"It's going to be all right," he told her, reaching for her hand. "I'll get you help."*

*She looked at him, opening dazed eyes. "Ju...Juliana?"*

*Then her breath heaved.*

*She didn't say anything else ever again.*

LOGAN STOOD AT THE TOP of the stairs as the memories rolled over him. He'd fought to keep that dark night buried for so long, but here, in this place, with Juliana once more…the past had gotten to him.

Some nights could never be forgotten, some mistakes never erased.

The life he'd known had ended that night. Two people had died. He'd…

"What are you doing?" Juliana's soft voice came from the darkness behind him.

Logan stiffened. "Just doing a sweep." Total BS. But he couldn't face her yet. Not after what he'd done.

Back then and…now.

Juliana had fallen asleep in his arms. Sleep wouldn't come so easily for him. Never had.

He'd searched the house. The agents and cops had already done plenty of sweeps. *He'd* done his share of searching before, too, but he'd had to look again.

*Because there'd been something in Susan's eyes…*

The woman had wanted Juliana to go into Aaron's room. Now Logan knew why.

He'd found the safe, conveniently left open. He'd seen the documents inside.

That safe had been empty just days before—well, empty except for the small gun. The senator had always seemed to be keeping guns close.

*Too close.*

Juliana hadn't seen her father's body after the suicide, but Logan had. He'd never forget the image.

But those files hadn't been in the safe days before. He knew because he'd cracked it himself and made sure the senator hadn't hidden any evidence inside. Since the safe had been empty then, it meant that someone else— *Susan*—had deliberately placed the files and the car-crash photos he'd discovered in that safe.

Susan knew what he'd done, what the senator had done. And she'd wanted Juliana to find out, too.

*Why? So she'd turn against me?*

He couldn't afford to have Juliana turn away from him, not now. It would be too dangerous for her.

"Dawn's close," she said, her voice husky. Sexy.

Dawn was coming. He could see the sky lightening behind the big picture windows. Faint hues of red were streaking through the darkness.

They'd have to get ready for her press conference soon. More plans. More traps.

Her fingers were on his back, tracing lightly over the scar that slid down near his spine. "What happened here?" she asked him softly.

Her touch was light, easy.

Logan swallowed and tried to keep his body from tensing. "A mission in the Middle East. Hostage rescue. It didn't go…quite as planned." He'd had to take the hit in order to protect the hostage. At the time, he'd barely felt the pain. And he'd killed in response to the attack—instantly. No second thought, no hesitation. In the field, there wasn't ever time for hesitation.

*Kill or be killed.*

Her fingers slid around his side. So delicate on his flesh. Logan turned to face her.

"And here?" Juliana asked. She was tracing the jagged wound that was too close to his heart. As she leaned forward to study the scar, her hair slid over his arm.

Logan took a breath and pulled her scent deep into his lungs. "A bullet wound in Panama." A drug lord hadn't liked having his operation shut down. Too bad for him. And that shot had almost been too close for Logan.

Her head tilted back as she studied him and let her fingers rise to slip under his chin. "And here? What about this one?"

His smallest scar. He stared into her eyes. "That one came from a bar fight…in Jackson, Mississippi."

A furrow appeared between her eyes.

*Why not tell her?* "One day, I lost my girl, so I got drunk in the nearest bar I could find." The only time he'd gotten drunk. *Won't be like him. Can't.* "There was a fight." His fingers lifted, caught hers, moved them away from the scar. "A broken whiskey bottle caught me in the chin."

Her gaze searched his. "You didn't lose me."

"Didn't I?"

She pulled her hand away. Logan saw that she was wearing a robe, long and silky. He wanted to pull her back into his arms but—

The phone in his back pocket began to vibrate. Logan pulled it out, keeping his eyes on hers. "Quinn."

"We just found McLintock," Jasper said, his voice rough.

"Where?"

"Cemetery. They dumped his body on the senator's grave."

Hell, that was a pretty clear message.

"He was carved up. Someone sure took their time with him."

Because Guerrero had wanted McLintock to talk, and Logan was betting that the guy had talked plenty, before his attackers killed him.

Guerrero and his men liked to get up close and personal with their targets. From the cases that he'd worked before, Logan knew that Guerrero's weapon of choice was a knife. He liked the intimacy of the blade. The control it gave him as he slowly tortured his prey.

That was why the cemetery bombing had never fit for him. Not up close and personal enough. The guy enjoyed watching the pain on his victims' faces.

"I'm going with the ME now," Jasper said, and there was the rumble of another voice in the background, "but I'll meet you at the press conference."

The press conference. Right. They still had their show to do. Logan ended the call. His eyes never left Juliana's. "You heard." She'd been too close to miss Jasper's words.

A faint nod. Her pupils had widened with worry.

"And you still want to go out there?" He pushed her because his instincts were to grab her and run. To hide her. To keep her safe and protected. *Not* to put her on display for the killer. "You still want to challenge Guerrero?"

"He killed Ben...."

"No, he tortured Ben, probably for hours, *then* he killed him." Brutal, but that was what they were dealing with, and they all had to face that truth. "You're going to bait Ben's killer on television. Taunt him. You ready for that?"

Maybe he expected her to back down. Maybe he *wanted* her to. Because then it would be fine when he kidnapped her and they vanished.

"How many others has he killed?"

He didn't even know. No one was sure. Hundreds. With the weapons that Guerrero had sold? Thousands.

"That's what I thought," Juliana said. Her chin lifted a little. Her shoulders seemed to straighten beneath the silk robe. "I'm ready for this. I'll do what I have to do, and we'll stop him."

And he knew there would be no running away. It was Juliana's choice, and he'd never take her choice away. He'd stand by her. Keep her safe. *No other option.*

He stared at her and realized...he'd *hoped* that she would want to run, but deep down, he'd actually expected her to do exactly what she was doing. Because he knew Juliana—the woman had a fierce core of steel.

She turned away from him, and he knew...things were only going to get more dangerous for them.

So he'd damn well stay by her side.

But she'd only taken a few steps when she stopped and pulled in a sharp breath, as if she were bracing herself. Then Juliana turned back to face him, her pretty face set with lines of determination. "There's something I have to tell you."

He raised a brow. Waited.

Her tongue swiped over her lower lip. "It was my fault."

Logan had no idea what she was talking about. "Juliana?"

"All of those men who died at your cabin, everything that happened there…it was *all because of me*."

He stepped toward her. "No, baby, it's not you. It's Guerrero. He's crazy. He'll torture, kill—do anything that he has to do in order to get what he wants."

Logan tried to take her into his arms, but she moved back.

"There was… I didn't tell you everything." She wrapped her arms around her stomach and rocked back on her heels. Pain glinted in her dark stare. "When I was in Mexico, when I was with John—"

Not John. Guerrero.

"We talked for so long. About everything. Nothing. Things that I didn't think mattered to anyone but…me."

A knot formed in his gut. "What did you tell him?" They'd gone over this before, on the plane ride back from Mexico, but they'd just focused on any revelations she might have made about her father. And now that he thought about it, Juliana had never quite met his gaze during that interrogation. She'd kept glancing away, shifting nervously. All the telltale signs of deception had been there, but he'd just thought—

*Not her.*

Juliana wouldn't lie. He was the one who lied. She'd just been nervous, in shock from everything that happened.

"I never realized what I said would matter." She was meeting his stare now. With guilt and stoic determination battling the pain in her gaze. "I should have told you sooner."

"Told me what?"

"Guerrero knows about you. About us." She looked down. "I told you…he wasn't asking about my father's work. He was just asking about me, my life."

And she'd mentioned him? "Why?"

After a moment, her gaze came back to him. "I thought that I was going to die. I didn't expect a rescue."

As if he'd ever leave her to that hell. He'd been ready to bring that whole place down, brick by brick, in order to get her out.

"John…asked me if I'd ever been in love." Her laugh was brittle. "That's one of the things you think about before death, right? Did you love? Are you dying without that regret?"

That knot was getting bigger every moment. "You told him that you loved me."

"I even gave him your name," Juliana admitted in a sad rush. "With his connections, it would have been so easy for him to do a check on you and to—"

"Find the cabin under my name." Hell. The pieces fit. And that sure explained how Guerrero's men had tracked her so quickly.

"When you got me out, I didn't think what I'd said mattered." Sadness trembled in her tone. "I mean, I'd told him how you felt so I never expected—"

Logan caught her hands, pulling them away from her body. The tumble of her words froze and she stared up at him with parted lips. "How did I feel?" It scraped him raw on the inside to think that she'd been talking with Guerrero, laying her beautiful soul bare.

Juliana swallowed. "I told him that you didn't love me back."

His focus centered only on her. On the rasp of her breathing. The scent of vanilla. The ghost of pain in her eyes.

"So I thought he'd know there was nothing between us. I never thought he'd go into your life or that he'd—"

Logan put his mouth on hers. His tongue slipped past her lips. The kiss was probably too hard, too rough, but so was he right then.

*I told him that you didn't love me back.*

Her hands rose to his shoulders. Her mouth moved against his, gentling him.

After a few moments, Logan forced his head to lift. He stared down at her. "You didn't…you didn't do anything wrong." His voice came out as a growl.

She gave him a faint smile. "Yes, I did. But I won't make any more mistakes again. I promise." Then she turned, pulling away. With slow steps, Juliana headed back to the bedroom.

But she had it wrong. The fault wasn't hers. He was the one who'd screwed up. The one who'd never told her the truth.

"Logan…come back to bed with me."

His head jerked up. He'd been staring at the floor. At nothing.

Now he saw that she'd looked back over her shoulder at him. Her hand was up, reaching for him.

He should tell her the truth. She wasn't a kid any longer. Neither was he. He *would* tell her. Because of Susan, he'd have no choice.

If he didn't tell Juliana about that dark night, Susan would.

*Guerrero will.* The guy would be digging into his past, learning every secret that he could. And he'd try to use those secrets against her.

Maybe Juliana thought that Logan didn't care, but Guerrero…

"Logan?"

Guerrero would figure out the truth.

He rushed to her. Took her hand. Kissed her.

*I loved you back.*

Juliana might have gotten over him. She might just be looking for pleasure in a world gone to hell, but she mattered to him.

Always had.

He lifted her into his arms.

She always would.

SUSAN WALKER WATCHED as the poor little rich girl stepped toward the microphone. Looking dutifully mournful but determined. *Cry me a river.*

"The allegations that you've all heard about my father are true." Juliana's voice was clear and pitched perfectly to carry to all the microphones that surrounded her. "Senator Aaron James was using his position to perpetrate criminal acts. He was working with an arms dealer, a man that the government has identified as Diego Guerrero, and selling weapons off to the highest bidder."

There was an eruption of questions as the reporters attacked like sharks.

Juliana held up her hand. "My father took his life because he couldn't face what he'd done, but he left evidence behind." She glanced toward the men in black suits beside her. Men who screamed FBI or CIA. "That evidence has been recovered and is being turned over to the authorities."

Susan fought to keep her expression cool as Juliana continued talking. The reporters were eating up her every word. The woman looked like a perfect victim, sad-little-me, having to be so brave and struggle on after daddy's treachery.

The mob around Juliana would probably make her into a celebrity. Hell, there was no *probably* about it.

And there stood Logan. Just a few feet away from Juliana. The reporters hadn't noticed him. They'd followed Juliana's gaze to the other agents, not ever seeing the real threat right under their noses. Blind fools.

"The authorities have told me that Diego Guerrero is in the country, possibly operating under one of his aliases…" Now Juliana was staring straight into the cameras. "John Gonzales is a name he's used before."

One of the suits rushed forward. He held up a picture.

"This is a sketch of Diego as his Gonzales persona," Juliana continued. "We'll make sure you all get a…"

Susan spun away, took two furious steps forward and slammed into the man she now knew was called Gunner.

Gunner just stared down at her with a raised brow. "Going somewhere?"

She forced a smile. "I just… It's too much, you know?" She waved her hand back to the crowd. "I don't know why you insisted on escorting me here today. I told you already—you and the other agents—I had no idea what—"

"Ben McLintock said he had no idea, too." Gunner's dark stare seemed to measure her, looking for secrets.

*You won't find them.*

"But we still found his body this morning. Dumped on the senator's grave."

Susan staggered back. She hadn't expected…

"I guess Guerrero thought he was holding back." Gunner lifted one shoulder in a faint shrug. "By the looks of things, I'm thinking McLintock talked to Guerrero, told him everything he knew. Guerrero *made* him talk."

Her heart beat faster. Her palms started to sweat. Damn Mississippi heat. Even in the spring, she was melting.

"So maybe you should be rethinking that offer of protection," Gunner murmured with an assessing glance.

Rethinking it? Why? So they could get close and find out exactly what she'd done and lock her away? No dice. She'd gone that prison route before.

She'd lost two years of her life to a juvie jail. She wouldn't ever be going behind bars again.

It had taken Susan too long to build her life again. Or rather, to steal the life that she had. Before she got in trouble, she'd been Becky Sue Morris. After juvie…

*Hello, new me.*

"I don't know anything," Susan said. Juliana was still talking, feeding her lines to the reporters. Why? "Guerrero wouldn't learn anything from me."

"No, but he'd still kill you. Slice you open just like he did your friend McLintock."

Ben hadn't been her friend. He'd just been an annoying lackey who stood in her way. He'd been working for Aaron before she'd arrived on the scene, and while she might have gotten access to Aaron's bed, Ben had been the one to know his secrets. Yes, she bet that Ben had known all about the deals with Guerrero. The twit had probably been in on everything.

How much money had they made? And she hadn't seen so much as a dime.

Now Juliana was walking away from the microphones. The big show was over. No, Juliana's show was over.

Susan's show was just beginning.

Her gaze moved back to Juliana. Logan was being her shadow. Her guard dog. What else was new? Juliana must not have found the file she'd left for her.

Logan glanced up then and his gaze cut right to her.

*He found it.*

Susan kept her breathing easy and smooth. That gaze of his seemed to burn her flesh.

"Is there a problem?" Gunner asked quietly.

She put her hand on his arm, stumbled a bit. "It's...so much. Ben. Aaron. I need a few minutes." She glanced up, offering him a tired smile. "Give me a little time, okay?" Her voice was weak. Lost. She thought it sounded pretty perfect.

Gunner nodded. Right. What else was a gentleman supposed to do?

After taking a deep breath, she made her way to the nearest ladies' room. Susan checked, making sure that no one else was around. Then her glance darted around the small room...and landed on the window to the right.

Time to vanish.

"WHERE'S SUSAN?" Logan demanded as he headed toward Gunner.

The agent jerked his thumb toward the restroom.

Eyes narrowed, Logan immediately headed toward the ladies' room door.

"What are you doing?" Juliana grabbed his arm. "You can't go in there!"

*Watch me.* He knew that Susan was trying to drive a wedge between him and Juliana, and he also knew...

*I don't trust her.*

So he knocked on the door, a hard, fast rap. "Susan! Come out! We need to talk." Just not in front of Juliana. He glanced over his shoulder at Gunner. "Take Juliana to the car. I'll be right behind you."

Juliana was looking at him as if he was crazy.

And he heard no sound from inside the bathroom.

*Hell.* "Susan?" Another hard knock at the door.

No response. Not so much as a whisper of sound.

His instincts were screaming now. Logan shoved open the door. Scanned under the stalls.

Gone. And only an open window waited to the right.

He spun back around to face Gunner. "What did she say to you?"

Gunner was shaking his head. "Out the window. Who would have—"

"What did she say?" Logan demanded again. Juliana stood behind Gunner in the doorway. Her gaze was watchful. Wary.

"We talked about McLintock. I told her what happened—"

"She got scared," Juliana broke in. "She must have run because she was afraid she'd be targeted, too."

Maybe.

But he doubted it. There were plenty of reasons for people to run.

He yanked out his phone and had Syd on the line in an instant. "Susan Walker is gone," he said. "We need to start searching the area for her, now." The bright sunlight hit him when he stepped outside and began to sweep the lot.

"Her car's gone," Gunner said from beside him. The man's voice was tight with anger.

The vehicle sure as hell was gone. Gunner had driven Susan's vehicle to the press conference, but it looked like the lady had reclaimed her ride. "Get the cops to put out an APB on her," Logan said. He wanted to talk to Susan, *yesterday*.

He glanced to the left and saw Juliana staring at him with her brows up. "It's for her protection," he said, the words half-true.

Half lie.

Susan was a dangerous woman—she knew the truth

about him, and he was willing to bet she knew plenty of secrets about the senator.

If Guerrero got ahold of her, the man would make her spill those secrets, just like he'd done with McLintock.

SUSAN NEVER EVEN saw the man approaching. She was fumbling with her keys, trying to rush back inside her old apartment—*good thing I kept the lease*—when hard arms wrapped around her.

"Someone wants to see you." She felt the blade bite into her waist.

A whimper rose in her throat. No, this couldn't be happening. She had planned too well.

But then the guy yanked her away from the apartment. There were no neighbors to see her.

He shoved her into the trunk of a black car. She tried to scream for help, but there was no help. The car sped away quickly, knocking her around in the trunk, sending her rolling back and forth.

Susan shoved and kicked at the trunk. Her breath rasped out. It was so dark. Only one faint beam of light trickled into the trunk. Without that light, it would be as if she was in a tomb.

Buried alive.

Susan screamed as loud as she could. The car kept going.

*"Help me! Help me! Somebody, please!"* She'd hated the dark for years. Ever since her mother had gone away.

Susan had been six. Her mother had just…put her in the closet. "Be a good girl. Mommy has to leave for a while. And you…you have to be quiet until I get back."

She'd put her in the closet, then never come back. Just…*put me in the closet.*

"Help!"

Her mother had been an addict. A whore. Social services had finally come to find Susan…because her mother had overdosed. They'd taken her out of that closet.

*"Get me out!"* Susan screamed as she kicked toward the back of the car.

She'd promised herself never to go back into the dark again. She'd fought for a better life. Clawed her way to that promise of wealth and privilege.

She couldn't go out like this. Not in a trunk. Not cut up with a knife, like McLintock.

She should have more.

The car stopped. She rolled, banging her knees, still screaming for help.

Then she heard the voices. Footsteps coming toward her.

The trunk opened. Light spilled onto her. Susan stopped screaming.

And she started plotting.

*I'm not dead yet.* Her heart thundered in her ears.

*Survive.* That was all she had to do. Stay alive. Escape.

She just had to play the game right.…

# *Chapter Nine*

Juliana didn't know why she went into her father's room. Despite what Susan had said, Juliana didn't expect any big revelations. She and her father—they hadn't been close.

Not in years.

She stood in the doorway, feeling like an intruder as her gaze swept over the heavy furniture. The room was cold but opulent. Her father had always insisted on the best for himself.

He just hadn't cared about giving that best to others.

Such a waste. Because when she tried hard enough, Juliana could almost remember a different man. One who'd smiled and held her hand as they walked past blooming azalea bushes.

She turned away, but from the corner of her eye, she saw...

*My paintings.*

Goose bumps rose on her arms, and she found herself fully entering his room. Crossing to the right wall, she stared at those images.

*Storm Surge.* The painting she'd done after the horror of the last storm had finally ended. On the canvas, the fury of the storm swept over the beach, bearing down like an angry god.

*Eye of the Storm.* The clouds were parted, showing a

flicker of light, hope. The fake hope that came, because the storm wasn't really over. Often, the worst part was just coming.

Her hand lifted and she traced the outline of her initials on the bottom left of the canvas. Her father…he'd told her that her art was a waste of time. He'd wanted her in law school, business school.

But he'd bought her art, framed it and hung it on his wall.

So he'd see it each day when he woke?

And right before he went to sleep each night?

"Who were you?" she whispered to the ghost that she could all but feel around her in that room. "And why the hell did you have to leave me?" There had been other ways. He shouldn't have—

A woman was crying. Juliana's head whipped to the left when she heard the sobs, echoing up from downstairs.

She rushed from the room, leaving the pictures and memories behind. Her feet thudded down the stairs. She ran faster, faster…

Susan stood in the foyer, her face splotched with color, and streaks of blood were on her arms and chest.

Gunner waited behind her. His face was locked in tense lines of anger.

"What the hell is going on?" Logan demanded as he rushed in from the study.

"Some of the guards near the gate found her…." Gunner picked Susan up and carried her to the couch. "She was walking on the road outside of the house."

Susan was still crying. Her eyes—they didn't seem to be focusing on anyone or anything.

"We need an ambulance!" Juliana said, grabbing for the nearest phone. There was so much blood… She could see the slashes on Susan's arms.

Juliana glanced up and met Logan's hard stare.

"The bastard just dumped her in the middle of the road, like garbage," Gunner growled, but though fury thickened his voice, the hands that ran over Susan's body were gentle.

Juliana started to rattle off her address to the emergency dispatcher.

"No!" Susan jerked away from Gunner and her gaze locked on Juliana. "Don't let them take me! I don't want to go! I want—I want to be home!" Tears streaked down her cheeks. "Let me st-stay, *please*."

Gunner grabbed her hands and began to inspect the slices on her body.

Juliana hesitated with the phone near her ear. The operator was asking about her emergency.

"Does she need stitches?" Logan leaned in close.

Gunner's tanned fingers slid over Susan's pale flesh. He caught her chin in his hand, forcing her to look at him. "Are there any other wounds?"

She just stared at him, eyes wide.

"Susan, tell me...*are there any other wounds?*" When she still didn't answer, his hands moved to the buttons on her shirt.

She jerked, trembled. "No! No, there aren't any more..." Her gaze darted back to Juliana. "I want to be home." She sounded like a lost child. "Please, I told them that I just wanted to go home."

Logan gave a small nod. Juliana's fingers tightened on the phone. "Never mind. It's my mistake. We don't need any assistance." She put the phone away and hovered near the couch. She could see bruises already forming near Susan's wrists. And those cuts... Someone had definitely used a knife on her.

Susan's breath choked out. "Thank you."

"Don't thank us." Gunner's voice still shook with fury. "We're gonna have to take you in."

Her face crumpled. "Why?" Desperate.

"Because there's evidence on you," Logan told her, his own face grim. "The techs can check you. Whoever attacked you—there'll be evidence left behind."

Susan's laugh was brittle and stained with tears. "We both know who attacked me. Guerrero—or rather, his men." Her lip quivered but she pulled in a deep breath. "He took me from my apartment, threw me in a trunk."

"He? You *saw* Guerrero?" Juliana asked, stunned. If Susan had seen Guerrero and gotten away...

Susan gave a slow shake of her head. "I never saw anyone. The man—at my apartment—came at me from behind. Took me someplace, but when he opened the trunk, he had on a ski mask." Her gaze found Gunner's again. She kept turning back to him. "I can't tell you anything about him. I don't have any evidence or DNA on me. I didn't touch him, didn't claw him, didn't fight." She swiped her hand over her cheek. "I was too scared."

"How did you get away?" Juliana asked. She hated seeing Susan like this. She'd wanted to protect her, but...

It seemed she couldn't save anyone.

"I didn't know anything." Another swipe of Susan's hand across her face. "I *didn't!* I kept telling him that, over and over..."

Juliana fired a fast glance over at the grandfather clock. It had been five hours since the press conference.

Five hours of torture for Susan.

"It felt like I was there forever," Susan whispered. "Then...then he said I could go if I delivered a message."

Logan's gaze locked on Susan. "What message?"

"Guerrero...said to tell you...there is *no* evidence.

There's no escape." She looked at Juliana. "And you're going to die." A sob burst from her. "I'm so sorry!"

Susan was apologizing to her?

"He's coming…he'll kill you, and he said he'd kill your lover." A fast glance toward Logan. "He knows what Logan did. I told him, I had to tell him! He was cutting me and I wanted him to stop. I didn't have any information on Aaron, and it was the only thing I could say—"

Juliana shook her head, lost. "What did Logan do?"

Silence. Then the grandfather clock began to chime.

Susan's jaw dropped. "I don't…" She fired a wild glance at Logan. Then Gunner. Then Juliana.

Juliana gripped the back of the leather sofa. "What did Logan do?" Something was off. Wrong. She could see the fear in Susan's eyes, and Logan…

Why had the lines near his mouth deepened? Even as his gaze had hardened.

"We should talk," Logan told her softly.

Susan was still crying. "He knows…" she whispered. "I told him what Aaron…how he kept you away from her…"

Her father had kept Logan away? Since when? Logan had *walked* away. Hadn't he?

"The man who took me, he said—" Susan was talking so quickly that all her words rolled together "—he would kill Juliana…make you watch…"

Logan's gaze seemed to burn Juliana. "No, he's not." He jerked his head toward Gunner. "Take Susan upstairs, then call Syd. I want techs out here to check her out."

But Susan tried to push against Gunner. "No, I don't want anyone else to see what he did! No!"

Gunner lifted her into his arms once more. "Shh. I've got you."

She'd never expected him to be so gentle. So…easy.

Susan's cries quieted as she stared up at him with hope in her eyes. "He won't come back?"

"No."

Juliana didn't speak while they climbed the stairs. Her palms were slick on the leather sofa. Logan's face had never looked so hard, so dark before.

*He knows what Logan did.*

She pushed away from the couch and marched to him. "What's going on?"

"The sins of the past…Guerrero thinks he can use them against me." His smile was twisted. "And he can." His hands came up to rest on her shoulders. "When I tell you… you can't leave. You're going to want to leave. To get as far from me as you can. That's what Guerrero will want."

He was scaring her. What could he possibly have to say that would be so bad?

"I can't let you leave me. Guerrero will be out there, just waiting for the chance to get you. He's trying to drive us apart, and I won't let him."

*"Tell me."*

He braced himself as if—what? He were about to absorb a blow? Did he actually think she'd take a swing at him? If she hadn't done it before, it wasn't as if she was going to start now.

"It wasn't just chance that led me to that diner all those years ago." His voice was flat, so emotionless. "I was there because I'd been looking for you. I wanted to talk to you. I *needed* to."

She remembered the first time she'd met Logan. She'd been at Dave's Diner, a dive that high-school kids would flock to right after the bell. She'd been home from college on summer break, hanging out with some girlfriends. Juliana had been leaving the diner and she'd run into him, literally. His hands had wrapped around her arms to steady her, and she'd looked up into his eyes.

She'd always been a sucker for his sexy eyes.

Juliana held her body still. Inside, a voice was yelling, telling her that she didn't want to hear this. Susan had been too upset. This wasn't good. But she ignored that voice. Hiding from the truth never did any good. "Why?"

"I came to find you...because I wanted to apologize."

That just made her feel even more lost. "You didn't know me. There was nothing you'd need to apologize for."

His gaze darted over her shoulder. To the picture that still hung over the mantle. The picture of her mother. "I didn't know you, but I knew her."

Her breath stalled in her lungs.

"I told you about my father."

He had. Ex-military, dishonorably discharged. A man with a taste for violence who'd fallen into a bottle and never crawled out. Logan had told her so many times, *I won't ever be like him.* As if saying the words enough would make them true.

"The military was his life, and when they kicked him out, he lost everything."

She waited, biting back all the questions that wanted to burst free. Her mother? She wouldn't look at that picture, couldn't.

"I tried to help him. Tried to stop him, but he didn't want to be stopped. He was on a crash course with hell, and he didn't care who he took with him to burn."

She *wouldn't* look at her mother's picture.

"I tried to stop him," Logan said again, voice echoing with the memory, "I tried..."

THE BEDROOM DOOR shut softly behind them. Susan could feel Gunner at her back; his gaze was like a touch as it swept over her.

He saw too much. She didn't like the way he looked at her. As if he could see right through her.

She swiped her hands over her cheeks once more. No matter how hard she wiped, Susan could still feel the tears. "I need to shower. I have to wash away the blood."

But he shook his head. "You'll just wash evidence away. We told you—"

"I'm not a crime scene!" The words burst from her. "I'm a person! I don't want to be poked and prodded by your team. I just want to forget it all."

His dark gaze drifted over her bloody shirt. "Is that really going to happen?"

*No.*

She glanced around the room, her gaze sweeping wildly over every piece of furniture. Every picture on the wall. *Every. Picture.* Her heart kicked into her chest.

"I know what it feels like," he told her, and the gravelly words pulled her gaze back to him.

"I was taken hostage by a group in South America." He lifted his shirt and she gasped when she saw the scars that crossed his chest. Not light slices like the ones she'd carry on her flesh. Deep, twisting wounds. Ugly. Terrifying. "They took their time with me," he said. "Five days... five long days of just wishing that pain would stop."

She'd had five hours. Susan never, ever wanted to imagine having to go through days of that torment. It wouldn't happen. She wouldn't let it happen.

Her gaze swung back to the wall. Juliana's canvases. Those storms. Surging.

A storm was at the door. A hurricane that was going to sweep them all away.

Not her. She wouldn't let it hurt her.

"What did you do?" she asked, taking a small step toward him, unable to help herself. "What did you do to get away?"

That stare was like black ice. "I killed them. Every single one of them."

Susan shivered. She hadn't been strong enough to kill the man who came after her. He'd been too big. That knife…

"I just cried," she said, voice miserable. "I cried, and I told him everything he wanted to know." Because she'd just wanted the pain to end.

She'd always thought she was so tough, but in the end, she'd broken too easily.

"You'll get past this," Gunner promised her as he lowered his shirt, hiding all of those terrible, twisting scars. "I did."

But she wouldn't.

"I WAS ALWAYS dragging my father out of bars. Or finding him in alleys passed out. But even when he was sober—days that were far too few—my father…had a darkness in him."

It seemed as if every word came slowly. The grandfather clock's pendulum ticked off the time behind him, with swinging clicks that seemed too loud.

"My father was a good killer. An assassin who could always take out his targets." Logan's breath expelled in a rush. "He told me, again and again, that I was like him. Born to kill."

And Logan had told her—again and again—*I won't be like him.*

"Why—why was he discharged?" Juliana asked.

"Because on his last mission, he had what some doctors called a psychotic break. He had to be taken down by his own team. He wasn't following orders. He was just *hunting*."

And that broken man had come home to Logan? "Where was your mother?"

"She left him."

*And you?* She forced the words out. "And what about *my* mother?"

He lifted his hand as if he'd reach for her, but his fingers clenched into a fist before he touched her. "That night, I found him at another bar. He jumped in his truck and wouldn't give me the keys." He lifted that clenched hand to his jaw and rubbed his skin as if remembering. "He punched me. Hit me over and over then got in that beat-up truck. I couldn't…I couldn't just let him leave like that. I climbed in. I thought I could get him to stop."

She didn't hear the grandfather clock any longer. She just heard the drumming sound of her heartbeat filling her ears.

"He was going too fast, weaving all over the road. I was trying to get him to stop…." A muscle flexed along the hard length of his jaw. "I saw the other car coming. I yelled for him to stop, but it was too late."

*Too late.*

"I guess I got knocked out for a few minutes, and when I opened my eyes again, he was dead."

She blinked away the tears that she wouldn't let fall. "And my mother?"

His gaze held hers. "She was…still alive then."

Her knees wanted to buckle. Juliana forced herself to stand straighter.

"I rushed to her. I tried to help." He drew in a rough breath. "She said your name."

Her heart was splintering.

"It was…the last thing she said."

She stumbled back. But he was there, rushing toward her, grabbing her arms, holding tight and pulling her close.

She didn't want to be close then. She didn't want to be anything.

"She loved you," he said, voice and eyes intense. "You were the last thought she had. I came to find you… I was in that diner because you should have known how much she loved you. I wanted to tell you, I *needed* to. But then you looked up at me." He broke off, shaking his head. "You looked at me like I was something—*somebody*—great, and no one had ever looked at me like that before."

She couldn't breathe. Her chest hurt too much.

"You loved me," he said. His eyes blazed. "With you, then, everything was so easy. I knew if I told you that I was there that night, that my father was the one driving when your mother died…you'd hate me."

Her whole body just felt numb. "I read…the reports. Talked to the cops. The man driving the car, his name was Michael Smith." She'd dug through the evidence when the memories and pain got to be too much for her.

Her father had never talked about the crash. She'd been seventeen when she went searching for the truth herself.

"After he died, I took my stepfather's name." His fingers were still tight around her. "My mom had remarried another man. Greg Quinn. Greg…was good. He tried to help us."

Her heartbeat wouldn't slow down. "The reports… The police said a minor was in the car." They'd told her…the teenager had been the one to call for help. When they'd arrived on scene, he'd been fighting to free her mother.

*Logan?*

He would have been what then, fourteen?

"I went by Paul back then," he said. "Logan's my middle name."

All these years…he'd kept this secret?

"I was arguing with him," Logan told her, his voice slipping back into that emotionless tone that she hated. "He wasn't paying attention. I was arguing, he was drunk…"

"And my mother died."

A slow nod. He released her and stepped back. "If I'd been stronger, I never would have let him in that truck. If I hadn't been yelling at him, maybe he would have seen her car coming.… *I could have saved her, but I didn't.*"

Her face felt too hot. Her hands too cold. "My father knew."

"Yes."

Another secret. More lies.

Juliana held his gaze. "You asked me to run away with you. You said you wanted us to start a life together." Kids. A house. "And all that time…"

"I wanted to be with you more than I ever wanted anything else in my life." Now emotion cracked through his words. "Your father investigated me, found out who I was. The son of a killer."

He was more than that.

"He was going to tell you. He told me to leave, or he'd—"

"And that made you just walk away? His threat?" She wasn't buying that line. Time to try another one.

But he gave a hard shake of his head. "No, I left because he was right. You deserved more than me. My father was right, too, you know… In a lot of ways, I am just like him." He lifted his hands, stared at his fingers. "I was made to kill."

"Maybe you were made to protect." She was tired of

this bull. "You don't have to be like him. Be your own person! You didn't have to leave me alone—"

"You looked at me like I was a hero. I never wanted you to look at me…the way you are right now."

She stepped back. "You should have told me from the beginning." Everything could have been different between them. No secrets. No lies. "You just left me!"

Juliana took another fast step away from him.

"I came back."

Her eyes narrowed.

"Six months," he said, jerking a rough hand through his hair. "I'd joined the navy. Tried to forget you. *I couldn't*."

"You didn't come back for me." The lies were too much. Why couldn't he ever tell her the truth?

"You weren't alone."

Juliana blinked.

"You called him Thomas. He was blond, rich, driving a Porsche and holding you too close."

"How do you know about him?" Thomas had been her friend; then after Logan left, he'd been more. She'd just wanted to forget for a while. To feel wanted, loved by someone else.

"You were sleeping with him."

There was anger, jealousy—rage—vibrating in his voice now. She almost wished for that emotionless mask.

"I couldn't breathe without thinking of you, but you'd moved on. Gotten someone better."

She and Thomas had broken up after a few months. He'd been a good guy, solid, dependable, but he hadn't been…

*Logan.*

"You had what you needed. I had no right to come back in and screw up your life."

He'd come back.

"So I stayed away." His hand rose to his chest. Pressed over the scar that was a reminder of the battles he'd faced. "I did my job."

SUSAN STARED UP into Gunner's face. Not a handsome face. Too hard. Too rough. This wasn't an easy man before her.

She let her head fall forward, so weary she could hardly stand it. "I never wanted things to be like this."

His hands came up to her shoulders. "You're safe."

She wasn't. "I grew up with nothing." Nothing but the looks of pity others gave her. "I swore that one day I'd have everything." But Aaron was dead. His daughter was still alive. The will gave Susan *nothing*.

*Just what I've always had.*

Unless Juliana died, Susan would just get scraps.

Now she had Guerrero out there, waiting in the shadows.

Her shoulders hunched as she leaned toward him. "This isn't the way I wanted my story to end."

"It's not over," he told her as his hands tightened around her shoulders. "You think I didn't want to give in when they had me in that pit? Giving up is easy. Fighting to live is the hard part."

Yes, it was, but... "I'm a fighter." Always had been.

"Good, you should—" His words broke off, ending in a choked gurgle.

Susan didn't look up at his face. Her eyes were on her hands—on the knife she'd just shoved into his stomach.

*You should have searched me.* Guerrero had been right. An injured woman could get past nearly any guard. Some men just had blind spots. *I slipped right past yours, Gunner.*

She twisted the knife. "I'm not going back to nothing."

Another choked growl.

Susan looked up into his eyes. His hands had fallen from her. "Sorry, but this time, you need to give up. There's no point in fighting."

Because he wasn't going to keep living.

He slumped over and hit the floor with a thud.

A FAINT THUD REACHED Juliana's ears. She frowned and glanced back up the stairs.

"We can't change the past. If I could, hell, yes, I would," Logan said, "but we—"

Glass shattered. Logan jerked—and red bloomed on his shoulder.

Then he was leaping toward her. He threw his body against Juliana's, and they fell to the floor, slamming down behind the couch.

She heard shouts. Screams. More gunshots.

It sounded as if an army was attacking.

With Guerrero, that might be exactly what was happening. They had guards outside, local cops who'd been assigned to protect the house and her. Surveillance was watching, and backup would come, but...

More gunfire.

She grabbed Logan's arm. Felt the wet warmth of his blood. "Logan?"

He raised his head. Stared at her with an unreadable gaze.

"Guess he took the bait," he said.

The words were cold.

"Stay here, and keep your head down."

What? He was leaving?

She held him tighter. Logan winced, and her hand dropped. "You can't go out there!"

"I'm a SEAL. That's exactly where I need to go."

*Into the fight.*

"You won't be afraid anymore. We'll get his men. I'll make sure one stays alive, and we *will* track Guerrero." Then he kissed her. A hard, fast press of his lips. "Stay down."

And he was gone. Rushing away and his blood was on her hands.

Juliana crouched behind the thick couch, breath heaving in her chest. Then she heard the scream. Wild, desperate and coming from upstairs.

*Susan.*

The guards outside were already under attack. Susan couldn't get caught in the crossfire. The woman had suffered enough.

*Because of my father. Because she was close to us.*

Juliana knew she had to help her. Keeping low, she rushed across the room and used the furniture for cover as best she could.

Her hand was on the banister when another round of gunfire erupted in the room.

# Chapter Ten

They were outgunned.

Logan grabbed the injured cop who'd been slumped near the porch and pulled the guy back, giving him cover. He let out two fast shots as he fired back at the attackers, who just weren't stopping.

A quick sweep counted ten men. Twelve.

The cops at the front door were both down. Gunner was in the house. *He'll be out soon.* Gunner never could stay away from a gunfight.

Jasper was firing, attacking from the distant right side, back near the heavy gate—a gate that was currently busted open.

*Blasted your way in.*

Syd would be coming. The woman was always their eyes and ears. She'd be watching the video surveillance, sending backup and joining the fight herself.

The woman could be lethal.

Logan grabbed the cop's hand and shoved it against the guy's wound. "Keep pressure on it." The uniform was as pale as death, shaking, but he'd be okay. Provided he didn't take another bullet.

Logan ignored his own injury, barely feeling the pain. He didn't have time for it then. These men—they weren't getting into the house. They wouldn't get to Juliana.

He eased away from the cop and began to stalk his prey. He'd been trained for up-close-and-personal kills. He could get close and the prey wouldn't know it. Not until it was too late.

Jasper kept firing and distracting the attackers so that Logan would have time to sneak up on them.

*Leave some alive.* He wanted to take them down but would kill only if necessary. These men had to be brought in alive—*we'll make you turn.*

No one would be pulling knives and taking the easy way out of this mess.

Logan wasn't going to allow for easy.

He snuck up on one of the gunmen, grabbed his hand and broke the wrist. The man's weapon flew to the ground but he tried to kick out at Logan.

Logan punched him in the throat. The man never even had time to scream. In seconds, he was on the ground, and he wasn't going to be getting up anytime soon.

*One down.*

CHIPS OF WOOD FLEW from the banister as Juliana rushed up the stairs. That last bullet had come too close for any kind of comfort.

She jumped off the stairs and hurried down the hallway. Just a few more feet…

Juliana shoved open her father's bedroom door. "Susan!"

Susan spun toward her, a knife in her hands.

Juliana shook her head, stunned. "What—"

Her paintings were behind Susan. They'd been slashed.

"Run…"

A whisper. So faint she almost didn't hear it, but Juliana's gaze jerked toward that hoarse sound.

Gunner. On the floor. Covered in blood.

But then Susan leaped toward her and grabbed her hand. "You're not running anywhere." That knife flashed toward Juliana.

*When you attack, use the strongest part of your body.*

Juliana grabbed for the knife with her right hand even as she slammed her left elbow into Susan's stomach. Susan stumbled back and grunted in pain.

The knife skittered across the floor.

"What the hell are you doing?" Juliana screamed because she didn't want to believe what she was seeing. Susan couldn't be in on this mess.

But then Susan yelled and launched herself at Juliana. The two women hit the floor, rolling in a tangle of limbs. Susan was the same size as Juliana, and the woman was fighting with a wild, furious desperation.

But she wasn't the only one desperate to win this battle. Juliana felt more than a little desperate, too.

"Should have…died at the…cemetery…" Susan snarled as she slammed Juliana's head into the floor. "Should have…"

Juliana shoved her fingers toward the other woman's eyes. Susan shrieked and leaped back.

"*You* set the car bomb?" Juliana lurched to her feet as she tried to prepare for another attack.

Only, Susan wasn't advancing on her. Instead, she'd run toward her father's open safe. As far as Juliana knew, the only thing her father had ever kept in that bedside safe was a gun.

Juliana dived for the knife. It was close. She could get it and attack—

"Don't move." Too late. Susan had the gun. She had it aimed at Juliana. And the woman was…smiling.

Gunfire echoed from outside and Juliana tensed, but Susan just kept staring at her. "I went to so much trouble…

had everything timed perfectly. But you wouldn't get in the car."

Juliana licked her lips. Susan's back was to the large picture window in her father's room. Gunner was to the right, lying in a growing pool of blood. The knife was a light weight in Juliana's hand, but what good would it do against a gun?

*Not much.*

"Why?" Juliana asked with a shake of her head. "Why are you doing this?"

More gunfire erupted from below. A man's pain-filled cry was abruptly cut off.

"Is Guerrero forcing you to help him?" Juliana pressed. She lowered the knife to her side, wanting Susan's attention to shift away from the weapon.

But Susan just laughed. "The bomb was *me.* You think you know me? You don't know anything about me or where I come from. Aaron didn't know, either. He thought I was just another one of the brainless whores who'd be happy jumping at his beck and call."

From the corner of her eye, Juliana thought she saw Gunner shift just a bit.

"I've seen things…done things…" Now Susan's laugh held a desperate edge, but the gun in her hand never wavered. "I'm not going back to nothing because of you!"

"Susan, I haven't done anything—"

"*It all goes to you!* The money. The house. Everything. He promised, but I saw the will—*it's all yours.*"

Was this what it was about? Money? "Charles died in that bomb blast."

"Am I supposed to care?" Susan lifted the gun. "I have to look out for myself. If I don't…who will?"

There was no more gunfire from below. Was that good?

Or bad? *Logan, be safe.* "I don't care about the money. Take it."

"I will." Susan's smile was grim. "When you're dead. When everyone thinks that Guerrero took you out, I'll take the money." Now Susan did glance back over her shoulder toward that big window.

Susan had led Guerrero's men to the house. The woman might have even given them security codes to get past the gate and inside the house. She had access to everything there, so getting those codes would have been easy for her.

"Guerrero wanted the evidence…." Susan's gaze flickered back to the slashed paintings and hardened. "I thought I could give it to him."

Juliana was guessing she'd thought wrong.

"Doesn't matter," Susan muttered. "He can still take you. Take you, kill you, and this mess will be over!"

Juliana inched forward. Slowly. Carefully. "You think he's going to just let you walk away? That's not how he works. No one walks away from him and survives."

Susan's smile twisted her lips. "That's okay. Susan Walker was never meant to live forever."

The woman was insane. How had she hidden this craziness for so long?

"Susan never existed, but Becky Sue Morris…Becky Sue existed—and she'll keep existing. Becky Sue is going to wire the money to her accounts. She's going to take all the jewelry. Take everything she can." She swiped her tongue over her bottom lip and glanced back at the window. "Becky Sue…knows how to survive. How to wire a bomb. How to put a price on someone's head so they get taken out." Her breath heaved. "She learned early how to do all of those things."

And she learned how to blend in and become someone else. Juliana stared at the gun and realized she didn't have a choice. Susan or Becky Sue or whoever the hell the woman really was—she wasn't going to let her escape.

Death wasn't an option. Juliana wasn't ready to die. She had too much to live for.

She took another step forward. Susan didn't even seem to notice that only a few precious feet separated them now.

*Can I move fast enough?*

She'd have to because there wasn't another option.

But first, Juliana knew she had to distract the other woman. "He's going to torture you before he kills you. Just like he did with Ben."

Susan was sweating. "Shut up."

"That's what he does. Sure, he'll kill me. That's a given, but he'll kill you, too. You won't get the money or the house or anything because you'll be rotting in the ground with me."

Another step.

Susan's eyes were wild. "Shut...*up!*"

"Why? I'm already dead, right? What more are you going to do to me?"

"I'll kill your Logan."

*No, you won't.*

"Some men just don't see the attack coming. They think we're weak, helpless...all because of some tears and a little blood."

A little blood? Susan's shirt had been soaked with her blood.

"Their mistake," Susan whispered.

"You're not going to hurt Logan." Juliana's fingers had clenched around the knife so hard that her hand ached.

Susan's head jerked. "You still care about him." Now she sounded shocked. "You know what he did. I mean, I had to spell it out for you! The guy killed your mother, used you—then walked away."

Another step, close enough to strike.

"And you still love him."

*Rat-a-tat.* The sudden burst of automatic gunfire had Susan's head whipping toward the window.

"Yes," Juliana growled. "I still do." Then she lifted her knife and lunged for Susan. Susan sensed the attack a few seconds too late. She screamed as her head swung back toward Juliana.

The knife shoved into Susan's left shoulder, and Juliana twisted her body, bending low for another attack.

Susan's fingers tightened around the gun and—

Gunfire erupted. Not down below, not outside. But from *in* the room. Gunner had crawled forward, and Juliana saw that he'd reached into his ankle holster and pulled out his backup weapon.

"Don't think—" his voice was a rough rasp "—you're… helpless…"

Susan staggered back. A balloon of red appeared on her chest. Her eyes were wide, her mouth hanging open in shock. She took another step back, another, her feet stumbling.

Then her eyes closed. Her head fell backward—her whole body fell—and she tumbled straight through that glass window.

LOGAN WHIRLED AT THE sound of shattering glass, and when he saw a woman's delicate form plummeting from the window, his heart stopped.

He lurched forward, all of his instincts forgotten. It was too dark. All he could see was the tangle of hair on the ground. A broken body. Blood.

*No!*

A knife shoved into his back.

"Don't worry," a voice whispered in his ear, "I'll make sure the pretty lady joins you in hell."

*Not Juliana.*

Through the moonlight, he could just see the woman's face. Not Juliana. Susan.

He spun around and grabbed the man behind him by the throat. "You're not…touching her."

This time, the man drove a knife into Logan's chest.

Logan attacked. He shattered the man's wrist, pounded with his fists, went for the man's throat. His prey was near death when…

Another man appeared and drove a needle into Logan's neck. Logan roared and tossed him back. The second attacker fell, his body crumpling into a heap.

But it was too late.

Logan's body began to shake. His vision blurred. He tried to swing out at the man charging him, but Logan's body slumped to the ground. He wanted to shout a warning, to Jasper, to Gunner, to *Juliana,* but he couldn't speak.

Shadows closed in on him, faces he couldn't see. Then a blade pressed over his throat.

"YOU'RE GOING TO BE all right," Juliana said as she pressed towels against Gunner's wounds. "I'm getting you help, okay?" She'd tried to call an ambulance, but the telephone upstairs had been dead. With the firefight going on out there…where was the backup?

More cops had to be coming. Cops and EMTs. They'd fix Gunner. They had to.

He caught her hand. His fingers were bloody, and they slipped over her skin. "Hide."

She shook her head. "I'm not leaving you."

"No more…gunfire."

He was right. But there'd been a lull in the gunfire before. She wasn't about to think it was safe just to have bullets start blasting again.

"Stay…down."

Now he sounded just like Logan. She tried to smile for him. Hard, when she was sure the man was bleeding out right in front of her eyes.

"I'm going to my room and getting my cell phone." She'd call for help. She wasn't letting him die while she did nothing. So those attacking might have cut the lines that connected the house phones, but they wouldn't be able to stop her from using her cell. "Everything's going to be okay." Juliana hoped she sounded more reassuring than she felt.

Gunner's dark, tired gaze called the words a lie, but he didn't speak. Maybe he couldn't speak any longer.

Juliana lurched to her feet. She took a staggering step forward and—saw a faint glint from the corner of her eye.

She spun back around, her gaze flying to the painting. Susan had slashed it over and over, and there, hanging out from the bottom of the canvas, Juliana could just see the faint edge of…

A flash drive.

*He said he gave you the evidence.*

She grabbed the drive with her bloodstained fingers. People were dying outside because of this tiny thing. She shoved the drive into her pocket and rushed for the door.

*Get. Help.*

She was almost to her room when she heard the creak of the stairs. Juliana tensed. It could be Logan, but if it were him, then wouldn't he have called out to her?

Her fingers reached for the doorknob. Then she heard another creak. Another. The soft pad of footsteps heading toward her father's room.

*Gunner.*

Juliana spun around. She had taken Gunner's gun, and the weapon felt slippery in her palms. "Stay away from him!" She rushed forward.

And nearly ran into the man who haunted her nightmares.

Juliana skidded to a halt. She'd expected to face his flunkies. The hired killers. Not...

John.

He smiled at her. The same tired, slightly crooked smile he'd given her when they were trapped in that hell. "Hello, Juliana."

Ice chilled her. Logan would never have let the arms dealer get inside the house. The only way this man could have gotten past him...

*No, Logan's not dead.*

John's stare—no, *Guerrero's stare*—dropped to the gun. "Give that to me."

No way. "I'll give you a bullet to the heart!"

His smile stretched. "I don't think so."

"You need to think again." She wasn't backing down. This man had destroyed her world. She wasn't about to just stand there and be a lamb for his slaughter. She had the gun. She had the perfect chance to shoot.

Then Guerrero lifted his hand, and within his grip, a bloody knife blade glinted. "This is your lover's blood."

*No.* "Is he dead?" Her heart already felt as if it was freezing.

"My men will make sure that he is if you don't come with me now." Guerrero dropped the knife on the floor and opened his hand to her. "I'll let him keep breathing, but you give me the gun and we leave."

"He's already dead." The man thought she was a fool. "And so are you." *Logan*. The scream was in her head, desperate to break out, but she saw herself calmly aiming the gun right at his chest. One shot would be all that it took. Of course, she couldn't aim with her trembling fingers, so maybe she'd just empty the gun into his chest.

That would work.

His smile vanished. "*You're* killing him. Every moment you waste, every second. My men are so eager to pull the trigger…"

Only, there wasn't any thunder from gunfire outside. Just silence.

"Jasper…he's there." Jasper would still be fighting. And there were other guards. Other cops.

"The one at the gatehouse? The sniper? It took some doing, but we took him out, too." His hands were up in front of him. "There's no one out there to help. Backup might be coming, but they'll get here too late." No Spanish accent coated his words. "By the time they arrive, Logan will be dead."

"*He's already dead.*" And Guerrero was just jerking her around.

"Come with me," he said, his voice low, emotionless. "I'll prove that he's alive."

She wanted to believe him.

"Or stay here," Guerrero said as his dark eyes glittered, "and you will be responsible for killing him."

"Move," Juliana ordered. "Head down those stairs and keep your hands up!"

He laughed, but he moved, taking slow, measured steps

as he headed down the stairs. She expected him to try for the gun, to attack her, but he didn't.

He didn't even glance back at her as he walked.

The front door hung open. He was just about to head out that door now.

*"Wait!"* She hated to get close to him, but there wasn't a choice. Juliana rushed forward and shoved the gun into his side. She didn't know what might be waiting out there, and she wanted a shield.

He grunted when the barrel of the gun dug into his body. "So different...than the girl in Mexico."

"Maybe you didn't know that girl so well."

His eyes flashed at her.

"Anyone comes at me, I'll kill you." Just so they were clear.

His head inclined toward her. "I think you mean it."

"I do."

"Pity..." Then he started walking, nice and slow. "Don't you wonder why more cops aren't here? Why it was just your lover and the skeleton staff of guards?"

Yes, she did. Where the hell was the backup?

When she went outside, all she saw was carnage. Bodies on the ground. Men moaning, twisting. Shattered glass. Susan—

Juliana jerked her gaze away.

"Money can buy anything in America. A slow response time from cops. The right intel from a disgruntled detective who feels like everyone is going over his head on yet another case."

Two men had risen from the ground. They were bloody, bruised, but coming right toward them.

"Tell them not to come any closer," Juliana whispered.

"Don't come any closer," he called out easily enough.

"Such a shame that things had to be this way between us. You know, I became quite fond of you in Mexico."

The man was the best liar she'd ever met. "Where's Logan?"

She didn't see him. Hope had her heart racing too fast in her chest. Guerrero was a liar, but maybe, maybe Logan wasn't dead.

*Don't be dead.*

Guerrero pointed to a black van that was idling on the right. "In there."

She kept her gun to his side. They walked slowly toward that van. It seemed to take them forever to reach that spot.

*Where is Jasper?* He should be out there but she sure couldn't see any sign of him.

"Open the door," Juliana ordered when they drew close to the van.

Guerrero moved forward. He grabbed the side door on the van and yanked it open. It was dark in the van, but Juliana could just see the crumpled form of…a man inside. She couldn't tell if the body was Logan's. It could have been anyone. Any—

*Gunfire.*

Blasting right near her body. No, near Guerrero. Her head whipped up. Gunner was leaning out of the broken second-story window, firing down on them.

Then Juliana was hit from behind, rammed so hard that she stumbled forward and fell into the back of the van.

More gunfire.

Coming from behind her now. Jasper? Finally?

But the van door had closed behind her. The gun had fallen and she'd slammed face-first onto the van's floor. Her forehead hit hard and pain splintered through her skull.

And she hit—someone. The man in the van. The man who wasn't moving. She shoved her hands against the van's metal floorboard even as the vehicle lurched forward. She was tossed back a bit and tires squealed. More gunfire.

The van kept going—racing away.

She lifted her hands, afraid, and touched warm skin. Her hands slid over the man's body nervously. Wide shoulders. Strong muscles. She touched his neck and felt the thready beat of his pulse.

Her finger smoothed higher. Felt his chin…and the faint scar that raised the skin there.

*Logan.*

She wrapped her arms around him and pulled him close and—felt the wetness of his blood on her. "Logan?"

"Isn't that sweet?" Guerrero's voice. Her head jerked up. In the darkness, she could make out two men in the front of the van. The driver—and the shadowy form of the man who held a gun on her.

"Told you he was alive," Guerrero said as the gun's barrel swung between her and Logan. "And if you want him to stay that way, you hold him tight, and you don't so much as *move* until I tell you to do so."

They were leaving the senator's mansion, heading down the twisting roads of the swamp. Roads that could take them to a dozen secluded locations.

"This time," Guerrero promised, "we won't be interrupted, and if you don't tell me everything I want to know, then you'll watch while I slice your lover apart."

He'd already started slicing.

"He'll be the one who screams soon, Juliana. You could hardly bear it when you heard the sound of a stranger screaming. Tell me, what will you do when those cries come from someone you love?"

*Anything.*

And Guerrero, damn him, knew it.

## Chapter Eleven

Logan opened his eyes, aware of the pain that throbbed through his body in relentless waves. It was the pain that had forced him to consciousness.

The darkness hit him first. Wherever he was, there were no windows, no fresh air. He was sitting, bound with his arms pulled behind him and tied to the wooden slats in the back of his chair.

He also wasn't alone. He heard the soft rasps of breath coming too fast. So close to him.

There was a faint beam of light on the floor to the right, just a sliver that came from beneath what Logan suspected to be a door.

He tried to shift in his chair but the pain doubled, knifing through him.

Hell, yeah, he'd been knifed all right—

"Logan?"

He stilled. That was Juliana's voice, and when he took a breath, he smelled vanilla. Beyond the blood and dust and decay in the room, he smelled her.

*No.* Gunner should have been keeping her safe. He'd made a dumb move; Logan knew it. He'd seen the body falling and fear had made him reckless for a moment, but Juliana—

"Please, Logan, talk to me. Tell me you're okay."

"I'm…" He cleared his throat because his voice was no more than a growl. "I'm okay, baby." A lie, but he would have told her anything right then. He didn't know how much blood he'd lost; Logan just knew he was too weak.

*The cops have been working for Guerrero.* He'd figured that little fact out too late. From the sounds of the battle that had echoed in his ears, he knew Jasper had reached that same conclusion.

*Too late.*

You couldn't even trust the good guys these days. But then, maybe there weren't any good guys.

"I was afraid… I thought you were dead."

"Not yet."

Her laughter was choked. Desperate. "That's what Guerrero said."

And Logan knew how the guy had gotten her out of the house. *This time, I was the bait.* "G-Gunner?"

Silence from her, the kind that told him something had gone very wrong.

*Of course something went wrong. We're both being held in this hole, and Guerrero is about to come in and start his sick games.*

Games that Logan couldn't let the man play with Juliana.

"Susan stabbed him. When we left…he was alive. He was shooting at Guerrero."

If Gunner was still breathing, then they had hope. He'd get Sydney. They'd track Juliana through the implant.

All his team needed was a little bit of time.

Logan could give them that time. He could take torture, as much as necessary. *As long as Juliana makes it out.*

He'd suffered plenty over the years. It wasn't the first time he'd been taken hostage. He'd gotten out before. He would now.

"I'm sorry." He had to tell her that. He couldn't stand to be there, to all but feel her next to him, and not say the words. When he'd last seen her eyes, she'd looked as if she hated him.

If they weren't in the darkness, would that same hate glitter in her stare?

"I didn't want to hurt you." Truth. "I didn't want—"

"Logan, we can talk about that later." Something thudded—her chair. Her leg brushed his. *So close.* He wanted to reach out and touch her, but the rough rope just dug into his wrists and arms.

"You will get out of here."

"*We're* getting out." Her voice vibrated with intensity. "I've been in this dark, you weren't talking, I was afraid— I *never* want to think that you're dead again, got it? You were so close, and I thought you had died."

His hands fisted. "I won't die." But he had to warn her. He wasn't going to lie to Juliana, not ever again. "But it's going to be bad, baby. What comes…" He swallowed and said what she had to hear. "I can take it, understand? You stay strong and just know that I'll be all right."

Guerrero and his torture games. Logan had seen the bodies left behind after Guerrero's playtime was over.

"I'm not going to let him slice into you!" Her voice was fierce. "I'll give him what he needs. I don't care."

But they didn't have anything to give him. Even if they did… "The minute you talk, we're dead." She was only alive because Guerrero couldn't stand the idea that evidence was out there floating around. Evidence that could lead a path back to him.

"He's not letting us escape," Juliana whispered, her voice so soft in the darkness.

Logan kept pulling at those ropes. She was right. Guerrero wasn't going to let them slip away.

"What happened?" Juliana asked. "What went wrong?"

They'd trusted the wrong local cops.

The silence must have stretched too long because she said, "Logan?", her voice sharp.

He exhaled slowly. "The cops were working for him. When I went out, they turned on me instead of fighting off his men." Those who'd been left alive, anyway. The cops on their side had been taken out or injured instantly. Money could talk, and Guerrero sure had a lot of dough. "Guerrero probably had a contact at the P.D., one who knew just which cops would turn for the cash." Enough cash could make even the strongest men weak. "Hell, some of 'em might not have even been cops, just plants who were sent in."

But he'd been fighting them back. He and Jasper had been holding their own against them all.

Until he'd lost his control. He'd seen the body and… "I thought it was you." He'd never forget the fear. How could he? Echoes of it still burned in his bleeding gut.

"What was me?"

"When the body fell, for an instant…" He wished he could see her through the darkness. His eyes had adjusted, and he could make out the outline of her body, but that wasn't good enough. He wanted to look into her eyes. To *see* her while he had the chance.

Time was all they needed. *Hurry up, Syd.*

His breath expelled in a rush. "I thought it was you, and I've never been so scared in my life." Not even that horrible night when his father had destroyed three lives.

The night that was between them. Always would be.

His fear, that crack in his control, had cost them both. Guerrero never would have gotten the drop on him if he'd stayed focused.

But with Juliana, focus had never been his strength.

"Logan, I need to tell you…" Juliana began, her voice soft.

He wasn't sure he could stand to hear what she had to tell him. He heard footsteps coming in the hallway, heading toward them.

"Lean toward me," he told her.

He heard the rustle of her clothes. The creak of her chair. She was bound just like he was, but when they leaned forward, they were just close enough—

*To kiss.*

Logan's mouth took hers. He kissed her with all the passion he felt. The need. The hunger. But he kept his control. He just wanted her taste on his lips. Wanted the memory to hold tight and to get him through the pain that would come.

His lips slipped from hers. "I always loved you." He hadn't meant for the confession to come out, but as soon as the words rumbled from him, Logan didn't regret them. It was the truth, one he'd hidden, one he'd carried, and in case Syd didn't get there fast enough, he wanted Juliana to know.

"What?"

"You deserved better than to be with a killer's son." No, he'd tell her everything. *No more lies.* "You deserved better than to be with a killer. That's what I am. What I've always been, inside. My father, he knew. He saw it in me. Told me I'd be just like him, and when I got in the military…" It had all been too easy for him.

He pulled in a breath. Still tasted her. "You're the one good thing that I've known in my life. I walked away from you because…hell, Julie, how could you not hate me knowing what happened? But I carried you with me every place I went. *You were there.*" She'd gotten him out of more hells than he could count.

Silence. Then "Logan…"

The footsteps were closer. Their time was up. "Just remember that, okay?" He wanted to touch her, so he kissed her again. "Remember." No matter what came.

The door creaked open. Light poured onto them. He saw Juliana's face then, pale, beautiful, but marked by dark bruises near her forehead and on the curve of her left cheek.

"You son of a bitch," he snarled and turned his head. His gaze locked on the man advancing in that bright light. A man with dark hair, dark eyes and a grin the devil could wear.

"Hello, Mr. Quinn," Diego Guerrero said, his voice calm and flat. "I was wondering how much longer you'd be out."

Because he'd been drugged. Yeah, Logan had figured that out fast enough. He remembered the slice of knives, but he also remembered the prick of a needle that had taken him down during the battle. Guerrero had wanted a live hostage. *So you could use me against Juliana.*

Guerrero was a man who knew how to plan well. Just not well enough.

Logan smiled at him. "Tonight, your empire's going down. You're about to lose everything."

Guerrero laughed at that. Two men followed him into the room. Men who already had knives in their hands.

"No, Mr. Quinn…or shall I just call you Logan? Logan, tonight, you're the one who's going to lose…" Guerrero walked over and stood behind Juliana. His hands wrapped around her throat. "You're going to sit there and watch while you lose everything that matters to you."

SHE HADN'T EXPECTED a bloodbath. Sydney Sloan raced through the senator's mansion, her gun in her hand. Jasper hadn't been outside. He should have been out there, waiting for her.

Instead, she'd just found the ground littered with bodies. Some still alive, some way past dead. Cops. Men in ski masks. Men with pain contorting their faces.

But she hadn't seen the two men that she needed most. *Gunner and Jasper.* Where the hell were they?

She'd called her boss, Bruce Mercer. Federal agents were minutes behind her. Whatever screwup had happened with the local law enforcement, it wouldn't be happening again. The agents would take care of the cops and men who still lived. She just needed—

A ragged groan came from the right. Sydney tensed as adrenaline spiked through her body. She flattened her body against the wall, sucked in a deep breath.

Then she rushed into the room with her gun ready to fire.

"Freeze!" she yelled.

But the men before her didn't freeze. Jasper was crouched over Gunner, and they were both covered in blood. Gunner wasn't moving. He barely seemed to breathe.

She grabbed for her phone. "Where's the ambulance?" Sydney demanded. This scene—it was too similar to one she'd seen before. Only, that time, she'd lost her fiancé.

She wasn't losing her best friend.

Sirens wailed outside, answering her question before the other agent on the line could.

"Get those EMTs into the house," Sydney ordered. "Second floor. First room on the right. We've got an agent down, and he's priority one."

The only priority for her then.

Sydney dropped to her knees. Jasper had his hands over Gunner's wounds, trying to keep the pressure in place. She added her hands, not caring that the blood soaked through her fingers. "What happened?"

Jasper grunted. "Susan—she was working with Guerrero. She got too close to Gunner."

Because Gunner always had a weakness for the helpless damsels. She shook her head and blinked eyes that had gone blurry. When would he learn?

"Guerrero took Logan and Juliana." Jasper's voice vibrated with his rage. "I tried to stop them, but…"

Then she realized that all of the blood wasn't Gunner's. Her eyes widened.

"I knew if I didn't stay with him he'd die." Jasper didn't even glance at his own wound. He came across as a tough SOB.

And he was.

But he also cared about his team.

"We'll get them back," she promised. There wasn't an alternative for her. She'd lost others she cared about over the years. She wasn't losing any of her team.

Shouts came from downstairs and drifted up through the broken window. Sirens yelled. The ambulances had arrived. Backup.

"Hurry!" she screamed.

Soon there was the thunder of footsteps on the stairs. The EMTs pushed her back, but…but Gunner grabbed her hand.

His eyes, weak, hazy, opened and found her. "Syd…"

She swallowed and tried to pull back. "It's all right, Gunner. You're going to be fine." He'd have to be.

He tried to smile at her, that disarming half grin that had gotten to her so many times, but his lashes fell closed and his hand slipped from her wrist.

Her heart slammed into her chest but the EMTs were working on him. They got Gunner out of that room, into the ambulance. The lights were swirling. Agents were racing around the scene.

She wanted in that ambulance, too. She wanted to be with Gunner, holding his hand.

But she stood back and watched the lights vanish.

Jasper was behind her. He had barely let anyone see his injured shoulder. He'd just growled, "Back the hell off."

That was Jasper.

She swallowed and hoped the mask she usually wore was back in place. "You ready to hunt?" she asked him. Not waiting for his answer—she already knew what it would be—Sydney yanked out her phone, punched in the code.

The GPS screen lit up instantly.

*Got you.*

Because Guerrero might have taken Logan and Juliana, but they were going after them. They would get them back.

And Guerrero would get exactly what he deserved.

GUERRERO BROUGHT HIS blade against Juliana's throat. "You have proven to be so much trouble…"

"Then maybe you should have just killed me in Mexico."

Logan blinked, surprised by the rough words that had tumbled from Juliana's lips. No, no, she didn't need to be antagonizing a killer. Logan wanted Guerrero's anger directed at him.

Not her.

The blade bit into her flesh. A rivulet of blood slid down her pale throat. The lights were on now, too bright, too stark. "Maybe I should have," Guerrero agreed.

"But then, you knew you'd never get your hands on that evidence!" Logan snarled at him. "And your house of cards would fall on you."

Guerrero looked up at him. "I'm beginning to think that evidence doesn't exist." But he lifted the blade from Juliana's throat.

Logan's heart started to beat again.

But then the goon on his right shoved his blade into the wound on Logan's side. Logan clenched his teeth, refusing to cry out as the blade twisted.

"I mean, if Juliana had the evidence, if she knew anything about it…she'd say something…*now,* wouldn't she?" Guerrero asked, glancing down at the blood on his blade.

*"Stop!"* Juliana screamed. "Stop hurting him!"

"Oh, but we're just getting started." Guerrero nodded to his henchman, and he shoved that blade in even deeper.

Logan's hands fisted and he yanked against the ropes. "Have your…fun…" he rasped. "When I'm free…I'm… killing you."

"Promises, promises," Guerrero muttered.

"Yeah, it's a…promise." One he intended to keep. Guerrero and his torture-happy guards weren't getting away.

The knife slid from his flesh. Logan sucked in breath, but he hadn't even brought it fully into his lungs when Guerrero waved his hands and said, "Cut off his fingers."

*"No!"* Juliana lurched forward in her chair, yanking against the binds that held her. "Don't!"

Logan braced himself. The guard came around him and—

Logan kicked out with his feet. Idiots. They should have secured his legs. One kick broke the hand of the guy with the bloody knife. The weapon flew away. He caught the other guard in the knee and there was a solid crack that made Logan grin.

He stopped grinning when Guerrero put his knife to Juliana's throat once more.

Guerrero glared at him and said, "Always the hero…"

The guards scrambled back to their feet. They lurched forward as they came for Logan again, only this time, they stayed away from his legs. One slugged him in the jaw. The other grabbed his fallen knife and charged at Logan.

*That's right. Focus on me. Leave her alone.*

"Stop!" Guerrero's order froze the men.

And Logan realized…Guerrero was still focusing on Juliana. He'd grabbed her hair and tangled it around his fist. That knife was pressed against her throat, and Juliana's eyes were on Logan.

There was fear in her stare. But more, trust. Faith. She thought he'd save her.

*I will.*

There was more emotion burning in her eyes. But he didn't want to let himself believe what he saw. Not then.

Guerrero yanked back hard on Juliana's hair. "You both have information that I want. She has my evidence."

"I…don't," Juliana gritted. A tear leaked from the corner of her eye.

"And you…" Guerrero's eyes narrowed on Logan. "You're EOD."

Logan shook his head. "What the hell is that?"

The blade dug into Juliana's skin. "Don't lie, agent," Guerrero snapped. "I can see right through lies."

Oh, right, because he was clairvoyant? No, just your standard sociopath.

"My men have been digging into your life. Ever since Juliana here was so helpful in sharing her lover's name.

A SEAL, but you're not working in the field any longer. At least, you're not supposed to be."

Because he was with a new team now and had been for the past three years.

"The pieces fit for you. The more I dig, the more I know."

Guerrero's eyes reminded him of a cobra's watching his prey, waiting for a moment of weakness so he could strike. *Come on. Strike at me. Leave her alone.*

"The EOD has dozens of teams in operation."

Guerrero's intel was good.

"I want to know about them all. Those agents…their names…their lives. I can sell them all to the highest bidder."

And there would be plenty of folks willing to pay. "Don't know about them." He tried for a shrug, but the ropes pulled on his arms. "I'm just an ex-SEAL who did a favor for a senator."

Guerrero's laugh called him on the lie. "And after the senator died, you stuck around because…?"

"Because I asked him to!" Juliana tossed out before Logan could speak. "I was scared. After the explosion at the cemetery, I asked him to stay with me."

She was protecting him.

But Guerrero wasn't buying it. "He took out my men at the cabin. Eliminated them in an instant."

"What can I say? Once a SEAL…"

Guerrero lifted the knife from Juliana's throat. His eyes were on Logan's arm. On the blood that dripped to the floor. Logan wasn't moving, not making a sound.

"Trained to withstand anything, were you?" Guerrero asked.

*Just about.*

"She wasn't." Then he put his blade just under Juliana's

shoulder, in the exact spot the guard had sliced Logan's arm. "So when I start cutting her, I bet she'll scream."

He sliced into Juliana's arm.

*"Stop!"* Logan roared.

Juliana gasped but made no other sound.

Guerrero frowned. "Interesting…"

"No, it's not." Rage was choking Logan. "Get. Away. From. Her."

Guerrero lifted his knife. "Juliana, I believe you were wrong about him. I believe your lover does care…and he's about to show you just how much."

Juliana's eyes met Logan's.

"Two things can happen here," Guerrero said, and there was satisfaction in his voice. "One…I start cutting her, and she breaks. She can't handle the pain—no one ever can—and she tells me where I can find my evidence. I mean, she has it, right? That's what she told the reporters."

Juliana was still staring at Logan. *Keep looking at me, baby. Don't look away. Everything's okay.*

"Or we have option two…" Guerrero walked behind Juliana and the blade moved to her right shoulder. "I start hurting her, and *you* talk, Logan. You talk…and I make her pain stop."

Logan's teeth ground together.

Guerrero sighed. "You think I don't know about the EOD? Those agents have caused plenty of trouble for me and my…associates over the years. I know I'd enjoy some payback time."

Too many would.

"You talk, you tell me about the agents, where I can find them, any aliases they have, and I'll make Juliana's pain stop."

The ropes were cutting into Logan's flesh. Thick, twisted, they held him so tight.

"Tell me, and I'll make her pain stop." The blade dug into Juliana's arm. Her teeth sank into her bottom lip, and Logan knew she was trying to hold back her cries.

He'd never loved her more. *"Let her go."*

Guerrero bent near her ear. His lips brushed over the delicate shell when he asked, "Where's the evidence, Juliana? What did you do with it?"

"We…lied to the reporters," she whispered.

"Where is it?" he pressed.

Juliana shook her head.

Logan marked Guerrero for death. He stared at him, knowing this was one target that wouldn't be brought in alive. "You made a mistake," Logan told him.

Guerrero yanked that bloody blade from her flesh. Juliana's shoulders sagged.

"You should never have brought me in alive." Guerrero had let him get close, and Logan definitely intended to kill El Diablo.

"So tough." He lifted the blade again, and drops of blood fell to hit the floor as he turned back to Juliana. "Now, where were we?"

"Mexico," she said, voice trembling.

The guards weren't looking at Logan. They were focused on Guerrero. On Juliana. There was eagerness on their faces.

They liked the torture.

Guerrero was still crouched near Juliana's side, his mouth too close to her ear. "What about Mexico?"

"Why didn't you just…torture me then?"

"Because getting under your skin was half the fun." His fingers slid down her arm, sliding over the blood. "You've got such lovely skin."

*"Guerrero,"* Logan snarled.

"She does, doesn't she?" Guerrero murmured. "A beautiful woman." Now the knife rose to her face. "But you won't be that way for long."

Logan's vision bled red. He heaved in his chair.

"I don't think you wanted to hurt…me." Juliana's fast words froze Guerrero—and his knife. "We talked in Mexico for so long. Had you done that before? Ever gotten close with…someone like me?"

"I've lied to more men and women than I can count." He glanced at his knife. "Pain tells me what I want to know. But sometimes, lies are easier."

"And less bloody," Juliana whispered, swallowing. "Because I don't think…I don't think you wanted blood. I don't think…you wanted this life."

"This is the only life I want."

Juliana shook her head. Her eyes weren't on Logan any longer. They were on Guerrero. "You told me… You said you weren't perfect…. You said I didn't deserve what was happening to me…. You meant that, didn't you?"

A muscle flexed in Guerrero's jaw. Juliana kept talking, pressing her point as she said, "You didn't want to kill me then. That's why you kept me in that room…why you talked to me for so long."

"I was using you, getting intel from you. Keeping you alive long enough to make the senator squirm."

"Was John all a lie? Or was he…was he the man you could have been? What happened…" she asked him, speaking quickly, keeping the man's focus on her and keeping that knife off her body, "to change you? Why did John die…and El Diablo take over?"

"Because only the strong survive." A flash of pain raced over Guerrero's face. "I learned that lesson when I walked in my mother's blood."

Juliana flinched at that revelation.

Then Guerrero straightened, moving back a bit from

her. "It's a lesson you're going to learn now, too, Juliana." He frowned down at her, seemed almost lost an instant, then he said, "I'm sorry…" and lifted the knife to her face.

# Chapter Twelve

Juliana braced herself, knowing that there was nothing she could do to stop that knife from cutting her face. She wouldn't scream. She'd hold back the cries no matter what.

The knife pricked her skin. The pain was light, the faintest press, but she closed her eyes, knowing what was to come.

But then she heard a choked cry, the thud of flesh on flesh, and her eyelids flew open even as the knife was ripped away from her skin.

Logan had leaped from his chair. The ropes were behind him, some still dangling from his wrists. He had Guerrero on the ground and he was punching him again and again and again.

Guerrero's men seemed to shake from their stupor, and they lunged for him.

"Logan!"

His head whipped up. His eyes were wild. She'd never seen him look that way before. *His control is gone.* "Behind you!" But her shout was too late. One of the guards, a big guy with thick, curling hair, plunged his fist into Logan's back even as the other raced forward with his knife.

Juliana shoved out her feet, tripping the man with the knife. The weight of his body sent her crashing to the floor. Her chair shattered, and it felt as if her wrist broke, but Juliana twisted like a snake, moving quickly, and thanks to that broken chair, she was able to get out of the ropes.

She rushed to her feet. The guards were both attacking Logan now. One had a knife, but before he could attack, Logan just ripped that knife out of his hands. Then Logan knocked that guy out with a flash of his fists.

The other guard froze, glanced down at his buddy. She could feel the man's fear. But…Logan was bleeding. His body shuddered. The fool must have thought that was a sign of weakness.

He went in for the kill.

Logan stepped back, half turned and caught the man in a fierce grip.

"Wrong move." The whisper came from right beside Juliana. She jerked, but Guerrero already had her. He grabbed her, his arms wrapping around her from behind.

*"Juliana!"*

She didn't waste time looking at Logan. She hunched her shoulders and dropped instantly from Guerrero's grasp, just like Logan had taught her. Then she drove her elbow back into Guerrero's groin. He groaned and stumbled back.

*Not such easy prey, am I?* Not this time, she wasn't.

Logan rushed past her and crashed into Guerrero. They both hit the ground, rolling in a ball of fists and fury.

The second guard…he was still moving, trying to crawl for the discarded knife.

Thunder echoed outside.

Juliana grabbed the chair that Logan had been tied to. She lifted it as high as she could and slammed it down onto the guard's back.

He stopped moving then.

Juliana spun back around. Guerrero had a blade in his hand. A blade he was driving right at Logan's throat.

Juliana screamed and ran forward.

Logan grabbed Guerrero's hand, twisted it back and shoved the blade of the knife into Guerrero's throat.

A choked gurgle broke from Guerrero's lips.

"Told you," Logan growled, "you never should have brought me in alive."

Guerrero's body shuddered. He tried to speak, couldn't.

And as she watched, as Logan rose to his feet, El Diablo died. He was crying when he died. The tears leaked down his face even as the blood poured from his neck.

Her breath heaved out of her lungs. Juliana looked down and realized that she was dripping blood. She'd forgotten her wounds. She'd been too worried about Logan. But now…

Now she *hurt*.

He turned toward her. "Julie…"

Footsteps raced outside the room. Logan swore. He grabbed the knife and yanked it from Guerrero's throat. Then he pushed Juliana against the wall, sheltering her beside his body as he waited for the next wave of guards to come into the room.

A man raced in, a gun in his hands.

Logan kicked the gun away and put his knife at the man's throat in a lightning-fast move.

"Don't!"

Not Juliana's cry. Sydney's. Juliana saw the woman rush through the door. Her eyes were wide and worried and locked on Logan—Logan and Jasper.

"Here to…save you…" Jasper wheezed.

Logan lowered his arm. "Little late, buddy. Little late…"

Sydney and Jasper glanced at the bodies on the floor. "Yes, it looks that way."

Logan used the knife to cut away the last of the ropes that dangled from his wrists. She'd barely even noticed them during the fury of the fight. "Are we clear outside?" Logan demanded.

Sydney nodded. "I don't think Guerrero was expecting us to come so soon." Sydney edged closer to the body. "Only a handful of men waited outside."

Juliana didn't want to look at the body. Her hand lifted, and she touched the raised skin on the back of her neck. The tracker had come in handy, just like Logan had said it would. "It's over," she whispered, almost afraid to believe the words were true.

Logan's head whipped toward her. His eyes—the wildness was still there. A beast running free. And there was fury in his blue stare.

Fury...and fear?

Juliana dropped her hand. He'd told her that he loved her. Sure, they'd both been about to die, but she wasn't about to let him take those words back.

Sydney was talking into her phone, asking for more men. A cleanup crew. Boots on the ground.

Jasper had bent over the guards. He gave a low whistle. "Someone plays rough." He looked back up at Logan.

Logan shook his head and jerked his thumb toward Juliana. "That one was hers."

Jasper blinked and stared at her with admiration. "I think I'm in love."

"Get in line," Logan muttered.

Juliana wrapped her arms around her stomach. Maybe they were used to this kind of scene, but she wasn't. The smell of blood and death was about to gag her, and her wounds ached and throbbed and—

Logan was there. "She needs medical attention."

A choked laugh slipped from her, and she didn't know where that had come from. Wait, she did. *Shock.* "You're the one who was gutted."

"Barely a scratch," he dismissed as he lifted her arms to study the wounds, but his face was pale, and the faint lines near his eyes and mouth had deepened.

When he stumbled, it was her turn to grab him. "Jasper!"

The other Shadow Agent was there instantly. "Damn, man, you should have said…"

Logan gave a quick shake of his head and cut his eyes toward Juliana.

The flash of fear instantly vanished from Jasper's face, but it was too late.

*It's bad.*

"Let's get out of here," Logan muttered. "I want… Juliana safe."

"I am safe," she said quietly. "Whenever I'm with you, I know I'm safe." A man who'd kill to protect her. How much more safety could a girl ask for?

His gaze held hers. *I always loved you.* The words were there, between them. Had he confessed out of desperation? Because he'd thought they were going to die?

And did the reason why even matter? *No.*

*I always loved you.*

They made their way outside. Juliana stayed close to Logan and she tried not to notice the trail of blood he left in his wake.

They were at the edge of the swamp. Insects chirped all around them. Armed federal agents were swarming the scene, and an ambulance was racing toward them along that broken dirt road.

"Maybe we'll find evidence inside," Sydney said as she

rubbed the back of her neck and watched an EMT work on Logan. "Maybe we'll be able to connect his network and shut down some of the—"

"Here." Juliana reached into her pocket and pulled out the flash drive. Guerrero hadn't bothered to search her. His mistake. He'd just tied her up. Started his torture. When all along, the one thing he needed was right in front of him.

Silence. Even the insects seemed to quiet down.

She glanced up. Logan had been put on a stretcher, but he was struggling to sit up and get to her. "What the hell?"

Jasper shook his head. "The evidence. You had it all along?"

"No. I found it when I was fighting with Susan." A shiver slid over her as she remembered Susan's scream when the woman had been shot. Juliana could still hear the shatter of the breaking glass as Susan had fallen. "My father...he hid the flash drive in one of my paintings, one that he kept in his bedroom."

Syd took the drive. A grim smile curved her lips. "You just made my job a whole lot easier."

Juliana glanced at the blood on Logan's body. At the injured men on the ground. "If I'd found it sooner, it would have been easier for everyone."

The EMTs were loading Logan into the back of the ambulance. Someone else—another EMT, a woman this time—was reaching for Juliana.

Pulling them apart.

She didn't want to be apart from him any longer. They'd already wasted so many years. Too many.

She stepped toward the ambulance. "I was going to give it to him." Logan should know this.

He stared at her with glittering eyes.

"I wasn't going to sit there and let him kill you. I was going to trade the drive for your life."

"Ma'am, you're going to need stitches," the EMT next to her said. "We have to get you checked out."

She didn't want to be checked out. "Logan…"

He was yanking at the tubes the EMTs had already attached to him. Trying to get out of the ambulance, even as the two uniformed men beside him attempted to force him back down.

Juliana rushed forward and leaped into the ambulance. "Don't! You'll hurt yourself!"

He caught her hand in his and immediately stilled. His fingers brushed over her knuckles.

"Let's get the hell out of here," one of the EMTs muttered, a young man with close-cropped red hair, "before the guy tries to break loose again."

The ambulance lurched forward.

Logan wasn't fighting any longer. He let the men tend to his wounds. Juliana let them examine the deep cuts on her arms.

Logan kept holding her hand.

She kept staring at him.

There was so much to say, and she wasn't sure where to start. They'd been through hell. Death. Life.

Could they go back to the beginning and just be two people again? Two people who wanted a chance at love?

He brought her hand to his lips and pressed a kiss to her knuckles. "Don't leave me."

Her chest ached. "I won't."

The sirens screamed on, and they left the blood and death behind them.

WHEN LOGAN OPENED his eyes, the first thing he saw was Juliana. She was in the chair next to his bed, her head tilted back against the old cushion. Heavy bandages covered the tops of her arms. She was holding his hand.

He stared at her a moment and watched her sleep. She'd always been so beautiful to him. So beautiful that his chest burned just looking at her.

When Guerrero had threatened to use his knife on Juliana's face, when she'd braced herself, drawing in that deep breath and trying to be strong, something had broken inside of Logan.

He'd killed before. Killing was part of his job, part of surviving.

But this time, it had been pure animal instinct. Savagery. The primal urge to protect what was his.

Juliana was his. That was the way he'd thought of her for years.

But there weren't any secrets between them now, and he didn't know… *What does she think of me?*

His fingers tightened around hers, and almost instantly, she stirred in her chair. Her lashes lifted and her gaze locked on him. Then she stared at him. A slow smile curved her lips and her eyes—

*She still looks at me like I'm some kind of hero.*

When she, more than any other, knew he wasn't.

"Took you long enough," she said as she leaned toward him. Her voice was a husky caress that seemed to roll right over his body. "I was starting to wonder when I'd get you awake again."

"How long…" He paused and cleared his throat so he'd sound less like a growling bear. "How long was I out?"

Shadows darkened her eyes as her smile dimmed. "They had to operate on you, stitch you back up from the inside out."

Yeah, he could feel the pull of the stitches. He ignored the pain.

"And you've been sleeping for a couple of hours since then."

"You were…here, with me?"

She nodded. "You told me not to leave." One shoulder lifted, stretching the bandage on her arm. "I got stitched up while you were in surgery, and they let me come back once you were stable."

She rose from the chair and his fingers tightened around hers automatically, a reflex because he didn't want to let her go.

She glanced down. A frown pulled her brows low, and he forced himself to release her.

"Gunner's going to be all right, too," she said, and her words came a little fast, as if she were nervous. "Sydney's with him. She's been in his room…well, almost as long as I've been in here."

He knew why Sydney would stay with Gunner. Those two…there had always been something there. Something neither would talk about.

While he'd spent his years thinking about Juliana, Gunner had spent his time watching Syd—when he thought she wasn't looking.

"So I guess everything is over now," Juliana continued, easing away from the bed a bit. "The bad guy is dead. The EOD has the evidence and I can get my life back."

"Yes." The word was even more of a growl than before. Logan couldn't help it. Fear and fury were beating at him. *Don't want to lose her.*

"Thank you." Her gaze was solemn. "You risked your life for me. I won't ever forget that."

She turned on her heel, began to head for the door.

*No damn way.* "I wouldn't have much of a life without you."

Juliana stilled.

"I lost you once, and if you walk away…" Like she was doing. *Hell, no.* "Don't, okay? Don't walk away. Give me a chance. Give us a chance." And he was getting out of that bed. Yanking at the IV line attached to his arm. Swearing at the bandages and stitches that pulled his flesh.

Juliana turned back around. Her eyes widened when she saw him and she rushed back to his side. "Why do you keep doing this?" She pushed him onto bed. "I was just going to tell Jasper that you were awake. I wasn't leaving you."

So he'd panicked. A guy could do that when the woman he loved had almost died. And he did still love her. He'd tried to deny it, tried to move on.

Hadn't happened.

"I meant it," he told her, and yeah, he was holding tight to her hand again. He just felt as if she was about to disappear. Slip away.

"Logan?"

"When I said I loved you, it was true. I wanted you to know in case…" In case Guerrero had carried through on his threats. Logan shook his head. "I know you hate me—"

"No, I don't."

He wouldn't let the hope come, not yet. Not hating someone was a long way from loving the person. "I should have told you the truth about your mother the first day I met you. I was scared," he admitted as he stared her straight in the eye. "Scared you'd walk away. Scared that I'd see disgust in your gaze."

"Is that what you see now?"

"No." But he wasn't sure…

"I read the reports about my mom's accident. Her death wasn't your fault. I know you tried to save her."

It hadn't been enough. It would never be enough.

"You aren't your father. You aren't like him." Her lips pulled down. "And I'm not like mine." Her breath whispered out in a sad sigh. "Maybe things could have been different for them, too, but now it's too late."

Too late for their fathers. But… "What about us?"

Her lashes lowered. "What do you want from me, Logan?"

*Everything.* "A chance. Just give me a chance, Juliana, to show you what I can be."

"I already know what you are."

The pain in his chest burned worse than the stitches. "No, you—"

"You're the man that I love." Her lashes swept up. "I've known that since the first time you kissed me."

Hope could be a vicious beast. It bit and tore inside of him, ripping past the fear and driving him to pull her ever closer.

Her legs bumped against the bed. Her lips were just inches from his. "Juliana, don't say it unless…"

"Unless I mean it? But I do mean it." Her left hand lifted and pressed lightly against the line of his jaw. "Logan, I love you."

He kissed her. His mouth took hers, rough, hungry, because he couldn't hold back. He needed her too much. Always had.

The pain of his wounds didn't matter. The pain of the past years—being without her—didn't matter. She was with him now. In his arms.

He pulled her even closer. She stumbled against the bed and laughed against his mouth. That laugh was the sweetest sound he'd ever heard.

He wanted to spend the rest of his life making her happy, hearing her laugh and seeing the light in her dark eyes.

He wanted forever with her.

His tongue slid past her lips and tasted that laughter. So sweet. Just like her.

"Logan…" she whispered as she pulled her lips from his. "We can't. You'll get hurt…"

"The only thing that can hurt me is being away from you." That had gutted him before. Hell, this wasn't the time. Not the place. But… "Marry me."

Her eyes widened. She tried to pull away. He wouldn't let her.

"Logan, you just asked for a chance, and now you want forever?"

He smiled, and for the first time in longer than he could remember, it was a real smile. His chest didn't burn anymore. He didn't feel as if he'd lost a part of himself.

*She's right here.*

"I'm a greedy bastard," he confessed.

An answering smile, slow and sexy, tilted her lips.

"Besides, I've had your ring since you were twenty years old." He'd kept it, not able to let it go. "And I'd like to start making up for lost time."

"You had a ring…all this time?"

Because maybe he hadn't ever given up hope. Maybe he'd thought…one day.

That day was today.

"Let me make you happy." He had to make up for all the pain. The grief. The anger. He could do it. "I *will* make you happy. I swear."

This time she kissed him. Her head dipped toward him. Her mouth, wet, hot, open, found his. She kissed him with a passion that had his body tensing and wondering just how much privacy they'd be able to get. Because he was tempted…so tempted.

By her.

"You do make me happy," she told him. Her eyes searched his. "And yes, I'll marry you. I just want to be with you."

That was what he wanted. To spend his nights with her. To wake up in the morning and see her beside him. Every day. Always.

"I love you." He had to say the words again.

The hospital door opened behind Juliana.

Jaw clenching—*not now*—Logan glanced at the door. Jasper stood there with his brows raised.

"Guess you're going to be all right," Jasper said, his lips twitching.

"I'm going to be better than all right…." Logan laughed. "Man, I'm going to be married!"

Jasper's jaw dropped.

Before his friend could say anything else, Logan turned back to Juliana. His Julie. The angel who'd been in his heart for so long.

The woman he'd love until he died.

"Thank you," he told her as his forehead pressed against hers.

"About time," Jasper said as his feet shuffled across the floor. "If I'd had to spend another day watching you moon over her…" The door swooshed as he left the room.

"What do you have to thank me for?" Juliana asked him.

*"For loving me."*

"It's not going to be easy, you know," she said. "We'll have to adjust, both of us. You have your job, I have mine. You're not perfect…"

He laughed at that. "No, but you are."

Her grin flashed. "And when the kids come…"

*Yes.* "I can't wait." For the dream he'd wanted. For the life that he'd thought was long gone.

He'd fight for that dream, every damn day. Just as he'd fight for her.

The woman he loved.

His mission. His job.

His life.

* * * * *

**"They had a proposition for me,"
Rafe said. "One they tried to make
very difficult to refuse."**

She frowned. "What kind of proposition?"

"They wanted me to use our past to try to get on
your good side and convince you to cooperate."

Her eyes hardened. "And did you agree to this?"

"No," Rafe said forcefully. "Of course not. I would
never do anything to put you or Chloe in danger."

They let that hang in the air for a moment, then she
laced her fingers through his and squeezed. "You
don't know how much I've missed you, Rafe. How
many times I've cursed myself for letting you go."

"You don't think I feel the same?"

Her eyes looked hopeful. "Do you?"

# INTERNAL
# AFFAIRS

## BY
## ALANA MATTHEWS

MILLS &
BOON

All the characters in this book have no existence outside the imagination of the author, and have no relation whatsoever to anyone bearing the same name or names. They are not even distantly inspired by any individual known or unknown to the author, and all the incidents are pure invention.

All Rights Reserved including the right of reproduction in whole or in part in any form. This edition is published by arrangement with Harlequin Enterprises II B.V./S.à.r.l. The text of this publication or any part thereof may not be reproduced or transmitted in any form or by any means, electronic or mechanical, including photocopying, recording, storage in an information retrieval system, or otherwise, without the written permission of the publisher.

This book is sold subject to the condition that it shall not, by way of trade or otherwise, be lent, resold, hired out or otherwise circulated without the prior consent of the publisher in any form of binding or cover other than that in which it is published and without a similar condition including this condition being imposed on the subsequent purchaser.

® and ™ are trademarks owned and used by the trademark owner and/or its licensee. Trademarks marked with ® are registered with the United Kingdom Patent Office and/or the Office for Harmonisation in the Internal Market and in other countries.

First published in Great Britain 2013
by Mills & Boon, an imprint of Harlequin (UK) Limited,
Eton House, 18-24 Paradise Road, Richmond, Surrey TW9 1SR

© Alana Matthews 2013

ISBN: 978 0 263 90349 2
ebook ISBN: 978 1 472 00702 5

46-0313

Harlequin (UK) policy is to use papers that are natural, renewable and recyclable products and made from wood grown in sustainable forests. The logging and manufacturing processes conform to the legal environmental regulations of the country of origin.

Printed and bound in Spain
by Blackprint CPI, Barcelona

**Alana Matthews** can't remember a time when she didn't want to be a writer. As a child, she was a permanent fixture in her local library, and she soon turned her passion for books into writing short stories, and finally novels. A longtime fan of romantic suspense, Alana felt she had no choice but to try her hand at the genre, and she is thrilled to be writing for Mills & Boon® Intrigue. Alana makes her home in a small town near the coast of Southern California, where she spends her time writing, composing music and watching her favorite movies.

Send a message to Alana at her website, www.alana matthews.com.

# Chapter One

She opened her eyes with a start, not sure what had awakened her.

She was alone in the room, which was quiet except for the sound of an autumn breeze outside her window and the faint metallic squeak of the bed springs.

Had it been Chloe?

Squinting at the clock—which read 4:32 a.m.—she stilled herself and listened carefully, using the supersonic hearing only a mother possesses, tuning it in to Chloe's frequency.

But she heard nothing.

No whimpering. No cries in the night.

Even as a baby, Chloe had been a sound sleeper. And now that she was just past her third year, she was nearly impossible to get out of bed in the morning. The girl liked her rest and, unlike her mother, could snooze through a thunderstorm.

But what Lisa Tobin had heard was not thunder.

The noise, if she hadn't dreamed it—and she didn't think she had—was high-pitched and abrasive. Like glass shattering.

A window?

Was there an intruder in the house?

Icy dread sluiced through her bloodstream as the thought took hold. She listened awhile longer, hoping it was just her overactive imagination, and the moment she convinced herself it *was,* she heard another sound—a faint, muffled crash—coming from downstairs.

Definitely *not* her imagination.

There was someone down there.

Could it be Beatrice? Had she awakened in the middle of the night and decided to get an early start on her housekeeping?

Not likely. Bea was efficient, but she wasn't overly ambitious and was as sound a sleeper as Chloe. And even if she *were* tidying up, she had never been the clumsy type. The woman was as stealthy as an alley cat.

So intruder it was. Probably that punk kid from next door trying to prove himself to his punk buddies.

There had been a rash of break-ins up and down the street in the past few weeks and everyone pretty much suspected the kid. He was the product of a broken home—something Lisa was all too familiar with—and had been acting out ever since he'd reached puberty. In the year and a half she had lived in this house, the boy had been arrested three times. Twice for drugs, and once for burglary. And he was undoubtedly working his way toward arrest number four.

So what should she do?

Sit here and let him clean the place out?

Lisa's first instinct was to call the police, but as she reached to the nightstand for her cell phone, she remembered that she had left it in her purse, which was sitting on the table in the foyer downstairs. She had never had a landline installed, and now cursed herself for it.

So she had two choices. Stay put and hope the punk didn't work his way up the stairs…

Or confront him.

Neither choice thrilled Lisa, but she was not the shrinking-violet type and she wasn't about to sit here, waiting to be victimized.

So option number two it was.

Throwing her blankets aside, she sat up, swung her legs over the side of the bed, then got to her feet and pulled her robe on. She would need protection, of course. You don't go into a situation like this without it.

But what kind of protection?

A gun?

Lisa didn't like guns. Hated them, in fact. Had only held one in her hands twice in her lifetime and had felt extremely uncomfortable each time. But before he moved out, her ex-husband, Oliver, had insisted on putting a pistol in a lockbox on the hall closet shelf, telling her not to hesitate to use it if necessary.

It was a typical Oliver move. He was no stranger to violence—something she had learned only in the last days of their marriage, and part of the reason she had filed for a divorce. His stubborn refusal to consider her feelings—the pistol, for example—was the other part. She had thought she was marrying a prince charming but quickly discovered that there was something deadly beneath that charm. Something dangerous and controlling.

And intimidating.

A Dr. Jekyll who had quickly morphed into Mr. Hyde.

But Lisa had never been turned on by bad boys. She had too much self-respect for that. And where she had once felt warmth, she now felt trepidation whenever she encountered him. An uneasiness that wormed its way into her gut every time she saw him.

As much as she hated to admit it, however, Oliver had been right about the gun. And despite the punk's young age, confronting him without a weapon would be foolhardy.

She didn't have to use it, of course. Merely wave it at him to scare him away. Get to her cell phone and call the cops.

So that was the plan.

One she desperately hoped wouldn't go awry.

Sucking in a deep breath, she moved to her bedroom door and opened it a crack, peering out into the dark stillness of the second-floor hallway.

Empty.

Steeling herself, she stepped into that stillness and quickly made her way to Chloe's bedroom. She wasn't about to confront *anyone* without first checking to see that her little girl was safe.

She carefully turned the knob and pushed the door open. To her relief, Chloe was wrapped in her blankets, her tiny figure illuminated by the moonlight from the window, her shallow chest rising and falling.

Despite her trepidation, Lisa felt a sudden warmth spread inside her. The sight of Chloe sleeping always had that effect on her. It had been a lousy couple of years, yet Chloe had been the one constant, the one shining star, in Lisa's universe.

Reassured that her daughter was safe, she clicked the lock button, then pulled the door shut. She didn't like the idea of locking Chloe in, but didn't want to take any chances, either.

Turning now, she headed back down the hallway toward the stairs, stopping at the narrow closet on the left side of the landing.

Checking the darkness at the bottom of the stairs, she quietly opened the closet door, reached to the overhead shelf and found the wooden box where Oliver had left it, almost a year ago. It was secured by a small lock with a combination that was easy enough to remember: Chloe's birth date.

Dialing it in, Lisa unfastened the lock, opened the box, then carefully removed the loaded pistol. She didn't feel comfortable hefting it, but what choice did she have?

"Just point it and shoot," Oliver had told her during one of his more generous moments. "That's all you have to remember."

*Easier said than done,* she thought.

Returning the box to the shelf, she closed the closet door and turned again toward the mouth of the stairs, listening for more sounds from below.

It was eerily silent now.

No rummaging noises, no whispering voices—assuming there was more than one intruder—no footsteps…

Nothing.

Lisa had all but come to the conclusion that the burglar had left when she heard it: the faint, almost imperceptible clink of a glass and the sound of pouring liquid.

Someone was still down there all right—but whoever it was wasn't ransacking her house. He was helping himself to a drink from the wet bar.

What the heck?

Lowering the pistol to her side, Lisa started down the stairs, her heart thumping with every step. She was barefoot, but like the stairways in many old St. Louis homes, this one was made of wood and was full of creaks and groans, the carpet covering it doing little to muffle the sound of her descent. She may as well have announced her entrance with the trill of trumpets.

As she reached the living room, clutching the gun tightly at her side, a lamp next to the sofa came to life, startling her. She was about to swing the gun upward when she stopped herself, realizing who it was.

Oliver. Drunk or stoned, as usual, sitting on the sofa with his feet up on the coffee table, a glass of vodka in hand.

"You've gotta work on your stealth skills, babe. I could hear you at the top of the stairs."

As her heartbeat slowed, anger rose in Lisa's chest, crowding out the fear she was already feeling. "I almost shot you, Oliver. What the heck are you doing here?"

She glanced around the room and saw what had made the noise that got her out of bed: a picture frame lay on the polished wooden floorboards, its glass shattered. The photo inside was one she had always loved—she and Chloe in front of the lake house, Chloe squirming happily in her arms. It had been taken at a better time in her marriage, nearly two years ago, before Oliver had released Mr. Hyde from his cage.

She had no idea if he had purposely knocked it from the end table or had merely stumbled into it. Whatever the cause, she'd now have to clean up the mess and replace the frame. Another black mark in a string of them as far as Oliver was concerned.

He didn't answer her question immediately. Instead, he took a sip of his vodka and gave her a long, slow smile.

"What's the matter, Leese, you don't like me darkening your doorstep? This is, after all, *my* house."

"Tell that to my attorney."

"Ah," he said, "your attorney. I'll bet you'd love to have a reason to give him a call. Real movie-star material, that guy."

"I hadn't noticed."

"Uh-huh. Sure. The two of you probably had this planned from the very beginning."

"Had what planned? What are you talking about?"

Oliver smirked, but there was a coldness in his eyes that frightened her. How could she not have known that he was a sociopath when she met him? How could she have let him seduce her into believing he was her man on a white horse?

"I've been thinking about this ever since you tricked me into the divorce," he said.

"Tricked you?"

"What else would you call it?"

"Surviving," she said, then sighed. "It's been nearly a year, Oliver. Time to move on."

"You and your pretty-boy lawyer planned this, didn't you? You knew I was a rich, successful businessman and you targeted me, roped me in, used that cute little rear of yours to break me down, take advantage of me. Started snooping around behind my back, sticking your nose in things you had no right getting into."

She thought about Harvey, her handsome but overly earnest attorney who was nearly twice her age, married and had three kids. Their relationship had always been strictly professional.

"You're insane."

"Am I? You got your hooks in me good, babe. I take one look at you in that robe, I get as a randy as a teen-ager."

Lisa felt her dinner backing up on her. The thought that she'd ever had the desire to take this man to bed gave her an urgent need for a box of gingersnaps. Or a chug of Pepto Bismol.

"Don't flatter yourself," she told him.

"I was *trying* to flatter *you*."

She stared at him. "Get out of here, Oliver. You don't live here anymore, and you know what's at stake. So go home."

"And what if I don't?" He shifted his gaze to the gun at her side. "You gonna put a hole in me?"

She frowned at him, then moved to the long table against the wall and set down the gun down, glad to be rid of it.

As she stepped away, she said, "You can take it with you, as far as I'm concerned. I don't ever want you thinking I owe you any favors."

The coldness filled his entire face now as he swung his feet off the table and stood up. "Let's talk about fa-vors, why don't we?"

He moved toward her, and Lisa found herself back-ing away slightly, wondering now if she should have been so quick to put down the gun. Oliver carried with him such a sense of menace that she was unsure of what he might do.

Despite his history of violence, however, he had never threatened either her or Chloe and she hoped that would continue to hold true.

"You weren't so anxious to refuse my favors when I got you out of that dump of an apartment you lived in. I didn't see you protesting when I put you in a brand-new Volvo. Made sure you and Chloe had all those pretty little clothes to wear."

"I've never said I'm not grateful, Oliver, but none of that means you own me. And right now you're trespassing."

He moved in close, trapping her against the wall. "Trespassing? I haven't been around here in months and this is how you treat me?"

Lisa's heart started thumping again. "Get out of here, now, or I swear I'll—"

It came suddenly and without warning. Oliver's hand shot toward her, grabbing her by the throat, slamming her roughly against the wall.

Lisa struggled, feeling her air cut off. She tried to speak but couldn't.

"I'm sorry," Oliver said. "What was that? Were you about to threaten me again? Tell me I don't have the right to come into a house I bought and paid for? You think some computer file you've got stashed, or some piece of paper your lawyer drafted up is gonna change that?"

Panic rose in Lisa's chest. She could barely breathe.

Upstairs, Chloe started to cry, the sound muffled by her door. But Lisa doubted it was their voices that had awakened her. Her usual sound sleep had instead been disturbed by that sense of menace that Oliver carried with him wherever he went. A malignant contagion stirring the air around them.

As Lisa struggled to breathe, he loosened his grip on her throat and she stumbled sideways. But before she could move away from him, he grabbed hold of her arm and shoved her back against the wall.

She was too stunned to move. This was the first time he had ever laid a hand on her.

"Don't you talk to me like that again, you little gold digger." He held her in place and slipped his free hand inside her robe, grabbing her right breast, rubbing his thumb over her nipple. "You may have snagged the gold, but the way I see it, you've got a long way to go before you earn—"

A ratcheting sound cut him off. They turned and saw Beatrice standing at the foot of the stairs, a shotgun in her hands, leveled at Oliver.

"You'd best get your paws off her real quick, son. I wouldn't want to muss up the lady's new robe."

Tears of relief filled Lisa's eyes. She hadn't even known Bea *owned* a shotgun—wouldn't have approved if she did, not with Chloe in the house—but the old woman looked as if she knew how to use it and Lisa welcomed the sight.

"If you think I'm kidding," Bea continued, "just try me."

Oliver released Lisa, but his body went rigid, the coldness in his eyes turning into a hard, angry stare. "You don't have the guts, you old bat."

"Don't I?" She moved forward. "My daddy taught me how to use this scattergun when I was twelve years old. I've never shot at nothin' but tin cans, but I'm all too happy to find out what a round of buck can do to a grown man's face. I don't imagine it'll be pretty."

"I didn't come here alone," Oliver told her. "I've got men outside and all I have to do is sound the alarm."

Bea smiled. "You go right ahead and do that, son, see what it gets you."

He studied her a moment longer, then did as she asked and backed away, throwing his hands up as he moved. "Never argue with a shotgun."

"Damn right."

Lisa took a deep breath and said, "Get out of here, Oliver, and don't come back."

He snapped his gaze toward her. "Or what?"

"Or I go to the police."

"Why? Because I copped a feel?" He grinned. "Judging by the way your body reacted, I'd say you were enjoying it."

"You know what I'm talking about," Lisa said.

His face got hard and Bea gestured with the shotgun. "Son, I'm about two tics away from squeezing this trigger—and it isn't much of a target, but I'll be aiming at your talliwacker."

Oliver's eyes narrowed. "You're gonna regret this," he said, then looked at Lisa. "Both of you."

He walked to the front door and yanked it open, then turned in the doorway and smiled at them again, using his thumb and forefinger to form a gun.

"You're about to find out what happens to women who dump on Oliver Sloan…"

He pretended to pull the trigger, then turned again and went outside.

## Chapter Two

The call came in two hours earlier. Gunshots heard by an insomniac, coming from the auto repair shop next to his apartment building.

"Unit Fourteen, we've got a possible 142 in progress, can you respond?"

"Roger, dispatch. I'm on it."

Sheriff's deputy Rafael Franco was in the middle of his usual graveyard shift, happy to have the distraction after a night of shoveling up street drunks and carting them to the holding tank. It was a part of the job he had never enjoyed, mostly because his skill and brains were being underutilized by the department.

His college diploma still had a bit of wet ink on it, but he was frustrated that he hadn't yet been promoted.

Rafe had been with the Sheriff's department for nearly three years now, the newest and greenest member of the Franco family to wear a badge. The Francos and law enforcement went all the way back to his great-great-grandfather Tomas, an Italian immigrant who had joined the St. Louis police force when it was little more than a ragtag group of men with guns and good intentions.

Rafe knew he had a lot to live up to, but he felt restless working the streets, and figured he had already paid his dues. He was tired of patrol duty. What he really wanted was to join his sister, Kate, on the homicide squad, where brains and reasoning and solid evidence-gathering far outweighed your ability to heft a drunk into the backseat of your cruiser.

Unfortunately, Rafe didn't get the impression he'd be bumped up anytime soon. But a report of gunshots gave him hope. Not that he wished any other human being ill, but if he happened to luck into something big, maybe he'd get a chance to demonstrate his investigative skills.

He also didn't mind the distraction from his thoughts tonight. As always, he had taken a long nap before reporting to duty, and a dream he'd had was haunting him—a vague, half-remembered remnant from his college years, featuring a girl he had once loved. He had awakened from it feeling disoriented and a little sad, filled with a vague, undefinable yearning that he couldn't quite shake.

Rafe hadn't seen the girl in over three years now, but she still showed up on the doorstep of his mind every now and then and he'd often thought of trying to contact her. Their breakup had been mutual—both convinced that they were too young to be getting serious—but Rafe often regretted the decision and wondered if she did, too.

He hadn't met a woman since who had made him feel the way she had. And that dream, as hazy as it was, hadn't done him any favors.

THE AUTO BODY SHOP was located on a deserted city street, nestled between a run-down apartment building and an abandoned drive-in liquor store.

The place was dark when Rafe pulled up to the curb. A sea of cars in various states of disrepair crowded the lot out front, making the place look more like a junk-yard than a body shop. The garage—a large rectangular structure—was located in back and, by Rafe's count, sported nine repair bays, each with its aluminum roll door closed and locked for the night.

Off to the right of the building was a connecting of-fice with its front door hanging open, nothing but dark-ness beyond.

Something obviously wasn't right here.

To Rafe's mind, this was an indication that the caller might not have been hearing things. Too often reports of gunshots are nothing more than a car backfiring or kids playing with firecrackers, but that open door sug-gested something far more sinister.

Rafe called it in, told the dispatcher he was on the scene. That he'd stay in radio contact as he checked it out.

Grabbing his flashlight from the glove compartment, he killed his engine and climbed out of the cruiser. He moved off to his left, not wanting to approach the open door directly, in case the shooter—assuming there was one—was still inside.

Stepping into the sea of cars, he stayed low and care-fully made his way around and through them, drawing closer to the office, making sure to come at the door-way from an angle.

He was about ten yards away when he stopped, crouched behind an old Chevy Malibu missing its grill, and peered into the darkness beyond the threshold, look-ing for signs of life inside.

Nothing but still air in there.

Nobody home.

Satisfied that he was alone out here, Rafe stood up, clicked the radio on his shoulder.

"Dispatch, this is Unit Fourteen. Looks like it's clear out here, but I'm headed inside for a closer look."

"Do you need backup?"

"I think I'm good for now," Rafe said. "I'll stay in radio contact."

"Roger, Fourteen."

Switching the flashlight on, Rafe pointed it toward the building, then dropped a hand to the holster on his hip and unsnapped it, resting his palm against the grip of his Glock.

Using the beam to guide him, he approached the doorway and stepped through it, finding nothing but your typical cluttered office—a desk piled with paperwork, an adding machine, a few metal chairs, a bookshelf full of repair manuals, an old computer. There was a faded calendar on the wall featuring the *Motor Babe of the Month* wearing a barely there bikini and holding a wrench provocatively as she posed in front of a souped-up Ford Mustang.

Off to the left was another doorway that opened into a garage bathed in moonlight, which filtered in from a bank of high windows. It was about half the size of a football field, and there were cars parked in each of the nine bays, all but one in various states of disassembly.

Rafe smelled the odor of a cooling engine and ran the flashlight beam over the car closest to him—a shiny Jaguar XJ that looked as if it was in fine condition, no body work needed. There was a thin layer of road dust covering it and it didn't seem to have been repaired at any time in the recent past.

So why was it parked in here?

Was it the owner's car?

And, if so, where was he?

Before Rafe could ponder these questions, the beam of his flashlight caught something dark and glistening on the cement directly beneath the Jaguar's front passenger side—

A small pool of red liquid that looked very much like blood.

It was coming from the crack beneath the door.

Rafe's body tensed. Drawing his Glock from its holster, he shone his light through the car window and saw two figures slumped inside, both male, both very dead. Eyes wide. Mouths agape. Judging by their appearance—unshaven, rumpled clothes, with matching bullet holes adorning the middle of their foreheads—they weren't Sunday school teachers.

And this was definitely the work of a professional.

Rafe was about to call it in when he heard a sound coming from across the garage—the faint clang and scrape of metal against concrete, as if someone had accidentally kicked a stray hubcap.

He wasn't alone in here.

Jerking his flashlight beam toward the source of the sound, he illuminated the far end of the garage.

"Sheriff's department," he called out. "Show yourself and take it slow, hands in the air."

He caught a glimpse of movement and reacted instinctively, diving sideways, just as a muzzle flashed and the bark of gunfire filled his ears. One of the Jaguar's side mirrors exploded above his head and he dove for cover behind a tall, rolling tool cabinet.

Dropping the flashlight, he reached for the radio on his shoulder and clicked it on.

"Dispatch, this is Unit Fourteen. I'm under fire. Repeat, I'm under fire."

"Roger, Fourteen, we're sending backup."

More gunshots punched holes in the Jaguar and the tool cabinet, landing way too close for comfort. Rafe quickly snatched up the flashlight and closed it, tucking it into its loop on his belt.

No point in giving this guy a target.

He returned fire—once, twice—then retreated into the darkness behind him and waited.

The gunfire stopped, followed by the longest stretch of silence that Rafe had ever experienced. His heart pounded wildly as he waited for the perp to make a move. He figured the guy would either start shooting again—assuming he had the rounds—or make like a jackrabbit.

Rafe didn't have to wait long for the perp to decide. A dark figure popped up from behind the equally dark silhouette of a car and took off, heading for a door on the left side of the garage.

Rafe shot to his feet and shouted, "Hold it!" as he took off after the guy, leaping over stray tools and car parts that lay on the garage floor.

A moment later he was at the door and about to crash through it, when he stopped himself, thinking that might not be a wise move.

What if the perp was out there waiting for him?

Instead, he stepped to the right side of the doorway

and crouched down to avoid being in the line of fire. Then he reached a hand out, turned the knob, and flung the door open.

As it swung wide, he half expected another flurry of gunshots—

But nothing happened. All he heard was the distant drone of street traffic.

Getting back to his feet, he carefully peeked around the door frame and saw the perp several yards away, working his way through the maze of cars in the front of the lot.

"Police!" Rafe shouted as he took off after him. "Stop right now!"

The guy didn't slow down. He was nearly to the sidewalk now, only feet from where Rafe had left his cruiser. As the perp barreled past the last of the cars, he brought his gun up and shot at the black-and-white, shattering the windshield and puncturing one of the tires.

Rafe swore under his breath and kept running, moving into and through the maze—

Now the guy was on the street and jumping into a gray BMW. The engine roared to life as Rafe vaulted the hood of a junked Mazda and scrambled after him.

Just as he reached the street, the BMW's rear tires began to spin and smoke, the car laying rubber as it tore away from the curb.

Rafe tried to read the license plate, but the streetlight was too dim and the plate was obscured by darkness. He whirled around, hoping his cruiser was still good to go, and found that the shooter had hit his mark. The right front tire was shredded and leaking air. Fast. No way he'd get very far.

Swearing under his breath again, he watched the BMW disappear down the street, then reached for his radio.

"The suspect has escaped," he said. "He's headed north on Davis Avenue in a gray BMW, license plate unknown. My vehicle has been compromised."

"Roger, Fourteen. Patrol's been alerted and backup is on its way."

As he waited for his fellow deputies to arrive, Rafe went back into the garage. He found the switch for the overhead lights and took a closer look at the bodies inside the Jaguar.

Two males, approximately thirty years old, one with a tattoo of a spider on his neck. They both looked Slavic to Rafe, maybe Russian, which immediately brought to mind the Russian mob.

Were these guys connected?

Was it a contract killing?

Judging by the placement of the wounds, Rafe had no doubt it was a professional hit, but he'd failed to get a look at the shooter and had no idea if he'd been chasing another Russian or someone else entirely.

Knowing full well that he was breaking protocol, Rafe untucked and used his shirttail for protection as he reached for the passenger door handle. He'd have a heck of a time explaining any stray prints. Swinging the door open, he leaned inside and carefully checked the pockets of the victim closest to him.

Nothing. No wallet. Keys. Coins. Cigarettes. Not even a stick of gum. Rafe closed the door, then moved around to the driver's side and did the same thing with the other victim, getting the same results. The shooter had obviously cleaned house after he'd made the hit.

Rafe was about to close the car door when he spotted something on the floor mat near the driver's left foot.

A small, narrow slip of paper.

He reached down, snatched it up and tilted it toward the light, noting that it was a receipt for a fill-up at a Western Star service station just across town.

The time stamp read 2:45 a.m.

Rafe knew this could very well be the key to identifying the victims—and, by extension, the shooter. He also knew he should return it to the floor mat where he'd found it. But as the sound of approaching sirens filled his ears, he stuffed it into his jacket pocket and closed the car door.

A moment later, he stepped outside to greet his colleagues.

# *Chapter Three*

"Let's go through it one more time," Kate said.

Rafe balked. "Seriously?"

They were standing outside the auto repair shop. The roll doors had all been raised, the garage overheads lighting the yard as a flurry of crime scene techs moved in and out of the building.

"Look, Rafe, I know it's late, I know your shift is almost over, but if this is a mob hit, things could get sticky. I want to make sure all our bases are covered."

Rafe hadn't been surprised when his big sister, Kate, showed up at the scene. She was the Homicide Squad's best investigator, specializing in organized crime, and anything that smacked of a professional hit was usually passed off to her. She took her job very seriously and had the tenaciousness of a bulldog. She also got results and was the envy of every investigator on the squad.

Growing up in Kate's shadow had not been easy for Rafe. Ever since he'd graduated from college and had joined the department, he had been trying to live up to her reputation. He had put in extra hours, volunteered for event work, even worked the holidays no one else wanted to—all in hopes that he could make just the fraction of the impression that his sister had made. Unfortunately, nobody seemed to have taken notice of these sacrifices.

Including Kate.

"I don't care about working a little overtime," he told her. "I'm here for the duration."

It wasn't as if he could go anywhere anyway. His cruiser was being towed to the police garage as they spoke and he'd have to hitch a ride with one of the other deputies to get back to the station. He was bound to be here at least another hour.

"Good," Kate said. "So let's go through it again."

Rafe sighed. "As I said, I got the call out at about 0300 hours, give or take. Dispatch'll have the exact time."

"And no ID on the caller, right?"

"Right," Rafe said. "Although he said his apartment overlooks the lot."

Kate turned to her partner, a burly guy named Eberhart who stood nearby. Rafe got the feeling the guy had always regarded him as an irritant, and the feeling was mutual.

She signaled to him. "Charlie, get a canvass going on the apartment building. We need eyes on this thing."

Eberhart smirked. "Maybe your little bro here would like to volunteer. He's gotta be good for something."

Kate frowned. "Just get it started, all right?"

Eberhart gave her a salute. "Your wish is my command, O Great Leader." Then he turned and called to a couple of deputies who were huddled near their cruisers. "Look alive, knuckleheads, you've just been recruited."

The guy was a jackass.

When he was gone, Kate returned her attention to

Rafe. "Okay, so you responded to the call and arrived at approximately what time?"

"About 3:10. The place was dark, so I notified dispatch and decided to take a look around."

"Did you request backup?"

"We didn't even know for sure that shots had actually been fired at that point, so I didn't think backup was necessary."

Karen gave him a stony look. "And as a consequence, you almost got your rear end shot off and the suspect got away."

Rafe felt his cheeks go red. As a big sister, Kate had never been much of a nurturer, and it was just like her to point out any mistakes he may have made.

He frowned at her and said, "Are you going to bust my chops or let me talk?"

"Go on."

"When I got close to the building, I saw the door was ajar—"

"And you *still* didn't call for backup?"

Rafe sighed. "What exactly are you investigating here? Me or the murders? I told dispatch what I was doing every step of the way. I'm not exactly a rookie, you know."

Her frequent interruptions and insistence that he repeat his story made *him* feel like a suspect, as if she were expecting to expose him in some kind of lie. But he knew from previous conversations with her that this was merely a technique she employed to try to jog a witness's memory and draw out more details.

"Just tell me what happened when you got inside," she said.

"I saw the Jaguar, the bodies, then the shooting started."

"And where was the suspect?"

"Across the garage." Rafe pointed to the building behind them. "He came out that door and was gone before I could stop him."

"Did you at least get a look at him?"

"My answer hasn't changed since the last time you asked me. It was too dark. And he was wearing a hoodie."

"And no license number from the car he was driving?"

Rafe just gave her a look.

"Okay," she said, reading his unspoken message. She flipped her notebook shut and clipped her pen to it before putting it in her coat pocket. "Enough business for now. How are you doing? It isn't fun getting shot at."

"The only thing that's hurting is my pride," Rafe said. "I wish I could've caught the guy."

"Sounds like you did what you could, little brother. I wouldn't sweat it, if I were you."

"Thanks. What do you want me to do now?"

Kate waved a hand at him. "You're done here. Find your ride, go back to the station and write up your report."

"That's it?"

Her eyebrows went up. "You have a better idea?"

He shrugged. "I thought I might be able to assist somehow. Maybe help Eberhart with that canvass. Or help you inspect the crime scene." He paused. "I'm thinking the owner of the auto repair shop must be connected to these guys somehow. Otherwise, what were they doing here?"

Kate smiled. "You just can't wait to get rid of that uniform, can you?"

He hadn't realized it was so obvious. The last thing he wanted was to come across like an anxious puppy. At twenty-five, he was still young, but he'd always thought he was pretty mature for his age. Ready to take the next step in his career.

Maybe he'd been deluding himself.

"As I said, I just want to help."

Kate's smile disappeared and she suddenly looked very serious. "You can help by being patient and doing your job, Rafael. Your time will come, but it may not be as soon as you want it to be, and that's something you'll just have to live with."

Spoken like a true big sister, he thought. With just the right amount of condescension. Rafe had the urge to tell her where to stuff it, but remained professional.

"So are we good?" Kate asked.

"We're good," Rafe said.

She turned away and was about to start toward the garage when she stopped. "Just one last question."

"Which is?"

"You didn't touch the car, right? Didn't try to do a little investigating of your own?"

Rafe felt his heart kick up and thought about the gas receipt that was still in his pocket. He'd meant to give it to her, but now he wasn't so sure that was a good idea. Surely they'd be able to identify the bodies through fingerprint analysis, and his breach of protocol would never have to come to light.

If worse came to worst, he could give it to her later, claim he'd found it on the garage floor and in the excite-

ment that followed had forgotten about it. But handing it
over now would be a mistake. Especially after she had
just treated him like a redheaded stepchild.

"Rafe?"

He blinked at her. "Give me some credit, sis, I'm not
stupid enough to interfere with a crime scene."

"You're sure about that?"

"Yes," he lied. "Absolutely sure."

She studied him skeptically. The woman had always
had the uncanny ability to read him. Had caught him in
a number of lies as they grew up, but had always been
merciful enough not to tell their parents.

Kate was a good six years older than Rafe and that
gap had given her enough insight to avoid the pettiness
of sibling rivalry. She may not have been a nurturer,
but she wasn't a traitor, either. And nobody could ever
say that the Franco kids didn't look out for one another.

Even so, she really annoyed him sometimes.

"I'm going to trust you on that," she said. "But if any
fingerprints show up, you're on your own."

"They won't," he told her, relieved that he'd had the
wherewithal to use his shirttail for protection. "I promise."

She studied him a moment longer, then nodded and
walked away, heading into the garage.

When she was gone, Rafe let out a long breath and
tried not to feel too guilty.

CITY OF LIMERICK PUBLIC LIBRARY

## Chapter Four

"So is your sister seeing anyone these days?"

The deputy he'd snagged to drive him back to the station was a guy named Phil Harris. Harris was what qualified in the patrol division as an old-timer, although he couldn't yet be over forty. He'd been with the department since he was Rafe's age and had never progressed further than a RS-3 pay grade.

Harris was a good cop, but not the most ambitious guy in the department.

"Sorry, Phil, I don't keep track of her love life. You'd have to ask her."

Harris wasn't the first deputy to approach Rafe about Kate. One of the hazards of working in the same department as your sister was that you had to put up with every hot-to-trot single—and sometimes married—guy on the job, looking to get into her pants. Rafe would be the first to admit that Kate was a looker—she *did* have the Franco genes, after all—but the last thing he wanted to think about was who she may or may not be sleeping with.

"I was hoping you'd put in a good word for me," Harris said. "Let her know I'm interested."

What was this—high school?

Rafe shook his head. "First, I've got zero influence over Kate. And second, you might as well stand in line. You're about the fifteenth deputy who's asked me about her in the last month alone—and the competition is stiff."

"How stiff?"

"Like County Undersheriff stiff."

Harris's eyebrows shot up. "You're telling me she's been hitting it with Macon?"

"That's the rumor," Rafe said. "But, as I told you, I don't keep track. I'm having a hard enough time with my own love life."

Harris turned. "I thought you were dating that blonde in dispatch? The one with the big—"

"That's been over for months," Rafe said. "In fact, it was over before it really got started. No chemistry. Besides, I don't have time for romance. I've got to think about my career."

Harris snorted. "You sound like me about twenty years ago. I passed up on a perfectly good relationship—a gal I could have had a life with—all because I thought I didn't have time for that nonsense. Now look at me. I'm alone and going nowhere. And believe me, it isn't much fun."

Rafe found his mind wandering back to last night's dream and the girl he'd left behind. He shook the thought away.

"Boo-hoo," he said. "I'm still not going to set you up with my sister."

Harris grinned. "You saw what I was trying to do there, huh?"

"From a couple hundred yards away."

THEY WEREN'T TWO MILES from the station house when Harris's radio came to life.

"Dispatch to Unit Ten, do you read me?"

Harris snatched up his handset. "This is Ten. What do you got?"

"A possible 273 D in Forest Park. Can you respond?"

*Two-seventy-three D* was code for a domestic dispute, every deputy's least favorite type of call. Too often it was a husband being abusive to his wife, and Rafe had no tolerance for such men. It took everything he had to keep himself from giving the abuser a very painful life lesson.

Harris turned to him. "You in?"

Rafe was already supposed to be off the clock, but despite his reservations, he found that he still had a lot of pent-up energy coursing through his veins.

"Sure," he said.

Harris clicked the handset. "I'm on it, dispatch. Deputy Franco assisting. Give me the address."

Ten minutes later they pulled into Forest Park, an affluent section of St. Louis, not far from the Hill, where Rafe lived. The neighborhood featured a mix of 2-million and 3-million-dollar homes. Tudors. Dutch colonials. A couple of Cape Cods thrown in for good measure. It was the kind of place that made deputies like Rafe and Harris feel as if they were little more than servants to the rich and powerful.

Rafe had to fight against this feeling as they pulled up to the house in question, a two-story colonial. The front door was nearly the size of his entire apartment.

They got out and he waited as Harris knocked.

A voice on the intercom came to life. "Yes?"

"Sheriff's department," Harris said. "You called us about a domestic dispute?"

A moment later, the door opened and an elderly woman who was built like a bull terrier, ushered them inside.

"Come in, come in," she said. "The no-good creep is gone, but we want to file a formal complaint against him."

"Against whom?" Rafe asked as they followed her into a large foyer.

"The former man of the house. He broke in through the back door and raised quite a fuss."

"Is anyone hurt?"

"No, but it got pretty dodgy there for a minute."

Rafe nodded. "So who is this guy? Your husband?"

The old woman laughed. "Me? No. I'm just the hired help. But I had to scare him off with my scattergun. Couldn't have him treating Lisa like that."

"Lisa?"

"The lady of the house."

Just as she said this, they stepped into an expansive, tastefully furnished living room and Rafe's heart momentarily seized up as his gaze shifted to the woman sitting on a large white sofa in the center of the room.

The name *Lisa* was not uncommon, but the face that went with it was all too familiar. One that Rafe knew quite well but hadn't seen in over three years.

Except in his dream last night.

Call it fate or luck or serendipity, but the woman sitting on that sofa—the woman holding a sleeping child in her lap—was none other than Lisa Tobin.

His college sweetheart.

## Chapter Five

Lisa thought she must be dreaming.

Or simply mistaken.

But one of the deputies Beatrice had just escorted into the living room looked a lot like…

She swallowed, felt her pulse quicken. "Rafe? Rafe Franco?"

He stopped at the edge of the foyer, nearly frozen in place. He looked a little older—especially in that uniform—no longer the boy she had known in college, but a man. A man who had filled out with muscle and angular edges and broader shoulders. A man who had obviously spent the past few years working out and had the body to prove it.

But it was him, all right. It was Rafe.

A new and improved Rafe.

His eyes went wide at the sight of her, his voice tinged with disbelief. "Lisa?"

Lisa's mind suddenly flooded with images from the past—the pain, the heartbreak she'd felt in those days following their breakup. The sense of loss and confusion and, most of all, fear. Especially when she found out she was…

She stopped short, pulling herself back to the present. She carefully laid Chloe on the sofa and got to her feet, moving to Rafe, who now looked like the proverbial deer caught in the headlights.

She felt pretty much the same way.

"My God," she said, overcome by a kind of surreal numbness. They met in the middle of the room, Rafe pulling her into a hug as Bea and the other deputy looked on in surprise.

Lisa could feel Rafe's taught muscles pressing against her, and it gave her a small thrill to be back in his arms after all this time. It felt different, yet much the same.

His smell hadn't changed. The smell of his hair and his skin and the faint remnants of aftershave...

She reluctantly pulled away from him now, holding him at arm's length, trying to process this unexpected turn of events.

"What are you doing here?" she asked. "How...?"

"I've been living here for a few years now."

"I know your family's from St. Louis, but I thought you went to California after college. All that talk about beaches and surfing and..."

"That lasted about two months before I realized I really don't like sand. So I decided to go into the family business." He gestured. "I tried to get ahold of you when I came back. I even called your mother, but she had no idea where you'd gone."

Not surprising, Lisa thought. She and her mother had never gotten along.

She nodded. "It's a long story. And not worth repeating."

"When did you move to St. Louis?"

"About a year ago. I moved here with..." She hesitated, not wanting to talk about her marriage and divorce. As if talk of Oliver would spoil this moment. "As I said, it's a long story."

Now Rafe's gaze shifted to the sofa, to Chloe, his eyes clouding with confusion. "She can't be yours."

"I'm afraid so," Lisa said, her heart kicking up a notch. "All thirty pounds of her."

"How old is she?"

Lisa hesitated. "She was three last month."

She half expected him to start doing the math, but the significance of the timing seemed to be lost on him.

"I guess you were busy while I was pretending to be a beach bum," he said. "I'm happy for you, Leese. She's beautiful."

*Because she looks like you,* Lisa thought, suddenly overwhelmed by an intense, gut-wrenching guilt.

But this wasn't the proper time and place for confessionals. She wasn't sure if there *was* a proper time and place. Not over three years and another life later. Not when part of her past had been sprung on her without warning or preparation. This was a delicate situation that needed to be dealt with in private—with tact and sensitivity.

Lisa couldn't count the number of times she had wanted to pick up the phone and call Rafe. Tell him that long story in detail. But it was too much to handle right now, too much to process.

So she merely nodded in response and said, "Her name is Chloe."

She saw confusion in Rafe's eyes, and maybe a hint of disappointment, too. Not because of Chloe, but because she had somehow managed to move on with her life in a much bigger way than either of them could have expected back in college. A life that, despite the circumstances, hadn't included Rafe.

But before he could speak again, his partner said, "I hate to interrupt this happy reunion, folks, but we *are* here for a reason." He looked at Lisa. "Do you have a complaint to make?"

Lisa pulled herself from her thoughts and shook her head. "Calling you was Bea's idea. I don't really want to stir up any trouble."

"Oh, for God sakes," Bea said. "The creep broke into your house and started manhandling you."

"What creep?" Rafe asked, looking concerned. "The so-called former man of the house?"

Lisa nodded. "My ex. But it really wasn't that big of a deal. He has a few boundary issues, is all."

Rafe frowned. "Tell me about the manhandling part. Did he hurt you?"

Lisa hesitated. "He…he pawed me a little."

"Pawed you?" Bea cried, turning to Rafe. "He had her up against the wall and was slobbering over her like a Saturday-night sex fiend. And if I'm not mistaken, he had her by the throat at one point. As I told you, if I hadn't turned my scattergun on him, he'd probably still be here."

Now Rafe's partner stepped toward them. The name above his badge read Harris. "Ma'am, we can't force you to file a complaint, but it sounds to me as if things got pretty nasty here."

Lisa nodded reluctantly. "Maybe."

"And if I know anything about human nature," Harris continued, "this isn't the last you'll see of this creep. Especially if there's a child involved."

Lisa caught herself glancing at Rafe, but said nothing. Rafe, however, took this as a cue to say, "Has he ever hurt you before?"

"No. That's why I'm so hesitant to press charges. He can be violent, but he's never been violent with me. Or Chloe."

"So what changed?"

Lisa shook her head. "I don't know. He was drunk, maybe a little stoned. We've been separated for nearly a year and the divorce became final three months ago. But I was the one who filed and he still hasn't accepted it."

Rafe's brows furrowed. "You couldn't have been together very long."

"Long enough for me to realize what I'd gotten myself into."

"Meaning what?"

"As I said, it's a long story."

Rafe nodded. "You also said he can be violent. What did you mean by that?"

"The people he sometimes associates with are not exactly the nicest people in the world. I told him I didn't want them around the house, but he ignored me."

"That still doesn't explain the violent part."

Lisa hesitated again, not sure how much she should say. But she knew that if *she* didn't tell them, Beatrice would, so she might as well put it out there.

She slunk to the sofa. "He had a girlfriend while we were together. I only found out about her when she wound up in the hospital. A friend of mine works at County and saw him when they brought her in."

"For what?"

"A broken jaw. She had to have it wired shut."

Rafe's brows went up now. "And you think he did that to her?"

"I know he did. He told me as much when I confronted him. Said she was a loudmouthed little witch who didn't know when to shut up." Lisa sighed. "That was the last straw. I filed for divorce less than a week later."

She remembered the look in Oliver's eyes when he'd confessed to her. A look that she could only describe as pride. He had been proud of what he'd done to that poor girl. As if he were the king ape who had punished a disobedient subject.

That's when she realized he was a sociopath.

Filing those divorce papers had been another turning point in Lisa's life, and the moment she did it, she felt liberated. Yet, before then, she hadn't even realized she was a prisoner. She had allowed herself to block out the truth simply because Oliver had provided her and Chloe with a home. A family.

And the illusion of happiness.

When she thought about it now, however, maybe Oliver was right. Maybe she *was* a gold digger.

Rafe said, "I know you, Lisa. You always *did* try to avoid confrontations. But if this guy is starting to get violent with you, you need to press charges and file for a restraining order. Deputy Harris is right. He *will* be back."

"I can handle him," she said.

Bea snorted. "By letting him rub you up like a $2

tart? Seems to me *he* was the one doing all the handling."

Lisa felt her face flush, but said nothing. With Bea, you could always count on the truth, no matter how unflattering it might be.

"I'll tell you what," Rafe said, then moved to the sofa and sat next to her. "You don't have to file charges, but at least give me his name."

"Why?"

"I'll go talk to him. Tell him he needs back off."

"You'd better take my scattergun if you do," Bea said.

"Trust me, I've handled my share of tough guys. Most of the time they're more talk than action, and I'm pretty sure I can convince him to leave Lisa alone." He looked at Chloe, who was still fast asleep. "I assume you have custody?"

The question caught Lisa off guard. "Uh, yeah," she said. "Sole custody."

"Good. Then it shouldn't be a problem. What's your ex-husband's name?"

"Sloan," Bea said. "Oliver Sloan."

And to Lisa's surprise, Rafe and Deputy Harris exchanged a look that told her they'd heard the name before. The shock on their faces was hard to miss.

"Oliver Sloan?" Harris said. "You've got to be kidding me."

"You know him?" she asked.

"Better than I'd like to. There isn't anyone in law enforcement who doesn't. Not in St. Louis."

"I don't understand," she said. "Why?"

"Are you serious?"

"Yes," Lisa said. "Oliver's in real estate. He may have

problems and a poor choice of friends, but he's a glorified salesman. Why would the police care about that?"

"Because of what he sells," Rafe told her.

Lisa was bewildered. For all his faults, she'd never thought Oliver was involved in anything that would raise the interest of the police—except maybe a bit of real estate hanky-panky that she was convinced he was trying to pull. There was also the incident with his girlfriend, but the woman had never pressed charges.

"I don't understand."

"It's simple," Rafe said. "Your ex-husband is up to his eyeballs in organized crime."

# *Chapter Six*

Oliver Sloan.

When the name came out of the housekeeper's mouth, Rafe wasn't quite sure he'd heard her right.

Oliver Sloan was a bad man.

A very bad man.

Oliver Sloan was nothing less than the local king of organized crime. Drugs. Prostitution. Extortion. Gambling. If it was a thriving illegal enterprise, Sloan's involvement was a given.

The problem, unfortunately, was proving it. Despite years of trying, neither the Sheriff's department nor the St. Louis police had been able to come up with any evidence against him. Too many crime scenes had been sanitized. Too many witnesses had disappeared. Too many suspects had kept their mouths shut and taken their punishment, refusing to reveal who had given the orders.

Oliver Sloan had somehow managed to stay above it all. Had even presented himself to the public as an altruistic businessman. A real estate mogul. But as Harris had said, everyone in St. Louis law enforcement circles knew he was dirty. As dirty as they come.

What Rafe had a hard time stomaching, however,

was that Lisa had not only been involved with the guy, but also had actually been *married* to him. Had a *child* with him.

That was just one surprise too many.

Rafe had been feeling shell-shocked ever since he entered the house and saw Lisa sitting on that sofa. And the thought that Oliver Sloan had sired that child was almost too much to bear.

Rafe remembered what he and Lisa had meant to each other in college and how their breakup was largely due to their inability to commit. Even though it was only a little over three years ago, they had seemed so young then. So immature.

But they'd both done a lot of growing up since then. And apparently Lisa herself hadn't had much trouble committing. Not for a while, at least. She had gone straight from that breakup into the arms Oliver Sloan.

But how could she not know what kind of man he was? Was he that good at hiding it?

"Let me get this straight," Rafe said. "You had no idea your ex-husband was suspected of being part of a crime syndicate?"

Lisa shook her head in dismay. "You must have the wrong Oliver Sloan. I've sat in his office, watched him make deals. If anything mob related was going on, I think I would've noticed."

"His company's a front," Harris said. "But, trust me, you aren't the only one he's snookered. There are a few people on the city council who think he's God, and he's got more connections than the pope."

"I can't believe this," Lisa said.

"Well you'd better start wrapping your head around

it, because if this guy's giving you grief, you're in a lot more trouble than you—"

"That's enough, Phil." Rafe approached his partner. "We came here to help Lisa, not scare her half to death."

He turned to the sofa, chastising himself for letting this go on as long as it had. Lisa's expression was a mix of fear and disbelief.

"Look, Lisa, I won't kid you. You're probably making the right move, not pressing charges. But that doesn't mean Sloan won't answer for what he did here tonight."

"You're still going to talk to him?"

"As soon as I get off duty. I don't think a civil conversation will hurt, and I doubt he'll do anything stupid. He's not a stupid man."

Rafe felt Harris's gaze on him, probably wearing a look of disbelief himself. Probably thinking *Rafe* was the stupid one. But Harris had maintained a career as a patrol deputy by playing it safe, and what he thought right now wasn't of much interest to Rafe. He was merely a ride back to the station house.

Lisa got to her feet and approached them, pulling Rafe into another hug. He smelled the familiar scent of lavender and was pleased to know she still used the same perfume. He knew it was an odd thing to remember or be comforted by, but that scent had defined her somehow and smelling it now sent a cascade of memories tumbling through his head.

"Thank you," she said. "But be careful. I don't want you getting hurt because of me."

"Don't worry, I'm not the scrawny kid you knew in college."

She laughed. "Believe me, I noticed."

She squeezed him tighter, then pulled away, her look telling him that she suddenly felt awkward about this whole situation. They both needed to step back for a moment, evaluate this unexpected reunion, then proceed from there.

But Rafe hoped she wouldn't mind if he called her. "Is there a number where I can reach you?"

Their gazes connected for a moment, then Lisa moved to a table along the wall, opened a drawer and scribbled something on a scratch pad. Tearing the top sheet off, she folded it twice and handed it to him.

"My cell," she said. "But whatever you do, don't let Oliver get hold of it. Otherwise, he'll start texting me day and night."

"It's safe with me," Rafe said, then looked across the room at little Chloe, who was stirring on the sofa. She was indeed a beautiful child, a reflection of her mother.

Too bad her father was scum.

Rafe nodded toward the girl and said, "My grandmother always told me that children are God's way of granting us eternal life. You're a lucky woman, Leese. And I'm sure you're a wonderful mother."

She smiled wistfully. "Thank you, Rafe."

He gestured to Harris and they went back into the foyer. And as he turned at the front doorway for one last look at the girl he had once loved, he thought he saw tears in her eyes.

"ARE YOU OUTTA YOUR MIND, Franco?" The words flew out of Harris's mouth before he even had the cruiser's engine started. "You think you're just going to walk up to Oliver Sloan and tell him what's what?"

Rafe shrugged. "You have any better ideas?"

"Damn straight I do. Walk away and leave it alone. There's a reason we've never been able to pop this guy. Rumor has it he's even got the *mayor* in his pocket."

"I've never been big on rumors," Rafe said.

"Well, I hope you aren't too big on your job, either, because this guy can ruin your career with a snap of his fingers."

Rafe chuckled. "You watch too many crime shows."

"What I watch is my back, and you'd better watch yours, too. But if you *are* stupid enough to confront this clown, leave my name out of it. I don't need him knowing I'm alive."

Rafe wasn't surprised by Harris's lack of internal fortitude, but it grated on him nevertheless. "Come on, Phil, are you a cop or a glorified Girl Scout?"

"I'm a guy who knows his place in the world. And until somebody with more juice than me puts this stinker behind bars, I plan on doing my shift and keeping a low profile. I'd suggest you do the same."

"Sorry, no can do."

Harris shook his head in disgust and finally started the engine. "I don't know what that lady means to you, but after what I saw, I've got a pretty good idea. And if you don't start thinking with the brain in your head instead of the one in your pants, you're gonna be knee-deep in trouble."

Rafe supposed he had this coming, but it wasn't like that at all. He was just doing his job.

"Doesn't matter how many times you say it, Phil, I'm not going to change my mind. I don't see any harm in having a nice, civil talk with the man."

Harris huffed and put the cruiser in motion. "It's been a pleasure knowing you, hotshot. Say hello to St. Peter for me."

BACK AT THE STATION HOUSE, Rafe typed up an incident report on the shooting at the garage and dropped it off on Kate's desk. It had taken considerable effort to concentrate on the task, his mind continuously drifting back to Lisa.

Had Phil been right?

Was he thinking with his libido?

The scene in Lisa's living room kept replaying through his mind. Seeing her on that sofa with a sleeping child in her arms. Thinking how time had a way of expanding and contracting. How three years seemed like an eternity—and *had* been when you considered the changes they'd both been through. Yet as he had pulled her into that hug, it felt as if no more than a handful of minutes had passed since he'd last held her.

The feel of her body pressed against his had been so familiar, so comforting—so electric—that he'd had a hard time letting her go.

He thought about the dream he'd had. The one that continued to haunt him. Lisa holding him by the hand, urgently pulling him along a tree-lined trail toward a house near the water.

"Where are we going?" he had asked.

"I want to show you something. Something wonderful. Something glorious."

She continued to pull him along.

"What?" he said. "What is it?"

She threw her head back, the air around them coming alive with the music of her laughter, a high, sweet trill that had always filled him with joy. "It's a secret, silly. But you'll find out soon enough."

Before they reached that house, however, the house that held the secret, the sound of his alarm had jarred him awake. He had opened his eyes feeling cheated, the remnants of the dream swirling though his head, leaving him with a vague, undefined yearning in the middle of his chest.

In the middle of his heart.

It had been an effort to shake it off and go to work, but he'd done his best, never suspecting that he was about to walk right into that dream. To feel Lisa's touch again, after accepting long ago that she was gone for good.

Was he some kind of psychic?

Was it fate that had brought them together again?

Rafe didn't know or much care. It had been a shock, and a delight, and maybe Phil *was* right. Maybe he was letting his emotions, his desire, override his reason. But he had been trained to protect and serve, and who better to protect than someone he knew? Someone he had loved?

Oliver Sloan was a bad man—worse yet, a bad man with connections—but if Rafe didn't confront him about Lisa, who would?

Rafe had seen Sloan's type time and again, and he knew full well that unless someone called him on his behavior, it wouldn't change. Unless Sloan was told, in no uncertain terms, to leave Lisa alone, he would be back, and the violence would escalate.

It always did.

So when Rafe finished his report and dropped it on Kate's desk, he didn't bother to shower, didn't bother to change out of his uniform. He ran a quick address check, then went straight to the department garage and signed out a new patrol car.

Then he headed across town to talk to Oliver Sloan.

## *Chapter Seven*

Sloan despised himself sometimes.

It didn't happen often, and it was never because of the things he'd done—and he had done quite a few sketchy things in his life.

No, this occasional self-loathing came down to one thing. How he felt. About Lisa, in particular.

His entire life, Sloan had never had trouble getting women. He was, after all, a good-looking guy—something he'd been well aware of since his second birthday.

His mother used to dote on him, call him her little movie star. The girls in middle and high school used to stare at him as he walked the halls, hoping he'd grace them with a glance of his piercing blue eyes. And if you were to put him in a lineup with Brad Pitt and George Clooney, well, let's just say those two cretins would have to fight for attention.

This wasn't ego at work. Sloan merely saw what he saw when he looked in the mirror, and knew what he knew. And when he snapped his fingers, the women came running as if they hadn't had a meal in a week and were just dying to get a taste of Oliver Sloan.

But that Lisa, she was different.

No amount of good looks and charm could crack its way through that cement wall she'd built around her, and that aggravated Sloan no end. Yet she had gotten so deep under his skin that he felt an itch every time he was around her. A desire so strong that he lost control. Almost felt powerless in her presence.

And Sloan didn't like feeling powerless.

Sloan despised feeling powerless.

As a consequence, at those moments—as rare as they were—he despised himself.

HE HAD WANTED HER the moment he met her, and could still remember the day with great clarity.

He had taken a field trip to the Chicago branch of his real estate firm, and the moment he walked in the door, he saw her, sitting there behind the reception desk. A fresh-faced twenty-three-year-old with a look of innocence that could only be measured in terms of what it did to his body.

Sloan had seen his share of beautiful women in his time, but the sight of Lisa had nearly stopped his heart— a reaction no woman had ever before had on him.

First, there was that face. Like an exquisitely lit photograph of feminine perfection, with flawless white skin, cobalt-blue eyes, and a pouty mouth that was made to do naughty things to naughty boys.

Then there was the body. He couldn't see much behind the reception desk, but what he saw sent a rush of adrenaline coursing through his veins, and he knew he had to have her.

She smiled as he stepped off the elevator, and said, "May I help you?"

Apparently, she hadn't gotten the memo that he'd be visiting today.

"I'm Oliver Sloan," he said, thinking she must be new if she didn't already know that. "I'm here to see Gary Orbach."

She got to her feet then and held out a hand to shake. "Mr. Sloan, I'm Lisa Tobin, and I want thank you for giving me a chance here. This job couldn't have come at a better time."

Sloan didn't do the hiring or firing—that was beneath him—but he was all too happy to take credit for hiring her. To his surprise, however, now that she was standing up, he could see a slight bulge in the front of her dress.

Was she pregnant?

Not that this killed the effect. In fact, in some odd way it made her even more attractive to him. Maybe because it meant she wasn't a stranger to the kind of carnal activities he was imagining at that very moment.

To his further surprise, he found himself checking her hand for a wedding ring.

There wasn't one.

So did this mean she was one of those unconventional brides who had decided to forgo wearing one in some lame attempt to show her independence? Or was she simply not married at all? And if she wasn't married, was there a boyfriend in the picture? A biological father?

The fact that he even cared was a bit disconcerting. He had never hesitated to hit on a married woman. He was, after all, Oliver Sloan, and nine times out of ten such advances were successful. In fact, *eight* times out of ten even the husband knew what was going on and had the good sense to keep his mouth shut and stay out of the way.

But for some unknown reason, Sloan wanted this one—this Lisa Tobin—this specimen of perfection with the alluring pregnancy bump—to be unattached.

Because he knew the moment he saw her that he had to have her all to himself.

From now until forever.

THEIR COURTSHIP had been short, but fraught with frustration. For Sloan at least.

He quickly discovered that Lisa wasn't like other women. Was not impressed by his looks and his money and his standing in the community. And this, Lord help him, made her even more attractive to him.

It wasn't until long after their separation that he realized that it must have been a ploy. She had manipulated him into wanting her. Wanting her to the point where he broke his cardinal rule and got down on one knee and asked her to marry him.

They had been dating several weeks by then. Dates that had started out tentative and full of hesitation on her part. She had told him that she didn't ever want him to feel that she was taking advantage of him because of the baby. And he had believed her. For no other reason than he was madly, head-over-heels in love with her— an emotional malady that he had always scoffed at.

The powerlessness he felt when he was around her niggled at him, worried him. Made him wonder if he was losing his edge. He remained on his best behavior around her because he didn't want to upset her, take the chance of losing her.

In those first weeks he had even taken a hiatus on bedding other women. And when he finally got *Lisa* into bed, it was the most sublime experience he'd ever been part of. He didn't know where or how she had learned to do what she did, but he didn't care as long as it was with him.

And when she said "yes" to marriage, it was the happiest day of his life.

IT WASN'T UNTIL the baby was born, five months later, that things began to go sour. After Chloe came into the world, Lisa became less attentive and a lot less interested in taking him to bed.

At first he blamed it on postpartum depression, but he quickly grew impatient with her. A man should only have to put up with so much.

And her obsession with Chloe was relentless. Didn't she realize she had a husband to tend to? Didn't she understand that it was only his generosity that had allowed her to spend so much time with the child?

He had offered to get Chloe a nanny, so that Lisa would be free of the responsibilities of raising the kid, but Lisa had balked at the idea. Said she was only interested in raising Chloe herself, and wished that Sloan would be more attentive to the little girl he had promised to raise.

He didn't remember making such a promise, but he supposed somewhere in the haze of bedding Lisa and asking her to marry him, he must have made noises in that direction. But surely she had to understand that such promises were never meant to be kept. He was all too happy to support the kid, but he didn't have time to be developing a relationship with her, any more than his father had had time for him.

This seemed to be a sticking point with Lisa, however, and he soon realized that she didn't love him the way she once had. That the freshness of spirit that was there in the beginning of their relationship had all but disappeared.

And this made him need her even more. He found himself constantly consumed by thoughts of her, wondering what he could to do to regain what they'd lost. He found himself taking out his frustration on the other women he bedded. Had even broken the jaw of one of them when she'd had the audacity to ask if Lisa cared that he had strayed.

And when Lisa found out about it and confronted him, he had been open and honest with her in hopes that she would realize what she was doing to him.

Instead, she had gotten crafty. She'd begun sneaking around in his personal files and had told him that if he didn't grant her a divorce, he would pay the consequences.

It was only then that Sloan realized he had been used. That she had only pretended not to care about his money. That there was undoubtedly another man out there telling her what to do. How to manipulate Sloan.

Yet, oddly enough, none of that mattered.

He still wanted her, more than ever. The year of separation had been sheer torture for him and he couldn't convince himself that it was over.

No matter what it took, he would get her back. And this time, it would be on *his* terms, not hers. He was,

after all, the man in this relationship and it was time he
made her realize that.

This morning may have backfired with that nosy
maid of hers brandishing a shotgun, but there would be
other days. Other mornings.

And sooner or later, Sloan would have what right-
fully belonged to him.

# *Chapter Eight*

It wasn't a surprise that Sloan didn't live in a house. No, a guy like him only *owned* houses. Living in one would be far too conventional for him. He was a mover and a shaker who considered himself to be movie-star cool. So what better way to prove it than to live in a hotel suite?

But not just *any* hotel. Sloan lived in one of the most luxurious establishments in St. Louis. The one with a five-room penthouse suite priced at four grand a night, with a name fit for a king.

*The Palace.*

Rafe had only been here on a couple previous occasions. Callouts in the middle of the night when some of the guests had gotten unruly. The hotel staff usually handled such matters in-house, with their private security squad, but sometimes things got out of hand and the Sheriff's department was called in to clean up.

Rafe had always been a meat-and-potatoes kind of guy. Not one for fancy trappings and over-the-top displays of wealth and power. So when he stepped into the Palace lobby, he took in its stark, postmodern decor with a jaundiced eye, thinking about how much meat and potatoes you could buy just by auctioning off its contents.

You could probably feed a small, developing country.

Rafe had no problem with wealth—people deserved to be rewarded for their hard work—but such displays got him wondering about the world's priorities. And it didn't surprise him that Oliver Sloan would choose a place like this to live.

What better cover for his thuggery?

But then Sloan was a new kind of thug. One who used money and power and influence rather than guns—unless, of course, they were absolutely necessary. He wore the finest clothing, dined at the most popular restaurants, smiled for photographs with the elite of St. Louis, pretending to be an upstanding citizen, as he worked his shady deals in back rooms and private offices.

Rafe knew that if he tried to go through channels to see Sloan, if he went to the front desk and sent up a message, he would be turned away. And if he pressed it, if he insisted on being seen, then Sloan's cronies would be alerted, management and security staff would appear out of nowhere and Rafe's boss would be dragged out of bed by a call from someone on high asking how some insignificant sheriff's deputy had the audacity to show up on Sloan's doorstep at six o'clock in the morning.

That was a scene Rafe would just as soon avoid. So the moment he walked into the hotel, he turned to the bellman on duty and gestured abruptly.

"Follow me," he said.

The bellman's eyes widened slightly at the sight of Rafe's uniform, but he didn't balk, didn't resist. Instead, he nodded politely and came around from his desk and followed Rafe straight to the bank of elevators on the far side of the lobby.

Rafe pushed the button, waited for the doors to open, then gestured the bellman inside. "After you."

As they turned to face the closing doors, Rafe said, "Take me to the penthouse."

He had known that getting there would require special access and only a bellman or the hotel manager would have the key.

But now the bellman balked. He just stood there without moving.

So did the elevator.

"Well?" Rafe said.

"I, uh, I'm not supposed to let anyone up there."

Rafe had been expecting this.

"I feel your pain, but you're just going to have to steel yourself and make an exception."

"But we have strict orders from Mr. Sloan to—"

"You see this uniform?" Rafe said.

"Uh…yeah."

"You think I'm wearing it just for fun?"

"Uh…no."

"I'm a deputy with the St. Louis Sheriff's Department, and I don't care what Mr. Sloan ordered you to do. When I tell you to take me to the penthouse, you'd better take me to the penthouse or you'll find yourself facing a possible obstruction of justice charge. Do you want that?"

The bellman swallowed, said nothing. He just reached into his pocket, took out a key card and slipped it into a slot on the elevator panel, punching a button with his index finger.

The elevator glided into motion. Rafe put his trust

in the numbers that lit up the panel above the doors to be sure they were actually moving.

When they reached the penthouse, a faint bell chimed and the doors slid open again. Beyond them was a long, richly appointed hallway, bathed in white. There was another set of doors at the far end, two dark-suited guards keeping watch in front of them.

Rafe thanked the bellman and started down the hall, wondering if he should have brought a pair of hiking shoes for the trek. He once again marveled that Lisa had been married—if only briefly—to a guy this far out of touch with reality, and decided he'd definitely have to get that "long story" on record.

Not that she owed him any explanations. But he was curious, and hoped she'd be willing to share.

He was about halfway down the hall when one of Sloan's guards said, "Excuse me, deputy, but we weren't informed of your arrival. Do you have an appointment?"

"It's six o'clock in the morning," Rafe said. "Who makes an appointment at six o'clock in the morning?"

"Then I can only assume you got off on the wrong floor." The guy may have looked classy and all in his suit, but the tenor and tone of his voice betrayed him as just another thug.

"You can assume all you want," Rafe told him. "But I'm here to see Mr. Sloan about his early-morning activities. So wake him up if you have to."

The thug smiled as Rafe came to a stop in front of him. "I'm getting the impression you don't know how this works."

"You *should* be getting the impression that I don't care. Tell Sloan I'm here."

"You aren't too smart, are you?" the other guard said.

"Smart enough to make it through college, for what it's worth. What year did *you* drop out?"

"Hey, Frank," the first one said, apparently addressing his partner. "We got ourselves a comedian."

"I think you're right," Frank said.

"Remember that funny guy out in Vegas? The one who kept cracking jokes about your crew cut?"

"The guy who kept calling me G.I. Joe? Yeah, I remember."

"Wasn't he a fed or something?"

"Narcotics detective," Frank said. "And come to think of it, he tried to get in to see Mr. Sloan without an appointment, too."

"You ever find out what happened to him?"

Frank shrugged. "Last I heard, the brace was off, but he was still in physical therapy."

Now they both turned their gazes on Rafe, their faces abruptly hardening, their eyes full of quiet menace. These were two men who took their jobs very seriously and answered only to one master.

And it wasn't Rafe.

He said, "Come on, guys, why the hostility? All you have to do is open that door and step aside and let me talk to your boss. I'll even apologize for the 'dropout' crack."

Rafe knew he was wasting his breath, but he was simply waiting for one of them to make the inevitable move. They were done talking and ready to introduce Rafe to their fists, and he was trying to decide which one would take the lead.

As is turned out, they moved simultaneously, like a

well-choreographed dance duo, one reaching for Rafe's jacket as the other took a swing.

But Rafe hadn't spent the past few years just lifting weights. A month after joining the department, he had signed up for a self-defense class, led by a guy who specialized in Krav Maga. He had gotten so good at it that he now led the class himself, every Tuesday and Thursday night.

It took four precise moves to put Frank out of commission and pin his partner to the floor, all without breaking much of a sweat.

Now Frank was unconscious and the other one was looking up at Rafe with eyes that were no longer filled with menace, but with the kind of desperation that only a man fearing for his life can produce.

But Rafe wasn't a sadist. He gave the guy a polite warning, then released him and stepped toward the hotel suite doors.

"Don't worry," he said, "I'll announce myself."

RAFE HAD BEEN EXPECTING more thugs inside the suite, but was pleasantly surprised when no one came rushing forward.

The suite, which was triple the size of his apartment, looked like something out of a lifestyle magazine, with a flawless white carpet and a handcrafted sofa and chairs that were clearly more expensive than the pieces he sat on at home.

Off to his right was a full kitchen featuring a state-of-the-art espresso bar. Being a Franco, Rafe was a sucker for a good shot, so it immediately caught his attention.

To the left were two open doorways that he assumed

led to bedrooms. And judging by the sounds emanating from one of them, and the long trail of male and female clothing leading directly to it, his assessment was accurate.

He didn't doubt that it was Sloan in there. The guy had worked up an appetite with Lisa and was now quenching it with someone who would give him what Lisa hadn't been willing to. They were making quite a racket, those two, so Rafe went to the espresso bar, made himself a shot, then settled in on the sofa to wait for them to finish up.

# Chapter Nine

"Who the hell are *you?*" Sloan barked.

He stood naked in the bedroom doorway, his muscular body bathed in sweat, a scowl on his face as he stared at Rafe with eyes full of rage. He was about thirty-five, with short dark hair, and held a pair of boxer shorts in his right hand—which he had scooped up from the floor before realizing Rafe was there.

Lisa had said he was drunk when he came to her house, and the effects of the alcohol—and whatever else he was ingesting—didn't seem to have worn off.

Rafe set the espresso cup on the coffee table and got to his feet, nodding to the scattered clothes. "You want to get dressed, Mr. Sloan? I can wait."

But Sloan obviously wasn't embarrassed by his nakedness. He made no move to cover himself. "How did you get in here?"

"Your guards let me in."

"*What?*"

"I was as surprised as you are," Rafe said. "I guess my people skills are a lot better than I thought they were."

Sloan finally started pulling the boxers on. "Do you have a warrant?"

"For what? I'm not here to search the premises. I just want to talk."

Sloan scooped up a pair of dark slacks. "Then make an appointment. I want you out of here. Now."

Rafe smiled. "You know, it's funny. I'm pretty sure that's what Lisa Tobin wanted when you paid her a visit early this morning. Yet it took a shotgun to get you to leave."

"Lisa?" Sloan said incredulously. "You're here because of Lisa?"

"You assaulted her, Mr. Sloan. Physically."

Sloan scowled again. "I didn't do any such thing." He started jabbing his legs into the pants, angrily punctuating his words. "My ex-wife is a pathological liar. And you're an idiot if you believe a word she says."

"Oh? What about the housekeeper? Beatrice. Was she lying, too?"

Sloan scoffed. "Do you know I hired that ungrateful witch? She's as nutty as Lisa is."

"Maybe so, but Ms. Tobin seemed very upset, and I have a hard time believing she was lying about what happened."

"Lisa Tobin is very good at manipulating men into thinking she's some kind of victim. But what she really does is use them, then discard them when they're no longer useful to her."

"Or maybe she just doesn't like being cheated on," Rafe said. "By men who brutalize their mistresses."

Sloan was in the middle of buttoning his shirt now, but stopped abruptly and looked at Rafe. "You're gonna want to watch your step, deputy."

"Or what?"

Sloan moved toward him and Rafe instinctively dropped his hand to his Glock.

"How old are you?" he said. "Twenty-five, twenty-six? You're barely out of diapers and you think you know it all, don't you? Think because you wear that fancy uniform and that star on your chest that you can barge into a man's home and make accusations about his character."

"You can't be that clueless about your reputation," Rafe said.

"My reputation? I'm a businessman."

"Is that what they're calling it these days?"

Sloan raised his right hand and held his thumb and forefinger in a pinch, leaving less than a quarter-inch of space between them. "You're that close to getting your butt kicked, hotshot."

"By whom? Frank and his girlfriend in the hall? They've already tried and it didn't work out so well."

Sloan studied him a moment. "I've got to admit you've got brass in your pants, deputy. But I can't help wondering why you're really here."

"Just to tell you to back off. Leave Lisa alone."

Sloan smiled. "So it's Lisa now, is it? Did she bat those baby blues at you and get you all aquiver inside?" He paused. "Or maybe it's more than that. Maybe she gave you a little taste of the goods and you came up here to play knight in shining armor."

"You really like to hear yourself talk, don't you?"

Sloan shrugged. "I can think of worse ways to spend the day."

"Well, maybe you should listen for a minute. If you

think you can walk into a house, a house with your own child in it, and—"

"My own child?" Sloan chuckled. "You don't know *anything,* do you?"

"I know it's my job to butt heads with jerks like you," Rafe said. "And if you think you can terrorize women without consequences, keep pushing, buddy. I'm all too happy to push back."

Sloan stared at him and Rafe returned the stare, the tension between them palpable. Volatile. Part of Rafe hoped that Sloan would make a move. Give him a reason to bring out the cuffs.

But Sloan was no dummy. He suddenly relaxed. Finished buttoning his shirt. "As I said, deputy, I didn't go anywhere near that house this morning. I've been in this suite since ten o'clock last night, and I've got half a dozen witnesses who'll vouch for me. Including the little gal you just heard moaning and groaning." He grinned. "And she wasn't faking it."

"You're pathetic, you know that?"

"Be that as it may," Sloan said, "I live in a world you can only dream about, and that gives me certain privileges. You made a big mistake coming here, hotshot. I figure by this time tomorrow morning you'll be looking for a way to pay your rent, and you're usefulness to my ex-wife will have come to an abrupt, unceremonious end."

"Or I could just beat the crap out of you and claim self-defense. Arrest you for attempted assault on a sheriff's deputy."

Sloan smiled again. "Ah, but you wouldn't do that, would you? I know your kind. You're Deputy Dudley

Do-Right, who helps damsels in distress and believes in the letter of the law." He tucked his shirt in and turned, heading toward the doorway he had emerged from. When he reached it, he turned back, still smiling. "I think you can find your way out, deputy. And when you go, be sure to tell Frank and Bobby that their services are no longer—"

"Hey, baby, what's the holdup?" A naked woman with tousled blond hair appeared in the doorway behind him. "Do you want another toot or not?"

She was carrying a baggie full of white powder, her pinky extended toward him, the hollow of her long, scarlet-colored fingernail loaded with the stuff.

Rafe couldn't believe his good fortune. Fate once again stepping in when he least expected it, giving him an excuse to draw his weapon and point it at Sloan and the woman.

"Down!" he shouted. "On your knees! Now!"

The woman yelped in surprise, dropping the baggie as Sloan gave her a murderous look, then threw his hands in the air and sank to the carpet.

"Don't shoot, don't shoot!" she cried, quickly mimicking Sloan.

As she dropped to her knees, Rafe reached for the radio still clipped to his shoulder and flicked it on. "Dispatch, I've got a 190 in progress and I need backup."

He gave them the address, then gestured to the clothes that remained on the floor and told Sloan's companion to put them on.

Sloan looked up at him, fire in his eyes. "Better start getting that resume in order, hotshot. And I sure hope you've got experience cleaning toilets, because when

I'm done with you, that's about the only job you'll be able to get."

"Stop," Rafe said. "You're scaring me."

But as he looked into Sloan's eyes, he could see that this was far from over.

# *Chapter Ten*

Lisa wasn't able to go back to sleep that morning.

After Rafe and his partner left, Beatrice had scooped up Chloe from the sofa and carried her upstairs, announcing that she was headed back to bed.

"I bought some eggs if you want breakfast," she said. "And the coffeemaker's set on automatic."

Lisa knew Bea wasn't happy with her. Her words had come out in a clipped monotone that telegraphed her displeasure. Bea felt that failing to press charges against Oliver was a mistake. That he had gotten away with too much in his life because people were afraid of him.

And maybe she was right. Maybe Lisa *should* have pressed charges. But, until tonight, Oliver had never laid a finger on her and she knew that much of what had happened here had been fueled by the drugs and alcohol.

There was actually a time when Oliver had been sweet to her. Kind. And despite that sense of menace she felt around him now, despite the episode with that other woman—the one that had led to their divorce—Lisa had a hard time equating the man she had married with the picture Rafe and his partner had painted.

So when it came time to pull the trigger—to use one of Oliver's favorite phrases—she couldn't bring herself to do it. A mistake, perhaps, but it was *her* mistake and she would own it, just as she owned all the others she'd made.

Her inability to sleep, however, had nothing to do with Oliver. The significance of what had happened with him in this room paled in comparison to what had followed.

Lisa had long ago given up on the thought of ever seeing Rafe Franco again, had convinced herself that he no longer mattered to her. She had assumed that he had stayed in California and was spending his weekends on the shores of Malibu or Zuma Beach or one of the other sun-and-fun hot spots they'd seen on television.

But suddenly here he was, the man she had loved so fervently. The first—and only—real love she had ever known. He was no longer a confused, idealistic college student, but a grounded sheriff's deputy who commanded a room when he entered it.

The transformation Rafe had undergone was startling to Lisa, but in a good way. Three years ago, when they parted ways, she had been convinced that he was too young and restless to commit to her. That trying to tie him down would be a mistake, even if she loved him more than anyone she'd ever known.

It was *because* of that love that she had let him go. Had even pretended that she, too, was restless. That she, *too,* wanted to explore the possibilities of life. They had talked about going their separate ways many times in that last year of college, and she knew that Rafe needed time to find himself.

So she had given it to him, even after she found out she was pregnant.

When the doctor sprang the news, Lisa's first instinct had been to try to contact Rafe. To tell him he was about to be a father. Rafe was just the type of guy to drop everything, to put his life on hold and do the right thing. To marry her and help her raise their child.

But the last thing she wanted was a marriage based on obligation. Her parents had married because of *her,* and they had been miserable for as long as she could remember.

So she had never picked up that phone, had never sent him that email. Had convinced herself that *this* was the right thing to do. To grant Rafe his freedom.

But seeing him walk into her living room had changed everything. Seeing him look down at Chloe and smile, hearing him tell her how beautiful Chloe was, had made her realize that the choice she'd made might very well have been the wrong one. That it wasn't fair to Rafe.

Or to Chloe.

But after more than three years, how could she possibly break the news to him? She couldn't simply blurt out, "Oh, by the way, Chloe is yours."

She had to find the right moment.

The perfect moment.

But when, she wondered, would that be?

"So TELL ME ABOUT that hunk of a deputy," Bea said.

She had awakened an hour later in a much better mood. Had poured herself a cup of coffee and sat at the kitchen table, where Lisa was staring forlornly at a bowl of fruit and yogurt.

"He's just a guy I knew in college," Lisa said, trying to downplay the relationship. Bea had no idea that Chloe was that "hunk" of a deputy's baby. Nobody did.

Bea grinned. "*Knew?* As in the biblical sense?"

It was just like the woman to get straight to the point. Lisa didn't bother to respond, but she felt her face grow warm and Bea's grin widened.

"Atta girl, Leese. Believe me, if I were forty years younger, that's one piece of man-candy I wouldn't mind taking a tumble with."

"That was a long time ago," Lisa said.

"Oh, who cares. At least you've got the memory. And I'll bet he was pretty memorable, too."

Lisa felt a smile coming on and tried but failed to stifle it. "I won't deny we were pretty good together."

"Well," Bea said, "he seemed happy to see you, and I noticed he didn't have a ring on his finger."

Lisa had to admit that she'd noticed, too. And the moment she did, she had experienced an inexplicable feeling of relief, and maybe a little hope. But then her mother—who was a virulently unhappy woman—had always said that hope was for dreamers.

Besides, Lisa wasn't interested in trapping Rafe now any more than she had been after college.

"I'm not looking to get married again," she said to Bea. "Not after this last disaster."

"Well, I can't blame you for that. But don't let one nasty apple spoil the entire barrel for you. Besides, I've got a feeling Deputy Studly will keep to his promise and do a little damage repair on your behalf."

"And what if it doesn't stick?" Lisa asked.

"Then you do what you should've done in the first place and file charges against that no-good ex of yours."

"And what if that doesn't stick, either?"

"Then I guess Mr. Oliver Sloan'll find out just how good of a shot I really am…"

# Chapter Eleven

"I don't think you realize just how dangerously close you are to getting yourself fired."

Harold Pine was captain of the Patrol Division, a thirty-year veteran who hadn't been in the field in more than half that time.

He sat behind his desk, his tailored uniform masking his considerable bulk. There was little he could do, however, about his slightly misshapen dome, which he regularly shaved bald in an attempt to look slick—an attempt that failed on many different levels.

Rafe shifted in the chair in front of Pine's desk. "I was just doing my job," he said. Which wasn't strictly true, since Lisa hadn't filed a complaint against Sloan.

"Your job?" Pine barked. "Your job is to follow protocol. Nothing more, nothing less."

After calling for backup at Sloan's hotel suite, Rafe had done a quick sweep of the rooms and found another cache of cocaine, along with several tabs of what looked like ecstasy. But now Sloan's girlfriend was claiming the drugs were hers, and his attorney was screaming illegal search and seizure, charging that Rafe had been in the hotel suite not on police business, but as a private citizen.

In other words, he had been trespassing and had no probable cause for the search. And to Rafe's surprise, not only had the judge at the morning arraignment agreed with Sloan's attorney, but so did Pine.

"No, what you did was screw up, Franco. I talked to Deputy Harris and I know exactly what happened. You aren't the first cop to get his weenie in a knot over a woman, but you chose the wrong ex-husband to go after."

"Why?" Rafe said. "Everyone in the department knows Sloan is dirty. This was our chance to put him away."

"There's just one small problem with that."

"Which is?"

Pine smiled patiently, then got to his feet. "There are some people who want to talk to you."

He gestured and Rafe stood up, following him out the door. They moved down a long corridor to a conference room, Rafe wondering what was going on until Pine threw open the door to reveal who was inside.

The were four people seated at the conference table, two of whom Rafe had seen earlier that morning: his sister Kate and her partner, Charlie Eberhart. Sitting beside them was Kate's boss, Captain Weeks, and at the head of the table was none other than the County Undersheriff himself—the man Kate was rumored to be dating—Daniel Macon.

As the door closed behind Rafe, Macon gestured. "Have a seat, deputy."

Rafe did as he was told. He glanced at Kate, but her face was a mask. He had no earthly idea what this was all about, but figured he would soon find out.

And he knew it couldn't be good.

Once Rafe was settled in his seat, Macon said, "I'm sure you're aware, Deputy Franco, that Oliver Sloan has long been a target of this department."

Rafe nodded. "I know he's been a thorn in our side for quite some time."

"And I'm sure," Macon continued, "that you thought arresting Sloan on a petty drug charge was a way to put him behind bars where he belongs."

"I didn't go there to arrest him," Rafe said. "Just talk to him. I saw the drugs, and did my duty."

"Be that as it may," Kate said, "you also jeopardized a nine-month-long investigation."

Surprised, Rafe swiveled his head toward her. "Investigation?"

"The woman you arrested along with Sloan was an undercover operative for this department. She's been one of my confidential informants for years."

"That's right, genius," Eberhart told him. "You just cowboyed your way into an ongoing investigation and nearly blew the whole thing."

Rafe was speechless. What was there to say? No words he uttered would change what had happened.

But how could he be blamed for this? He may have gone to Sloan's hotel suite for personal reasons, but the bust he'd made had been righteous. By the book.

Was he about to be hung out to dry for doing his duty?

"Fortunately," Macon said, "the judge saw fit to drop the charges against him. A judge we think could very well be in Oliver Sloan's pocket. Only this time it worked to our advantage."

Kate leaned forward. "But do you see the stakes we're dealing with here? This isn't just about Oliver Sloan. It's about the network he's built and all the people who are beholden to him."

"Including his ex-wife," Eberhart said.

Rafe stiffened, felt the hairs on the back of his neck rise. Were they suggesting that Lisa was part of Sloan's criminal organization?

That was ridiculous.

First, Rafe knew she'd never get involved in any illegal activities—not now, not ever. Three and a half years couldn't have changed her *that* much. And second, her reaction to the truth about her ex-husband's activities had been genuine. Even if she had suspected that Sloan was up to no good, it was obvious that such suspicions had been vague and ill-formed, and nothing to do with organized crime.

"We understand his ex is an old girlfriend of yours," Macon said.

Rafe nodded. "We dated in college."

"And where was that?"

"University of Illinois."

"He pretty much kept her under wraps, too," Kate said with a smile. "Only brought her out here once during all that time and I never even got a chance to meet her. I guess he didn't want to expose her to the fighting Francos."

Rafe chafed. "Why does any of this matter?"

Kate's boss, Captain Weeks, spoke up. "Because," he said, "we think this unexpected reunion is extraordinarily fortunate. A turn of events that could be used to our advantage."

Rafe felt his gut tighten. "What do you mean?"

"It's simple," Macon told him. "We want you to turn her. We want you to nurture the relationship and convince her to be our confidential informant."

Rafe couldn't quite believe what he was hearing.

"So let me get this straight," he said. "You want me to betray a friendship in order to get at Sloan?"

"Not betray," Kate said. "Merely talk her into helping us."

"What about the blonde? Your CI?"

"Unfortunately, I've already heard from her. Even though she claimed the drugs, she says that Sloan blames her for the bust and told her to get lost. She thinks it'll be a long time before she can get him to trust her again."

Rafe considered this for a moment. He had no intention of agreeing to their demand, but he was curious what they figured they could get out of it.

"And if I were to turn Lisa," he said, "what exactly would you expect her to do?"

Macon spread his hands out. "Judging by that domestic call, it's obvious that Sloan still harbors some feelings for his ex-wife and his child. We'd want her to encourage his affection and try to—"

Rafe abruptly stood up. "You're out of your mind if you think I'd do that to her."

"We aren't really asking, Deputy Franco. Your future with the department could well depend on your decision."

Rafe shot Kate a look, surprised that she would be part of this.

She gave him a brief, apologetic shrug, as if to say

*This wasn't my call,* then quickly looked down and studied the tabletop.

"Well, Deputy Franco? You do value your future here, don't you?"

"Not if it means taking advantage of someone I care about. I took this job to help people, not manipulate them. That's the kind of thing Sloan would do."

"Law enforcement can sometimes be dirty business," Captain Weeks said. "And we have to fight fire with fire."

Rafe shook his head. "Not with me, you won't."

Then he turned and walked out the door.

KATE CAUGHT UP TO HIM in the hallway. "Rafe, wait."

He stopped, turned, his body stiff with fury. It was bad enough they were asking him to betray Lisa, but he couldn't quite fathom why his own sister would be part of it.

"I know this stinks," she said. "And I'm sorry you got caught in the middle of it. But the truth is, you kind of put yourself there."

"I busted a man for possession of drugs. Last I heard, that was considered a good thing."

"You have to understand the stakes here, Rafe. We've been after this jerk for nearly a year now and so far we've got nothing."

Rafe's eyebrows went up. "Not even from your CI?"

Kate shook her head. "Sloan's been very careful to keep his business to himself. My CI has even tried searching his computer, but couldn't find anything incriminating."

"Then maybe you're wasting your time. Maybe you should've been happy with the drug bust."

Kate snorted. "Oh, yeah," she said. "And if we got lucky, if Sloan was actually convicted, he'd get maybe five years. Less for a first offense. In the meantime, his network stays intact and he gets out of prison even richer and more powerful than he is now."

Rafe stared at her. "I'm not going to try to turn Lisa, Kate."

"And I'm not asking you to, Rafe. Do you think I wanted this? I know how much she meant to you back in college, even if you did keep your love life under wraps."

"Then why are we even doing this?"

"For two reasons," Kate said. "First, Oliver Sloan is a very bad man. You know those bodies you found this morning? We think he may be behind that."

Rafe had figured the hits were mob-related. So it made sense that Sloan was somehow involved.

But that didn't change anything.

"The second?" he asked her.

Kate's eyes softened. "I'm worried about you, little brother. I know it took you a long time and a lot of soul searching before you decided to join the family business. And I'd hate to see this decision destroy it for you before you've really had a chance to prove yourself."

"If proving myself means what you people seem to think it means, then maybe I'm not cut out for the family business."

"Just think it over," she said. "Who knows? This could even mean that bump up to Homicide you want so badly. Take a day or two. I'll stall the others."

"You can stall them all you want," Rafe told her. "I'm not going to change my mind."

"Believe me, I know how stubborn you can be. And I don't want you to do anything that would compromise your beliefs. But take the time anyway, okay?"

"Whatever you say, sis."

Rafe gave her a look, then turned and walked away.

# Chapter Twelve

Sloan wanted Rafe Franco's head.

All he could think about as he sat in that disgusting, foul-smelling jail cell was how miserable Deputy Do-Right was about to be.

This guy Franco thought he had it all figured out. Thought he could come into Sloan's hotel room, terrorize his woman, slap cuffs on his wrists and actually get away with it.

Hadn't he gotten the memo?

Nobody messed with Oliver Sloan.

Nobody.

Rafe Franco was about to be educated. You don't go after a man like Sloan and come out smelling like roses. Instead, you'd be smelling like what those roses are *planted* in, and the stench won't be going away anytime soon.

In fact, you'd be very lucky if *you* weren't planted along with them.

Five hours, Sloan thought. Five hours he sat fuming in that cell, hours he'd never be able to get back. Hours he could've spent boffing that little blond Gloria—if she hadn't been stupid enough to come trotting out of his bedroom buck naked with a bag of coke in hand.

Stupid, stupid, stupid.

Then there were Frank and Bobby. Those two were supposed to *prevent* guys like Franco from getting into the hotel suite.

And what had they done?

Folded like a couple of lawn chairs.

When Franco booked him, the first thing Sloan did was demand his phone call. He pulled his lawyer out of bed and put her to work. Sloan had three things he wanted taken care of by the time they got to court that morning.

First, a nice little payoff arranged for the judge who was scheduled to do the arraignment. Fortunately, it turned out they already had a standing financial agreement with the guy, so the problem was easily taken care of.

Second was to get him a decent suit to wear to court. The clothes he'd managed to put on before the shouting started and the cuffs came out were wrinkled and soiled—partly with Gloria's cherry-red lipstick. Sloan had a reputation to maintain, and refused to appear in public without a perfectly pressed suit, a crisp shirt and a neatly knotted tie. His old man had always told him that you're more often judged by what you wear than what you do or say, and it was Sloan's experience that those words were absolutely true.

The third item on his lawyer's agenda was to check into this idiot Rafe Franco. Sloan had sensed that Franco hadn't come to the hotel as an officer of the law, and he wanted to know exactly what the nature of his relationship with Lisa might be.

Was he her boyfriend?

Had he been sleeping with her?

If so, how had he escaped Sloan's surveillance? Sloan had been putting teams on Lisa since the day they separated. Not *every* day, mind you, but enough to keep tabs. And he couldn't for the life of him figure how they had managed to miss her playing nighty-night with a six-foot-two-inch hunk of stone.

So finding out what Lisa and Franco had between them was high priority. Sloan would be damned if he'd let some cop steal Lisa's heart. For better or worse, that heart belonged to Sloan and Sloan only, whether she liked it or not. It was bought and paid for, baby. Same as her body.

And *that* was something Sloan was willing to kill for.

"THERE HE IS!"

The shout came from a punk of a reporter who looked all of twenty years old. A snot-nosed little creep who probably thought he was the next Woodward or Bernstein. Except in these days of blogs instead of newspapers, pretty much anyone could make that claim. Didn't mean they had what it took to live up to it.

A crowd of reporters and video cameras waited just outside the prisoner processing room, where Sloan had picked up his wallet and personal effects. The crowd wasn't as big as he had expected, and he was a little disappointed by that. There was no such thing as bad publicity as far as he was concerned, and he planned to spin this disaster in his favor.

As she escorted him outside, however, his attorney—a luscious little number in a tight skirt, named Lola Berletti—told him to keep his mouth shut.

"You can't be serious," he snapped.

"You don't want to give them ammunition," she told him. "They'll cherry-pick whatever you say and use it against you."

Sloan huffed a chuckle. "I didn't get where I am by being shy, baby. How about you keep *your* mouth shut and let *me* worry about the press."

Before she could say anything more, the reporters surrounded them, hounding Sloan all the way to the limo. His bodyguards—Frank and Bobby's replacements—made a path as he smiled for the cameras and ignored the inane questions being hurled at him.

But as his driver opened the limo's rear door and Berletti climbed inside, Sloan stopped and turned, facing the cameras and video cam lenses.

"This is much ado about nothing, folks. Much ado about nothing."

A voice rang out above the others. "Is it true there were drugs found in your hotel suite?"

Sloan smiled. "This is simply a case of an overzealous sheriff's deputy who decided to jump to conclusions and arrest everyone in…"

He paused, and the reporters seized the moment, jumping in with more questions. But Sloan's thoughts had been abruptly interrupted. Just beyond their heads, directly in his line of sight, was Rafe Franco, standing in the doorway of the processing center, giving him the cold eye.

Sloan gave it right back, thinking how much he was going to enjoy crushing this jerk.

He cleared his throat and returned his attention to the reporters. "Any drugs that were found in my hotel," he said, "belonged to the young woman I was entertaining and had nothing to do with me. I wasn't even aware she had them—and the court record reflects that." He gave them another smile. "I guess this is ultimately a lesson in how to choose your friends."

More questions came at him rapid-fire, but he again ignored them, shooting Franco one last look as he climbed into the limo and let his driver close him inside.

Berletti was frowning at him. Her skirt was so tight she had to sit at a kind of sideways angle on the seat. She had unbuttoned a couple of buttons on her blouse, revealing that nice mound of cleavage that Sloan had always admired.

"Glad you decided to take my advice," she said.

"I don't pay you for advice," he told her. "I pay you for results. Did you get that information on Deputy Hotshot?"

"Of course. Did you think I'd fail you, O Mighty One?"

Sloan scowled. "Stow the sarcasm, all right? Just give me the info."

Berletti leaned forward, giving him a better look at the valley between her breasts, and reached into her briefcase, pulling out a small computer tablet. She pressed a button, bringing it to life, then tapped an icon, opening a data file.

Rafe Franco's Sheriff's department ID filled the screen, along with a printed narrative.

"Rafael Thomas Franco," she read. "Twenty-six years old this coming July, graduated with honors from the University of—"

"Now why do I give a flying fruitcake where this guy graduated from college?"

"Because it's pertinent information."

"How so?"

"He attended the University of Illinois at Chicago. Which is where he met Lisa Jean Tobin."

Sloan was surprised. Lisa had never mentioned the guy. Had they been in contact all this time?

"So what are you saying? They were college sweethearts?"

"Well," Berletti told him, "that's a little hard to determine on short notice. But take a look at this photo. It's from the *Chicago Maroon*."

She touched the screen and showed him a page from what looked like a college newspaper featuring a color photo of an art exhibit at the school. Standing in front of an iron sculpture were a young man and woman holding hands.

Sloan had to squint, but he had no doubts that the woman in the photo was Lisa. He'd recognize that angel face anywhere. And the guy holding her hand looked about thirty pounds of muscle lighter, but it was definitely Deputy Franco.

"That seems pretty conclusive to me," he said.

"Well, it's easy to jump to conclusions, but I'd say it's a safe bet they were intimate." She paused. "And the timing is interesting, as well."

"How so?"

"This photo was taken in the latter half of 2009. If they were intimate before they eventually split, then there's every possibility that…" She paused.

"That what?"

"That Mr. Franco is Chloe's father."

Sloan felt a slow burn coming on. Now that he knew that Franco might well be the guy who had put that kid in Lisa's belly, he had to wonder if Franco had been behind the scenes from the very beginning. Using Lisa to steal Sloan's heart and get to his money.

It didn't seem that far-fetched.

"I want to hurt this creep," he said to Berletti. "I want to hurt him bad."

Sloan thought about this. He could have the guy whacked and it would be over and done with.

But where was the fun in that?

No, he wanted this clown to suffer first. Maybe spend some time in a stinking jail cell himself. Get Lisa and every one of his friends and coworkers looking at him as a loser, a no-good. Get Lisa thinking that maybe she was better off with a real man, like Sloan.

*Then* he'd have him killed.

He told Berletti all this, and, true to form, she came up with a plan.

"You know those two Russians we took care of last night?"

"Yeah. What about them?"

"Turns out Deputy Franco was the officer who handled the call."

"So?"

"So what if we play with the evidence a bit and make his associates at the Sheriff's department wonder if he did more than just answer a call?"

Sloan smiled. "You can arrange that?"

Berletti smiled right back, then leaned forward in her

seat and kissed Sloan on the mouth. Her breath was hot and her lips tasted like apples.

She took hold of his hand and placed it on one of those voluptuous mounds. "I can arrange anything you want, darling. All I have to do is mention your name…"

# *Chapter Thirteen*

When the doorbell rang, Lisa called out to Beatrice and told her she'd answer it. Chloe was awake now and wreaking havoc on a coloring book at the coffee table, so Lisa patted her head and crossed to the foyer.

"I'll be right back, hon."

When she opened the door, she was surprised and thrilled to see Rafe standing there. He was still wearing his uniform, but the car in the drive behind him was a red Mustang.

"Is this a bad time?" he asked.

The truth was, she hadn't been able to stop thinking about him. Her mind was a mix of emotions—elation, concern, fear—and she still hadn't figured out how to tell him about Chloe. Part of her just wanted to blurt it out, but another part knew that such a strategy—if you could call it one—was ill-advised.

She had no idea where Rafe's head was right now, and was terrified by the thought that he might not consider this welcome news.

What exactly was she supposed to say?

*Oh, by the way, you see that little girl who looks a lot like a cross between you and Shirley Temple? The*

*one with the blond curls and the blue eyes and the cute
little dimples? The one you said was beautiful?*

*That's your daughter, Rafe.*

Your *daughter*...

*Sorry I never mentioned her to you.*

"Leese? Is this a bad time?"

Lisa pulled herself from her thoughts and smiled at
him. "No, of course not. I'm just a little distracted by
everything that's happened this morning."

He nodded. "I can't blame you. That's why I'm here."

Lisa eyed him hopefully. "You got Oliver to back off?
To promise he won't bother me anymore?"

Rafe's expression said he'd done anything but. He
looked crestfallen and maybe just a little angry.

"May I come in?"

"Sure," she said, gesturing him into the living room.
"Would you like some tea or something? Bea's in the
kitchen as we speak, and—"

"No, I'm fine," he told her, then followed her to the
sofa.

He looked down at Chloe decimating the coloring
book and the anger seemed to melt away. He smiled. "I
see she's got her mother's talent for art."

Lisa laughed. "I'm afraid so."

The memory he'd invoked was a warm one. In college Lisa had taken several art classes but was woefully
bad at every single one of them—a running joke in their
relationship. For a while he had called her Picasso, a
good-natured dig and a term of endearment.

That was something she had always cherished back
then. His affection. He gave it freely and without expecting anything in return. Especially in bed. He was the

most attentive man she had ever been with, and she still remembered, with great clarity, their nights together.

Ah, but that was then and this is now. And while she felt a certain warmth from Rafe, there was also a reserved, almost professional politeness to it. Something he had no doubt learned on the job.

She watched as he crouched next to Chloe and seemed to take great interest in her task.

"What're you coloring there, kiddo?"

Chloe barely looked up at him. She wasn't normally a shy child, but she was too busy working her blue crayon to be bothered with some stranger in a uniform.

"A kitty cat," she murmured.

"A kitty cat with blue fur," Rafe said. "I like it. I wish I could have one just like that in my apartment."

She looked up at him now, and as Lisa watched, her heart was breaking.

*Tell him, you idiot.*

*Tell him.*

"You can have this one, if you want," Chloe said. "He's almost done."

"Are you sure?" Rafe asked. "I wouldn't want you to miss him. And he might get lonely at my place."

Chloe seemed confused for a moment, then squinted at him. "Do you live all by yourself?"

"I'm afraid I do, kiddo."

"Then you can be friends and he can live with you," she said, then went back to coloring.

Rafe smiled again, tousled her head, then got to his feet, turning to Lisa. "Where were we?"

*Trying to keep from bursting into tears,* Lisa thought.

She said, "I'm not sure. You wanted to talk about Oliver?"

Rafe nodded solemnly. "I'm afraid things didn't go as well as I hoped they would. In fact, it was a disaster. Your ex isn't exactly an agreeable man."

"I'm pretty sure I warned you about that. Did he try to hurt you?"

"I only wish he had. I might've been able to make the charges against him stick."

"Charges? What charges?"

Rafe told her about his early-morning confrontation with Oliver, about the woman in Oliver's bed, the bag of cocaine, the arrest and court, and by the time he was done, Lisa's head was whirling.

But she wasn't surprised by any of it.

Nothing about Oliver surprised her anymore. She just wished he was out of her life for good.

"So why are you here?" she asked. "To warn me?"

"Emphatically," Rafe said. "I got the distinct impression that Sloan is not happy with you right now, and I'd bet a year's salary that he'll be back here, late one night. And you may not be able to get rid of him this time."

A feeling of dread worked its way through Lisa's bloodstream. "You think I'm not safe here?"

"Not in the least," Rafe said. "I think you should pack some things and get out. You, your daughter and your housekeeper. As soon as you possibly can."

"But where will we go? A hotel?"

"I wouldn't advise that. As I told you, your ex has some very powerful associates and they'd undoubtedly find you at a hotel."

Something caught his eye and he reached to the end

table and picked up the photograph Oliver had shattered when he broke into the house. The one with her and Chloe standing in front of the lake house.

"Nice photo," he said. "What about this place? Looks like Carlyle Lake."

She nodded. "We spent a lot of time there before we moved to St. Louis."

"A rental?"

She shook her head. "No, it's Oliver's. He kept it in the divorce settlement. He's pretty attached to the place. I think because it was the only time in our marriage that we were actually happy."

"Scratch that idea, then." He set the photo back down. Then he said, "You remember back in college, when we came out here for the weekend?"

She nodded, the pictures flooding her mind. "We stayed at your grandmother's house."

"That's right. Grandma Natalie. That house is way too big for her now, and she's all alone, so I'm sure she'd be happy to have the company."

"I wouldn't want to impose," Lisa said.

He shook his head. "Don't worry, I'm her favorite grandson. She'll be more than happy to do me the favor."

Lisa nodded again, thinking that if she could get Rafe alone in that big house, sharing a bit of quiet time as they'd had during that visit many years ago, she might be able to level with him. Tell him the truth about Chloe.

Assuming she could work up the nerve.

"All right," she said. "We'll start packing right away."

"Good. I've been up all night, so I'm gonna go catch a quick nap and I'll be back to pick you up early this evening. Will that work?"

"Of course."

"And if Sloan shows up on your doorstep again, tell your housekeeper not to hesitate to pull the trigger this time."

A FEW MOMENTS LATER, Rafe drove toward his apartment, but soon realized he was much too wired to take a nap.

As he had stood in Lisa's house again, had knelt next to her beautiful little daughter, Undersheriff Macon's demand kept running through his head.

*It's simple. We want you to turn her.*

*We want you to nurture the relationship and convince her to be our confidential informant.*

Rafe could fully understand why they'd want to use Lisa to spy on Sloan, but he would never allow it. He'd never put her in a position of danger like that. His job was to protect people like Lisa, not throw them to the wolves.

It was one thing to bust a criminal and make him your confidential informant in exchange for leniency or a free pass. But Lisa was an innocent. A woman who had met the wrong guy and fallen for his ruse. It would be heartless to use that mistake against her, even if it meant bringing Sloan's criminal enterprise to its knees.

And there was no guarantee of that. Sloan was dangerous enough to Lisa as it was. If he were to somehow find out that she was working with the Sheriff's department, he might very well kill her.

Or keep his hands clean and have her killed.

So the thought that Rafe would ever try to turn Lisa was insulting and ridiculous, and it annoyed him that his sister Kate had asked him to take a couple days to think about it. Even the carrot she'd dangled—a promotion to Homicide—wouldn't make him change his mind.

After seeing Lisa today, still as lovely and alluring as she had been in college, all thoughts of his career had abruptly vanished. Worrying about a promotion suddenly seemed so unimportant to him that he couldn't believe he'd been fretting about it.

He couldn't stop thinking about Lisa and his last days with her, that moment when he knew she was afraid to commit and was looking for a way out of their relationship.

He had made up all those stories about wanting to go to California and be a surf bum, because he was trying to let her off the hook. He'd pretended that he, too, wanted to explore options, but his only *real* desire had been for them to stay together. Instead he'd done what he thought would make her happy. Had even headed out West after graduation—a pointless exercise if there ever was one.

He had all but convinced himself that he'd never see her again—and that she had no desire to see *him*—until he walked into her living room.

It had been a struggle to maintain his distance. To remain professional. Yet despite the facade, he'd felt more attracted to her than ever. He'd even felt an instant and unexpected connection to her daughter, Chloe, who was, quite possibly, the cutest kid he'd ever seen.

Before he left, Chloe had carefully torn the page with the blue cat out of her coloring book and handed it to him. And in that moment, Rafe felt an inexplicable hitch in his throat. Something about the child had gotten to him, very quickly, and he was touched by her generosity.

She certainly hadn't inherited this from her father.

Maybe what Rafe had felt was the power of his regret welling up on him. His failure to fight for Lisa rather than let her go. Her daughter, Chloe, was a kind of symbol of that regret. She was what *could have been*.

Had he and Lisa stayed together, Chloe—or someone very much like her—could have been his child.

But fate has a way of throwing curveballs at you, and Rafe knew that what was done was done.

As he drove toward his apartment, however, a thought occurred to him. If he could get Lisa and Chloe squared away, if he could get a toxic presence like Sloan out of their lives forever…maybe he and Lisa could rediscover what they once had.

And maybe, just maybe, he could call that little girl his own.

# *Chapter Fourteen*

Rafe had nearly reached his apartment house when he suddenly remembered something: the receipt he'd picked up in the Jaguar this morning. The one he'd found near the dead driver's foot.

If, as Kate suspected, those two hits were the handiwork of Oliver Sloan, maybe Rafe could find a way to pin it on the guy and send him away forever.

Assuming the brass would let him.

Such a move might not topple an entire criminal network, but Rafe frankly wasn't concerned about that. His only interest at this point was in helping Lisa. Though he'd already gotten himself into trouble with the department by going rogue this morning, he didn't figure another trip off the rails could hurt him that much.

And he was more than happy to sacrifice his job to protect Lisa.

He had no idea if Kate and her crew had yet identified the dead Russians. But he had every intention of checking into it himself.

Suddenly energized, he dug into his jacket pocket and pulled out the receipt. According to the time stamp, the gas had been pumped at approximately 2:45 a.m. at a service station on Davis. There was no indication whether or not the customer had paid cash or used a credit card, but there was a way to find out.

It might amount to nothing, but he had to try.

Shifting his Mustang into gear, Rafe hit the accelerator, made a wide, squealing U-turn and headed across town.

THE DAVIS STREET service station was your typical low-end franchise that boasted nine pumps, a repair garage and snack shop about the size of Rafe's living room.

The pumps looked as if they hadn't been replaced or refurbished in ten years, but the gas was cheap and the snack shop served cherry super slushes.

So maybe the place wasn't all that bad.

The guy behind the counter wasn't a week past sixteen and carried the scruffy aura of a high school dropout. He glanced up nervously as Rafe, still in his uniform, stepped inside and dug the receipt out of his pocket.

"Your supervisor around?"

The kid was staring at the Glock holstered on Rafe's hip. "Huh?"

"Your boss. Is he on the premises?"

"Uh, no, he only shows up for a couple hours in the morning. He's gone for the day."

Rafe had no idea if this kid would have the wherewithal to help him, but figured if there were any questions, he'd be a lot easier to manipulate than the guy who owned this franchise.

He put the receipt on the counter.

"I'm investigating a homicide," he said. "The guy who was killed bought gas here this morning at 2:45."

"No kidding?"

"No kidding," Rafe said. "I need to know what he used to pay for the gas. Is there any way to check that?"

The kid hesitated. "Aren't you supposed to have, like, a warrant or something?"

"I'm not asking for his hospital records," Rafe said. "Just a simple gas purchase. Can you give me that?"

The kid scratched his head, a mop that looked as if it hadn't been washed within the past week or so, and was undoubtedly full of lice, then gestured to the register in front of him, which was part calculator, part personal computer, complete with a flat-screen display.

"It should be in here," he said. "If the thing didn't crash, like it does every other transaction."

*Transaction* seemed like a big word for him, but he'd managed to get it out.

Rafe said, "Well, why don't you take a look at that receipt, then do what you have to do to find out."

"Okay…"

The kid picked up the piece of paper, squinted at it, then slowly began punching in a string of numbers on the register keyboard. After a moment, the computer bleeped and something came up on screen.

"It was paid for with a debit card by a guy named… Serge…" He squinted at the screen now, and Rafe could see he was having trouble trying to figure out how to pronounce the customer's last name.

"Just spell it for me," Rafe said.

The kid did as he was told and Rafe took one of the station's business cards from a holder, then used a pen next to the register to write the name on the back.

*Serge Azarov.*

When he was done, he noticed the kid was looking at his Glock again. "You ever use that thing?"

"It's been known to happen," Rafe said.

"You ever kill anyone?"

"Once."

The kid's eyes lit up. "Yeah? Who?"

"A guy about your age, as a matter of fact."

The kid swallowed. "Really? What'd he do?"

"He dropped out of high school," Rafe said.


RAFE ACCESSED the LAWCOM database with his smartphone. The only Serge Azarov listed was a forty-two-year-old, two-time offender, who had been busted on a weapons charge four years ago, and had only recently been released from jail.

His photo matched the face of the dead driver.

Since his release, he'd taken up residence is a run-down apartment house in a notorious section of a city that was already considered by some to be one of the most dangerous in the world.

Rafe had seen a lot of violence in St. Louis, and the city certainly had its share of troubles, but statistics also had a way of skewing people's perception of the world, and he thought much of that perception was colored by paranoia.

That didn't keep him from remaining very alert as he entered the neighborhood Serge Azarov had called home. And because he had to assume that Kate and her partner might also be looking for this guy, Rafe had decided to park his Mustang a few blocks away, chuck his uniform into the trunk, and change into the jeans, T-shirt and hoodie he kept stored there.

The last thing he needed was nosy neighbors ratting him out to Eberhart and his sister.

He stuck his Glock in the waistband of his pants, near the small of his back, then put his hood up and walked to the apartment house, which was a ratty, ten-story walk-up with graffiti-stained, wrought-iron bars protecting the lobby door.

He punched a bunch of buttons on the security com until someone finally buzzed him in, then climbed two flights of stairs to a corridor dotted with doors. He could hear a couple screaming at each other at the far end of the hall, and a baby crying just two doors away.

Rafe found apartment 211, and rapped his knuckles against the door, hoping Azarov had lived alone.

The was no answer. A good sign. And after a couple more tries no one came to the door.

Rafe pulled out his wallet, and removed the slender lock picks he kept tucked inside it. He was about to lean forward and go to work, when a door down the hall flew open and an elderly woman in a bathrobe looked out at him.

"You look for Serge?" she said in thick Russian accent.

Rafe turned his head slightly, but didn't look directly at her, hoping the hoodie would give him some protection. He didn't need anyone seeing his face, just in case things went south. "Yes, ma'am. I'm a friend of his."

"Serge no home," she said. "He supposed to have breakfast with his aunt Luba, but he no show."

*Small wonder,* Rafe thought. "Do you have any idea when he'll be back?"

She eyed him suspiciously. "What you want from him?"

Rafe took a chance. "He borrowed one of my tools and I need it to fix my car."

"Here," the woman said, then disappeared inside. She came back, holding a set of keys, then shuffled toward the doorway. "I let you in to get it."

She shot Rafe a look as she approached and he backed up to give her room. He couldn't avoid her gaze this time.

"I can trust you?" she said.

"Yes, ma'am, of course."

"Not all Serge's friends are good boys. Sometimes even Serge isn't a good—"

A phone rang, the sound coming from her open doorway. The woman looked startled, then quickly handed Rafe the keys. "That might be him now," she said. "You bring them back when you finish."

"Yes, ma'am," Rafe told her, and watched her shuffle off the way she came.

Letting out a breath, he found the right key, then opened the door and stepped inside, buffeted by the strong stench of cigarettes. He closed the door behind him and locked it, just in case the old woman came back.

The place was early dump, with a threadbare carpet and walls that featured tobacco-stained, flowered wallpaper that looked as if it had been installed sometime in the fifties. It was a one-bedroom unit, with a simple sofa, chair and television in the living room, with an attached kitchenette.

There was an abandoned, drying bowl of cereal on the coffee table, an ashtray full of Russian cigarette butts—the source of the stench—and a jacket draped over the couch. Rafe picked it up and rifled through the pockets but found nothing.

He wasn't really quite sure what he was looking for. Something that might tell him who Azarov's friends and associates were. But the guy didn't seem to have lived here long, which made sense, considering he'd only recently been released from prison.

Rafe went to the kitchenette and rifled through the drawers and cabinets, but all he found were a few chipped dishes and some tarnished silverware that should have been replaced a decade ago.

Rafe knew that if he didn't take these keys back soon, Aunt Luba was likely to come snooping. Kicking into higher gear, he headed into the bedroom and found an unmade twin bed covered with a stained flat sheet and ratty blankets, butted up against the wall next to a window with a fire escape.

The closet was hanging open and bare except for a couple more jackets, which Rafe quickly searched.

Nothing.

A battered dresser stood in a corner and he yanked open the drawers, finding nothing but a few pairs of underwear, three T-shirts and two pairs of socks. No receipts, no photographs, no letters—nothing.

In other words, this was big fat waste of time.

Rafe was turning toward the bedroom door when he heard muffled voices in the hallway.

"I tell him to bring them back when he finish," Aunt Luba was saying, "But he no come. He must still be in here."

"You have any idea who this guy is?" another voice said, and at the sound of it, Rafe's heart stopped.

It was Eberhart. And Kate was undoubtedly with him.

Uh-oh.

"Do you have another set of keys?" Eberhart asked.

"No," Aunt Luba told him.

The small apartment suddenly filled with the sound of pounding, fist on wood, the door rattling loudly with every jolt. "Sheriff's department! Open up in there!"

Rafe stood frozen in place, knowing he was toast, knowing that this was likely the end of his job, and despite all his self-proclamations earlier, he wasn't quite ready to give up on it. Not just yet.

And as he heard the pounding on the door again, Eberhart shouting for him to open up, he knew that the next sound would be splintering wood.

Rafe didn't think, just reacted. Turning on his heels, he launched himself toward the window with the fire escape.

He was across the room in three strides, hands grabbing for the lock, struggling to push the window open, when the inevitable happened behind him, the front door crashing wide, as Eberhart and Kate entered the premises.

Mostly likely with guns drawn.

Rafe yanked at the window, trying to force it open, and finally, thankfully, it scraped upward, just enough for him to squeeze through—

And a sound just loud enough to be heard in the living room.

He dove through it just as Kate shouted behind him, "Police! Stop!"

But Rafe didn't stop, didn't slow down. He scrambled onto the fire escape and started his descent, glad that the window was dirty and that his face was obscured by the hoodie. Fortunately, he was only two flights up and it took him no time at all to navigate the steps and leap to the blacktop below.

He stood in the alleyway at the rear of the building, heard footsteps clanging on the metal above him, Kate once again shouting for him to halt.

"You! Stop right there!"

He took off running, heading for the mouth of the alley, a sudden sense of guilt sweeping through him— he was running from his own *sister*—but he couldn't risk being caught.

Kate kept shouting and he could tell by the sound of her voice that she was working her way down the fire escape. He hit the mouth of the alley and turned, picking up speed, but he'd run plenty of races with Kate as a kid and he knew just how fast she was.

A moment later he heard her shouting again as she came around the corner behind him. Rafe suddenly flashed back to early this morning when he was chasing the suspect at the auto repair shop and it was hard for him to believe he was now on the receiving end of such a chase.

He bore down again and picked up speed, his lungs drawing in ragged breaths. Kate had stopped shouting and he knew she was now concentrating on breathing and quite possibly gaining on him. But he couldn't look back. He didn't want her to recognize him.

Rafe reached the end of a street, darted across the intersection, nearly colliding with a car that had sped up to jump a red light, then shot across to another alleyway, hoping that Kate had been slowed at the intersection.

But a moment later, she shouted again, struggling to breathe herself, and he knew she was much too close for comfort. "Stop! Stop right now!"

Rafe almost expected her to call out his name, because surely she must recognize him even from behind, but he didn't waste time worrying about it. He put the hammer to the pedal and picked up even more speed, heading toward a pair of metal doors in the side of the building.

One of them was ajar.

"Stop!" Kate shouted once again, and he could tell by the faltering tone that she was starting to get winded, losing speed.

Rafe reached the doors and launched himself against them, flinging them open to reveal nothing but darkness inside. This was a warehouse of some kind or a storage facility.

As he got inside, he kept moving through the darkness, waiting for his eyes to adjust and hoping he wouldn't bump into anything. After a moment, it became clear that this was a file depot of some sort, the massive place crowded with numbered legal boxes sitting on low rows of shelves.

Rafe could hear Kate's footsteps behind him. She would be inside at any moment now and, per protocol, would slow herself down and draw her weapon.

He wondered for a moment if he should just give this up and cop to the truth, but there was a large part of him that resisted for one simple reason—he didn't want to look like a complete fool in front of his older sister. Rafe had spent his entire childhood trying to impress both Kate and their older brother, Vincent. And he knew Kate would not react well if she discovered the man she was chasing was her own kid brother.

So he kept moving, working his way through the rows of shelves, looking for another door. A way out.

He saw one on the far side of the second row he entered, visible mostly because of the light seeping under the door. He abruptly shifted direction and was halfway to it when Kate shouted, "Freeze!"

A flashlight beam illuminated Rafe's back, throwing his elongated shadow onto the floor and up onto the boxes.

Rafe stopped in his tracks, raised his arms and knew what was coming.

"Down on your knees!" Kate commanded.

Rafe's heart was thumping in his ears.

*Oh, well,* he thought. *At least I tried.*

He was about to drop to his knees when another voice shouted, "What is this? What's going on here?"

Rafe recognized the indignant, authoritative tone of what had to be the building security guard, probably pulling his own weapon from his holster as he spoke.

Rafe froze in place, knew that Kate would have to respond, and she did immediately. He also knew that she'd be showing the guard her weapon in a nonthreatening manner to keep him from firing his own.

"County Sheriff, sir! Don't fire. Do not—"

That was when Rafe bolted. Made a beeline straight for the door, Kate again shouting for him to halt or she'd shoot. But he didn't falter, didn't slow down, knowing that she would aim for his legs.

He zigged and zagged and the first shot didn't ring out until he reached the door, gouging the floor nearby. It ricocheted harmlessly, just as he slammed through the door and burst onto the street, once again running for all he was worth.

Rafe had a better lead on her this time and he wasn't about to let himself get caught. His lungs felt shallow, each breath harder than the next, but he didn't let it slow him down, couldn't let it.

He took a right at the next block, then darted across the street, ran to the next corner and took a left, finally chancing a look behind him.

No sign of Kate. Or Eberhart, wherever *he'd* gone to. Probably still back at Azarov's apartment, relaxing and smoking a cigarette.

Rafe took two more turns, left, then right, then stripped off the hoodie and dumped it into a trash can on the street. Crossing the next intersection, he spotted a coffee shop and went inside, finding a booth in back that allowed him a view of the street.

A waitress nodded to him as he slid into the booth, gave him a small smile and he smiled back, even though he didn't much feel it.

He sat there trying to catch his breath, then gestured for the waitress to bring him a cup of coffee.

He waited in the booth for nearly an hour before going back to Azarov's neighborhood to retrieve his Mustang.

## Chapter Fifteen

"Are you sure this'll be okay with your grandmother?"

"I've already called her," Rafe said. "She's more than happy to have the company. Thrilled, in fact."

They were driving at a clip in Rafe's Mustang, Lisa up front next to him, Chloe and Bea in back. Lisa felt uncomfortable and nervous, but wasn't really sure why. She had met Grandma Natalie during her junior year, when Rafe had brought Lisa home for the weekend.

Maybe the nerves were caused by the way Rafe was driving, which was a tad too fast for her. When he had shown up at the door looking disheveled in jeans and a T-shirt—as if he had just returned from a jog at the park—she'd had to wonder what he'd been up to.

She was immediately reminded of how gorgeous he was, but he seemed distracted and a little out of sorts. Something was weighing on his mind.

Maybe some of that had rubbed off on her.

Or maybe her nerves were simply caused by the secret she knew she had to reveal. The one sitting right there in the backseat, playing Crazy Birds on an iPad.

The closer they got to Grandma Natalie's house, the more trepidation Lisa felt. She had spent half the day wondering how she would break the news to Rafe, and still hadn't come up with an idea that would guarantee a happy outcome.

But then she supposed nothing could.

This feeling was compounded by her mixed emotions about Rafe himself. He had only been back in her life for a few short hours—and only a small portion of *that,* when she thought about it—yet she felt as if something had been awakened inside her. Some long-abandoned emotion that had lain dormant, quietly percolating below the surface of her heart for the past three years.

Why, she wondered, did it matter to her how he reacted to the news about Chloe?

Was she still in love with him?

After everything she had been through with Oliver, was she still even capable of love?

All she knew was that, despite the turmoil inside her, she felt good being with Rafe again, riding beside him in this Mustang that he'd had for so many years. It was the same car they drove here as juniors, and she felt at home in it. Just as she had back then.

She felt safe with him, protected.

It was the role Rafe had always taken. Lisa had grown up very much the independent woman, but when she'd met Rafe in her freshman year—or the tall, reedy teenager he was back then—she had quickly discovered that she didn't mind his old-fashioned, chivalrous ways. He opened doors for her, pulled out chairs for her, gave her his coat if they were caught in the rain, stood up to boys who made drunken passes at her at frat parties or disparaging remarks when she turned them down.

Yet he did all this without ever robbing her of her independence. Without ever undermining the essence of who she was as a woman.

Now he here was again, falling so easily into the old role. Looking out for her. Helping her.

He was staring intently at the road as he drove and she wanted so much to ask him what he was thinking about right now.

"You seem preoccupied," she said. "Is something wrong?"

He shook his head. "Nothing I can't handle."

"Does it have something to do with Oliver?"

He glanced at her, smiled. "Don't you worry about that jerk. He's my number-one case now."

"Meaning what?"

"That sooner or later I'm gonna find a way to put him behind bars, where he belongs."

Lisa shook her head. "I still can't believe all this stuff about his being involved in organized crime. I mean the mob?"

"This isn't like the old days, Lisa. Gangsters don't dress up like the godfather or threaten people with tommy guns. Organized crime is fronted and populated by people who look like legitimate businessmen, and are often so far removed from the actual wrongdoing that it's nearly impossible to put them away."

"So then what makes you think you'll be able to do anything about Oliver?" she asked.

"Determination," he said. "Pure determination."

GRANDMA NATALIE LIVED on the Hill, a largely Italian-American neighborhood marked by the brick and terracotta Roman Catholic church that stood on the corner of Wilson and Marconi Avenues.

The house itself was a two-story, red-and-white, bungalow-style affair with a large front porch overlooking Shaw Avenue, which was fairly busy at this time of day.

Rafe pulled the Mustang into the drive, and before they even had their doors all the way open, Grandma Natalie emerged from the front doorway—looking just as Lisa remembered her—arms extended to Rafe.

She was a small, plump Italian woman in her mid-eighties, with a smile that was big and wide and friendly.

Lisa watched as Rafe went to the foot of the porch and pulled her into a hug.

"Rafael," the old woman sang. "My sweet little Rafael."

Not so little anymore, Lisa thought. He dwarfed the old woman.

"Good to see you, Nonna. How've you been?"

"I work, I eat, I sleep," she said. "Then I start all over again." She pulled away and held him at arm's length, studying him. "You look tired, Rafael. Have you been sleeping?"

He shook his head. "I never made it home after my shift," he told her. "I'm pretty beat."

"Well, come then. Come sit inside in your grandfather's chair and take a nap. I'll make some tea and keep your friends company."

This was Rafe's cue to turn to Lisa, Bea and Chloe. "Nonna, you remember Lisa, don't you?"

Now the old woman turned her smile on them, and in that moment Lisa could swear she felt warmth flowing through her. Almost magical in its energy.

"Ah, yes," Grandma Natalie said, taking Lisa's hands in hers. "Of course I remember. The one who got away."

Lisa and Rafe exchanged a brief glance, an embarrassed smile, then Rafe gestured to Bea and Chloe and introduced them.

Natalie nodded to Bea, then stooped toward Chloe, reaching a hand out to tousle her hair. "What a beautiful little…"

She paused, a question forming in her eyes.

She glanced up at Lisa, then Rafe, then at Lisa again, who quickly averted her gaze. Rafe didn't seem to notice the look, but in that moment, Lisa knew that the old woman had seen something familiar in Chloe. Probably the same thing Lisa saw every time she looked at her daughter's face.

*Rafael Franco's eyes.*

"Lovely child," the old woman said. "Let's see if we can find you some cookies."

Chloe's face lit up. "Really?"

"As long as your mama approves."

Lisa smiled. "Of course. Thank you so much for having us, Mrs. Franco."

"Call me Nonna," she said, then lightly flicked a finger under Chloe's chin, provoking a giggle. "You, too."

"Okay."

Then she straightened and turned to Rafe. "Rafael, don't just stand there looking handsome. Get their things and carry them to their rooms upstairs. I'll start the tea."

THE INTERIOR of the house was a museum. A perfectly maintained replica of 1920s St. Louis, with antique furniture, polished wood floors and a gleaming wooden staircase that led to the bedrooms.

Lisa had forgotten that feeling she'd had so long ago, when she had first stepped foot inside the house. It seemed to hold the same welcoming warmth as Grandma Natalie's smile. A house that said, *Come in, come in. Make yourself comfortable.*

"I remember the first moment I saw you," Nonna said to her as she poured tea into delicate porcelain cups.

They were seated in the large but intimate living room, the air so still that every clink of the porcelain seemed magnified.

"I was in the kitchen," she continued, "with the window overlooking the drive, and Rafael drove up in that infernal machine of his, and a moment later you stepped out." She smiled. "I thought, oh, my, what has that grandson of mine gone and done?"

Rafe, who was slumped wearily in a worn leather chair, cracked open his eyes and said, "What's that supposed to mean, Nonna?"

"That as handsome and charming as you are, young man, I couldn't quite believe you had managed to steal such a beautiful treasure. Especially after some of the ungodly young women you dated in high school."

Bea, who looked a little uncomfortable being served, let out a snort. "I like this woman."

Nonna smiled at her. "I'll bet you'll like my lasagna even better. Just you wait and see."

"Come on, Nonna," Rafe said. "Cut me a break."

The old woman ignored him and turned again to Lisa. "And when I met you, I was quite delighted that he'd finally managed to find someone who was not only beautiful, but also had brains, too. Rafael's a wonderful boy, but he doesn't always think straight. He needs to be grounded in reality sometimes and you seemed like just the woman to do it."

Rafe sat up now, blinking at her. "How long are you planning to go on like this?"

"You just go to sleep, son. Let the ladies talk."

"I feel like I'm under a microscope."

Nonna waggled a hand at him. "Just be happy anyone's talking about you at all. You could do worse."

Rafe gave her a good-natured scowl, then settled back in his seat and closed his eyes. "I couldn't stop you if I wanted to, so carry on."

"Boys and their grandmothers," Bea murmured with a grin.

Nonna finished pouring her own cup of tea, stirred in some sugar, then settled onto the sofa, again addressing Lisa.

"Where was I?" she asked.

"Talking about how Rafe needs grounding," Lisa said, more concerned about where the old woman was *going* with all this. During the entire monologue she had kept glancing at Chloe, who was once again in deep communion with her crayons.

"Ah, yes," Nonna said. "So you'll understand why I was surprised and disappointed when the two of you broke it off. I had gotten the impression that Rafe was quite enamored of you, and you of him."

Rafe opened his eyes again. "Okay, Nonna, now you're really pushing it. Time to change the subject."

She glanced at Chloe again. "A grandmother can't be

concerned about the choices her grandson makes? Especially when he may have certain responsibilities…"

Rafe frowned. "What the heck are you talking about?"

Lisa knew exactly what the old woman's concern was and she immediately moved to allay it. "The breakup was a mutual decision, Nonna. And it didn't come easily." She smiled. "I'm just happy we've had this chance to reconnect, even if it's under unfortunate circumstances."

Grandma Natalie looked at her. "Then I take it he doesn't…"

She stopped, letting the unspoken question hang in the air, and Lisa felt a sharp, painful stab of guilt.

"Doesn't what?" Rafe asked.

Lisa looked directly at the old woman, mentally imploring her not to go any further. She didn't want Rafe to find out like this.

"Nonna?"

The message seemed to get through, as Nonna relaxed. "Never you mind, son, you're half asleep. You'd better take that nap before dinner. The stomach won't wait."

Rafe studied her curiously for a moment, glanced at Lisa, then threw his hands up in an exasperated gesture that implied that women were a mystery to him.

Then he closed his eyes again.

## Chapter Sixteen

Dinner crept up on them faster than anyone had expected. Chloe unpacked the toys she brought in the living room as Lisa and Bea helped Grandma Natalie in the kitchen and a still-groggy Rafe set the dining room table.

Lisa remembered what a wonderful cook Grandma Natalie was. One Sunday every month, the entire Franco clan gathered here at the house to break bread and catch up with one another. Grandma Natalie would prepare a feast and the wine flowed as if it were coming from a fountain in the floor.

Lisa had been part of one of those Sundays. Had met Rafe's brother, Vincent, and his aunts and uncles and cousins, all of whom seemed to have some connection to firefighting or law enforcement. Sheriff's deputies, firefighters, beat cops, detectives, arson investigators. The Franco family was permeated by the culture and seemed to revel in it.

On the drive in, back then, Rafe had warned Lisa that she was about to be surrounded by some of the toughest cops she had ever encountered—not that she had encountered many—and that she shouldn't let them intimidate her. That they were loyal to the badge, but they were also good people. Compassionate people.

"My family," he had told her, "lives and breathes by our own code."

"Code?"

"It's based on what's informally called Code Blue, the police code of conduct."

"Sounds a little ominous to me," she had said.

Rafe shook his head. "Just the opposite. Since childhood, I've always been taught by example to respect others, show empathy and humanity, do no harm unless it's justified, protect those who can't protect themselves, trust and help one another when needed…and…"

"And what?"

"Avoid bringing shame on the family. I know it all sounds a little goody-goody, but it works for us."

At the time, Lisa had thought this code painted a vivid portrait of the Rafe she knew. He had always been a man—a boy then, really—of integrity, who seemed very sure about who he was and what he believed in. Cop confidence was part of his DNA, but never in that annoying, holier-than-thou way demonstrated by so many of the campus police officers.

Rafe was the picture of solid, but gentle, self-assurance. A picture Lisa had found quite attractive.

Still did.

Not that Rafe didn't have his doubts at times. He had often told her about his reluctance to follow in his siblings' footsteps and join the force. But that had come more from a fear of disappointing them than anything else. He was afraid he wouldn't live up to the Franco family name.

He was especially concerned about living up to the example set by his sister, Kate—whom Lisa hadn't met that Sunday. She was apparently one of the shining stars of the Franco family and Rafe said he often felt inadequate around her.

But now it looked as if he had finally conquered that fear and had grown and matured since making his decision to join the department. And helping her with Oliver proved that he still lived by the credo the Francos so cherished.

It was the last part of it, however, that bothered her. *Avoid bringing shame on the family.*

These were modern times, sure, but the Franco clan struck her as a bit old-fashioned. So would the news that one of their favorite sons had fathered a child out of wedlock be greeted as a source of shame, or of celebration?

It was probably a pointless worry, but such things weighed on Lisa's mind. Especially when the matriarch of that family was busy making pasta primavera right next to her, and knew darn well that the little girl now helping Rafe set the table was her great-granddaughter.

Lisa ached inside, knowing she needed to tell Rafe the truth, but still unable to think of a way—or a time—to do it.

But it had to be done.

No matter what the consequences.

DINNER WAS SUBLIME. Lisa couldn't remember the last time she'd had food so delicious.

Grandma Natalie was an amazing cook.

They ate for what seemed like hours, sharing a bottle of wine, Rafe forgoing a glass because he had to work a shift tonight. Somewhere in the middle of it all, Chloe began to yawn and Lisa decided it was time to put her to bed.

"Let's get you upstairs, hon. You've got to wash up and change into your jammies."

"Can Mr. Rafe take me?"

This provoked a smile. "I don't see why not," Rafe said. "But none of this mister, stuff. Just call me Rafe."

*Or Daddy,* Lisa almost blurted out, but caught herself just in time. And she half expected Grandma Natalie to say it instead.

Getting to her feet, Lisa said, "We'll both do it, hon. Make it a party."

"A party!" Chloe squealed. "Make it party!"

"How about a teeth-brushing contest?" Rafe asked.

"Yea!" Chloe squealed.

Laughing, Rafe got to his feet, then went around the table and scooped Chloe into his arms. "I'll bet I can get mine cleaner than yours."

"Uh-uh," Chloe said.

"We'll see about that," Rafe chuckled, then carried her out of the dining room toward the stairs.

Laughing now, Lisa got to her feet and followed, but before she reached the doorway, Grandma Natalie called out to her.

Lisa turned. "Yes?"

"You may not think this is any of my business, child, but does my grandson know who he's carrying upstairs?"

Lisa's laugh died and she said, "He will soon, Nonna. I promise. Just as soon as I figure out a way to tell him."

Beatrice frowned. "Tell him what? Am I missing something?"

Grandma Natalie patiently patted Bea's hand and returned her attention to Lisa. "Just open your mouth and say the words, child. That's all it takes."

Knowing the old woman was right, Lisa nodded solemnly then headed toward the stairs.

## Chapter Seventeen

"I made something for you," Chloe said.

Rafe smiled. "Oh? What is it?"

He was crouched over the bed in what had once been his mother's bedroom, a small space located near the back of the house. The window overlooked the back-yard where Mom's old swing set still stood, victim to a bit of rot and rust, but gleaming in the moonlight, an old, pleasant memory.

Rafe had spent quite a bit of time on those swings himself.

He pulled the blankets up toward Chloe's chin as she said, "It's in my backpack."

Rafe glanced at Lisa, who stood leaning in the door-way, watching them. There was a look in her eyes that puzzled him. A vague sadness, he thought. Something bothering her.

Undoubtedly thoughts of Sloan. It had to be hard raising a man's child when that very same man was a threat to you. She undoubtedly saw part of Sloan every time she looked at Chloe's face.

Rafe didn't see it, however. He couldn't bring him-self to equate this precious child with Oliver Sloan. She was too innocent, too…beautiful.

Her mother's beauty, he supposed.

It certainly wasn't Sloan's.

"Are you gonna look at it?" Chloe asked.

Rafe snapped out of his thoughts and reached for the backpack hanging over the bedpost—a lime-green frog with more zippered pockets than anyone could ever need, especially a child.

"In here?"

"Uh-huh."

Rafe unzipped the main pocket and reached inside, pulling out a sheet of paper that had been torn from a coloring book. It was another kitty cat. This one crudely colored pink.

"Do you like it?" Chloe asked.

"I love it," he said. "But you already gave me a blue one." Which, he realized, was still folded in the pocket of his uniform jacket in the trunk of his car.

"You said you didn't want him to get lonely, so I made him a friend."

For reasons he couldn't quite understand, Rafe felt a sudden warmth sluice through him. This was, quite possibly, one of the most heartfelt things anyone had ever done for him.

He again felt that unexplained connection to this little girl, and his chest filled with a yearning that came very close to bringing on tears.

He held back. Smiled. Ran a hand along Chloe's forehead. "Thank you, hon. This is the best present anyone ever gave me."

"Really?"

"Absolutely," Rafe said. Then he heard a quiet sob

behind him and swiveled his head to find Lisa turning quickly away from the doorway, heading into the hall.

"Leese?"

She didn't respond and he felt compelled to go after her, but didn't want to leave Chloe in a lurch. Instead, he turned back to the girl, smoothed her forehead again, and said, "You'd better get to sleep now, cupcake."

Chloe smiled. "I like cupcakes."

"So do I," Rafe said. "So do I."

HE FOUND LISA on the front porch, sitting on the swinging bench that his grandfather had built. The old man had been very proud of that accomplishment. He was a gruff old patrol cop who hated retirement and always had to be doing something with his hands. His death two years ago had been a deep blow to everyone in the family.

Rafe remembered how Lisa had spent a lot of time on this bench the weekend he'd brought her here during college. The Franco clan could be an overwhelming bunch and although she had never admitted it, Rafe sensed that her weekend among them had been plagued by sensory overload.

While Rafe was busy having fun catching up with family, Lisa had been a stranger in a strange land, and that couldn't have been easy for her. So it wasn't surprising that she'd spent time out here, trying to gather her thoughts.

And he supposed tonight wasn't any different. She'd been uprooted and moved out of her house and had to be feeling the stress of her situation. He didn't know what had triggered her sudden retreat from the bedroom, but he found himself falling into his old rhythms with Lisa, wanting to comfort and protect her.

He sat next to her on the swing, saw that she had a trace of tears in her eyes.

They hadn't had physical contact except for the hug this morning, and right now Rafe wanted to put his arm around her and pull her close.

But he resisted.

"It wasn't that long ago," he said. "You and me sitting here on a night like this, looking up at the sky. Yet it seems like some faded childhood dream."

Lisa nodded, wiped at her tears. "Were we really as in love as we thought we were?"

Rafe thought about this, but didn't really need to. He already knew the answer. "I know *I* was."

She smiled wistfully. Nodded. "Then what happened, Rafe? Why did we go our separate ways?"

"I've thought a lot about that over the last three years," he said. "I think maybe we were so much in love that it scared us. We were a lot younger then. Not only physically, but emotionally. I guess the thought of settling into some kind of permanent relationship, some happily ever after, didn't sit well with either one of us."

He paused, studying her a moment. She was nodding, vaguely, as if seeing that time through different eyes.

"But the thing is, Leese, I've always thought it was a mistake. I should never have let you go. I just thought you wanted—"

"Let *me* go?" she said.

He nodded. "It seemed like what you wanted. So I made up that stupid story about California, to make it easier for you. To let you off the hook."

Her face opened up in surprise. "You're kidding, right?"

"No," he said. "Why would I be?"

She started laughing now, more tears springing to her eyes. She wiped them with her sleeve. "I don't believe this. And all this time I thought *you* were the one who wanted to break up."

Rafe frowned. "What?"

"I was letting *you* off the hook. I figured you didn't want to be tied down to someone."

Now Rafe started laughing, not quite believing what he was hearing.

"You don't know how miserable I was," Lisa said. "There were so many times I wanted to call you, tell you we'd made a mistake, especially after…" She paused, looking like a woman who had nearly dropped a toe on the trigger of a bear trap. "I just never got up the nerve, because I figured the last person you wanted to hear from was me."

"I felt exactly the same way," Rafe said. "How stupid are we?"

Now they both laughed, but there was a bittersweet quality to it. Then Rafe sobered, thinking about the little girl who lay upstairs, asleep by now. The little girl who had given him a pink kitty cat to keep the blue one company.

"And look what I missed because of it," he said.

"What do you mean?"

"This'll probably sound crazy to you, but when I look at your daughter, when I look at Chloe, all I can think is what might have been. She could be *my* daughter, not Sloan's. And instead of going through all this nonsense with him, you and I could have been making a home and raising our child."

Lisa's face went through a series of shifting emotions, as if she couldn't quite figure out how to respond. He'd taken a risk, telling her this, but it was the way he felt. And he'd been feeling it since he walked into her living room just a few short hours ago.

He had never been able to put her fully out of his mind, so it was no surprise that he was still in love with her.

Lisa again wiped the tears from her eyes and said, "Rafe, I've been looking for a way to tell you this, so I guess it's best that I just come out and—"

She was cut off by the opening of the front door. Grandma Natalie stepped outside carrying a small tray, breaking the spell, jerking them back to reality.

"You two are looking quite cozy," she said.

Rafe smiled. "Just like old times."

Nonna glanced at Lisa as if they were in some sort of secret communication. "Am I interrupting something?" she asked.

That was odd, Rafe thought. Had they been talking about him? And, if so, why?

Then Lisa suddenly said, "No, no, Nonna. You're fine. We were just talking about the good old days..."

"You're sure, now?"

"I'm sure," Lisa said, and Rafe still wondered what the heck was going on between them.

Women and their talk.

But before he could give it too much thought, Grandma Natalie shuffled toward them with the tray, which held two cups of tea and a plate full of what she'd always called apostle's fingers. The dessert was made of ricotta cheese, sugar and cinnamon, and Rafe had been eating it for as long as he could remember.

"I prepared a treat for you," Nonna said. "I hope you aren't too full."

But Rafe was stuffed after dinner and took this as his cue to stand up. "As much as I don't want to, I'm gonna have to decline, Nonna. My shift starts in a couple hours and I need to get home to shower and shave."

"You're leaving? So soon?"

Rafe smiled. "Duty calls." He glanced at Lisa. "But don't worry, I'll be back."

He wanted to lean down and kiss her, especially after the conversation they'd just had. But agreeing that what they'd done in the past was a mistake didn't necessarily translate into how Lisa felt here and now. He sensed a hesitation in her, some kind of inner turmoil. But they'd have to finish their talk at another time. Hopefully soon.

So he merely nodded to her, said good-night, then turned to take the steps down to his car. He was only halfway through the turn when Grandma Natalie took hold of his elbow.

"Wait, now, Rafael. Don't let an old woman chase you away. You two have so much to talk about."

"I'd like to stay, Nonna, but duty calls."

"Duty, duty, duty," she said. "That's all I ever heard from your grandfather. Why is everyone in this family so dedicated to duty?"

She was one to talk. In her early years she had been a probation officer for the state, and quite devoted to the job.

Rafe shrugged. "I guess we're all just wired that way."

"You can't just stay for a few more minutes? Maybe the young lady has something to—"

"That's okay, Nonna," Lisa said. "I'll still be here when he's off work. I should probably be getting ready for bed."

Rafe still sensed that something was going on here, something he wasn't privy to, but he merely nodded again, said another good-night.

Then he took the steps down to the drive and got in his car.

AS THEY WATCHED him drive away, Grandma Natalie said, "Well, child? Did I just ruin your perfect moment?"

"I don't know if there is one, Nonna. Now probably wasn't the right time anyway."

"Oh, nonsense. The boy needs to know he has blood. Every man does. It isn't fair to keep him in the dark any longer. That girl isn't getting any younger and every minute is precious. She needs a father. One who will love her and cherish her and take care of her."

"And do you think Rafe's that man?" Lisa asked.

Grandma Natalie scowled. "What kind of a silly question is that? You *know* he is."

Lisa nodded. She was right, of course. Having all these doubts about how Rafe would react to the news was nothing more than her own insecurities showing through. And as much as she'd wanted to tell him, she had almost welcomed the interruption from Grandma Natalie.

Why was she making this so complicated?

Maybe her problem was not that she was afraid Rafe would reject Chloe. Based on how they were interacting, based on what he had just told her, that seemed unlikely.

But they had spent the past few moments talking about what *could* have been, not what was. And while Rafe might not reject Chloe—would he reject *her?*

Was it too late for them to paint that perfect portrait of a happy family?

Her fear of the answer was, in itself, an answer to the question she had asked herself earlier today.

Was she still in love with him?

Of course she was.

She had never *stopped* loving him.

Sitting here on this porch swing, talking about the silly mistake they had made—believing the other wanted to be set free—Lisa had felt that old chemistry ignite. For a moment she had thought Rafe was about to kiss her, but he had shied away from it.

The question was why?

Was it possible that he had indeed moved on?

Was it possible that he would never feel the way he'd felt back in college?

The way *she* felt *now?*

Was he merely caught up in the nostalgia of the moment, a feeling that would eventually fade, leaving nothing of substance in its wake?

As usual, she was overthinking. A habit she'd had since childhood.

But she couldn't help herself. Any more than she could help the knot in her stomach. The fear that what they'd once had could never again be duplicated.

# *Chapter Eighteen*

The moment Rafe parked in the underground garage, he felt something wrong.

It wasn't a feeling he could quantify. More of an animal instinct, really. But it permeated the air around him as he climbed from the car.

Was someone watching him?

He thought about the look Oliver Sloan had given him outside the processing center. Sloan surrounded by a group of reporters, but locking eyes with Rafe, telling him, *Don't think you're gonna get away with this, hotshot.*

Could Sloan be stupid enough to have sent a couple goons to Rafe's apartment building?

Did he think that Rafe could be so easily intimidated?

If so, he was sadly mistaken. Rafe was long past the time in his life when someone like Sloan could scare him. And he'd already proven that Sloan's goons were ineffectual thugs who were all posture and no follow-through. Rafe's skills in Krav Maga had taken care of that, and they surely would again.

Not that Rafe felt he was anything special. But one thing his martial arts classes had taught him was that there was never a reason to feel helpless in the arms of danger. On the contrary, if you stayed smart and acted decisively, 99 percent of dangerous situations could be neutralized in a split second.

And if that last 1 percent required deadly force, then so be it. Rafe had never had any desire to kill a man, but he wouldn't hesitate to use that option if the situation required it.

He stood by his car and scanned the parking lot. His apartment building wasn't huge, and the lot itself was small, full of narrow spaces packed with a couple dozen cars. Entry required a key card, which took you past a rolling steel gate, but such safeguards could be easily hacked by savvy people, either through electronics or simple social engineering.

But as he searched the dimly lit, cement enclosure, paying special attention to the dark pockets behind the parked cars, he saw nothing of concern. No movement. No subtle shifting of shadows.

Yet that feeling of being watched didn't fade. If someone *was* watching him, he was very, very good.

Locking up the Mustang, Rafe went to his trunk and retrieved his uniform, holster and Glock. Bundling up the uniform and holster, he tucked them under his arm and kept the Glock in his hand, just in case.

With another quick glance around him, he crossed from his car to the elevator about ten yards away, feeling the hairs on the back of neck rise as he pressed the button and waited.

He half expected someone to come up behind him, but the elevator arrived without incident, its doors sliding open at the sound of a bell.

HALF A MINUTE LATER, Rafe stepped into the tenth-floor hallway, which was dotted with several doors. His apartment was on the far side of the hall, and he moved toward it, only to stop short about three yards away.

His door was ajar.

Rafe tensed, chucked his uniform to the hallway floor. Raising the Glock, he studied the open door for a long moment, then stepped carefully toward it, coming in at an angle, approaching it from the side.

He stopped again, just shy of the door. Gave it a nudge with the toe of his right boot.

The door creaked. Swung open just wide enough to fit through. Dark inside.

Rafe waited. Listened.

Heard nothing.

Yet he sensed that someone was in there, the hairs on the back of his neck still tingling, those animal instincts again kicking in.

He waited a moment longer, then decided to move. Inching laterally toward the opening, he nudged it wider, then quickly slipped through, immediately stepping to the side to stay out of the light from the hallway.

Pressing his back against the wall, he gripped the Glock with both hands, waited again. He listened for the sound of breathing.

Nothing.

He reached for the light switch next to him, flipped it on. The lamps on either side of his couch came to life, illuminating the small apartment, and he was surprised by what he saw.

The place was mess. A disaster. All the books had

been pulled from the bookshelves. The drawers and cabinets in his kitchenette hung open, several utensils scattered across the floor. The door to his bedroom hung wide and in the wan light he could see that his mattress had been overturned, the comforter and bedsheets lying in a heap on the floor.

His apartment had been ransacked.

But by whom? And what were they looking for?

These questions had only just entered his mind, when he heard a faint *click* and a lamp went on his bedroom.

Rafe crouched, raised the Glock, then froze.

His sister, Kate, was sitting in the armchair he kept in the corner near the bed.

What the heck?

"Nice entry, little brother. But I had you for two or three milliseconds when you stepped into the doorway. You should've killed the hallway light first."

Rafe stood up, his heart pounding. "What is this?" he barked. "What are you doing here?"

Kate gestured. "You want to put the weapon away?"

He'd almost forgotten he was pointing it at her. He lowered it, tucked it into his waistband and said, "That doesn't answer my question."

Kate got to her feet and approached him. He noticed now that she was holding a manila folder with a department tab on the side. A case file.

"Why don't we start with your answering a couple of mine?"

Rafe frowned. "What's going on here?" He gestured to the mess. "Did you do this?"

She shook her head. "But I know who did."

"Who? Sloan?"

She shook her head again and waggled a hand toward his small two-seater dining table. "Let's talk, all right?"

Moving to the table, she dropped the manila folder on top of it and sat, waiting for him to join her. He crossed to it, scraped the second chair back and sank onto it, feeling the Glock pinch at him. He pulled it free and laid it on the table.

"Okay," he said. "Start talking."

Kate nodded. "I have to say, little brother, I'm disappointed in you."

"About what?"

She stared at him a long moment.

"Well?" he said.

She drummed her fingers on the folder. "You mind telling me where you were at around 3:30 today?"

Rafe felt his gut tighten. All at once he knew what this was about.

He'd been made.

He didn't know how, but Kate wouldn't be here if she didn't suspect, or know for certain, that he'd been at Azarov's apartment this afternoon. That *he* was the one she'd been chasing.

"I guess I don't need to tell you that," he said. "Because you already know."

Her fingers went still and she slid the manila folder across to him. Rafe stared down at it, saw that the label read CASE 13-2257. HOMICIDE.

He flipped it open and found a photograph inside. One taken by a traffic cam as a car passed through the red at an intersection.

The car that had nearly hit him.

Rafe hadn't even noticed the flash of the cam, but

there he stood in living color, dodging that car, his face presented directly to the camera. Identification wasn't iffy, it was crystal clear. The guy in the hoodie was, without a doubt, Rafael Franco.

"You care to explain?" Kate said.

Rafe lowered his head, could barely look at her. Kate had always had this uncanny ability to make him feel small. In her presence he was the screwed-up younger brother who couldn't get anything right.

It was an unfair characterization, sure. But he felt it, nevertheless. Even though he knew she loved him fiercely and with all her heart.

What he always saw in her eyes at times like this was disappointment.

He finally looked at her again. "I was trying to get a lead on the killings," he said. "I know I was out of line, but I was hoping to find a connection to Oliver Sloan."

"Because of the ex-wife? Lisa?"

He nodded. "I need that guy put away. I don't want him going near her again."

"Sounds like you're letting a certain part of your body do your thinking for you."

"Yeah," Rafe said. "My heart. I'm still in love with her, Kate. And I don't want that creep terrorizing her."

"Are you sure that's all it is?"

He furrowed his brow at her. "What do you mean?"

She gestured to the folder in front of him. "Look at the next page."

Rafe moved the photo aside and stared down at a department ballistics report. He quickly read through it, saw that the techs had found a match between the bullets found in the bodies of the Russians to a SIG Sauer that had been recovered in a search.

"You found the murder weapon?"

"Yes, we did."

"Where?"

Kate was again silent for a long moment. Then she said, "I think you already know the answer to that."

Rafe was at a loss. "I do?"

Kate nodded and hooked thumb toward his bedroom doorway. "They found it under your mattress, Rafe. Pretty stupid place to hide it."

Intense heat rushed to Rafe's face and his stood up, feeling his heart start to pound all over again. *"What?"*

"Sit down, Rafe."

"I don't know what it is you're accusing me—"

"Sit *down,* Rafe."

Big sis again.

He took a breath, sat back down, waited for Kate to explain.

"I've known you all your life, little brother. You were never a stupid kid, and you're certainly not a stupid man. Your work in the field, until now, has been exemplary, and I'm pretty sure you were on the fast track to Homicide. I don't know that for sure, but there was talk about it." She paused, reached across the table and tapped the ballistics report. "But this doesn't look good, Rafe. As soon as Eberhart saw the photo and we realized who we were chasing this afternoon, he went straight to Internal Affairs."

"What?"

"I tried to talk him out of it, begged him to give me

a chance to speak to you first. But you know Charlie. Always by the book, and he never has liked you."

"No kidding," Rafe said.

"Internal Affairs tossed the apartment, found the gun, then rushed through the ballistics report."

"This is complete nonsense," Rafe said. "That gun isn't mine."

"Maybe so, but as I said, they found it under your mattress. And that isn't all they found."

Rafe furrowed his brow again. "I'm listening."

She took hold of the ballistics report and flipped it aside. Beneath it was a printout of some bank records, the name RAFAEL FRANCO and his account number referenced at the top of the sheet.

Kate tapped one of the entries. "There's a new deposit this morning. You want to tell me where you got that kind of money?"

Rafe zeroed in on the entry. It read $10,000.

He swallowed hard, his heart pounding again, not quite believing what he saw.

Where the heck had this money come…?

Then it hit him. Sloan. Oliver Sloan. The creep wasn't coming at him with his ineffectual goons. No, that was too obvious, and likely to get Sloan in trouble.

This was a frame job, pure and simple. Sloan was framing him for the hit on the Russians.

*Don't think you're gonna get away with this, hotshot.*

"I'm being set up," he said.

"Believe me, I tried to tell them that, but the boys in Internal Affairs aren't buying it. They think you were paid to do the hit and were probably in Azarov's apartment trying to plant evidence, pin it on Sloan."

"You've gotta be kidding me. So, what…is IA in Sloan's pocket, too?"

Kate shook her head. "They have to go where the evidence leads, Rafe. You know that. We all do. And right now it points to you."

Rafe closed his eyes. "I can't believe this is happening."

"It took everything I had to convince them to let me talk to you first. That's why I'm here."

"You know I didn't do this, right?"

Kate nodded. "I know you'd never hurt anyone. Not like this. Not unless it was necessary force. You were raised under the code, just as I was."

He studied her eyes and knew she was being sincere. Not that he'd ever doubt her.

"So what happens next?" he asked.

"You know the drill. You'll be booked and interrogated, unless you lawyer up. And I'd advise you to lawyer up."

"I can't say anything incriminating if I don't know anything."

Kate sighed. "Come on, Rafael, I know Ma didn't raise an idiot. I'll make some calls, get an attorney for you."

"And then what?"

"What else? We fight this thing."

"We?"

"You may be a bonehead, little brother, but you're my blood. And blood is everything."

She gathered up the photograph and ballistics report, returned them to the file, then closed it and stood up.

"Are you handling the arrest?" Rafe asked.

"Nope."

"IA?"

She nodded, then took her cell phone from her pocket, dialed a number and murmured a few words into it.

As they waited for IA to arrive, Kate said, "By the way, you almost gave me heart attack this afternoon with that little running stunt. It took me ten minutes just to catch my breath."

"Sorry about that."

"Just do me favor," she said. "Next time I yell at you to stop, do what I say, okay?"

## Chapter Nineteen

The boys in Internal Affairs were a humorless bunch. But then Rafe figured it was hard to have a sense of humor when 90 percent of the department despised you.

They put him in an interrogation room and fired questions at him, using the usual IA bulldog approach, trying to intimidate him, wanting to know who had ordered the hit and why. But Rafe took Kate's advice and immediately lawyered up.

In his experience, a perp who called in an attorney right away only made himself look more guilty to the people investigating him. But at this point, Rafe didn't care what they thought. If he started flapping his mouth, they might misconstrue something he said as evidence of his involvement in the crime, or even an outright confession.

Most of the people they brought into these rooms were indeed guilty of what they'd been accused of. But Rafe was one of the exceptions, and much to their frustration, he wasn't about to give them ammunition against him.

The lawyer was there within an hour of his confinement. A small, compact, athletic guy with short-cropped hair and an expensive suit. And Rafe wondered if he'd be able to *afford* the guy.

But then he was $10,000 richer, wasn't he?

Sloan had made sure of that.

The next hour was spent being hammered by another round of twenty questions, only this time the lawyer, whose name was Chaplin, shut the investigators down at every opportunity.

They didn't like him much.

When they realized they were getting nowhere, they hauled Rafe off to a holding cell and let him sit there the rest of the night.

And all he could think about, as he stared at those cement walls, was finding a way to make bail, clear his name—and, most important, protect Lisa and her little girl.

Whatever it took.

HE WAS ARRAIGNED the next morning at 9:00 a.m., sharing the perp bench with an accused car thief and an armed robber. It was ironic to be sitting here in the very same court that Sloan had sat in yesterday—only Rafe, even with his cop family, didn't have the kind of connections that would spring him.

He was charged with two counts of first-degree homicide and gave the judge a loud and forceful "Not guilty" when asked how he wanted to plea.

Arraignments are by and large a formality in which every defendant pleads not guilty. It's rare for an arraignment judge to allow any other plea, for fear the defendant hasn't had a chance to consult with an attorney. Better to take a "not guilty" and accept a modified plea later, should the state and the defendant reach an agreement before trial.

It had always annoyed Rafe when the news media went into a frenzy of outrage over a high-profile defendant who had declared himself not guilty. If they were honest in their reporting, they'd tell their audience that this was standard practice in any criminal court.

Once Rafe pled, the judge said, "As to the matter of bail, what's the state's recommendation?"

The prosecutor, a fat man in a thin man's suit, cleared his throat. "This is a heinous crime, your honor. Two men shot dead in cold blood. So we ask that the defendant be held without bail."

Not what Rafe wanted to hear, but he wasn't surprised.

"You're honor," his attorney said. "My client is a well-regarded member of the law enforcement community. He has no prior record, no means for flight and is in no way responsible for these two deaths. We'd ask that he be released on his own recognizance."

"You can set that pipe dream aside," the judge told him, "but I'm not going with the prosecution's recommendation, either. Bail is set at $2 million."

"But, your honor," Chaplin cried, "that's as good as setting no bail at all. My client doesn't have the means for that kind of bond."

The judge pounded his gavel. "Not my problem, counsel. Next case."

As they moved aside to let the next attorney and his client step up to the bench, Chaplin said, "Not the outcome I was hoping for, but don't sweat it. You'll be out in about two hours."

"How?" Rafe said. "I don't have that kind of money. And neither does my family."

"But you do have an angel on your side."

Rafe studied him. "Angel? What are you talking about?"

The attorney hooked his thumb to the gallery behind them and Rafe turned, surprised to see Lisa sitting in the back row.

Had she been here all this time?

She was watching Rafe with concern in her eyes. Gave him a small wave.

He waved back, then turned to Chaplin. "Are you saying she's putting up on the bond?"

"Putting up her *house,* as a matter of fact. Which is kind of ironic, since it was paid for by Sloan."

"I can't let her do that."

"What are you, nuts?" Chaplin said. "It'll be at least two months before your trial starts. You want to be sitting in a cement room all that time?"

"But it's her *house,*" Rafe said.

"Relax, Franco, it's just collateral. She doesn't lose anything as long as you show up for your court dates. And you don't strike me as the kind of guy who would skip out on court."

"Why's that?"

Chaplin smirked. "You've got a family full of cops. Where you going to hide?"

"You really shouldn't have done this," Rafe said.

They were sitting in back of a cab, headed toward Rafe's apartment. He noted that Lisa was wearing a gray jacket for the occasion, one he had given her for her twenty-first birthday. It was a bit dated, fashionwise, and he was not only surprised she had worn it, but that she'd kept it at all.

Rafe had always loved the way the jacket fit her. A gentle caressing of her curves. He was suddenly reminded of the night she she had worn it—and nothing else—as she crawled atop him in bed and made him forget all about a looming trig exam. Made him forget about everything except her, wearing that simple swatch of tailored gray cloth over that magnificent—and pliant—body.

Was wearing it now a signal of some kind? Was she trying to tell him something? Was it a symbol of solidarity, love, or simply just a jacket?

"I had to do it, Rafe," she said. "I know this all happened because of me."

"Don't be ridiculous."

"I know this has to be Oliver's doing. He's done it out of spite and jealousy, and if he's as powerful as you say he is, he'd be able to call on the right people to make it happen."

Rafe had, of course, been thinking the exact same thing, but Lisa hadn't provoked Sloan. *He* had.

"You weren't the one who stormed into your ex's hotel suite and arrested him," he said. "You weren't the one who broke into a victim's apartment and ran from his own sister. Believe me, this is my own stupidity at work. But I was looking for a way to get Sloan out of your life without…"

He didn't finish the sentence.

"Without what?" she asked.

Rafe hesitated, wondering how much he should tell

her. But he knew he needed to be open and honest with her. He'd learned that the hard way.

"My bosses called me into a meeting yesterday. After Sloan was freed. They've been investigating him for months."

"If he's what you say he is, then that's a good thing, isn't it?"

"Yes," he said. "But they had a proposition for me. One they tried to make very difficult to refuse."

She frowned. "What kind of proposition?"

"They wanted me to turn you."

"Turn me?"

"They wanted me to use my influence with you, to use our past, to try to get on your good side and convince you to cooperate."

She stiffened. "Cooperate in what way?"

"They wanted me to convince you to encourage Sloan to return to you so that you could spy on him and report back to me."

Her eyes hardened. "And did you agree to this?"

"No."

She didn't seem to have heard his response. "So is that what this has all been about? Taking us to Nonna's house? Being so nice to Chloe?"

*"No,"* Rafe said forcefully. "Of course not. I would never do that to you. I would never do anything to put you or Chloe in danger. That's why I broke into that apartment. I was hoping to find something that would connect the guy's murder to Sloan."

She softened, considered this a moment. Then tears sprang to her eyes as she said, "So then this did happen because of me. I've made your life a mess."

He grabbed hold of her hand. "Stop that, Leese. *You* didn't do anything. This is all on me."

They let that hang in the air for a moment, then she laced her fingers through his and squeezed. "You don't know how much I've missed you, Rafe. How many times I've cursed myself for letting you go."

"You don't think I feel the same way?"

Her eyes looked hopeful. "Do you?"

He looked into them, tears and all, thinking what a waste these past three years had been without her. Thinking how a simple miscommunication between them had separated them for far too long. And of the irony that it was fate—and Oliver Sloan—that had brought them back together.

On the porch last night, he had hesitated. But not now. He leaned toward her, kissed her. Felt the heat of her breath, her desire.

And there were no mistakes this time.

They both knew exactly what the other wanted.

# *Chapter Twenty*

They made love in the shower.

When they first entered Rafe's apartment, Lisa was shocked by the mess, once again feeling guilty that this had all happened because of her. Despite Rafe's insistence that he was the one at fault, she knew that he would never have gotten into this trouble if he hadn't been trying to protect her.

She took one look at the open cupboards and drawers and the books and papers strewn across the floor and immediately pushed him toward the bedroom.

"Go get yourself cleaned up," she said. "You smell like the inside of a jail cell."

He had laughed, kissed her on the nose, then headed toward his bathroom.

When he was gone, Lisa got to work. The least she could do to thank him was clean the place up.

She started with the kitchenette, making sure the dishes, canned goods and paper products were all back in place, that drawers were all shut, then she moved on to the living room and started returning the books to their shelves.

She was halfway through the pile, listening to the sound of Rafe's shower, when she found a book that momentarily stopped her heart. It was a copy of Robert Frost's poems that she had given to him shortly before they'd split up.

There was a bookmark poking up from the pages and Lisa cracked the book open to it, finding a small strip of photo booth snapshots. Four photographs of her and Rafe mugging for the camera, taken at a shopping mall one day when they had ditched their classes.

Lisa remembered that day well, especially what they'd done that afternoon on Rafe's bed. The almost insatiable desire they'd shared.

In the book itself, there was a highlighted sentence, Frost's words staring up to her, speaking to her, as if the poet—and Rafe—had read her mind:

*Love is an irresistible desire to be irresistibly desired.*

A moment later, the books and the mess were forgotten and Lisa was in Rafe's bathroom, pulling off her clothes, looking in through the steamed glass at his newly toned body, as the water cascaded over his broad shoulders, the expanse of his chest, dusted lightly with hair, the trail that hair made downward past the ripple of his abs and below.

She stared openly at him, feeling the desire overwhelm her, moisten her, as she opened the shower door and stepped into his arms. She offered herself to him, pressing her nipples against his chest, feeling the brush of his firmness against her thigh. Feeling it grow and expand as if begging to be touched.

So she obliged, reaching a hand down to squeeze, remembering the feel of him as if it were only yesterday, yet experiencing it in a whole new way, now that he had grown from a boy into very much a man.

They immediately fell into their old rhythm, Lisa now dropping to her knees, feeling the warmth of the water rushing over her shoulders as she took him into her mouth.

She heard him groan and the sound empowered her, thrilled her, knowing that she was giving him the ultimate pleasure. He put his hands on her head, and she felt them tighten against her as she worked. She knew instinctively that it had been a long time since he'd experienced this. Knew instinctively that he was coming close.

She felt his hands tugging at her, trying to get her to stand up so that they could move on to even better things, but she stayed put, wanting to reward him quickly for his sacrifices, to thank him for being there for her. It wouldn't have to stop here, of course. She already knew that they'd be moving into the bedroom after this, throwing that mattress back on its bedframe and continuing where they left off.

So she ignored him and concentrated on her task, feeling him grow even harder, listening to his groans, his breaths become more rapid.

Then he stiffened, his fingers wrapped up in her hair, tightening against her head as he let out a final, tortured moan and released himself.

She held him there until he was done, then gently pulled away and got to her feet, falling into his arms again, holding him close as she waited for the wave to roll over him and dissipate.

And, as she predicted, they didn't stop there.

THEY DIDN'T BOTHER to dry off, didn't bother to put the mattress on the bedframe. They simply knocked it flat on the floor and fell on top of it, their drenched skin soaking the bedsheets.

But neither one cared.

Rafe's hands began to roam, finding her breasts, gripping her enflamed nipples between his fingers, a tingle of electricity shooting through Lisa as his mouth found hers, his tongue slipping urgently between her lips.

Then one of his hands slid down her belly, stopping for a moment to caress her navel, sending a jolt straight to the sweet spot. She moaned in his ear as he moved on, using those strong fingers, caressing her, pressing the heel of his palm against her pelvis as he explored.

More shutters of electricity shot through her, tunneling straight for her brain, tiny explosions of pleasure bursting like the *rat-tat-tat* of a machine gun, growing in intensity as his fingers continued to move, to caress, to press and pinch and pull.

Then he pulled his hand away and slid down her body, tattooing her with kisses along the way, moving his mouth to her pelvis, using his tongue in place of his fingers, the tiny explosions growing in intensity.

She suddenly realized that her legs were trembling uncontrollably, something that had never happened to her before, even with Rafe. She was almost embarrassed by her inability to control them, but decided to go with the moment, let her body react however it chose to.

This feeling was too exquisite to fight.

She knew Rafe was merely reciprocating for what she'd done to him in the shower, but she had forgotten how skilled he was at this, and the reminder was so raw and real that she could barely contain herself.

Even so, she wanted him inside her. It had only been a few minutes since they left the shower, but she was more than ready for him and hoped that he was up to the task.

He must have read her mind, because he stopped suddenly and got up on his knees before her. And she shouldn't have wondered about him, because there, below the ripple of his abs, he was ready to go again.

And he looked enormous. Bigger than in the shower.

Bigger than she remembered from their days together.

He put a hand on each of her knees and gently pushed her legs apart, lowering himself toward her, rubbing against her as if priming her for what was to come.

But she didn't need priming. She was more than ready. Was, in fact, desperate for him. She needed him inside her.

*Now.*

A split second later she got her wish as he thrust hard and deep, filling her completely, his heat radiating up through her, growing in intensity with each new thrust.

She heard someone moaning, and realized it was her. A loud, long, uncontrolled utterance, punctuated by those thrusts.

And now Rafe was moaning again, too, the sound filling her ears, heightening her excitement. She felt the current between them growing stronger, hotter, more electric, building and building, their breaths shortening, timed perfectly to the rhythm of their bodies.

Then, all at once, something gave way inside her,

something charged and fluid that worked its way toward her brain and blossomed there.

She squeezed her eyes shut and let go, drifting away on a wave of pleasure, letting it crash over her.

Then Rafe uttered a low moan and tensed, and she felt him throbbing inside her, releasing himself, his warm wetness filling her, feeding her, pleasing her.

Then he collapsed against her and brought his mouth to hers, his breath hot and earthy, as he said softly, "I... love...you..."

And despite everything wonderful about the passion that had consumed her—had consumed them both— those three words were the real magic. And the only thing that mattered to her.

LATER, AS THEY LAY curled in each other's arms, Lisa said, "I've been thinking about what you told me."

He smiled, nuzzled her neck. "Just now? That I love you?"

"Well...yes, but no."

He got up his elbow. "Because I do, you know. That wasn't just a heat-of-the-moment thing. I've never stopped loving you, Leese. I don't think it's humanly possible."

She smiled and pressed her nose against his chin. "I feel the same way, Rafe, but that's not what I mean."

"Then what?"

"I'm talking about what you told me in the cab. About your bosses wanting you to turn me."

"Forget that. I didn't even entertain the notion for a second."

"I know," she said, "but maybe you should have."

He froze, narrowed his eyes at her. "What are you talking about?"

It was a thought she'd harbored since the moment he told her.

"Maybe I should do what they want," she said. "Maybe I should go undercover, so to speak, make Oliver think he still has a chance with me. Try to help their investi—"

"Forget it. That's not going to happen."

"But what if I can find some way to—"

He sat upright. "I said forget it. There's no way I'm letting them put you in that kind of danger. If he were to find out what you were up to, I have no doubt he'd have you killed. You'd wind up just like Azarov and his partner, sitting in a Jaguar with a bullet in your head."

He was heated now. Obviously troubled by the mere notion of her doing something like this. So she backed down, didn't press it.

"All right," she said. "You're right."

"You better believe I am."

"It was just a thought. I want to help in some way. I want to…"

She paused as the name he had spoken finally resonated.

*Azarov.*

"My God," she said.

"What's wrong?"

"That name. Azarov. I've heard it before. Well, not really heard it, but I've seen it on a document."

He nodded. "He would've been listed on the prosecutor's complaint against me as one of the victims."

Lisa shook her head. "No, no. Not today. A long time ago. Over a year now."

"What are you talking about? Where?"

Lisa took a breath, thinking about what she'd done in hopes that it would keep Oliver from contesting the divorce and ensure that he'd back away from her. She had always thought what she had found had something to do with a shady real estate deal, but now she wondered if it was much more than that.

"When I asked Oliver for a divorce," she said, "he outright refused. Said there was nothing I could ever do that would persuade him to let me go."

"Yet he did."

She nodded. "Because I managed to get some leverage against him. I knew he was involved in some unsavory real estate deals, so I searched his home computer and found a password-protected folder containing documents that I thought were connected to one of them. Names, dates, addresses, amounts. It looked like an accounting of bribes that had been paid out to various recipients."

"How did you know the password?"

"Oliver's pretty easy to read. I just kept guessing until I got it right."

"And that's where you saw Azarov's name?"

"Yes," she said. "It didn't click when you first said it, but now I'm sure of it. And I'm wondering if what I saw wasn't evidence of a real estate scam at all. Maybe those documents prove that Oliver has ties to organized crime."

Rafe's eyes were alive now. "Tell me you made a copy."

She nodded again. "On a data chip. I hid it in a safe place, and gave Oliver an ultimatum. Divorce me or I turn it over to the police. I had no idea if it would pay off, but judging by the look on his face, it was something pretty damaging. And it was enough to make him leave me alone." She paused. "For a while, at least."

"I'm surprised he left you alone as long as he did. He's a creature of impulse."

"No kidding," she said. "Ninety percent of it fueled by testosterone."

"So where did you hide this data chip?"

She sat up now and kissed his cheek. "Get dressed."

## Chapter Twenty-One

They were halfway across town when Rafe realized they were being followed.

Three cars back. A gray BMW sedan that should have blended in with the rest of the traffic, but didn't.

Rafe had noticed it shortly after they left his parking garage, but hadn't given it much thought until the car made a couple of tricky maneuvers to keep pace with the Mustang.

So there was no question about it. There was somebody unfriendly back there.

There were two possibilities. Either it was IA, trying to keep tabs on their number-one suspect, or it was one of Sloan's goons, keeping tabs on Lisa.

Either way, the news wasn't good.

"This is going to sound like the biggest cliché in the world," he said, "but we've got company."

"What do you mean?" She started to turn her head to look behind them but Rafe quickly put a hand on her wrist, stopping her.

"Hold it," he said. "No point in letting them know we know about them."

Lisa looked worried. "Who do you think it is?"

"I've got a couple of guesses, but figure it could go

either way." He sighed. "No matter who it is, they don't need to know where we're headed and what we're up to. Not yet, at least."

"So then what's the plan?"

"You remember that roller-coaster ride we went on at Hampton Park our junior year?"

She made a face. "How could I forget? I threw up all over your car. Why?"

"Don't do it again," he said, then stomped on the accelerator.

The Mustang roared and shot forward through an intersection. Rafe spun the wheel, took a sharp right, then shifted, stomped again and shot into the left lane as he poured on the gas.

Checking his rearview mirror, he saw the Beemer take the turn behind him, coming toward them at a clip. If the driver had been trying to hide earlier, there was no such subterfuge now. The driver came after them like a sleek gray cheetah, obviously unconcerned about rising gas prices.

Rafe had seen his share of high-speed chases in the past couple years, but he'd never been on the receiving end of one of them. Cutting off a Chevy Malibu, he changed lanes and picked up speed. The switch was abrupt and jerky, Lisa's face going pale as she grabbed for the handbar above her door.

"Uh…uh…uh…" she said, her widening eyes on the road ahead, apparently unable to form any words.

"Hang on!" Rafe told her, then shot past another car, cut back into the left lane and made an arcing turn onto an adjoining street. The Mustang's tires screamed in protest as they burned up the road.

Checking the rearview mirror again, Rafe saw the BMW breeze through the turn with a smooth, steady hand.

This guy was good.

Rafe checked his speedometer. He was clocking a good seventy miles an hour on a city street and his pursuer wasn't even flinching. No way the guy was IA.

Not with those skills.

And Rafe doubted he was one of Sloan's usual thugs, either. The people Sloan surrounded himself with weren't exactly top-of-the-line.

So who was he?

Rafe decided there was only one way to find out. A face-to-face with the man. But not on *his* terms. It was time to reverse the trajectory of this chase and set it right.

Telling Lisa to hold on again, Rafe spun the wheel, tapped the brakes and roared into an alleyway on his right. He was familiar with this alley because of his patrol work and knew it led to an adjacent street.

On that street was another alleyway, this one long and narrow. But Rafe knew about an abandoned warehouse at about the halfway mark, and a service ramp that led into an empty cargo bay.

Sheriff's deputies routinely patrolled the alleyway to chase away squatters, and after a concerted six-month effort the vagrants had finally gotten the message and stayed away for good. The owner was supposed to have boarded the place up by now, but hadn't yet gotten around to it.

When Rafe saw the gray Beemer turn into the alley behind him, he stomped on the gas again and shot out into the street. Horns honked around him as he cut diagonally toward the second alleyway and turned into it, shooting straight for that warehouse ramp.

A few moments later, he pulled into the darkness of a cargo bay, then came to a stop and let the engine idle.

Lisa seemed to be trying to find her voice. "...You were right about the roller coaster."

"Sorry about that."

"What are we doing in here?"

"Waiting."

"For what?"

"The inevitable," Rafe said cryptically, feeling a little guilty for not explaining his plan. "I need you to get out of the car."

"What?"

"This could get nasty, and I don't want you getting hurt. You'll be safe enough here in the warehouse."

"But I don't understand. Where are you—"

Rafe put a finger to his lips to silence her as the sound of the BMW's engine reverberated through the alleyway. Getting the message, she carefully popped her door open and got out of the car. She looked frightened, but it couldn't be helped. Better she hide in here in case this guy had firepower.

Nodding to her, Rafe watched her back away into the warehouse darkness, then popped the Mustang into Reverse and looked out the rear windshield toward the bottom of the ramp.

A moment later, the BMW rolled into view, cruising at a slow crawl now, the driver undoubtedly wary as he searched for his prey.

Rafe hit the gas. Hard.

He rocketed backward down the ramp, ramming into the side of the BMW. Metal screamed as it collapsed inward and the Beemer was punched sideways. Before the driver knew what hit him, Rafe cut the engine and was out of the car in a quick, fluid move, the spare gun he kept in his glove compartment now in hand as he turned toward the crumpled BMW.

But to his utter surprise, the driver was gone, his door hanging wide. How he had managed to flee so fast was beyond Rafe's comprehension, but Rafe spun on his heels, looked down the alley and saw a man running, wearing a hooded sweatshirt—much like the one Rafe had worn earlier—much like the one he'd seen the hit man wearing at the auto repair shop two nights ago.

And Rafe knew this was the same guy.

It had to be.

He shouted and took off after him, and the guy turned suddenly, gun in hand, and fired off a shot.

The bullet whizzed past Rafe as he dove behind a garbage bin and returned fire, once, twice, but the guy was too far away now, heading into the street.

And then something completely unexpected happened.

Just as Rafe was about to get to his feet and give chase again, just as the guy had stepped onto the street—

An A-1 Furniture truck came out of nowhere and slammed into the man, killing him instantly.

Rafe stopped short and turned away, squeezing his eyes shut in horror.

"No ID," KATE SAID. "Nothing. This guy's a phantom."

"I'd bet my last nickel he was working for Oliver

Sloan," Rafe told her. "He's got to be a hired killer. I'm almost positive he's the guy I chased out of that auto repair shop."

They were standing in the mouth of the alley, a section of the street cordoned off as crime scene techs worked to bag the man's body and remove it.

Lisa stood nearby, looking pale and sickly, undoubtedly trying her best not to throw up. Kate's partner, Eberhart, was leaning against their cruiser, quietly smoking a cigarette as he eyed Rafe suspiciously.

Kate frowned at Rafe. "What do you think you're doing, little brother?"

"What do you mean?"

"It looks to me as if you're still trying to work this case. And now you've gotten the ex-wife involved."

"You're the ones who wanted her involved, remember?"

"That was before IA arrested you. If you had any sense, you'd be lying very low right now. You need to stay away from this. As it is, my partner wants to haul you in right now and start grilling you."

"Hey," Rafe said. "I didn't ask for this guy to come after us. What happened here was purely defensive."

"Well, I guarantee IA'll have plenty of questions, but right now, you need to go home, get some rest, catch up with your girlfriend—who looks scared witless, by the way—and try to forget that Oliver Sloan even exists."

"Can't do that," Rafe said.

Kate sighed. "Look, I'm not telling you this as your big sister. I'm telling you this as a fellow cop. We're going to stop this guy, I promise you that, but it's going to take time to get the goods on him."

"Maybe not," Rafe said.

She studied him. "What do you mean?"

He gestured toward Lisa. "Turns out she may have some evidence that proves Sloan's not only connected to organized crime, but also to one of the victims, as well. Azarov."

"What kind of evidence?"

"Some documents Sloan kept hidden on his computer with names, dates and what she thinks may have been bribe amounts."

Kate looked visibly excited. "You've got to be kidding me. Where are these documents?"

"On a data chip she's been keeping in a safety deposit box. We were on our way to retrieve it when the dead man started following us."

"You sure this is the real thing?"

Rafe glanced at Lisa, their eyes connecting for a moment, then returned his gaze to Kate. "She wouldn't lie to me."

Kate didn't need any more prompting. She immediately turned, calling out to Eberhart. "Rev her up, Charlie, we've got places to go."

Eberhart frowned, ditched his cigarette. "Oh, yeah? Where to?"

"We're going to make a withdrawal."

THE HAMPTON BRANCH of the Westland National Bank was located in a strip mall in southwest St. Louis.

Rafe's Mustang had to be towed from the alley, so he and Lisa rode in the back of Kate's cruiser to their destination, which was little more than an oversize box, sandwiched between a Taco Hut and a Gino's Pizza.

As they all climbed out of the car, Eberhart said, "So this is where we find the evidence to take Sloan down, huh? Fat chance."

Kate said, "Why don't you wait out here, Charlie?"

"And miss the look on your face when this turns out to be a big fat bust?"

"Smoke another cigarette," she said. "I think you might need it."

Eberhart shrugged. "Suit yourself."

As he pulled his pack from his coat pocket and turned back to the car, Kate, Rafe and Lisa moved toward the bank's entrance. Rafe opened the door, letting Lisa and Kate step past him.

The bank was small, nothing more than a satellite office for one of the large branches downtown. Which, Lisa had told them, was exactly why she had chosen it.

There were two teller windows and a manager's desk off to the right. Toward the back was a cage with the vault on the left, and a small room full of safety deposit boxes on the right. The safety deposit clerk sat at a desk nearby, and looked up with a smile as they approached.

Lisa introduced herself and gave the clerk her account number. The clerk checked her records, nodded, looked at Lisa's photo ID then stood and escorted them past the gate into the security box room.

The clerk and Lisa approached a small door in the wall marked 339, and used dual keys in the locks to open it. The clerk slid the box out and handed it to Lisa, then excused herself, telling her that she could have privacy in a small, curtained booth to the left of the room.

When she was gone, they all moved to the booth. Lisa slid the curtain back and set the box on a table inside.

As Rafe and Kate watched, she took hold of the lid and lifted it, Rafe feeling giddy with anticipation.

But disappointment soon followed.

The box was empty.

Her face filling with shock, Lisa shoved a hand inside and patted it—an instinctive, but ultimately useless gesture.

"I don't understand," she said. "I put it in here. I *know* I put it in here."

Kate glanced at Rafe as if to say, *Are you sure this woman's trustworthy?* But Rafe ignored her and grabbed hold of the box, turning it upside and shaking it.

Nothing fell out.

The data chip was clearly gone.

"Somebody must have taken it," Lisa said. "I don't know how they managed it, but—"

"We can certainly try to find out," Kate said, then turned and headed back toward the safety deposit clerk's desk.

They followed as Kate pulled out her badge and showed it to the clerk. "Excuse me, but I need you to check the records."

"For what?" the clerk asked.

"I want to know if anyone had access to that safety deposit box in the last several days."

"I'm afraid you'd need a warrant for that."

Lisa moved forward. "Are you forgetting that it's *my* box? Please do as she asks."

The clerk nodded, then jabbed a few keys on her computer keyboard, watching the screen. When she found what she needed, she said, "The records show that you came in three days ago to access the box."

Lisa frowned at her. "Oh, really? And do you remember seeing me?"

"I wasn't on duty that day. But it says here the customer complained of a lost key, so we used a master."

"You *what?*"

"It's all right here," the clerk said. "She had several forms of identification and there was no reason to believe—"

"This is ridiculous." Lisa shook her head in dismay, then staggered to a nearby chair and sat down.

Rafe and Kate moved to her.

"I can't believe it," she said. "I don't know how he found out where I was hiding it, but this has to be Oliver's doing. He must've found someone to pretend to be me."

"I wouldn't put it past him," Kate said.

Rafe nodded. "Which would explain why he suddenly showed up at your house the other night. You don't have any leverage against him. Not anymore."

Tears sprang to Lisa's eyes. "I can't believe this. Why won't he just leave me alone?"

"Because he's a psychopath," Rafe said. "He's fixated on you."

Lisa wiped her eyes. Rafe could see that she was beyond distressed. Terrified that she would never be rid of Sloan.

Unfortunately, that was a very real fear.

She looked at Rafe. "Maybe I need to do what your sister and your bosses want me to."

"Meaning what?"

"Make Oliver believe I want him back and—"

"No way," Rafe said. "Forget it. I already told you, that's not going to happen."

"But couldn't you put a wire on me? If I could get him to admit he set you up, if I could get him to confess to me that he had those Russians killed, wouldn't that be enough to—"

"Did you hear what I just said?" Rafe barked. "The guy's a psychopath. If he were to find out what you're up to… I'm not going to put you in that position."

"Well, maybe it's not your choice," she told him.

"It's the *only* choice, Lisa. Anything else is too dangerous."

She stood up now. "You know, I love you with all my heart, Rafe, but don't for a minute think you can tell me what to do any more than Oliver can. If you think you can control me…"

"I'm trying to *protect* you, Leese."

"And look what it got you," she said. "Maybe it's time I started protecting myself."

Then she turned and walked out the door.

## Chapter Twenty-Two

They were silent on the ride back to Grandma Natalie's house. The only one who had anything say was Eberhart, who seemed outright gleeful that he had been proven right. That nothing would—or had—come of their little jaunt to the bank.

He said to Rafe, "I'm holding you responsible for all of this, Franco. You're an embarrassment to your entire family."

Kate said, "Shut up, Charlie."

"You telling me I'm wrong? I'll leave it a jury to decide if he offed those two Russians, but you can't deny he's been stickin' his nose in where it don't—"

"Shut. Up. Charlie."

He would have kept going if Kate hadn't given him the death stare. The one she'd been perfecting since she and Rafe were kids.

Rafe had always sensed a lot of tension between her and Eberhart, and was pretty sure that Kate would just as soon trade the guy in for a new partner. But in the Sheriff's department you didn't always have a choice of who you'd be riding with. And unless the relationship was so fractured that the two of you were coming to blows, changing the situation was next to impossible. So you did your best to get along.

Not that Eberhart was making much of an effort. Yet for all his faults, he wasn't wrong. Rafe *was* an embarrassment to the Franco clan, and he'd be the first to admit it.

He just wasn't sure it mattered all that much at this point.

After Kate dropped them off, Rafe and Lisa went inside and Lisa scooped up Chloe in her arms and took her straight to the bedroom, closing the door behind them.

All she said to Rafe was that she had "some thinking to do" and that was that.

End of communication.

HE DIDN'T SEE HER again until close to dinner.

She came down to help Nonna and Bea in the kitchen as he took babysitting duty and watched cartoons with Chloe.

The girl sat close to him on the sofa, snuggling up against him, and Rafe put an arm around her, once again feeling that inexplicable connection.

He wondered if she ever missed her father.

How could she not?

Yet oddly, Chloe had yet to even mention Sloan. Maybe the guy didn't like pink and blue kitty cats.

That was the least of his faults, if true. Sloan didn't strike Rafe as the type to care much about kids, and Rafe had to wonder what his reaction had been when Lisa told him he'd gotten her pregnant.

Joy? Elation?

Doubtful. The only thing Sloan got elated about was

Sloan. He was a narcissist, pure and simple, and Rafe didn't get the impression that he'd ever spent more than obligatory time with his daughter.

Which was probably for the best.

Rafe couldn't imagine having a child like this and not wanting to spend as much time as possible with her. If she were his, if he were lucky enough to be her father, she would quickly become the center of his universe.

Kitty cats and all.

BEA DID MOST OF THE TALKING during dinner, telling them stories of her childhood in a small town in Texas. How her father had wanted a boy and had raised her to ride and shoot and wrestle pigs in the mud patch.

Chloe seemed to get a kick out of that one. The thought of this woman rolling around in the mud with a three-hundred-pound pig was too much for the girl to handle, and she giggled like crazy, asking Bea to tell the story again.

Lisa, on the other hand, seemed pensive, barely touching her dinner. Several times, Rafe was tempted to ask her what was going on inside her head, suspecting he already knew, but he resisted.

She would talk when she was ready to.

He thought about what she had said at the bank. About him trying to control her, just as Sloan always had.

Was that true?

If it was, that had never been his intention. Rafe had always had strong opinions, sure, but he wouldn't dream of trying to impose them on anyone, especially Lisa.

But he wouldn't shy away from telling her exactly how he felt, either. And to his mind, playing games with Sloan was far too risky.

HE WAS READING a bedtime story to Chloe when Lisa appeared in the doorway, fresh from a shower, wearing a terry-cloth robe.

"I need to talk to you when you're finished," she said.

She stepped into the room, kissed Chloe on the forehead and bid her good-night, then left them alone so that Rafe could finish the story. It was one his own mother used to read to him about Whacky Wednesday, where everything in the world seemed to have been turned upside down.

He was halfway through it when he realized that Chloe was asleep. Smoothing her hair back, he raised the blanket up to her small chest, then turned out the light and closed the door.

A moment later, he was in Lisa's room, surprised to find her dressed in tight-fitting blue jeans and an equally tight cardigan sweater. Her hair was brushed back and she'd put on enough makeup to enhance but not mar her natural beauty.

"I thought you were getting ready for bed," he said. "What's going on?"

"Sit down, Rafe."

He studied her a moment, saw the measured determination in her eyes, then sat on the edge of the bed.

She moved to him, took his hands. "I'm sorry I got so upset with you at the bank this afternoon. I shouldn't have lashed out at you like that. All you've ever tried to do was help me."

"I'm glad you understand that. But don't even worry about it. You had a right to be upset."

"Maybe, but there's something *you* need to understand. Do you think you can try to do that?"

"Of course," he said.

"Good. Because I have to make this right. You're in trouble because Oliver is obsessed with me. And while there's nothing I can do to control that, I can at least try to stop him."

Rafe stared at her. "You called Kate, didn't you?"

She nodded. "I told her I wasn't bluffing this afternoon. I'm more than willing to cooperate with their investigation and wear a wire. She's setting it up as we speak."

"For tonight?"

She nodded. "I've already asked Oliver to meet me at the house. Alone."

A mix of emotions tore at Rafe and he squeezed her hands. "Lisa, this is crazy."

"I'm not asking for your approval. But if we're ever going to have any kind of life together—and I'd like that, more than anything—then something has to be done about Oliver. Something that will keep him away from us forever."

"And if this goes wrong? What then?"

"I don't see why it should. All I have to do is play to Oliver's weakness—which is me."

"I don't like this, Lisa. You know I don't like it."

"You've made that abundantly clear. But how do we have any kind of relationship if you're doing time in jail? How will you ever get to know your daughter if the only way you see her is through a set of bars?"

The words had gone by so quickly that Rafe thought he must have misunderstood her. When he ran them through his head again, his heart momentarily seized up and he got a lump in his throat.

"My daughter?" He swallowed. "What are you telling me?"

"I wanted you to know three years ago, Rafe. I *should* have told you then, just as I should have told you the moment you walked into my living room and saw her. But I've been so afraid about how you'd react that I kept looking for excuses not to." She paused, moving in close to him. "But I can't keep it from you anymore, Rafe. Chloe isn't Oliver's child. She's yours. Every drop of blood she carries comes from you and me."

Rafe just sat there, staring at her, thinking he surely must have fallen asleep in Chloe's room and was dreaming this entire conversation.

But then he thought of that connection he had with the girl. That feeling of oneness whenever he interacted with her. And he knew this was real. That Lisa spoke the truth.

"Oh, my God," he said. "Oh, my God."

Rafe had never been one for tears—men raised in cop families would rather shoot themselves than ever shed one—but he felt his eyes growing wet. Couldn't have stopped it if he wanted to.

"I'm so sorry I didn't tell you sooner," Lisa said. "Can you ever forgive me?"

"Forgive you? There's nothing to forgive. This is the most wonderful news I've ever heard."

Then he pulled her close, wrapped his arms around her and kissed her.

*He was a father.*

Better still, he was *Chloe's* father.

But before he could revel in this notion, a horn honked outside and Lisa said, "I have to go. That'll be Kate and her team. It's time to do this."

Then she kissed him again, pulled herself free and headed for the door.

BY THE TIME Rafe reached the porch, Lisa was climbing through the sliding door of a telephone company van.

"Wait a minute," he called out. "Hold on."

She turned in the doorway. "You're not going to stop me, Rafe. I've made up my mind."

"Fine," he said as he crossed the lawn toward her. "I get that. But if you think you're going to do this without me, you're sadly mistaken."

Now Kate stuck her head out of the van. "Haven't you already gotten yourself in enough trouble? Stay home, little brother."

Rafe looked inside the vehicle and saw one of his cousins at the wheel, a St. Louis police officer named Billy Franco. In back with Kate was Mike Cuddy, a family friend and a freelance audio surveillance technician unconnected to the Sheriff's department.

In other words, neither of them were part of Kate's usual crew.

"What's going on here?" he asked. "Where's your partner? This doesn't look like a sanctioned operation."

"Don't you worry about that," she said.

"You haven't even passed this by the brass, have you? And you know Eberhart would blow the whistle if you tried to bring him in on it."

"I don't have time to deal with protocol. They always tie us up with endless planning and I just got word from one of my informants that Sloan may be gearing up to leave town on a business deal. I don't want to lose momentum."

"Or take a chance that Lisa will change her mind?"

"I'm not changing anything," Lisa said.

"Well, you're not doing this without me, either," Rafe told her, then looked pointedly at Kate. "Either you let me come along or I blow the whole operation."

Kate studied him with a scowl as if he were the pesky little brother threatening to tell their parents what she was up to. Then she said, "Well, then, don't just stand there, you little twerp. Get inside."

A moment later, they were on their way.

As Billy drove them through the city streets, Mike had Lisa remove her sweater and began wiring up her bra. A tiny microphone was attached to the fabric between her cleavage, with a lead running to a compact wireless transmitter taped to the small of her back.

When she put the sweater back on, it was impossible to tell she was wired at all. As long as Sloan kept his hands to himself, she would be safe.

But then there was no guarantee of that, was there?

"Okay," Kate told her. "These are the rules."

"I'm listening."

"First of all, you have to relax when you're with him. If he senses you're wearing a wire, if you offer him any kind of tell, you could find yourself in a very dangerous situation."

"Which is exactly what I'm afraid of," Rafe said.

Kate scowled again. "We've heard enough from you, buddy boy. You're either along for the ride or you get out now. Your choice."

She was once again pulling the big sister card, and under different circumstances Rafe may well have told her where to stuff it. But he said nothing.

She returned her attention to Lisa. "Now, when it comes to coaxing information out of this guy, you have to remember that he's been around the block a few times and won't be easily fooled."

"I was married to him, remember? I think I can handle him."

"Let's hope so, because we don't have time for me to instruct you in the finer art of extracting a confession. The thing you've got going for you is that the guy is apparently nuts about you."

"Or just plain nuts," Rafe said.

Kate ignored him and continued addressing Lisa. "When you called him, did you say what I told you to?"

Lisa nodded. "I told him that I thought things had gotten a little out of control and I wanted to talk. No promises. No enticements."

"Good. Because he'd probably be suspicious otherwise. Especially after a year of making it clear that you want nothing to do with him."

"I don't think he's suspicious at all," Lisa said. "I think this has led exactly where he wanted it to. My needing something from him. And a chance to put us in the same room without my threatening to call the police."

"Let's hope you're right," Kate said, then turned to

Mike and gestured to Lisa's chest. "What's the range on this thing?"

"We should be able to get a clear signal up to a block or so away."

She turned again to Lisa. "Okay. We can't very well drop you off in front of your house, so we're going to drive to a cabstand and let you ride the last mile home. But don't worry, we'll be parked about a half block south of your place, and we can hear every word you and Sloan say."

"And what if things go wrong?" Rafe said. "What's the emergency phrase?"

Lisa looked confused. "Emergency phrase?"

"A phrase that lets us know when it's time to move in," Kate said. "When you feel as if your life is in danger. Something that's unlikely to come up in normal conversation."

They all thought about this for a moment, then Rafe said, "How about pink and blue kitty cats?"

"Not one I would have chosen," Kate told him, "but it works as well as any." She looked at Lisa. "So that's the phrase. Pink and blue kitty cats. You think you can remember it?"

Lisa smiled and threw a glance at Rafe.

"I'm sure I'll manage," she said.

# *Chapter Twenty-Three*

When the cab dropped her off in front of the house, Lisa felt her knees shaking. She'd have to get that under control if she was going to make this work.

What she hadn't bothered to tell either Kate or Rafe, was that Oliver had always been a keen observer of human behavior, which was part of the reason he was so successful in business.

And Kate had been right. If he sensed even the slightest hesitation in Lisa's manner, she was done for. The choking incident from the other day was only a preview of coming attractions.

The one thing Lisa had on her side, however, was Oliver's ego. He was the type of guy with the kind of money that attracted women far and wide. And he was just vain enough to believe that it was *him* they wanted, and not the lifestyle he promised them.

The irony was that Lisa had never been much interested in that lifestyle. Money only served a purpose—putting food in her daughter's stomach and giving them shelter. Anything other than that was superfluous nonsense that held no real meaning for her.

It was Oliver's initial kindness that had attracted her to him, and the promise that he would take care of her

and Chloe when they most needed taking care of. And
on some level, it saddened her that things had gone sour.

But that sadness paled compared to the feeling of revulsion she now felt whenever she thought of him. She
just hoped she'd be able to use that giant ego against
him and get him to confess to his crimes.

When she got inside the house, she immediately
turned on the lights in the living room, then went upstairs for a moment to get something she needed.

By the time she came back down, she heard a car pull
into the driveway. She had asked Oliver to come alone
and hoped he had followed her wishes.

When she peeked out the window, she saw him
emerge from behind the wheel of his Lexus and head
for the front door.

A moment later, the bell chimed, and Lisa took a
deep breath, tried to steady her knees…then went to
the door to greet him.

"Hey, babe," Sloan said. "I was starting to wonder if
this day would ever come."

His voice came in crystal clear over the wire. Whatever microphone and transmitter Mike had used, it had
to be top of the line.

Rafe sat next to Kate inside the cramped van, listening carefully through a pair of headphones. He'd gotten
a knot in his stomach the moment Sloan rang the front
doorbell, and he didn't figure it would go away until
this whole thing was over.

He had checked and rechecked his spare weapon to
make sure it was loaded. Had done it so many times that

Kate had finally put a hand on his wrist and told him to
"Chill out, little brother."

"You're looking as hot as ever," Sloan said. "The
way you're wearing that sweater, I'd almost think you're
glad to see me. So are you gonna invite me in or what?"

"I'm surprised you haven't forced your way in."

She was playing it smart. Showing him that she was
still upset. Anything else would seem false and give
him reason to be suspicious.

"Hey," he said. "I was a little loaded, okay? I had
something to celebrate, so I was celebrating."

LISA NOTICED the twinkle in Oliver's eye and knew exactly what he was talking about.

"Let me guess," she said. "You were celebrating your
little victory at the Westland National Bank."

Oliver smiled. "Looks like somebody took a field
trip. Guess you didn't find what you were looking for,
did you?"

"You know I didn't," Lisa said. "But I'm not going to
stand here and cry about it. You might as well come in."

She opened the door wide and let him pass. He
brushed a shoulder against her breasts as he did, a tiny
smirk on his lips.

*And here we go,* she thought, figuring Rafe and the
others must have heard the scrape on the microphone
and gone into a panic.

She quickly said, "Have a seat. Do you want a drink?"

Sloan smiled and crossed to the sofa. "When's the last
time you ever saw me turn down anything you had to
offer? Like I told you the other night, babe. You pretty
much drive me crazy."

"I take it that means yes?" She moved to the wet bar in the corner.

"Vodka rocks. Same as always."

She put some ice in a glass, poured the liquid in, then turned and carried it to him. He was already sprawled out on the sofa, the king making himself at home in his castle.

The way he had his legs splayed she could clearly see the bulge in his pants. This was, she knew, a deliberate show, as if to say to her, *Look what you've been missing.*

Lisa stifled an involuntary urge to vomit all over him and handed him the drink.

He took a sip, then looked up at her. "You gonna stand there all night showing off that glorious rack, or tell me why I'm here? Not that I'm complaining, mind you."

"I'm surprised you don't already know," she said. "You seem to know everything else."

He grinned. "I do my best. But I've gotta say I was a little bowled over when my attorney told me about your cop friend."

"Oh? And what did she tell you?"

"She showed me pictures of the two of you in college. Quite the pretty little couple you were." He took a sip. "We sat there and did the math. Figured out when school ended, when you two parted ways—and the next thing I know, I realize I'm looking at a picture of Chloe's father."

She wondered what Rafe was thinking right now. She was relieved he had taken the news so well, but figured he might not be too happy with the subtle sneer in Oliver's tone.

"And that disturbs you?" she asked. She didn't really care one way or another, but she wanted him to feel relaxed. As if he could share anything with her.

Oliver shrugged. "I honestly don't give a rat's behind who knocked you up. But when he shows up in your life again and winds up storming into my hotel room all hot and bothered over something he thinks I did to you, I might have an issue or two about that."

"What kind of an issue?"

"Maybe I don't like the guy moving in on my woman."

Lisa shook her head. "You don't own me, Oliver. We're divorced, remember?"

"Only because you forced it on me. I figure I show a little kindness to a pregnant girl in need, give her a home, some clothes, welcome her kid into the world—"

"You didn't even come to the hospital."

"What can I say? I was busy. The point is, I *do* own you, Lisa. I own you just like I own that car out in the driveway, and all the people who work for me. Just like I own that cop boyfriend of yours, now that he's seen how the law really works."

Lisa laughed. "Don't you realize how pitiful that is?"

"What's that suppose to mean?"

"Think about it, Oliver. You say you own me, but in order to get me to pay any attention to you, you have to frame an innocent man. Yet the one thing you can't control is how I feel."

Oliver shrugged. "Feelings are overrated."

"So what is it you want from me? Is it the body?" She laughed. "You could walk into a nightclub, waggle your finger and half the women in St. Louis would come running. And most of them are better built than me."

"It isn't the body," Sloan said, "It's the way you use it. But even if they could give you competition in that department, they still wouldn't be you, would they now?"

"What's so special about me?"

Sloan chuckled, took another sip of his drink. "To be perfectly honest, babe, I have no idea. There's just something about you that turns me on. Always has, always will. And I figure if I can't have you, nobody else can, either."

"So is that why you framed Rafe Franco?"

A slow grin. "That's the second time you've said that, and I have no idea what you're talking about."

"I didn't just throw that data chip into my safety deposit box without looking at it first, Oliver. I saw what was on it. I saw names. And one of them was Azarov. The same guy Rafe is accused of killing."

"Well, isn't that a coincidence."

"No," Lisa said, "I don't think it is."

Oliver stared at her for a long moment, then knocked back the last of his vodka and held out the glass. "Hit me again, will you?"

*Oh, I'd like to hit you all right,* she thought, her frustration mounting.

Was she ever going to get him to admit to anything, or was she wasting her time?

She took his glass, then crossed back to the wet bar and poured more liquid over the ice.

"You know," he said, "I've gotta thank you for taking that stuff off my computer. I thought I was some kind of Mr. Wizard, keeping that folder hidden, but I figured if my own wife could find it, maybe the cops could, too.

Which is why I decided to wipe my hard drive, just in case you got chatty."

"I could have gotten chatty a long time ago," she told him. "But I didn't, did I? All I wanted was for you to leave me and Chloe alone."

"And all I've ever wanted is you, in this house, on your knees, in my bed, doing what I tell you to do when I tell you to do it, without complaint. So I guess we've got a bit of a problem, don't we?" He gestured. "You gonna bring me that drink or what?"

She crossed to the sofa, handed it to him. He tipped it back, drinking half of it down.

"What if I told you you could have that?" she said. "Me at your beck and call."

He stopped, gulped. Looked at her. "Is this some kind of trick?"

"No tricks, Oliver. A straight-up proposition. A business deal, if you will."

He furrowed his brow. "Business deal, huh? Are we finally getting to the meat of the matter? Is that why you invited me here?"

"Yes," she said.

She got down on her knees in front of him, framed by those splayed legs, then leaned forward and kissed him full on the mouth.

THEY HEARD THE RUSTLE of fabric accompanied by nothing but silence and Rafe knew she had to be kissing him.

What else could it be?

He and Kate exchanged glances as he racked and re-racked the gun in his hand, wanting desperately to use it.

"What the heck is she doing?" he said to Kate.

"Quiet. She's playing this perfectly. Just let her do her thing."

He was about ready to throw the rear doors open, run the half block to Lisa's house and barge in firing, when Sloan broke the silence.

"Well, well," he said. "Looks like you've still got the magic, babe. Not that I ever doubted it. But I have to admit I'm a little surprised."

"Why? It's what you wanted, isn't it?"

"That and a whole lot more."

"Well, that's what I'm offering," she said. "Me. The whole package. I'll even pretend I care about you some-times."

Rafe squirmed. Was this part of the script Lisa had planned or was she simply improvising?

"In exchange for what?" Sloan asked.

"Rafe Franco," she said.

ANOTHER SLOW SMILE came to Oliver's face. "Rafe Franco, huh? You want to illuminate me on this little demand?"

She kissed him again, lingering for a moment, mentally holding her nose as she flicked her tongue along his lower lip.

Then she said, "Doesn't matter what you admit to. I know you framed him."

"You ever gonna stop singing that tune?"

"You're a powerful man, Oliver, and you get things done. I don't care whose arm you have to twist, who you have to bribe, but you're going to do whatever you have to do to get the charges against him dropped."

Sloan chuckled. "You're giving me a lot more credit than I deserve."

"Really?" she said. "I thought you were the man who owned everything."

"Well, sure, but..."

Another kiss. This one longer, deeper. Lisa nearly gagged halfway through it.

Then Oliver reached forward and cupped her breast, running his thumb over the fabric, feeling the thin bra beneath, and the nipple beneath that. She felt a momentary stab of panic, worried he might find the microphone, but he wasn't anywhere close.

No, he was sticking to that one specific spot. She thought she might have to will her body to react, but the friction finally did its job and she grew harder against it.

She could feel *his* body growing harder as well, his splayed legs now pressed up against her abdomen. She halfway hoped that Rafe had taken his headphones off by now. He may not be getting a visual, but she didn't want him hearing this and letting his imagination go wild.

"You must really care about this guy," Oliver said.

"He's the father of my child. I don't want him to see her grow up from behind bars."

"You sure you don't want more than that?"

"That's all it *can* be, if you agree to my terms."

He kept working that thumb, and it took everything Lisa had not to flinch away from him.

"I wish I could, babe, believe me. But you've got me all wrong. I'm no fan of the guy, by any means, but I'm just a real estate developer. I don't have the kind of juice it takes to set him up *or* smooth it all out."

"Come on, Oliver, how stupid do you think I am? I saw those files, remember?"

"You saw some names and numbers," he said. "Doesn't mean a thing."

"So is that why you went to all the trouble of finding it? Of having someone pose as me to get it?"

"I'll have to plead the fifth on that one."

She reached forward and ran a hand along the side of his jaw, caressing it. "Are you going to plead the fifth on the man in the BMW, too?"

Sloan frowned. "I beg your pardon?"

"He came after us, Oliver. Shot at Rafe. He could have killed me, too. Probably would have, if he hadn't been hit by a truck. Are you going to tell me you didn't hire him?"

All of a sudden Sloan's face got ugly and his forefinger joined his thumb, pinching her nipple between them—hard. Sharp, searing pain shot through Lisa's breast and she stifled a cry, not wanting Rafe to know what was happening.

She didn't want him coming in here just yet.

"I don't know what you think you're playing at, you little slut, but you're treading on dangerous ground."

He bore down and the pain was relentless, and in that moment Lisa knew that this attempt at getting Oliver to talk had been an exercise in futility. That the only way she'd ever get this man out of her life was to take a page from *his* book. A contingency she had planned for when she went upstairs.

Wincing against the pain, she reached forward and shoved her right hand under the sofa cushion. She found what she had hidden there, pulled it free and pointed it directly at Oliver's forehead.

The gun from the upstairs closet.

Oliver's face went slack and he immediately released her. "Now wait a second, babe, you want to be very careful with that thing."

Lisa got to her feet and held the gun with both hands now, keeping it trained on Oliver, who looked as if he were about to pee his pants.

Then she said, "Pink and blue kitty cats."

## *Chapter Twenty-Four*

The words came so suddenly that no one in the van had expected them. A split second after Lisa spoke, she yelped loudly and three gunshots rang out.

*Bam. Bam. Bam.*

Rafe ripped his headphones off and bolted. Flew out of the van as if he had been launched by a catapult, covering the half block to her house in marathon time, his heart pounding, working its way up into his throat.

He heard footsteps behind him and knew Kate and the others were following his lead. A moment later, he crashed through the front door, gun high, expecting to find Lisa on the floor…

But to his surprise, the living room was empty.

What the heck?

"Fan out," Kate said behind him. "Check every room."

They moved quickly and efficiently, Rafe keeping his weapon extended as he moved down a hallway dotted with doors. He went room to room, kicking each door open, shouting "Clear!" when he saw that they were empty.

He heard more shouts of "Clear!" coming from other parts of the house, and when he'd checked every room he could find, he headed back to the living room where their cousin Billy was now waiting.

"I got nothing," Billy said.

"Same here," Kate told them, as she came down the stairs.

Rafe shook his head in disbelief. "This doesn't make any sense. Where did they go?"

"In here!" Mike shouted, and they all ran toward the sound of his voice, moving down another short hallway that led into what looked like a study. There was a desk in front of the window and floor-to-ceiling bookshelves full of hardback books.

Mike was standing near the center of the wall, pulling on one of the books. "They're fake," he said, then pressed inward on a panel and a section of the bookcase sprang open, revealing a door behind. "It's an escape route. It was hanging open when I came into the room."

Rafe was about to step into the hidden passage, when they heard the sound of an engine roaring.

The Lexus.

Sloan's Lexus.

Turning, Rafe rocketed out of the room and headed toward the sound, crossing the living room to the foyer in seconds flat. He burst onto the front driveway with his weapon raised, only to see the Lexus roaring onto the street, burning rubber as it went.

He ran for all he was worth, trying to catch up to it, but by the time he reached the bottom of the driveway it was halfway down the street.

Rafe pointed his gun at it, but he knew that taking a shot would be foolish. A tiny miscalculation and Lisa could get hurt—because Rafe knew damn well she was inside.

Kate and the others drew up beside him as the Lexus screamed around a corner and disappeared into the night.

Then he turned to his big sister and said angrily, "No time to deal with protocol, huh? How's that working for you now?"

LISA AWAKENED with a start, her head pounding, and realized they were in Oliver's Lexus.

And they were moving. Fast.

But before she could move herself, Oliver shot a hand to her throat and grabbed it, squeezing hard. "You try anything, babe, I won't hesitate to hurt you. So be good, okay?"

The pain was excruciating and she struggled to breathe. When he loosened his grip, she sucked big gasps of air, feeling as if she couldn't get enough.

She felt dizzy, her head still pounding, and it took her a moment to remember what had happened.

The gun. She had pulled the gun on Oliver. Because she'd known that was the only way. The only way that she and Chloe—and Rafe—would be rid of him.

It was an irrational move—she knew that now—but her fear had gotten the better of her. If she hadn't hesitated, if she hadn't taken just a split second to consider the weight of what she was doing, Oliver would be dead now. There was no doubt in her mind.

But she *had* hesitated. Pointing a gun at someone— someone you despise—is one thing. But pulling the trigger is another thing altogether, and in that hesitation, Oliver had seen an opening and pounced. Sprang from the sofa and tackled her. The gun was knocked upward and she had involuntarily fired off three shots.

*Bam. Bam. Bam.*

Then her head had hit something solid—the edge of the coffee table?—and the blow had sent her reeling, spinning away into darkness.

Now here she was in Oliver's car, struggling to breathe, her neck raw where he had grabbed her, and all she could think to say was, "Pink and blue kitty cats. Pink and blue kitty cats. *Pink and blue kitty*—"

"What's wrong with you?" Oliver barked as they barreled down a city street at top speed. "Why do you keep…"

He stopped himself, his face shifting expressions as if he suddenly understood.

"The cops," he said, his eyes going cold. "That's a code phrase. You've been working with the cops."

Then, without warning, he reached a hand out—the same hand that had grabbed her throat—and shoved it up inside her sweater, groping around until he found the transmitter taped to the small of her back.

"You little…"

Grabbing hold of it, he ripped it free, then rolled down his window and tossed it into the street. Shooting her a warning look, he reached into his pocket for a cell phone and hit speed dial.

When the line came alive, he said, "I've got myself a situation that I need you to take care of. Tell those new guys you hired that they're about to earn their keep."

Then he snapped the phone shut and hit the gas.

RAFE WAS BESIDE HIMSELF, couldn't stand still. He paced Lisa's living room like an expectant father worried about bad news.

They had searched for signs of blood, but found none, and could only assume that the gunshots had gone wild. That Lisa had not been hurt.

A least Rafe hoped so.

Prayed for it.

But that didn't change the fact that Lisa was gone.

"He's got her, Kate. You know he's got her. The question is where is he taking her?"

Kate was still studying the carpet. "Maybe *he* doesn't even know," she said. "I've put out an APB on the Lexus and sent some deputies to his hotel. But somehow I have a feeling that's the last place he'll go. Especially if he's on to us."

"If he wasn't before," Rafe said, "he will be as soon as he discovers that wire. Then all bets are off. I can't believe I was stupid enough to let you do this."

"Look, Rafe, I'm sorry, but there's always a risk with this kind of—"

"*Risk?*" he shouted. "We're talking about the woman I love, Kate, not some confidential informant you've been cultivating for years. This is an unmitigated disaster. And if anything happens to her, I'm holding you responsible."

Kate got to her feet. "Nothing's going to happen, little brother. I promise you."

"Oh? Another promise you can't keep?"

"Maybe we're overthinking this. Maybe she got hurt in the struggle and he's taking her to the hospital."

Rafe stared at her. "You can't be serious. The guy's a narcissistic sociopath."

"I'm just trying to think of all the possibilities, okay? I'm doing the best I can here. So will you please stop pacing and sit down?"

Rafe stared at her a long moment, then moved to sofa and sat. "You happy now?"

He buried his head in his hands. Why had he given in to this nonsense so easily? Why had he allowed Lisa to do something so foolish? If anything happened to her, if Sloan were to hurt her in any way, he'd never forgive himself.

He looked at his sister again. "We need to figure out where he's taking her, Kate. The longer she's with him, the better the chance he'll…"

Rafe stopped suddenly, saw something from the corner of his eye. Getting to his feet, he moved to the end table at the far end of the couch and found a framed photograph there, the glass broken.

"What is it?" Kate asked.

Rafe picked up the photo. It was one he had seen before, the shot of Lisa and Chloe standing in front of a house on a lake.

Carlyle Lake.

*It's the only time in our marriage that we were actually happy,* Lisa had said.

Kate moved toward him. "Rafe? What is it?"

He turned now and showed her the photograph.

"I think I know where he's taking her."

# Chapter Twenty-Five

It was a family operation.

Following protocol meant mobilizing an entire division, and with that came endless questions and wasted time spent debating whether or not the taxpayers should be paying for the search and rescue of someone who might not even be missing. Especially when that search and rescue required crossing state lines.

Considering that this problem had been caused by an unauthorized operation, the prudent decision was to handle the matter in-house—or in-family, so to speak—rather than put the brass in a bind should things go wrong. So Rafe, Kate, Billy and Mike were joined by Billy's brother, Mario, and Rafe and Kate's older brother, Vincent.

They convened in Lisa's living room, where Mario—who headed a cybercrime task force for the FBI—used a backdoor channel to hack into Oliver Sloan's real estate records.

"So what am I looking for?" he asked.

Rafe said, "Any properties he may own in Carlyle, Illinois."

Mario spent the next several minutes stabbing keys

on his laptop keyboard, then said, "Got something. Looks like an acre of land right off the lakefront."

"That's the one," Kate told him, then looked at Rafe. "If you're right about this, looks like we're back in business."

CALLING IT A LAKE HOUSE was something of a misnomer. According to the blueprints Mario downloaded, it was more of a compound than a house, and judging by the way Sloan had protected himself at the hotel, Rafe figured there would be plenty of security there.

Rather than go in guns blazing, and risk hurting Lisa in the process, they decided on a stealth assault, using the darkness to shield them. The trick was to get inside undetected and extract Lisa from the premises.

"We'll want to go for maximum coverage," Vincent said. He was the oldest of the clan and took charge immediately. His job as a squad commander required him to make a dozen different decisions every day. "With six of us working in pairs, we can come in from three different entry points." He pointed to the blueprint. "Here, here and here."

"What about security?" Rafe asked.

"It's my understanding that this clown Sloan is known for using over-the-hill mercenaries. But we shouldn't be overconfident. Some of these guys are very good at what they do."

"Do we use deadly force?" Billy asked.

"Only if necessary. There's no question they'll be ordered to shoot to kill, but let's do our best to neutralize them quietly. That leaves fewer questions to answer later on. So we're talking maximum efficiency, minimum violence."

*Good luck with that one,* Rafe thought. Once Sloan got wind of them, all bets were off.

"All right," Vincent said, pointing again to the blueprint. "Kate, you partner with Rafe and take the west flank. Billy and Mike you come in here, from the north. Covering the lakefront requires a boat, so we'll forgo that potential snafu and Mario and I will enter from the south flank." He looked at them. "Assuming she's in there, this should be over in a few short minutes."

"What about Sloan?" Kate said. "How do we handle him?"

Rafe's face hardened. "Just leave him to me."

HE PUT HER IN their old bedroom at the back of the main house. It had been a good year or so since Lisa had been here, and despite what their marriage had become, her memories of the place were fond ones.

Most of the time they'd spent here had been in the early days, shortly after they'd said their vows and Lisa still believed she had married a good man who wanted only to protect her and the child she would soon give birth to.

But that man had long since disappeared, only to be replaced by the creature who had brought her here, for reasons known only to him.

Was this his safe haven? His protection from the outside world and the people who were looking for her?

Or did he hope to recapture something here? Somehow find what they had lost so long ago?

It seemed to Lisa that Oliver had lost so much more

than a marriage. In these past few hours, she realized that he had also lost his mind. He hid it well with his charm and his good looks and his easy smile, but beneath that exterior was a monster whose only desire was to make her bend to his will.

It would almost be comic, if she weren't a victim of it. But she now had bruises on her throat and a sore, aching breast that proved what Oliver was capable of when provoked.

And it didn't seem to take much to provoke him.

Just before he locked her in the room, he had thrown one of her old negligees at her feet and told her to put it on.

"I've got plans for us tonight, babe. A little stroll down memory lane."

The thought filled Lisa with revulsion. And when he was gone, she stared at the negligee and told herself that no matter what Oliver did, no matter how much he hurt her, she would never bend, never break, never give him the satisfaction of letting him touch her that way again.

Not voluntarily, at least.

And if he tried, she'd break his neck.

THEY DROVE TO CARLYLE in the telephone company van, each of them lost in their own thoughts, remaining silent, as if the utterance of a single word might somehow jinx them.

When they found the compound, to no one's surprise it was lit up, signaling that the place was in full operation.

Parking in the shadows of a tree, several yards from the gated front entrance, Vincent leveled a pair of binoculars at the drive and said, "Bingo. We've got our-selves a Lexus."

Rafe felt his heartbeat quicken. His instincts had been right. Lisa was inside.

*Please be inside.*

There was a high stone fence and a lot of foliage sur-rounding the compound. A uniformed security guard stood near the gate with watchful eyes, undoubtedly warned to keep a lookout for the police. Any approach would be turned away with demands for a warrant—something Rafe and crew were unable to provide.

But the sight of this telephone company truck—if the guard had, indeed, seen them—did not seem to arouse any suspicions.

Pulling out of the shadows, they did a single sweep around the compound to assess their options and con-firm that the blueprints had been accurate. There were no neighboring houses for several hundred yards, and they decided the isolation could only work in their favor.

Rafe and Kate were dropped off near the west quad-rant, both carrying an extra weapon, a miniature flash-light and a lightweight headset that Mike had set them up with. Rafe wished he had a pair of night goggles, to boot, but this was a run-and-gun operation and they weren't exactly swimming in taxpayer-funded supplies.

The fence was about eight feet high. Rafe gave Kate a boost up, then she, in turn, pulled him up after. They each peered into the darkness and saw a wide stretch of lawn that led first to a guest cottage, then on to the main house beyond, and were relieved to see the area free of dog droppings.

Either the cleanup crew was very good at its job, or guard dogs had been forfeited in favor of manpower.

Earlier, they had discussed the possibility of alarm sensors, but a search of Sloan's credit card records—courtesy of a computer hack by Mario—showed no signs of any security company purchases in the past ten years.

Rafe and Kate waited a tense moment, in case their presence had been detected, then dropped to the ground inside the compound and darted toward the shadows of a nearby shade tree.

Rafe scanned the yard and saw no sign of a guard until his gaze fell on the main house. There were two men posted out front, and he assumed there would be more teams posted at the sides and in the back.

Kate gestured toward another shade tree, which was only a yard or so from the guesthouse. They waited until both security men had turned away, then took off, making a beeline for the shadows.

As they crouched down, Kate assessed their surroundings and said quietly, "I'm figuring at least eight hostiles at the main house and possibly a couple of outliers on patrol."

"Exactly what I was thinking," Rafe told her.

Kate touched her headset. "Team leader, we've only got two hostiles in sight, but have to assume there are more."

The radio crackled in Rafe's ear and Vincent said, "Roger, Kate, we can confirm two on our end."

"Same here," Billy said. "And we came very close to an encounter with a patrol jockey on the way in."

"Did they spot you?" Vincent asked.

"They would've lit the place up if they had."

"All right," Vincent said. "Let's do this the smart way. One man handles the security detail, the other takes the house. Move quickly and efficiently, and no screwups, or the hostage could wind up dead."

Rafe didn't like the sound of that, but he knew Vincent was right. He turned to Kate and they spoke quietly for a moment, agreeing that Kate would handle the guards.

A moment later, they were moving again, headed for the main house.

# Chapter Twenty-Six

Sloan wanted to kill something.

It was just that simple.

Ever since Lisa had told him that the hit man he'd hired had not only failed to do his job, but also had been hit by a truck, a nearly uncontrollable feeling of anger had risen inside him.

If the hit man had gotten himself killed, what had he left behind?

Was this something Sloan needed to be worried about?

His attorney, Berletti, had repeatedly insisted on the phone that there were no links to him, but Sloan had learned a long time ago—back in his early Chicago days—that if you relied on other people to do your dirty work, mistakes were sometimes made. And those mistakes could come back to bite *you* instead of the idiot who made them.

But as disturbing as this news may have been, it was nothing compared to the fact that Rafe Franco was still alive. Sloan had been promised that once the man was thoroughly humiliated and his reputation destroyed, he would become worm food.

But that hadn't happened. Franco was still out there

somewhere, probably looking for Lisa at this very moment. Because Sloan knew the deputy had to be behind the little sting operation she had tried to pull. He had probably been the one to talk her into it.

And that was the thing that angered him most of all. That Lisa had *allowed* herself to be manipulated like that, had even pulled a *gun* on him—and had actually tried to use it.

Here he had given this witch his heart, and she had been treating him like dirt, like used tissue, from the moment they'd met. She wasn't just a gold digger, she was a coldhearted tart who deserved to suffer some very serious pain before he snuffed her out for good.

Maybe if she was dead, he'd be able to forget about her. Maybe if she was dead, this uncontrollable feeling of yearning and lust he felt whenever he thought of her would go away. Because he desperately needed it to go away.

Sloan couldn't understand what it was about Lisa that cut so deep. He had slept with a hundred different women in his time, but he'd never had this feeling before. This sense of complete powerlessness.

And that scared him more than any thug with a gun could ever come close to.

Sloan sat in his kitchen, anger coursing through him, staring at a row of prescription bottles lined up on the table in front of him. He had seven doctors on retainer, and the narcotic cocktails they gave him helped dull the edge he often felt.

But they couldn't quell the anger.

Not this time.

Knocking back his fourth vodka rocks, he slammed

the glass on the table and got to his feet. He'd been sitting here stewing long enough. Lisa should have packed that dynamite body of hers into the negligee by now, and he planned to teach her a lesson before he killed her. Reduce her to a simpering mass of human waste and make her beg for mercy before he did the final deed.

Then maybe he could get some rest.

Maybe the anger would disappear.

Maybe this ache would go away once and for all.

WHEN KATE GAVE HIM the signal, Rafe darted across the lawn toward the side of the main house. The two security men posted near the door there had foolishly let down their guard, and Kate had taken the opportunity to sneak up behind them and neutralize them quickly and quietly.

Now Rafe was heading through the door, gun in hand, hoping there wouldn't be any surprises inside.

But the moment he got it closed behind him, he heard the faint rustle of fabric as another security man closed in on him. Whirling around, Rafe grabbed a handful of the guy's shirt, jerked him forward, then spun him and put him in a choke hold.

A moment later, the guy was on the floor, out cold.

Although Rafe had looked at the blueprints and had a general sense of how to navigate this house, there were unknown variables at work here. He had no idea how many more of these monkeys he'd have to deal with.

He scanned the area around him and saw that he was in the mudroom, a drain in the floor, a sink and hose in the corner, jackets and boots hung on hooks in the wall.

Beyond this would be a long hallway that, to the left,

led to a massive living room and kitchen. To the right were three of the seven bedrooms the house boasted, including the master, all the way in back.

Rafe figured Lisa could be in any one of these rooms. But knowing where they were located was one thing, and getting to them without sounding any alarms, was another thing altogether. His only sense of comfort was that Vincent and crew were bound to be in the house, as well.

To confirm this, he touched the button on his headset three times—the signal that he'd made it inside unscathed. A moment later, the signal came back, and he knew the game was on.

Pulling open a closet, he stuffed the security man inside, then moved to the doorway adjacent to the hall and carefully peeked around the threshold, checking both ends for any sign of hostile activity.

Seeing that it was clear, he stepped into the hallway and went to work.

LISA WAS STANDING at the window when the door opened behind her. She had thought for a moment that she saw movement out there. Someone slipping through the shadows. And for that split second, her heart had kicked up, a feeling of hope welling up inside her.

It was Rafe out there. It had to be. She knew he wouldn't rest until he found her.

But the hope died the moment she went to the window and saw nothing but the vast expanse of lawn, empty and untouched, lit by the lights from the compound and what little moon there was in the sky.

Then the door opened behind her and she turned, her heart sinking as Oliver stepped into the room.

There was a glassiness to his eyes that she immediately recognized. He was drunk and stoned and angry, and that had never led to anything good in their lives.

He was holding a gun. He let it dangle casually at his side, then used it to gesture to the negligee still lying on the floor.

"I thought I told you to put that on," he said flatly. "And when I tell you something you're supposed to do it."

Lisa eyed him defiantly.

"Or what?" she said. "You're going to shoot me?"

Oliver smiled drunkenly. "I'm saving that for later. Once you've admitted to me how much you love me. How you can't live without me. Which, come to think of it, is pretty much true."

"Go to hell," she told him.

"Yeah?" He moved toward her, raising the gun. He grabbed hold of her arm and twisted it, jerking her forward, pressing the barrel against her forehead. "The way I see it, that's already where you are. The bullet is just a formality."

Lisa struggled, wincing in pain. "Let go of me," she cried.

He pressed the barrel harder and she could feel it denting her skin. "You like that, babe? You like having this smoke stick poking at you? Or maybe you're interested in another kind of stick. Believe me, that can be arranged."

He released her arm and shoved her to the floor. Then he kicked at the negligee, flipping it toward her.

"Put it on," he said.

But she shook her head. "No."

He crouched next to her and pressed the gun against her forehead again.

"Put. It. *On.*"

"You're sick, you know that? You need help, Oliver. You're so drugged up and angry you don't even know what you're doing anymore. Why don't you let me help you?"

The offer seemed to surprise him, and he lowered the gun.

"Help me?" he said. "You want to help me? Is that what you were thinking when you drew a gun on me in our living room? You were gonna *help* me?"

"You were hurting me and I panicked," she said. "I didn't even realize what I was doing."

"If you think that was pain, Leese, you've got no concept of what real pain is. Now take those clothes off and get into this negligee, or you'll feel pain you've never in your life knew existed."

"You can't control me, Oliver. I won't do it. And nothing you can do to me will change my mind."

He nodded slowly. "We'll see about that," he said, then got to his feet again. "I grew up in Chicago, babe, and I learned from the best. Men who make the torture specialists for the CIA look like amateurs." He grinned. "By the time I get done with you, you'll be begging me to let you put that thing on. This is gonna be a night to re—"

Lisa lashed out suddenly, driving a fist straight into Oliver's kneecap. He howled and stumbled back, grabbing for it as Lisa jumped to her feet and swept past him, heading straight for the bedroom door.

But Oliver spun around and grabbed her by the hair, jerking her back with such force that she thought her scalp might come loose.

Pain rocketed through her skull. She grabbed at her head as Oliver pulled her backward into the room and spun her around again, pushing her toward the bed.

She sprawled across it and saw the white-hot heat in his eyes. A fury so intense that all rational thought had abandoned him, leaving nothing behind but the reptile. The animal brain.

"You just made a very bad mistake," he said. "A very bad—"

"Sloan!" a voice shouted as the door burst open behind him. And to Lisa's utter joy and relief, Rafe was standing in the doorway, gun raised, zeroed in on Oliver's back.

Oliver froze in place. Didn't move.

"Drop the weapon," Rafe told him. "Now!"

But Oliver didn't seem to hear him. As if he had disappeared inside himself and had lost all communication with the outside world.

"Do it now, Sloan! Or I'll put one in your back!"

Oliver finally nodded, and started to move. Crouching toward the floor, he lowered the gun to lay it on the carpet. But was only halfway there when Lisa saw something deadly flicker in his eyes.

Then suddenly he brought the gun up again, whirled around toward Rafe—

"*Die,* you son of a—"

And Rafe had no choice but to fire.

One. Twice. Three times.

The bullets punctured Oliver's chest and knocked him backward. He landed in a heap at the foot of the bed and didn't move.

Rafe stepped forward quickly, kicked the gun aside, looked at Lisa on the bed.

"I don't think I've ever been so scared for someone in my life," he said. "Are you okay?"

And that was when tears sprang into Lisa's eyes. She launched herself toward Rafe and fell into his arms.

## *Chapter Twenty-Seven*

The wedding took place on a Sunday morning in June.

They held the ceremony in Grandma Natalie's backyard, the entire Franco clan in attendance.

Rafe's brother, Vincent, served as best man, and Beatrice—dressed in her Sunday best—stood in as maid of honor.

The ceremony was brief and sweet. Lisa wore a beautiful lace chiffon wedding gown that was taken out of mothballs and dry-cleaned for the occasion by Grandma Natalie. It was the very same dress Nonna had worn sixty years and eighty pounds earlier, on the day she married her dear departed husband, Alonzo.

Everyone said that Lisa looked radiant that day. Rafe himself thought she had never looked more beautiful. It seemed as if a weight had been lifted—and indeed it had—and its absence had made her stand taller, prouder, as she held the hand of the man she loved and promised her heart to him forever.

Rafe, in turn, could not have been happier as he offered his vow to her:

"I've made a lot of mistakes in my years," he said. "And one of the worst was when I was stupid enough to let you go back in college. I won't make that mistake again, Leese." He paused. "I don't know whether it was fate or just good luck that brought us back together, but thank God that it did. Because you are my heart. You beat inside me every moment of every day. And from this day forward I will love you, cherish you and do everything in my power to protect you and our beautiful daughter."

By the time he was finished, they both had tears in their eyes.

And the kiss that followed was exquisite.

AFTER THE SHOOTING at Sloan's house, Rafe, the other Francos and their rogue operation had been roundly condemned by the police and the press alike.

Until, that is, the data chip was revealed.

When all the guards had been neutralized and an ambulance was called for Sloan—although resuscitation was a moot point by then—Kate conducted a search of Sloan's study and found a data chip in one of his desk drawers.

Plugging it into her phone, she quickly discovered that it was indeed the one taken from the bank, complete with promised names, dates and bribe amounts that exposed Sloan's entire network of sycophants, including some of the very people who had condemned the Francos.

But once the information came to light, the dominoes began to fall. The first to cave was Lola Berletti, Sloan's attorney, who volunteered to tell all in exchange for immunity. With her statement, Rafe was exonerated and the charges against him were dropped.

Kate and the organized crime unit were tasked with

the arrests of five judges, fourteen police officers, two city council members and an FBI agent who had been in Sloan's pocket for nearly fifteen years.

When the dust had cleared, Rafe did what he should have done three years ago in college. Because he'd known even then, despite their miscommunication, that he wanted his relationship with Lisa to last forever. And ever.

And ever.

So he asked her to marry him.

Now, standing here, exchanging vows with the woman he loved, in front of the *family* he loved, was a moment he would never forget.

But the highlight of the day was little Chloe.

Rafe's daughter had not only been the picture of perfection serving as flower girl for the occasion, but also she, with the help of Beatrice, had been in charge of decorating, as well.

And taped to the back of every folding chair lined up in Grandma's Natalie's backyard, were her carefully colored pictures.

Of pink and blue kitty cats.

\* \* \* \* \*

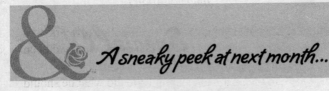

*A sneaky peek at next month...*

# INTRIGUE...

**BREATHTAKING ROMANTIC SUSPENSE**

*My wish list for next month's titles...*

In stores from 15th March 2013:

☐ Soldier Under Siege – Elle Kennedy

& Hostage Midwife – Cassie Miles

☐ Deadly Sight – Cindy Dees

& The Awakening – Jana DeLeon

☐ A Widow's Guilty Secret – Marie Ferrarella

& Colton Showdown – Marie Ferrarella

☐ Beyond Valour – Lindsay McKenna

**Available at WHSmith, Tesco, Asda, Eason, Amazon and Apple**

*Just can't wait?*

**Visit us Online**

You can buy our books online a month before they hit the shops! **www.millsandboon.co.uk**

0313/46

# Special Offers

Every month we put together collections and longer reads written by your favourite authors.

Here are some of next month's highlights— and don't miss our fabulous discount online!

On sale 5th April

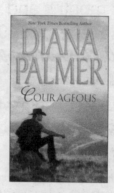

On sale 15th March

On sale 5th April

**Save 20%** on all Special Releases

Find out more at
**www.millsandboon.co.uk/specialreleases**

Visit us Online

0413/ST/MB410

# MILLS & BOON Book Club

## Save over £40

### Join the Mills & Boon Book Club

Subscribe to **Intrigue** today for 3, 6 or 12 months and you could **save over £40!**

We'll also treat you to these fabulous extras:

- FREE L'Occitane gift set worth £10
- FREE home delivery
- Books up to 2 months ahead of the shops
- Bonus books, exclusive offers… and much more!

### Subscribe now at
## www.millsandboon.co.uk/subscribeme

**Visit us Online**

Save over £40 – find out more at
**www.millsandboon.co.uk/subscribeme**

SUBS/OFFER/1

*The World of Mills & Boon®*

There's a Mills & Boon® series that's perfect for you. We publish ten series and, with new titles every month, you never have to wait long for your favourite to come along.

---

*Blaze.*
*Scorching hot, sexy reads*
4 new stories every month

By Request
*Relive the romance with the best of the best*
9 new stories every month

*Cherish*™
*Romance to melt the heart every time*
12 new stories every month

*Desire*™
*Passionate and dramatic love stories*
8 new stories every month

*Visit us Online*

Try something new with our Book Club offer
**www.millsandboon.co.uk/freebookoffer**

M&B/WORLD2

*What will you treat yourself to next?*

*Ignite your imagination, step into the past…*
6 new stories every month

## INTRIGUE…

*Breathtaking romantic suspense*
Up to 8 new stories every month

*Medical Romance*

*Captivating medical drama – with heart*
6 new stories every month

## MODERN™

*International affairs, seduction & passion guaranteed*
9 new stories every month

## n o c t u r n e™

*Deliciously wicked paranormal romance*
Up to 4 new stories every month

## RIVA™

*Live life to the full – give in to temptation*
3 new stories every month available exclusively via our Book Club

You can also buy Mills & Boon eBooks at
**www.millsandboon.co.uk**

*Visit us Online*

M&B/WORLD2

*Mills & Boon® Online*

## Discover more romance at
## **www.millsandboon.co.uk**

- ❧ **FREE** online reads
- ❧ **Books** up to one month before shops
- ❧ **Browse our books** before you buy

*...and much more!*

---

**For exclusive competitions and instant updates:**

 Like us on **facebook.com/romancehq**

 Follow us on **twitter.com/millsandboonuk**

 Join us on **community.millsandboon.co.uk**

*Visit us Online* | Sign up for our FREE eNewsletter at **www.millsandboon.co.uk**

WEB/M&B/RTL4

CANCELLED